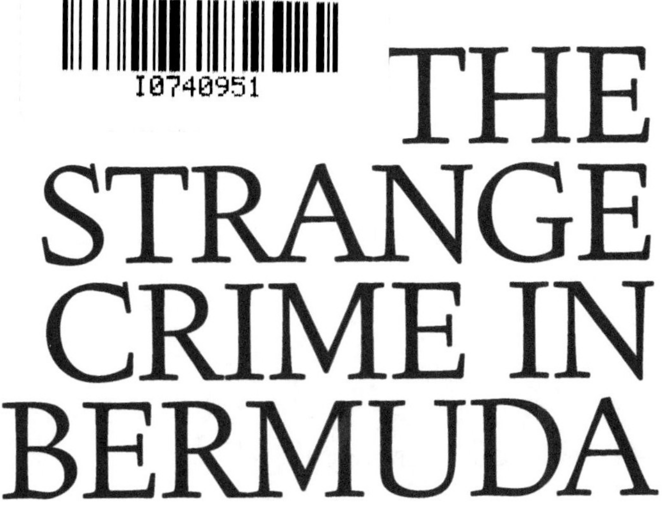

# THE STRANGE CRIME IN BERMUDA

# TOO MANY BOTTLES

## BY ELISABETH SANXAY HOLDING

STARK HOUSE

Stark House Press • Eureka California

THE STRANGE CRIME IN BERMUDA / TOO MANY BOTTLES

Published by Stark House Press
1315 H Street
Eureka, CA 95501, USA
griffinskye3@sbcglobal.net
www.starkhousepress.com



ISBN: 0-9749438-5-1

Cover and book design by Mark Shepard, SHEPGRAPHICS.COM
Proofreading by Rick Ollerman

*The publishers would like to thank Roger Schwed
for his help and assistance in the production of this book.*

PUBLISHER'S NOTE


First Stark House Press Edition: February 2005
Reprint Edition

## THE STRANGE CRIME IN BERMUDA

Hamish Grier receives a telegram from his old friend Hector Malloy asking him to visit him in Bermuda. On the ship down he meets Stephanie Rose, a brash young lady who turns out to be Malloy's island neighbor. But the day Hamish arrives, Malloy disappears. His beautiful wife, Faquita, believes there is something horribly wrong but Malloy's business partner, Reggie Cornwall, is positive that everyone is simply overreacting—Malloy will turn up. Rumors suggest that Malloy may have been involved with Miss Rose. Were they planning to run away together? Or could he be the victim of a strange accident? When Hamish finds one of Faquita's servants dead in a trunk, Malloy's disappearance takes on a sinister edge. And it's not long before Inspector Jesser becomes involved, with Hamish now in the very thick of it.

## TOO MANY BOTTLES

The cocktail party that night gives James Brophy a great idea for a new mystery story. He'll call it *The Party Was the Pay-Off*. But it's a challenge trying to write when his wife Lulu is always interrupting his thoughts. And she's in a real mood tonight. Maybe it's the pills. Pills for this, pills for that. She asks Brophy to get her the new bottle, but when she finally comes down to the party, Lulu is in such a horrible state she chases all the guests away. It's only the next morning when Lulu is found dead in her bed that Brophy realizes that his story title has taken on a new meaning. Her doctor suspects foul play. Her sister Norma believes it to be suicide. One of the party guests starts crying murder. And by the time Lieutenant Levy is brought in, it begins to look like Brophy is his prime suspect. After all, his marriage was failing, and who else had access to all of her pills? Someone had given Lulu the wrong medicine—and the pay-off was death.

# ELISABETH SANXAY HOLDING BIBLIOGRAPY


Invincible Minnie (1920)
Rosaleen Among the Artists (1921)
Angelica (1921)
The Unlit Lamp (1922)
The Shoals of Honour (1926)
The Silk Purse (1928)
Miasma (1929)
Dark Power (1930)
The Death Wish (1934)
The Unfinished Crime (1935)
The Strange Crime in Bermuda (1937)
The Obstinate Murderer [aka No Harm Intended] (1938)
Who's Afraid [aka Trial by Murder] (1940)

The Girl Who Had to Die (1940)
Speak of the Devil [aka Hostess to Murder] (1941)
Killjoy [aka Murder is a Kill-Joy] (1941)
Lady Killer (1942)
The Old Battle-Ax (1943)
Net of Cobwebs (1945)
The Innocent Mrs. Duff (1946)
The Blank Wall (1947)
Miss Kelly (1947)
Too Many Bottles [aka The Party Was the Pay-Off] (1951)
The Virgin Huntress (1951)
Widow's Mite (1952)

# Table of Contents


**INTRODUCTION**
By Gregory Shepard . . . . . . . . . . . . . . . . . . . . . . . . . . . . . . . . . . . . . . . . . . **7**

**THE STRANGE CRIME IN BERMUDA**
By Elisabeth Sanxay Holding . . . . . . . . . . . . . . . . . . . . . . . . . . . . . . **13**

**TOO MANY BOTTLES**
By Elisabeth Sanxay Holding . . . . . . . . . . . . . . . . . . . . . . . . . . . . . . **145**

# INTRODUCTION

We have the Depression to thank for Elisabeth Sanxay Holding's career as a mystery author. Until 1929, she had been writing serious, mainstream novels like *Rosaleen Among the Artists, Angelica, The Unlit Lamp* and *The Shoals of Honour.* She published six novels before the Depression, starting with *Invincible Minnie* in 1920, and ending with *The Silk Purse* in 1928. Early critics noted her expert characterization, and in the *New York Times* review of *The Silk Purse*, the reviewer said: "They are as real a collection of peoples as ever said yes when they wished to heaven they could say no."

So when the Depression hit in 1929 and she was no longer able to sell her leisurely character novels, Holding turned to writing mysteries. Or, more properly, suspense novels. Because, simply put, Elisabeth Sanxay Holding is the precursor to the entire women's psychological suspense genre, and authors like Patricia Highsmith and Ruth Rendell owe her a very large debt of gratitude.

Holding was one of the first to write mystery novels that didn't so much ask whodunit, but whydunit? In fact, we know whodunit because it's quite often the main character. It's the "why" that is always the most important part of her books. The psychological underpinnings of her novels form the basis of the mystery. Her characters always act from a very determined point of view. Whether from guilt, discontent, deception, misconception, or even pure altruism, they act out their dramas with very little consideration for other points of view. And therein lies the conflict. They have all got blinders on, seeing just what they want to see, each with their own misguided agenda. They lie when it will get them in the most trouble and tell the truth when it's in their own worst interest. In other words, her characters feel very real to us—we believe in them.

A rich, alcoholic husband grows tired of his well-meaning but lower-class wife. Everything she does irritates him. He decides he must get rid of her but his drinking is making him delusional and easily annoyed. Who can he trust? As he rushes from one hidden bottle, one seedy bar to another, the answer is clearly "no one." When his chauffeur comes to him with a plan to catch his wife with another man, he jumps at it. After all, sooner or later you've got to trust somebody.

This is the basic plot of *The Innocent Mrs. Duff.* What makes the book so compelling is the degree to which Holding gets under the skin of this self-deluded man. She wrote the story in a crisp, staccato style and makes the reader feel every bit of the scheming husband's mounting alcoholic mania. Though casual drinking was more a part of the daily lifestyle in Holding's day, she wasn't afraid to shed some light on its darker aspects. In fact, she had previously explored the theme of the alcoholic male in the *The Obstinate Murderer*—albeit more sympathetically—and clearly knew this personality well.

*The Innocent Mrs. Duff* and *The Blank Wall* (filmed twice, as *The Reckless Moment* in 1949 and *The Deep End* in 2001) are arguably two of her best works and the only two novels of Holding's that remain in print, thanks to Academy Chicago. Dell published several of her novels in paperback in the 50's, and Mercury published a few in digest form as well. And back in the 1960's, Ace Books published twelve of her books as Ace Doubles. But since then she has almost entirely gone out of print. A sad state of affairs for an author whom Raymond Chandler called "the top suspense writer of them all" in a letter to his British publisher.

All in all, Holding published eighteen suspense novels in her lifetime, beginning with *Miasma* in 1929, and ending with *Widow's Mite* in 1952. Many of these novels were also serialized in national magazines, and almost all were published in paperback and foreign editions, as well as by mystery book clubs. She also published quite a few short stories in magazines ranging from *McCalls*, *American Magazine* and *Ladies Home Journal* to *Alfred Hitchcock's Mystery Magazine*, *The Saint*, *Ellery Queen's Mystery Magazine* and *The Magazine of Fantasy and Science Fiction*. She even wrote a children's story, *Miss Kelly*, the story of a cat who could understand and speak human, and who comes to the aid of a terrified tiger.

Elisabeth Sanxay was born in Brooklyn in 1889, the descendant of an upper middle class family, and was educated in a series of private schools, specifically Whitcombe's School, The Packer Institute, Miss Botsford's School and the Staten Island Academy. She married a British diplomat named George E. Holding in 1913 and together they traveled widely in South America and the Caribbean, settling in Bermuda for awhile where her husband was a government officer. She also raised two daughters, Skeffington and Antonia, the latter of whom married Peter Schwed (until his recent death the executor of Holding's estate and a retired author and publisher with Simon and Schuster).

Holding was thirty-one when her first book was published. Right from the beginning she introduced the theme of discontent that she was to use so often in her mystery books. *Invincible Minnie* starts off slowly—telling at first when it should be showing—but evolves into a fairly lurid tale, the compelling story of a headstrong woman who uses sex to control men and get her way. There's no pat, happy ending either. Minnie runs roughshod over everyone, including her sister and children, and prevails through sheer determination. Holding's lean 40's style was only seen in glimpses in this first effort, but her characterizations were already taking shape in the relentless actions of Minnie and the various people she controlled.

With her second novel, Holding lets the story tell itself, vastly improving over the style of her first book. *Rosaleen Among the Artists,* a bit less melodramatic than *Invincible Minnie,* tells the story of a self-sacrificing young woman struggling to survive and find love in New York City. Though polished off with a sweeter ending, there is much travail as Rosaleen hits rock bottom before finally being united with her soul mate, Mr. Landry. In fact, the two are so matched in the stubbornness with which they hold onto their ideals—tenaciously sacrificing their own happiness at every turn—that they almost wear each other out by the end of the book. Ironically, it is their own principles that almost kill their only chance at love.

In 1929, when the Depression killed her mainstream career, Holding had to do something to help support her two daughters. She could have started writing nice, cozy romantic mysteries, but she just didn't have it in her. The characters she was creating were too contrary, too impulsive—too flawed—and not particularly romantic. They didn't act in their own best interests, holding onto ideals that invariably precipitated trouble. It's as if they felt compelled to do the very thing that caused the most havoc, even if for all the best reasons.

As a consequence, the mystery novels Holding began to write were dark affairs, having more in common with noir than standard detective fiction. It's easy to understand why she was such a favorite of Chandler's. Murder and mania are always lurking in the wings—and the menace doesn't always exist from the outside, but is quite often found from within. These are characters with something to hide. Sometimes there is a happy ending, sometimes not. Sometimes there is a detective, but he's usually as clueless as everyone else. You might say that Holding's characters are quite often lucky if they can make it to the last page with their health, if not their sanity, intact.

In *The Virgin Huntress* we follow young Monty on V-Day as he meets an older woman, Dona Luisa, and is brought into a world of class and culture he had always dreamed of. He is a charming if somewhat insecure young man, somewhat expedient—perhaps too expedient—in his past dealings with women. In fact, he is constantly nagged by secrets from his past, secrets that begin to fracture him as Dona Luisa's niece Rose begins to pry into his past life. By the end of the short novel, Monty has become completely unraveled, the victim of his own expediency. It's not a pretty portrait.

Another of Holding's favorite themes involves fractious family relationships and domestic disputes. *Dark Power* is a perfect example. In the first chapter we meet a young lady, Diana, who discovers that she is quite penniless and soon to be out on the street. Before this happens, however, she is suddenly rescued by an eccentric uncle she didn't know she had. He happily escorts her back to the family home, where she meets such a thoroughly dysfunctional collection of relatives that by the end of the book she barely makes it out alive.

Holding also loved to examine the way stress works on characters, particularly middle-aged men, and would combine this with her theme of domestic disharmony. *The Innocent Mrs. Duff* is an obvious example, but *The Death Wish* is another in which a man, Mr. Delancey, who had always thought himself happily married, comes to a moment of crisis in which he discovers that he actually hates his wife. She has slowly been emasculating him by controlling his purse strings, but when his best friend reveals a similar domestic situation and announces his plans to kill his own wife, Delancey is plunged into a world of self-doubt. At first he is shocked by his friend's confession, and when the wife is found drowned, he hopes that it is the accident that it seems to be. But a seed has been planted, and nothing in his formerly phlegmatic life will ever be the same.

Holding's deft hand at characterization makes all these situations ring true, giving them a psychological perspective that not only presents all her characters' foibles sympathetically, but creates the tension that propels her story along as well. Their actions are understandable, given the circumstances, and all the more frustrating because they are so identifiable. In *The Death Wish*, we watch Delancey try to convince himself at first that his wife is simply moody and a bit insecure. He wants to think the best of her. But the reader knows that his wife's insecure nagging is stifling him, her words little barbs that sink in and latch Delancey to her side, subtly but firmly controlling him. We feel his weakness and frustration, his mounting domestic horror, and nothing that proceeds from this realization seems anything less than inevitable. Not even murder.

This is Holding's true forte, that she can make the commonplace, the ordinary, so horrific and so suspenseful. But make no mistake, whether writing about dysfunctional families or failed marriages, her books are full of mystery. In *Lady Killer*, a young recently-wedded ex-model named Honey is on a cruise ship in the Caribbean with her older husband, who is turning out to be a fussy, fault-finding old crab. At the same time that she begins to realize that a life with this man will be completely intolerable, she also becomes aware that the man in the next cabin might possibly be trying to kill his wife. She begins to set about a campaign to protect this poor, plain and unfortunate woman, who doesn't really seem to want her help. In fact, no one on board seems to feel that Honey has any business stirring up trouble.

But the more Honey finds out, the more mysterious her fellow passengers begin to seem to her. Even her own husband begins to seem alien to her. And when she finds a body, even that isn't quite what it seems. But still the little mysteries pile up, and we are swept up in Honey's suspicions and doubts until even we begin to believe, like her, that *no one* is to be trusted.

*Miasma* presents us with another set of mysteries. A young doctor named Dennison has just about reached the end of his financial resources when he is contacted by a wealthy older doctor in town who wants him to take up residency in his house and assume the care of his patients. All well and good, except that the doctor's young nurse immediately warns Dennison to leave, mysterious patients come and go in the middle of the night, and his predecessor has gone missing. And then there is the weird drug that the older doctor prescribes to certain of his patients, one of whom is now dead from an apparent heart attack. Holding keeps the mysteries coming until both we and Dennison are wondering what the hell is going on here; daring us to put the book down no matter how late it is and how early we have to get up the next morning.

And then there is her rarest mystery, *Strange Crime in Bermuda,* a peculiar tale of a missing person on an enclosed island community. Young Hamish is asked to journey to Bermuda at the request of his old friend Malloy, but when he arrives, Malloy sets an appointment to meet him and then fails to show up for their meeting. It soon turns out that no one has seen the man that day, but everyone has a different idea of what of what has happened to him. A sense of confusion and dread sets in as we experience the unfolding events from Hamish's stubborn, narrow point of view. Hamish is continually misled by his various misguided allegiances, until he himself becomes the prime suspect. The resolution is both obvious and unexpected.

There is a reason that Dorothy B. Hughes said that "connoisseurs will continue their rush when each new Holding reaches publication." Her books are first and foremost very readable. Not only are they excellent examples of psychological suspense and first rate character studies, they move along at a nice, brisk pace. Holding was never one for overwriting. Her dialog always sounds just right, all the doubtful pauses and self-serving/self-deceptive lies in place. We may not always like these characters, but Holding makes us feel compelled to keep reading about them.

Elisabeth Sanxay Holding's mystery novels have been out of print far too long. Until her death in 1955, she was one of the best, and it is a pleasure to be able to bring her books back into print again, many of which have been unavailable in any edition for well over sixty years. It's time to rediscover Elisabeth Sanxay Holding. Her books may have gone out of print, but they have never gone out of fashion.

GREGORY SHEPARD
PUBLISHER, STARK HOUSE PRESS
SEPTEMBER, 2003

# THE STRANGE CRIME IN BERMUDA

To
Phyllis Wattley

# CHAPTER ONE

When Hamish Grier was eighteen he had pneumonia, and as soon as he was well enough to travel his father sent him on a West Indies cruise. He was a level-headed, serious boy, a little stiff in his manner, good-looking in his dark, unsmiling fashion; well-mannered. He could have had a good time on the ship.

But he did not. He had no gift for making friends easily; he was disconcerted if anyone made overtures to him; he was mortally afraid of making a fool of himself. He did not wish to be enthusiastic about anything or impressed by anything, and he was a little dismayed to find himself so stirred by this new beauty: the sea that was sapphire blue, or jade green; the regal purple of a bougainvillæa; the feathery light green of bamboo palms, outlined against a moonlit sky—all the hot bright colours of this world.

"I can see," he said to himself, "how the tropics could get you."

The tropics wouldn't get him, though, because his future was all planned, and it was to be in New York. This was only an episode.

His father had a friend in Trinidad who came to meet the tender there and drove Hamish off in his car to a club outside the town. There on the verandah sat a tall, lean, sunburnt fellow in white, with a little straw-coloured moustache and a bold nose. Malloy, his name was. He was drinking gin and tonic contentedly by himself, but when Hamish was presented to him, he was friendly and willing to talk. And in his talk he mentioned, casually, earthquakes, hurricanes, and revolution; a tea plantation in Ceylon; a snake farm in Brazil. He was like someone out of a play or a book, and Hamish didn't believe in him.

Even when his father's friend assured him that Malloy's yarns were fact and not fiction, and that he was a businesslike adventurer who made money out of his fantastic enterprises, Hamish still found him incredible. But he wanted to see more of him, and he was more flattered than he would admit even to himself to see that the older man liked his company. He had three days in Trinidad, and he went riding with Malloy, went swimming with him, sat on the club verandah with him; he learned to drink gin and tonic, he learned a lot about the habits of the barracuda and the black mamba. And he began to learn a little of what there is in the world.

The ship went on to Demerara and Hamish with it, and he left Malloy with a regret that surprised him. When they stopped at Trinidad northward bound, he was so pleased to learn that Malloy was coming with them as far as Martinique that he actually showed it.

They seemed to the other passengers an absurdly ill-assorted pair, the self-contained and wooden young Hamish, and the genial, rather battered rover, Malloy. But the friendship between them was soundly based; they had a profound mutual regard for each other.

"If I'd been like you—" said Malloy, "I mean to say, if I'd had some definite purpose when I was young.... But no. I wasted my time, played the fool, wouldn't settle down to anything."

He had an immense regard for Hamish's education.

"Latin..." he said. "Now, I hardly know a word of Latin. My father and mother did their best to make a scholar of me, but it was no good. I ran away from my home—in Ireland, that was—when I was sixteen, and I've never set foot there since."

He spoke with such regret that Hamish asked why.

"God knows!" Malloy answered with a sigh. "This life gets hold of you. One thing leads to another. And now, here I am, without a word of Latin."

"You speak Spanish."

"Oh, you pick that up," said Malloy. "Spanish and French, and a bit of Portuguese and Dutch, and you can get on anywhere. That's nothing. Now, these classics you've read...."

He wanted to know about the classics; he got Hamish to write out a list of books. They were at all times very serious together.

"We'll meet again, Grier!" Malloy said when he left the ship at Martinique.

He seemed certain of this, but Hamish thought he would never see Malloy again, or anyone like him. The tourists on board seemed to him flat and boring; he was homeward bound now, toward New York and his ambitious future, leaving behind him Malloy and Malloy's bright, enchanted world, and it depressed him.

But when he got home that passed. He went back to college, to his friends. He had taken a trip, that was all. He was surprised, and immeasurably pleased, to get a postcard from Malloy in Martinique.

```
Weather has been very good. This is an interesting place.
Empress Josephine born here. Historical associations.
                              Hector Malloy
```

He gave no address, and anyhow Hamish would not have known what to write to him; it was enough that Malloy, the adventurer, should remember him an hour.

The next year when Hamish was home for the Christmas holidays Malloy telephoned to him and proposed a visit to a night club; someone a thousand miles away had recommended it to Malloy. They met there, and Malloy was completely at home, cool, good-humoured, distinguished in his dinner jacket; not changed at all.

"Came to New York to get a ship to Mexico," he said.

He drank whiskey and soda as if it were water, and Hamish would at least have tried to keep up with him out of pride. But Malloy saved him from that folly; he began ordering beer for himself. It was a wonderful evening, and the next day Malloy was off to Mexico.

He sent Hamish a postcard from there, and at Christmas he sent him another card. Then a card came from Nicaragua. Two years later he telephoned again. This time he was on his way to Quebec.

Hamish was graduated from college and went into his father's business, exactly as he had planned. He was passionately interested in the business, he had plenty of friends, his life was altogether satisfactory to him. Only he never forgot that there was that other way of life, that other world. It was not for him; but sometimes he liked to think about it.

Malloy returned to New York on the way to Rio. He and Hamish dined together, and he was seriously interested in Hamish's progress.

"That's the life!" he said. "You'll get somewhere, my lad."

He had heard that there was a very fine Shakespearean actor now playing in New York, and he invited Hamish to see Hamlet with him. They went to a bar afterward.

"Now, there's a play..." said Malloy. "Makes you think."

He was unusually silent until he had had two drinks; then he came to, with a slight start.

"Well!" he said with a sigh. "All the world's a stage.... Yes. Some actors are not so good, eh? I wanted to ask you, Grier... I don't know how you feel about this sort of thing—speculative. It's a little deal in aquamarines. If you'd like to put a couple of hundred into it...."

Hamish was horribly embarrassed. He had had more experience now; responsibility had augmented his innate caution. He couldn't approve of this sort of business. But it occurred to him that perhaps Malloy was hard up, needed a bit of cash for the scheme. And Hamish gave it to him.

He was only a junior member of his father's staff, and his bank account was still very small; he had six hundred and fifty dollars, and he gave Malloy a cheque for five hundred. Did it with an air of hearty confidence, too.

That cheque was a milestone in their friendship. For one thing, it made Hamish realize how much Malloy meant to him. And it touched Malloy profoundly. He went off, and Hamish heard nothing from him for nearly six months. Then he got a letter.

Dear Grier:

Enclosed is a cheque—not so bad, eh? Excuse haste, but I am taking a plane to Montevideo. Will try to send you an account of this business from there. It was damned funny.

H.M.

The cheque was for eleven hundred dollars, and Hamish heard nothing from Montevideo. Two years went by, but Hamish never forgot him. He liked to think that somewhere, in some incredible place, Malloy was going about his business, cool, good-humoured, in a white suit and a helmet.

He was in his office on a bleak grey winter afternoon when Malloy telephoned again.

"Look, here, Grier!" he said. "Can you get away at once? Good! Come up to my hotel, will you, and see Faquita."

There was an unusual excitement in his tone, and Hamish felt an overwhelming curiosity. He did drop everything, and took a taxi uptown in the cold drizzle. What was Faquita, he thought? A girl? He had never known Malloy to take more than a casual interest in girls.

They were sitting side by side in the dark, solemn lounge of the hotel, Malloy and that girl. No one else, thought Hamish, could have found such a girl, so beautiful and so strange. A pale and slender young girl, with great, sorrowful, dark eyes; a rueful little smile; an undefinable, delicate charm.

The whole story had that charm and that strangeness. Faquita, for all her dark beauty and her trace of foreign accent, was an American, even a New Englander. Her father had been an engineer with a refrigeration plant in the Argentine; he had lived there with his motherless child until he, too, had died. An aunt in Vermont had sent for the girl, from a sense of duty; she hadn't wanted her, and Faquita hadn't wanted to go. And on the ship this forlorn young orphan had met Hector Malloy.

"We're going to be married on Saturday morning," Malloy said, "and at noon we sail for France on our way to Persia. Oil business."

Hamish was best man and the only guest at that wedding in the church vestry; he went down to the dock and saw them off. It was the most fitting thing that Malloy should be going to Persia with a beautiful, dark-eyed bride.

Hamish thought about them a great deal; even in the office, he thought about them. He had seen Faquita only twice, and for only a few moments; he had not exchanged a dozen words with her. Yet she haunted him. The other girls he knew seemed to him insipid, entirely uninteresting; he felt that he could never fall in love until he met another Faquita.

He imagined them in a Persia of his own invention, mosques, minarets, dim bazaars with incense burning; and he was always hoping to hear that they were coming back. Within six months he had a letter posted in Bermuda.

Dear Grier:

Here we are, very snug, nice little house and so on. Food and so on in Persia did not suit Faquita, so we came here. Have got an agency for one or two good British articles not doing half badly.

Thing is, when will you come down for a visit? Only two days on the ship, you know, and we can put you up. All the comforts of home. Let me hear when to expect you.

Yours sincerely,<br>Hector Malloy

Hamish wanted to go at once; the idea pleased him beyond measure. But whenever he was about to set a date, something came up in the office which needed his attention. Weeks went by, and months, and he was still thinking that maybe he could manage to get away soon. And then a cable came.

```
Can you sail Saturday. Wish discuss urgent matter.
Greatly appreciate if possible.
                    Malloy
```

That was on Thursday, and at nine-thirty on Saturday morning Hamish was on board the ship. It had been very much easier to get away than he had expected; he realized that the business could get on well enough without him for a week.

And as soon as the gangplank was up, a curious sense of release came over him, a sort of gay freedom. He remembered his other trip, and he was impatient to see that incredibly blue sea again, that hot colour; he was heading south, and on his way to see that very embodiment of the tropic world, Hector Malloy.

"If it's some business or financial scheme," he thought. "Well... I shouldn't mind putting what I've got into something like that."

He had saved two thousand dollars, and he was proud of it. But he would be still prouder to put it into some picturesque enterprise with Malloy.

"As far as that goes," thought Hamish, "I could manage to take a little time off, and look into the scheme. I could go to South America—Persia— down to Trinidad...."

It was a raw, dreary March day; under the grey sky the sea was leaden, the cold rain blew in his face as he stood at the rail. But he scarcely noticed that; he was thinking of Trinidad, of South America, Persia....

"Just the right sort of weather," said a girl beside him.

She was very pretty; her face was rosy above the fur collar of her coat, her grey eyes were alight; she was a tall young creature, with an extraordinary vitality about her.

"Right weather to go south, you mean?" said Hamish.

"That wasn't my idea," she said. "I mean I like New York in this weather. I like to come out of Carnegie Hall, and take a taxi—when I shouldn't—and go down Park Avenue in the rain, and stop at the Waldorf for a cocktail. I hate to be leaving."

"Well, you'll probably like Bermuda when you get there," said Hamish.

"I've lived there for over a year," said she. "And I'm still homesick."

She was very easy to talk to, a little too easy, he thought; too matter-of-fact. She told him that her name was Stephanie Rose, and that she had gone to Bermuda to do her writing in peace and quiet.

"Writing?" said Hamish, interested.

"A textbook," she said. "Elementary harmony."

That was not interesting.

"What hotel are you going to?" she asked.

"I'm going to visit friends," he said. "Fellow called Hector Malloy—"

"*Hector?*" she said, and said it in an odd way.

"Yes," said Hamish. "D'you know him?"

"I live next door to them," she said. "Well, I think I'll go below now. Shall we have a cocktail together before lunch? All right! I'll meet you in the bar at twelve-thirty."

Promptly at twelve-thirty she came into the bar, broad-shouldered and blonde, very handsome in her pink sweater and dark skirt. But so very matter-of-fact.

Hamish couldn't talk to her as he talked to other girls. She hadn't seen any new plays or movies; she told him candidly she didn't care much about reading. It was impossible to contemplate saying anything complimentary or flattering to her, or attempting even the mildest sort of flirtation.

She signed for her own drink, and he made no protest.

"If you haven't made a table reservation," she said, "let's sit together."

He arranged that. He had his deck chair moved next to hers; they swam in the pool together, walked the deck together, played ping-pong and shuffleboard. To the other passengers it must have looked like a sudden romance, but it was far from that. On the second night out they sat on deck; it was a sweet, mild night with a great orange moon sliding up over the rim of the sea. But even then she was matter-of-fact. She asked Hamish questions about the Gulf Stream, questions he was not able to answer.

"Someone told me that the Gulf Stream is changing its course," she said. "It's interesting to think what might happen if there was a big change, isn't it?"

That was the sort of thing that interested her; she was entirely impersonal.

Complete contrast to Faquita, thought Hamish, and a sensation stirred in him that had grown familiar, something that was half longing and half regret. He wondered if he was ever going to find that lovely, gentle girl of his own.

"Well, we'll dock tomorrow morning, Miss Rose," he said, for the sake of saying something.

"Steve to you," she said. "You must come and have tea with me."

His mind was full of Faquita; he was silent for a moment.

"Thanks, I will," he said. "If you live next door I suppose you see quite a lot of Faquita?"

"Faquita?" she repeated.

"Mrs. Malloy, you know."

"Oh!" said she. "Well, no. I don't go in much for social life."

He knew from some nuance in her tone that she didn't like Faquita.

"That's natural," he thought. "Couldn't imagine two girls more completely different."

But it was a black mark against Steve.

Hamish was up early in the morning, more eager than he would have allowed anyone to suspect. The sea was as blue as he had longed for it to be; the ship nosed her way between two little green islands surprisingly close. He saw the low, gentle hills; the white and pink houses: a scene tranquil and neat, lovely, yet in some indefinable way disappointing to him.

And Malloy, too, caused in him the same vague disappointment and regret. He was standing on the dock, in a dark-blue suit, and a grey felt hat; he was friendly enough, but preoccupied, businesslike about his guest's luggage.... Only Faquita was—right. She was waiting in a surrey that stood in the sunny street outside the shed; she wore a flowered dress of pink and black, a wide black hat; she was beautiful, gentle, and strange as Hamish remembered her.

"I'm so *glad*, Mr. Grier," she said, holding out her hand. She did not smile, but her little fingers clasped his warmly, and suddenly he was happy. Malloy sat in front with the coloured driver, Hamish got in beside Faquita, and the carriage set off along Front Street and turned up a hill.

"There's a new shop," said Faquita. "That's one of the big hotels."

They entered an avenue lined with cedars; before them a purple bougainvillæa was a startling glory of colour among the dark branches.

"The parish church," Faquita went on. "That's the athletic field.... They're building a new house here."

Hamish turned his head in whichever direction she indicated; he was touched by her efforts to entertain him.

"Did you have a nice trip, Mr. Grier? I'm glad we've had plenty of rain, and the tanks are full."

Hamish made proper responses. And presently the carriage stopped before a little bungalow that stood high on a bank above the road.

"Is this—?" Hamish began, and checked himself. He mustn't let them see how surprised, how dismayed, he was. It seemed to him impossible to imagine Malloy and Faquita, those two figures of romance, living in this tidy little suburban villa. And inside it was worse. It was appalling. A little sitting room crowded with cheap golden-oak furniture, stiff lace curtains at the windows, a grey carpet with garlands of pink roses.

"You'll want to wash and brush up before lunch," said Malloy. "I'll show you—"

"I'll show Mr. Grier," said Faquita, eagerly.

She led him along the narrow hall and opened a door. The shutters were closed; the room was dark. He saw in the dimness a white smooth bed, a green chest of drawers, a green iron washstand.

"It's nicer with the shutters closed," Faquita explained. "There's such a glare from the water."

But the moment she had gone, Hamish opened the shutters and looked out at a breath-taking beauty. Below him lay the sea, so blue and calm, green as jade in the shadow of the rocks; above him, blue sky without a cloud; and, far out, the white sail of a fishing boat. It delighted him, and his spirits rose and rose; he lit a cigarette and leaned out looking at this bright beauty, until a knock at the door startled him. A coloured boy in a white jacket stood there, with a gentle, deprecating smile.

"Sah…. Sorry to disturb you, sah, but Mr. Malloy say he like to see you at once, sah. In he office, sah."

"All right!" said Hamish.

"Excuse me, sah, but Mr. Malloy he say will you please come very *quiet,* sah?"

"Quiet!" Hamish repeated, surprised.

The boy smiled, an anxious, even entreating smile, and Hamish said no more but followed him along the corridor, walking as softly as he could on the bare floor. The boy led him out of a side door into a little walled garden to a wooden shed like a tool house.

"Mr. Malloy waiting for you, sah," he said.

Hamish opened the door and stepped into a bare little room bleached by the sun, with no furniture except a flat-topped desk, two straight chairs, and an army cot. The windows were barred, but outside was the blue sea. Malloy wasn't there, but Hamish was in no hurry; he stood by the window waiting. If Malloy wanted to see him 'at once' he would be here soon.

Ten minutes went by, and Hamish lit a cigarette. He finished the cigarette and then began to grow a little restless. He crossed the room; he looked at the articles on the desk—a tin of cocoa, a bar of soap, a bottle of toilet water. It was hot in here; he thought he would open the door.

The door wouldn't open. He thought at first that it had stuck, and he pulled it and pushed it. It wasn't stuck, though; it was locked on the outside.

Hamish didn't believe in that sort of thing. It was simply not possible that he should be locked into this shed. Anyhow, he intended to get out. He tried the bars at the window; they were rusty and he thought they might pull loose. They would not budge. The door would not open.

"All right!" he said to himself. "Malloy will miss me presently. The boy's made some fool mistake."

He smoked; he walked up and down the room. The noonday sun was making the place like an oven.... Half an hour.... It was nothing, simply a fool mistake. Three quarters of an hour.... Somewhere a whistle blew; twelve o'clock.... Over an hour now.... If this was a mistake, it was an extraordinary one.

Nothing on earth could have induced him to call for assistance; he would have baked alive first. But when he heard the sound of a light step on the gravel walk, he called, "Malloy?" pretty loudly, although he knew it was not Malloy. Someone tried the door.

"It seems to be locked," said Hamish.

"Oh!" said a voice he remembered. There was a moment's silence; then he heard a key being put into the lock, and Stephanie Rose opened the door.

# CHAPTER TWO

Hamish felt like a fool, and that made him angry. And the girl's composed and amiable smile did not soothe him.

"Thanks!" he said.

"No trouble at all," said she.

"Some mistake," said he. "Where did you get the key?"

For some reason that made the colour rise in her cheeks. "Oh…. In the door," she said.

And that was a lie. He had heard her put the key into the lock. "Did you?" he said.

"Probably some child just turned it," said she.

"Oh—very probably," said Hamish.

She stood for a moment, looking about her.

"Well… I'll be seeing you!" she said, and went off.

Hamish had been hot enough to begin with, and anger raised his temperature. He came out of the shed and walked toward the house; walked slowly, hoping to cool off a little. There was a great noonday calm over this brilliant world; he could hear the soft lap of the sea on the rocks.

"Must have been that house boy," he thought. "What the devil did he do such a thing for? What possible reason could he have for getting me out there and locking me in?"

He was so interested in getting to the bottom of this that he forgot about being polite. He went to the back door of the house, and through the glass he saw a neat, thin black woman in a print dress bending over the sink; he rapped, and she came toward him at once.

"I'd like to see that boy," he said.

"Raymond, sir?" she said, in a quiet British voice, with no trace of the boy's accent. "I'll fetch him, sir. Shall I send him to your room, sir?"

"No, thanks. I'll see him here," said Hamish, and stood on the kitchen steps, waiting with an undiminished anger. In a moment, Raymond came out of the house, with his air of gentle eagerness.

"Sah?"

"Why did you lock me in that shed?" said Hamish.

"Excuse me, sah. I did not know you in there, sah. Saw the key in the door, sah, and Mr. Malloy, he order me never to leave it so, sah."

"You knew I was there. You took me there yourself."

"Excuse me, sah. When I pass, I did not hear anyone speaking. And Mr.

Malloy, he order me not to leave it so, with the door unlocked—"

"Why didn't you look inside?"

"Oh, I ask your pardon, sah, but Mr. Malloy would not like me to look in, sah."

"Then why didn't you knock on the door?"

"Never think of that, sah."

Against his will, Hamish was impressed by the boy's fervent earnestness.

"But if Mr. Malloy wanted to see me at once," he said, "he must have missed me. Must have looked for me. Didn't he ask you where I was?"

"I did not see Mr. Malloy, sah. No, sah—he told me to fetch you, sah. I wait for him to ring, sah, while I lay the table for luncheon."

"Well, you've made some sort of mistake," said Hamish. "Where's Mr. Malloy now?"

"That I cannot say, sah."

"I'll find him," said Hamish, and went down the steps.

It was difficult to believe that Raymond had been lying; difficult to imagine any possible reason for such a lie. "But he must be lying!" thought Hamish. "If Malloy sent for me, and I hadn't come in a reasonable time, he'd certainly have looked for me and asked questions."

He went round to the front of the house, and there on the verandah he found Faquita, sitting in a rocking chair, embroidering.

"Have you had a little nap?" she asked.

"No...." Hamish began. Then he recalled that Raymond had said Malloy wanted him to come quietly. It was certainly possible that Malloy had never made the request, had not sent for him at all. But, if he had, perhaps he didn't want Faquita to know.

"Just resting," he said; and to himself, "I'd better shut up, until I know more."

It was his instinct to 'shut up' anyhow; he was never disposed to be over-communicative.

"Sit down, won't you?" said Faquita. "Hector had to go to his office, but he said he'd try to be back in time for lunch. Will you smoke, Mr. Grier?"

He offered his cigarettes to her, and she smiled up at him.

"Do you know I've never smoked? On the ship going to France I wanted to try. All the chic, attractive women seemed to be smoking. But Hector didn't want me to. He said he *liked* me to be old-fashioned."

She was old-fashioned, thought Hamish; she was like some girl out of an old novel. She talked to him about their house.

"It's the first real house I've ever had," she said, "and I couldn't tell you how I love it. I picked out all the furniture myself. It really is attractive, don't you think?"

He thought it was the most hideous house he had ever seen, and that made him sorry for her, and he praised it; he called it 'homelike.' He noticed now that she had no style in her dress, either; her thin dark-blue frock was too big for her. But that didn't matter. She was beautiful, and whatever she wore partook of her own fragile grace. He smoked two cigarettes, and encouraged her to talk about her cherished house and her way of living.

"I've *never* been so happy before," she said. "We've made such nice friends here. People drop in, in the evening—we have little dinner parties; we go out to dinner. It's quite gay! And yet, it's all so *nice.*"

She smiled, and held up her work. "A table cover," she said. "I really prefer all white; but Hector loves colours, so I'm using red and blue in the design."

Raymond came to her side. "Luncheon is sarved, mistress," he said, softly.

"We won't wait for Hector," said Faquita, rising. "I told Leah to make chicken creole, especially for you, Mr. Grier."

"Don't you think it could be Hamish?" he suggested, and she smiled again.

She was so happy; she sat at the head of the table in a dismal little dining room, the shutters half-closed, the walls a sort of mustard colour, the furniture over-large and heavy; she served, from plated dishes, the sort of food Hamish most disliked, soft and creamy foods, elaborate yet tasteless.

"Leah is a wonderful cook, isn't she?"

"She is!" said Hamish, warmly.

He found it a little difficult to talk to Faquita; it was rather like talking to a princess from a fairy tale. She didn't care for the movies, she didn't care for reading; she lived, he thought, in a world of her own, happy and innocent. When lunch was finished they went into the sitting room, and it became worse. An almost irresistible drowsiness came over him; his eyes filled with the tears of suppressed yawns.

"Do you ride a bicycle, Faquita?" he asked.

"Faquita!" she repeated. "That's my old name. I haven't heard it for so long. I like to hear it again."

He thought that a shadow came over her lovely face.

"Thinking of her father, probably," he said to himself. Another yawn made his throat ache. "This must be quite a change from the Argentine," he observed. "Don't you find it—a bit tame?"

"It's home," she said. And after a pause, she answered his question. "No, I don't ride a bicycle, Hamish. I don't swim; I don't walk. I'm a lazy creature."

A fragile creature, he thought; more than any other woman he had seen she needed protection, needed a home.

"Of course, Hector's tremendously active," she went on. "He's a magnificent swimmer; he rides; he does everything. He's the most popular man in Bermuda."

"I bet he is!" said Hamish, touched by this naive loyalty.

"I'll show you some snapshots," she said.

She brought out an album, and he did his best to show an interest in dozens and dozens of photographs. Hector on a horse, Hector in a motorboat; Faquita under a palm tree; pictures of people unknown to him and with that queer, squinting, suspicious look that unfamiliar photographs seem to have. He looked at them and made what comments he could, and his mind grew hazy with sleep.

"Where the hell is Hector?" he thought, in despair. "Why doesn't he come home?"

The hour he had spent locked in the shed no longer caused him any emotion; it was merged in the vast tide of boredom that rose and rose within him. A long silence came between them, and Faquita ended it with an obvious effort.

"Would you like to play backgammon?" she asked.

"The poor girl's as bored as I am," thought Hamish. "But she's too polite to say anything." So he must. "If you'll excuse me, Faquita," he said, "I'd like to unpack—"

"Oh, Raymond will do that for you!"

"I'd rather do it myself, thanks," he said.

When he got safely into his room, he undressed, put on a dressing gown, and immediately went to sleep. The shutters had been closed again, and he left them so; the warm, relaxing air blew in. He lay like a log.

When he opened his eyes it was dark, and for a moment he did not know where he was. Then, in alarm, he turned on the lamp beside him and looked at his watch; five o'clock. He dressed in haste, and went out of the room in search of Hector. But Faquita was alone on the verandah.

"Did you get a nice little nap, Hamish?" she asked. "Everyone is sleepy here for the first day or so."

He sat down on the rail and lit a cigarette. The road below them was busy: one of those carts, locally known as trolleys, went rattling by, the horse breaking into a clumsy gallop; a fleet of bicycles passed softly; Portuguese workmen were going home, their voices eager and plaintive. A carriage came with the lamps lighted, and after that everything had a light; a street lamp shone through the trees.

"Where the devil is Hector?" thought Hamish.

This had been the longest day in his life; he was scarcely able to believe that only this morning, only some seven hours ago, he had been on board the ship. He was very pleased to think that he had made a reservation for

Wednesday's sailing. Of course, it could be canceled, but it seemed to him that would be long enough.

"There's Reggie!" said Faquita.

Someone dismounted from a bicycle and carried the machine up the steps, a tall slight figure in white. Faquita rose and turned a switch, and an overhead light shone harshly on the verandah.

"Hamish," she said, "this is Mr. Cornwall, Hector's partner. Reggie, Mr. Grier."

Reggie advanced with a springy, bent-kneed gait, a good-looking young Englishman with innocent blue eyes, dark-lashed. He shook hands with Hamish and sank into a chair.

"Did you leave Hector at the office?" asked Faquita.

"Er—no," said Reggie. "No, I didn't. He's buzzing about somewhere. Come to think of it, I believe he took the train to St. George's. Business deal."

"He'll be along any minute then," said Faquita.

"Oh, certainly!" said Reggie, fervently.

Unexpectedly and loudly Faquita clapped her hands, and Raymond came hurrying out.

"Cocktails!" she said.

They sat there chatting, and Reggie's presence made matters very much better; he had a casual good humour that Hamish liked. Raymond came out with a shaker and glasses on a tray; with his air of gentle deference he poured out the cocktails.

"Raymond!" cried Faquita. "You fool! You've used those orange bitters again! Hasn't Mr. Malloy told you, time after time—"

"Yes, mistress. So sorry, mistress," said Raymond, bending his head to the storm.

She emptied her glass and the shaker over the rail. "Now make more!" she said.

She looked extraordinarily beautiful in her wrath, her dark eyes brilliant, a fine colour in her usually pale cheeks; she sat very straight, like a little queen, both hands on the arms of her chair. Hamish was amazed to hear Reggie laugh. She turned toward him, her delicate brows drawn together.

"She-Who-Must-Be-Obeyed," said Reggie, cheerfully.

"That is very ridiculous," she said coldly. "I'm *never* unreasonable."

There was a silence which lasted until Raymond came out again with more cocktails, acceptable this time to Faquita.

"Here's to a pleasant visit, Grier!" said Reggie, raising his glass.

Inside the house the telephone rang, and presently they could hear Raymond's voice answering.

"Yes, sah. This Mr. Malloy's boy, sah. One moment, please, sah." He came out on the verandah. "Mistress, Mr. Lenny in St. George's, he say he been waiting for Mr. Malloy since three o'clock. He say, Mr. Malloy made an important engagement with him, mistress, and—"

Faquita rose, her hand flew to her heart.

"Reggie!" she said. "Reggie, you told me Hector had gone to St. George's."

"May have been delayed in getting away," suggested Reggie, with undiminished cheerfulness.

"Three hours?" she demanded. "You know that's not possible."

"Mr. Lenny on the wire, mistress," said Raymond, softly.

"I'll speak to him!" said Faquita. "Reggie, do you know when Hector left the office?"

"No," said Reggie. "No, I don't, Frances. Wasn't there myself, you see. Why not tell Lenny that Hector will call him as soon as he gets home? Probably some misunderstanding about the afternoon. Hector may have thought the engagement was for tomorrow, or something of the sort."

"No..." said Faquita.

There was a very strange silence upon them all, Faquita still with her hand against her heart; Raymond looking anxiously at her; Reggie standing, cigarette in hand, and looking at no one; Hamish looking from one to the other, trying doggedly to understand. There was something he could not seize.

"Mr. Lenny on the wire, mistress," said Raymond again.

"Well.... Where is Hector?" cried Faquita.

Hamish started nervously, shocked by the question. And it brought everything to a head; all the nebulous doubts of the day gathered into one ominous cloud.

"Oh, he's somewhere about," said Reggie. "Don't worry! Look here! I'll speak to Lenny."

"No!" said Faquita, and went into the house. Hamish heard her gentle voice, sharpened by anxiety. "No, he's not, Mr. Lenny. Are you *sure* it was today?... No, I don't. I don't *know*.... But I can't help worrying.... Yes, I will.... Thank you, Mr. Lenny!"

She came out on the verandah again, stood in the doorway.

"Look here, Faquita!" said Reggie, persuasively. "Don't upset yourself. You'll hear from Hector—"

"What do you mean? Why should I hear from Hector?"

"Or see him, I mean. Sit down, Frances; there's a good girl."

Minding his own business was a passion with Hamish, but he felt obliged to intervene now on behalf of Faquita. The poor girl was alarmed, bewildered, and Reggie's air of blithe unconcern was making matters worse.

"If Hector doesn't show up by dinner-time," he said, "we'll make inquiries," he said.

"No!" said Reggie, vehemently. Then he resumed the persuasive tone. "Mean to say, Hector wouldn't like it. He's been delayed—some private business very likely, and he'd feel a bit of a fool if you called in the police—"

"Police!" cried Faquita, in a sort of scream. Her face grew white as paper; Hamish sprang to her side and took her arm.

"Don't be a dam' fool, Cornwall," he said, sharply. "No one mentioned the police. Probably Hector sent a message home, and it never reached Faquita. There's probably a perfectly simple explanation for the whole thing. I'll—" He paused, thinking. "I might ring up his club, for instance. Or, *you* ought to be able to make suggestions, Cornwall. You know where he's likely to be."

"Oh, yes," said Reggie in polite, earnest assent. "I'll see what I can do. I'll call you up after a bit. I'll have some news for you very soon. Simply carry on, and don't worry until you hear from me. Good night!"

He went, and his going was somehow startling. His tall white figure hastened along the path with that loose, springy gait. He carried his bicycle down the steps, mounted it, and sped off, noiseless as a moth. Hamish, still holding Faquita's arm, started after him.

"Yes, but—" he said, half to himself.

She drew closer to him.

"Hamish!" she said in a whisper. "I'm *afraid*."

She was trembling; her black eyes looked enormous in her pale face. He felt beyond measure sorry for her, and more than a little afraid himself. The facts, as he knew them, were bad enough; but his own secret knowledge made the affair still more inexplicable, and more disturbing. That message summoning him to the shed, his hour's imprisonment there....

"Hamish!" she said. "Do you think—we ought to call in the police?"

Then for the first time it occurred to him that *he* was in charge. He was responsible.

"*Hamish!* You do think so! You think something's wrong—horribly wrong."

"If she gets hysterical..." he thought.

He wouldn't know how to cope with that.

"Will you—lie down, Faquita?" he said in a very quiet, cool tone. "Rest a few moments, while I make an inquiry? I mean, will you not get yourself excited?"

"I'll try, Hamish," she said, her great, frightened eyes fixed on his face. "I'll sit here—and wait."

Hamish ran down the steps to follow up the one and only clue he held.

# CHAPTER THREE

When he reached the road, he didn't know which way to turn. Stephanie had said that she lived next door, but he didn't know on which side. The tide of home-goers had ebbed; the road was empty. He hesitated for a moment and then turned right at random. A few minutes' walk brought him to another villa very like Malloy's; he mounted the steps, rang the bell, and a young coloured girl opened the door.

"Miss Rose live here?" asked Hamish.

"No, sir," said she, and closed the door.

He went down the steps, and along the road in the opposite direction; he passed a long stretch of vacant land and came at last to a gateway in a stone wall leading to a long drive. At the end of this was the lighted facade of a very imposing house with a stone terrace before it. An elderly man was sitting there, smoking, and Hamish addressed him.

"Excuse me, but does Miss Rose live here?"

"Miss Rose?" said the elderly man, thoughtfully. "Now let me see.... Rose, hmmm...." He deliberated. "Sure it's not Ross?" he said.

"Rose," said Hamish, firmly.

"Rose, hmmm?" He deliberated again and then went toward the house. "Ellen!" he called, and a pretty girl of fifteen or so came out. "Ellen, this gentleman is looking for a Miss *Rose*—"

"Oh, yes! She lives in The Cottage!" said Ellen.

"Ah! The Cottage!" said the elderly man, delighted. "That's the next house, sir. Turn back in the direction you came from—"

"But the next house is Malloy's."

"The Cottage is between Mr. Malloy's house and this."

"You can't see it from the road," Ellen explained. "But there's a path.... I'll show you!"

She led Hamish down the drive lined with eucalyptus trees and into the road again; she showed him a faint little path cut in steps out of the rock.

"Just go along there," she said, kindly.

Hamish went up the little path, slowly, curiously depressed by the sensation of being a stranger. He didn't know the place; he didn't know the people; he didn't know anything. He really knew very little about Hector.... Reaching the top of the bank, he saw below him a queer little house with no wall about it, no trees—a house that looked casual as one of the boulders on the shore. Lights shone from its windows, and, as he drew near, there was a thunderous outburst of music from a piano. He stepped up on the verandah and knocked at the door, but no one came; no doubt that tremendous music drowned out any sound he made.

He looked for a bell and saw none; he knocked again more loudly, and being still ignored, he looked in at the window. There was Stephanie at a grand piano, slim, straight as a dart, the lamplight making her hair bright, her lovely profile grave, even stern; her eyes fixed upon the music before her. Hamish rapped on the window, and she glanced up and stopped playing; she rose with an ominous frown and opened the door.

"Oh, it's you!"

"Sorry to interrupt you, but—I'd like to ask you a question."

"Come in!" she said.

The sitting room, he thought, must take up most of the cottage, for it was a good-sized room and looking larger, because it was so bare—whitewashed walls, three wicker armchairs with blue and white striped cushions, white bookcases, a small table, and the piano; nothing else—no pictures, no ornaments, no rug on the polished floor. She herself looked austere, in a sleeveless white dress, no smile on her face.

"'Mrs. Malloy is very much worried about her husband," said Hamish. "He hasn't come home. I thought you might be able to—" He paused. "To make some suggestion," he said.

"I?" said she, coldly.

"I thought it was possible that Malloy might have mentioned to you where he was going."

"And why to me?"

Hamish was not daunted by her haughty air.

"I thought you might help me," he went on, doggedly. "I imagine you know Malloy pretty well."

"What makes you think that?" she demanded.

"Well," said Hamish, "you have a key to his office."

"I told you I found the key outside."

"I heard you put it into the lock."

"I picked it up from the grass."

"If you can give me any information as to where Malloy is," said Hamish, "I'd appreciate it. And I shouldn't think I had to tell anyone where I got my information."

She was silent for a moment.

"Sit down, won't you?" she said, with a sudden friendliness. "Have a smoke?"

She sat down opposite to him and accepted a cigarette and a light from him.

"I didn't mean to be so cross," she said. "But I am likely to be like that, when my practicing is interrupted. Now tell me. What's all this about Hector?"

"He hasn't come home."

"It's not late."

"Yes, but he wasn't home to lunch. He didn't keep an appointment he made this afternoon. His partner doesn't know where he is."

"Honestly, I don't think I'd worry if I were you," she said earnestly. "Hector has so many irons in the fire—so many people to see all the time."

"I am worried, though," said Hamish.

"I suppose Frances has made you worry," said Stephanie. "She's a marvelous worrier, of course."

"I think she has good reason to be anxious."

Stephanie smoked for a time in silence.

"Why did you come down here?" she asked, abruptly.

That was not a good technique to use with Hamish. He was not to be rushed; the tone and the question made him alertly wary.

"To visit Malloy," he answered promptly.

"Yes, but why did you come just now?"

"Just now?" he repeated, with a look of innocent surprise. "I don't quite understand—"

"It's really nicer at Easter time," she said.

"I didn't know that," said Hamish.

It was a deadlock. He meant to break it if he could.

"Well..." he said with a sigh. "I suppose there's nothing for it but to go to the police."

He was startled to see her sunburnt face grow pale.

"Because Hector's not home by half-past seven?" she said. "Doesn't that seem rather ridiculous?"

"No," said Hamish judicially. "No. Not in the circumstances."

"What circumstances?"

"Oh, quite a lot of little things," said Hamish. "I can't understand them, but they may mean something to the police."

"If you go to the police, they'll—laugh at you!" she cried.

"The police, dear? Did you say the *police?*" asked a quavering voice, and glancing up, Hamish saw a stout old lady with woolly white hair and silver-rimmed spectacles standing in the doorway. He rose politely, and she gave him a dazzling smile.

"I thought someone said police," she explained, coming into the room and settling herself comfortably in an armchair. "I have a perfect horror of the police. Ever since my dreadful experience in Barbados."

"Mapesie, this is Mr. Grier," said Stephanie. "Mrs. Mapes, Mr. Grier."

"Mr. Grier," repeated Mrs. Mapes, in a tone of cozy satisfaction. "That's very nice, I'm sure. I do hope you'll agree with me about *not* calling in the police. Because, of course, those underworld characters *watch* the police and *follow* them. The police *employ* them, you know. To collect information. And, of course, that leads to trouble."

Hamish could think of nothing to say to this extraordinary statement; but it was not necessary for him to say anything. Mrs. Mapes talked on and on, in a soothing, even a soporific way, telling him an amazing anecdote about a ring she had lost in Barbados. Stephanie sat by, with a blank face, and Hamish grew more and more restless. At the first pause in the story, he rose.

"I'm sorry," he said, "but I'm in rather a hurry."

Mrs. Mapes bent her head with a pleasant smile, and Stephanie rose and went to the door with him, opened the door, and went out with him.

"Hamish!" she said in a low voice. *"Don't go to the police! Honestly, you'll be sorry if you do."*

But that friendly, confidential tone was no more effective with him than her former haughtiness.

"Well, of course if you can assure me that he'll be back very soon—" he said. "In an hour, perhaps?"

"Of course I can't. But—if Hector's gone somewhere on business he'll be furious at all this fuss, and no wonder. Wait until the morning, at *least*."

"You expect Faquita to wait all night without a word?"

"You can persuade her—"

"I'm not going to try to persuade her."

"Oh, Hamish, please!" she said, laying her hand on his arm. "For Hector's sake. He'd hate all this so."

"If you know where he is," said Hamish, "if you know anything at all, this is the time to tell it."

"I'm just advising you—not to make a fool of yourself."

"Thanks," said Hamish. "But I think I'll risk that."

Seizing him by the shoulders, she tried to shake him. He was amazed, and then he laughed.

"Oh, go to the devil!" she said, unsteadily, and walked away.

He was grinning to himself as he walked along the path, but after a moment he grew serious again.

"Why doesn't she want me to go to the police?" he thought. "Is it because she knows that Hector's all right—or is it because there's something she doesn't want anyone to find out? She must know that in the course of time we'll go to the police. Is that what she wants? To gain time? Well, for what?"

He could not imagine any good answer.

"She had a key to the shed," he went on. "She may have known Hector very much better than she admits. Love affair?"

He dismissed that idea at once. In the first place, it was manifestly impossible to imagine a man turning from the beautiful and gentle Faquita to the prosaic Stephanie; and in the second place, it was impossible to imagine Stephanie being in love with anyone.

"Perhaps Hector didn't know she had the key," he thought. "Why the devil did she have it? Was there something in the office that she wanted to check up on?"

Suddenly he was tired of these questions he could not answer; tired, impatient. He wanted to get out of this atmosphere of confusion and disquiet.

"Probably Hector's home now," he told himself as he approached the villa.

But as he set foot on the path, Faquita's voice came to him through the dark.

"Hamish, have you found him?"

Down came the sense of responsibility, like a physical weight upon him. He would have to reassure and fortify her; he would have to make all the decisions.

"I've been making enquiries," he said, in a voice which sounded pompous in his own ears.

"What did you find out, Hamish?"

Her voice was desperately anxious; as he mounted the steps she came to him and laid her hand on his arm. Stephanie had made the same gesture, but how differently! A faint and delicate fragrance surrounded Faquita; her voice, her touch, stirred him to a feeling of angry protectiveness.

"Nothing—very definite," he said. "But it's still very early, you know."

She took away her hand and went back up the steps onto the verandah, stood there beneath the harsh overhead light, her eyes lowered; when she looked up her dark lashes were damp.

"Then—you're going to the police, Hamish?"

"I think we'd better wait a little longer," he said., "After all, it's still early, you know."

"But, Hamish, he's missed both lunch and dinner, without a word to me! He's never done anything like this before!"

"He may have sent a message that you didn't get," said Hamish. "You see, Faquita, we don't want to get in the police and make a lot of fuss if there's nothing wrong. Hector wouldn't like it, naturally."

"How long shall we wait, Hamish?"

Her dark eyes were fixed on his face, so anxiously, so pitiably; she trusted utterly to him. And he had to make a pretense of being definite and sure. He glanced at his watch.

"If he hasn't come in by ten," he said, "I think we might make some further enquiries."

"Ten?" she repeated. "Then I think—if you don't mind—I'll lie down until then, Hamish."

Hamish sat on the verandah and smoked a cigarette; he had meant to sit there until ten, but a violent restlessness assailed him. He strolled up and down the path, he walked round the side of the house and through the kitchen window saw the neat, thin coloured woman. Hunger overcame him, but he denied it.

"I'll read," he thought, and entered the house.

The lamps were lighted in the sitting room; it had a pathetically cosy look. There were no books there, though, not so much as a magazine. In a sort of desperation he went down the corridor; a door stood open showing a dark room, with two pale squares denoting the windows. He didn't know whether Hector had a room of his own, but if he had, and this were it, there might be books in it. He hesitated; it seemed incorrect to go wandering about in someone else's house. But his longing for something to divert him from his anxiety, his hunger, and his boredom, overcame him; he felt for the switch, and a light sprang out. He was in a bare room with an iron bed, a chest of drawers, two chairs; he felt sure it was Hector's room, because he saw a shaving mirror on the wall, a pipe on a little table.

But he saw nothing at all to read. This seemed unnatural; he glanced about the bright, bare little room, and under the window he noticed a large chest of cedarwood, with the lid not quite closed. It looked like the sort of box into which one throws anything and everything; he thought there might be some old books in there. Even an old newspaper would be welcome. It was not locked, not even tightly closed; it seemed to Hamish permissible to raise the lid. He did so, and he saw a body huddled in there, face down.

He didn't believe it. Things like that didn't happen. He stood staring down at the thing, and the lid slipped from his hand and fell with a thud on the body's shoulder-blades. He felt a little sick, but he would not acknowledge it; he opened the lid wide so that it rested safely against the wall, and reaching down, he got hold of the body under the arms.

It was Raymond, and he was not heavy. Hamish was able to haul him out and lay him on the floor. Hamish had never before looked upon death, but he recognized it now; he knelt and listened for a heartbeat, but he knew he would hear none. Raymond was dead, his black face mournful and calm, his hands strangely cool.

"Yes..." said Hamish aloud. "But...."

He crossed the room and closed the door and locked it; he did that without reasoning, from a blind instinct to gain time. He had to think; he had to recover from his amazement. He would have to stop staring at Raymond.... He turned away, looked at the wall before him.

He abhorred the sensational; his instinct was to find some sensible, decent explanation for this.

"No blow," he said to himself. "No sign of violence. He looks—peaceful enough." He wished to deny any violence. "Probably a heart attack," he thought. "He was going to pull down the shades or something of the sort, and he had a heart attack and fell into the chest. I'll send for a doctor."

But he made no move. Little by little, his reluctant mind was facing the fact. Nobody could fall in that position.

"Somebody put him there," thought Hamish.

But there wasn't anyone who could have done such a thing. There was no one in the house except Faquita, and the cook, and himself.

"The poor devil is still limp," thought Hamish. "But of course I don't know how long it takes for a body to begin to stiffen."

He remembered phrases from detective stories he had read. "Rigor mortis had already set in...." Raymond had been serving cocktails after five.

"I'll have to notify the police," he thought.

A sort of horror came over him. The police would come, would ask questions; the little house would be filled with confusion; Faquita would be terrified. And what would they find out?

"It's obvious that somebody tried to conceal this boy's death," he thought. "I only found out by accident. Somebody else knows."

Somebody else had put the body into the chest, had left it there in the dark room.

"My God!" said Hamish to himself. "Was it—murder?"

No need to think that. No sign of violence. The boy had died, and someone had wished, for some reason, to conceal the death. This house wouldn't be difficult to enter, he thought; someone could have got in by one of the windows.

"I wish to God Hector'd come back! I don't know anything about these people and their customs," he thought.

But however matter-of-fact he wished to be, he could scarcely think of this event as a 'custom.' Nor could he wait for Hector, or anyone else to explain it to him. He would have to act at once. No use thinking of the consequences; they could not be avoided now. He left the room, locked the door, and put the key into his pocket; then he left the house quietly. He could not telephone there, where Faquita might hear him. He went back to the big house where he had met the elderly man and the young girl; he rang the bell, and a coloured maid admitted him.

"I'd like to use your telephone, please," he said.

The elderly man came out into the hall. He was courteous and friendly;

he led Hamish into a large, handsome library.

"I want to get the police," said Hamish.

He saw the man's face change; he heard a little exclamation from the girl.

"It's begun," he thought.

# CHAPTER FOUR

It had begun, and it was out of his hands now; it had a life of its own.

"I want to report a death," he said. "In Mr. Hector Malloy's house."

"What's your name, if you please, sir?"

"Grier. Hamish Grier. I'm just visiting there. I found the body in a chest."

"Very good, sir. We'll send someone at once. Please see that nothing is disturbed."

As he turned away from the telephone, Hamish had a glimpse of the elderly man staring at him, with a fascinated horror. But he gave him no sort of explanation; he said "Thanks," and went out of the house. Somehow he felt ashamed, as if he had been behaving in an absurdly theatrical way. "I found the body in a chest...."

Just as he reached the road, it began to rain furiously; he was drenched before he could reach the bungalow. He ran up on the verandah and stood there, startled by the sudden violence. The rain drummed loud on the roof, gurgling little brooks were running down the bank, the street lamp was veiled by a silver mist.

"Of course there's some explanation," he thought.

And in his heart he had a desperate hope that the police would at once find a decent, seemly explanation and shut up about it. The fellow who had answered the telephone had been reassuringly matter-of-fact.

"If only Faquita didn't have to know," he thought.

The rain came teeming down, with no wind, falling straight from the black sky in a solid sheet. Hamish moved his head restlessly inside his damp collar and lit a cigarette. He did not wish to go into the house; he intended to stay out here until the police came. But suddenly it occurred to him that this was scarcely a private matter between him and the authorities; after all, it was Faquita's house, and she had a right to know all that happened.

"My God!" he thought. "If she's asleep... I can't knock at her door and tell her a thing like that. She's worried enough already about Hector."

He turned in haste; the front door was unlocked, and he entered the house and went quickly and quietly along the corridor to the kitchen. He was very glad to see a line of light under the door; he found the thin coloured woman sitting in a chair, sewing. She rose.

"I'd like to speak to you," said Hamish, closing the door. "What's your name, please?"

"Leah, sir."

"Well, Leah…" he said, and paused. "There's been an accident," he went on, "and I think you'd better tell Mrs. Malloy."

"Yes, sir," said Leah, and waited. With immense reluctance, Hamish had to say a little more.

"The police are coming," he said.

"Oh, my dear Lord!" said Leah, sadly.

"Yes," said Hamish. "And you'd better—prepare Mrs. Malloy."

"What shall I tell her, sir?"

"I think it's better not to tell her much, until the police have investigated."

"Oh, she won't be satisfied with that, sir!" said Leah, crumpling her apron in her thin fingers. "She'll ask me who had an accident—"

"It was Raymond," said Hamish.

"Oh, my dear Lord!" said Leah again.

"Now, see here!" said Hamish. "I think you're a sensible woman. We've got to consider Mrs. Malloy."

"Yes, sir," said Leah, with admirable calm. "Is Raymond hurt very bad, sir?"

It occurred to Hamish that Raymond's death might well be more shocking to Leah than to Faquita, and he marveled for a moment at his own assumption that only Faquita was to be sheltered and protected.

"I'm sorry," he said, gently. "I'm very sorry…."

"He's dead, sir?"

"Yes," said Hamish. "I'm sorry…."

There was a good loud knock at the door.

"I'll go," said Hamish, "if you'll look after Mrs. Malloy, please."

He opened the door, to see a policeman in helmet and glistening rubber cape.

"Did you report a death, sir?" he asked, in a voice which Hamish thought rang through the house.

"Yes," he answered with a frown.

"I'm Sergeant Welcome, sir, from the Hamilton Police Station. If you'll kindly give me the details—"

"I—happened to go into one of the rooms here," said Hamish. "I was looking for something to read. I noticed this chest partly open, and I looked into it. And I found the body of the coloured house boy. Raymond, he's called."

"What steps did you take, sir, upon the discovery of the body?"

"I pulled him out of the chest," said Hamish. "Naturally, I didn't know whether he was dead or not. When I saw that he was, I locked the room and went to a house down the road, to telephone to the police station."

"No telephone here, sir?"

"Yes. But I didn't want to disturb Mrs. Malloy."

"I see, sir!" said Sergeant Welcome. "Now, then. If you'll show me the body—"

As they turned away from the door, Hamish was startled to see Faquita standing outside her room, motionless, in a long white robe, with big frills down the front, and her black hair in two heavy braids. She looked so foreign, so beautiful.

"Mrs. Malloy?" said the sergeant, with a certain hesitation.

"Yes," she answered. "It's not true, is it?"

"We'll see, ma'am," said the sergeant, briskly. "If you'll kindly return to your room, until I've made an investigation—"

She immediately went into her room and closed the door.

"Mr. Malloy not at home?" asked the sergeant, lowering his voice.

"He's out," said Hamish. And he thought that if he could have one wish in the world granted, he would ask for Hector to come into the house now.

He took the key out of his pocket and opened the door. It was true; Raymond lay there on the floor, just as he had left him. Sergeant Welcome took off his cape and laid it on the floor with his helmet; he knelt beside Raymond and examined him, briefly; he looked into the chest; he examined the window and everything in the room.

"The police surgeon will be here directly, sir," he said. "Now...!"

He brought out a notebook and pencil, and began to question Hamish. His name, his address, his age, his business or profession.

"Previous to the discovery of the body, sir, when were you last in this room?"

"I'd never been in it before," said Hamish.

"Will you give me a list of the members of this household?"

"Mr. and Mrs. Malloy and a woman, a cook—named Leah. There may be other servants. I don't know. I only arrived this morning."

"Can you give me any details about the deceased? Full name, address?"

"I don't know anything about him," said Hamish.

"Very good, sir. Now I'm afraid I've got to ask Mrs. Malloy a few questions."

"Couldn't you ask Leah, instead?"

"I'll have to question her, too, sir. In a matter like this we're obliged to interview everyone in the house. Mrs. Malloy isn't ill, is she, sir?"

"No," said Hamish. "No. She's not ill. But a thing like this...."

"Yes, sir. Very unpleasant. Can you tell me where I can get in touch with Mr. Malloy?"

"I don't know where he is," said Hamish.

The doorbell rang, and the sergeant looked pleased.

"That'll be Doctor Piggott," he said. And it was. A big, thick-set man came briskly down the hall; his ruddy face looked stolid, until one noticed his very bright, shrewd little eyes.

"'This is Mr. Grier, sir," said the sergeant. "Mr. Grier discovered the body and notified the station."

"Ha!" said Doctor Piggott, amiably. "See you later, Mr. Grier. You might see that I'm not disturbed for a few moments, sergeant."

The sergeant went down the hall and knocked at Faquita's door. And Hamish could not stop him; he could not protect Faquita from this. He couldn't, in fact, do anything but wait. Leah opened the door.

"Sorry to disturb Mrs. Malloy," said the sergeant, "but I'll have to ask her a few questions. And you, too. Don't leave the premises."

"I'm ready," said Faquita, and came out into the hall, still in her frilled white robe. "Will you come into the sitting room, please?"

She was pale; her dark eyes looked enormous, but she was composed enough.

"Wait in my room, Leah!" she said.

Then she and the sergeant shut themselves into the sitting room; and Hamish did not know where to go, what to do.

"I suppose I ought to tell them about being locked in the shed," he thought. "It may have some bearing on—the rest of it."

That was a train of thought he could no longer ignore. It was a plain fact that Hector Malloy was not here. And it was another plain fact that Raymond was dead. Unusual facts, both of them, to say the least—so unusual that it was impossible to think of them as sheer coincidence.

"Well.... If there's a connection..." thought Hamish.

Hector had not been seen since the morning, and Raymond had certainly been visible and alive at half-past five. What connection could there be? Hamish went into his room, leaving the door open, painfully alert for any sound.

"The doctor may find that the poor devil's death was an accident," he thought.

And then Hector might come walking in, and there would be an end to this vague horror that hung in the air.

"Anything's better than not knowing where you stand," thought Hamish.

Doctor Piggott came out into the hall.

"Finished?" asked Grier.

"For the moment," said Piggott. "Where's the bathroom? Thanks. We'll have to do a P.M."

"Did you— Do you know the cause of his death?" asked Hamish.

"Can't be sure—without an autopsy," said Piggott. "But I'd say, offhand, that it was opium."

"You mean—poison?" asked Hamish.

"Oh, yes!" said Piggott. "Not much doubt of *that*. Now I'd like to wash up, and then I'll call the superintendent."

"Do you think it's—not a natural death?" asked Hamish.

Doctor Piggott stared at him with a faint smile.

"Think the boy crawled into the chest to die, so that he wouldn't disturb anyone?" he asked. "No.... Even without a post mortem I'd be willing to assert that he was drugged and put in there while he was still alive."

He went into the bathroom, and again Hamish waited, leaning against the wall.

"Drugged," he said to himself. "Well, why couldn't it be suicide?"

He wished it to be suicide. He wished to believe that the doctor and the sergeant were being officious and obstinate.

"Raymond took some sort of drug. May have been an addict. He took this drug, and while he was pulling down the shade perhaps—he was overcome and fell into the chest and couldn't get out. Thing's obvious. But in a small place like this, where nothing much happens, I suppose they like to make the most of any accident. They want to make a dam' melodrama out of it."

He was angry. Why was the sergeant keeping Faquita in there so long? The doctor reappeared and went to the telephone in the hall.

"Get me Superintendent Jesser," he said, and while he waited he lit a cigarette.

"Ha, Jesser? Piggott speaking. Sergeant Welcome got me here. Hector Malloy's house. They simply reported a death, but it looks to me like homicide.... Oh, no! No! coloured boy. I think you'd better come.... Very well, I'll wait."

The sitting room door opened, and Faquita came out and went into her own room. And at once Leah crossed to the sitting room. The doctor stood smoking, staring at nothing. Hamish, too, lit a cigarette.

"Mr. Grier!" called the sergeant. "Will you step here a moment, sir?"

He looked exasperated; he was standing near the door, and Leah stood facing him, composed, a little sad.

"I can't get much information here," said the sergeant. "Maybe you can help me. Have you any idea where Mr. Malloy is?"

"No," said Hamish.

"What did he say when he went out?"

"I didn't see him."

"When did he go out?"

"I don't know."

"When did you last see him?"

"When we came back here from the ship."

"Mrs. Malloy tells me that she was worried about Mr. Malloy's absence, and that you advised her not to notify the police. Can you confirm that?"

"I advised her to wait until ten o'clock."

"Why?"

"It seemed to me reasonable," said Hamish.

"Did you have any particular reason for expecting Mr. Malloy to return by ten o'clock?"

"No," said Hamish. "I just set that as a reasonable time."

"Now, Mr. Grier, this woman—Leah—tells me that you had words with the deceased this morning. Have you anything to say about that?"

Hamish was silent for a moment, struggling against an immense reluctance to tell any more. But he knew that he must.

"I didn't have words with him," he said. "I thought he'd locked me in the shed, and I spoke to him about it."

"Who locked you in the shed, Mr. Grier?"

"Raymond did. But he explained it satisfactorily. The boy thought the shed was empty."

"How long were you locked in there?"

"An hour—more or less."

"How did you get out?"

"A—a Miss Rose happened to be passing. I saw her through the window, and she let me out."

"Had you expected to find Mr. Malloy in the shed, sir?"

"Yes. The boy told me Mr. Malloy wanted to see me at once."

"What time was that, sir?"

"About eleven."

"You didn't feel at all uneasy, sir, when you didn't find Mr. Malloy?"

"No. Mrs. Malloy told me he'd had to go to his office and that he'd try to be back to lunch. I thought the boy had made some mistake. I still think so."

The sergeant had written all this down; he closed the notebook now.

"Thank you, sir," he said. "I think that's the superintendent now."

There was a sound of horses' hoofs clopping along the road; a carriage stopped before the house, and presently deliberate footsteps mounted the steps to the verandah. Sergeant Welcome opened the door and stood at attention, and in came a slender grey-haired man in a raincoat, a felt hat pulled low over his thin, fine face.

"Mr. Grier, sir," said the sergeant. "He reported the finding of the body."

"How do you do, Mr. Grier," said Jesser, cordially.

"Ah, Piggott. Sorry to inconvenience you, Mr. Grier, but I'm afraid I'll have to ask you some questions, presently."

Then he and the doctor and the sergeant went into the room where Raymond lay, and closed the door, and again Hamish didn't know where to go or what to do. After a moment's consideration he went into the kitchen and looked for something to eat.

"Faquita hasn't had any dinner," he thought. "Poor girl! This is going to be hard for her."

He found cold ham, and bread and butter, and a bottle of beer, and he ate like a wolf. He was a little surprised, a little abashed by his appetite.

"But after all," he thought, "it would be nothing but sentimentality for me to pretend to be much upset by the poor devil's death. I'm sorry, of course. I'd be sorry for anyone who went like that. But it doesn't affect me personally."

He ate, and all the time he knew he was evading the issue. He knew that there was something which did affect him personally, something he was bound to face very soon. He had a curious feeling that he was going to be extremely unhappy in a little while. He cleared away the hasty meal and went into his room, and the rain had stopped. He missed it; the silence was disconcerting. He saw Jesser go down the hall to Faquita's room; he heard the doctor telephone for the ambulance and then leave the house; he saw Leah go by to the kitchen. And at last Jesser reappeared.

"Leah," he said, "better go back to your mistress. Now then, Mr. Grier! Suppose we go into the sitting room?"

He lit a cigarette and smoked for some time in silence.

"Rather an unfortunate introduction to our little island, Mr. Grier," he said. "You'll have to take my word for it that we don't go in for this sort of thing as a rule. I suppose you came down for a rest. Most unfortunate."

He leaned back in his chair, a look of fatigue on his fine-drawn face. Though he was tall and broad-shouldered there was a suggestion of delicacy in his slender wrists and ankles, his long narrow hands and feet; he gave the impression of a sensitive creature, overdriven.

"Most unfortunate," he repeated. "Very likely you needed a bit of a vacation."

He was courteous, very agreeable, but Hamish was well aware that he was being questioned again. And the only intelligent course was to be perfectly frank.

"Not exactly for a rest," he said. "I had a cable from Malloy. He said he wanted to discuss something with me."

"Mr. Malloy has extraordinary business ability," said Jesser. "Full of schemes—and all of them successful. I've always found him remarkably interesting. I only hope this wasn't an enterprise that would take him away from Bermuda. A great asset to the club."

Hamish saw that he was being encouraged to talk.

"I don't know yet what his idea is," he said. "I haven't had a chance to talk with him."

"Sergeant Welcome told me of your experience this morning. I wonder if Mr. Malloy could have left a note for you. It's easy enough for a thing like that to be mislaid."

"I didn't see anything like a note," said Hamish.

"Sergeant Welcome will make inquiries," said Jesser. "We'll try to get in touch with Mr. Malloy and clear up this misunderstanding. It shouldn't be too difficult. That's one advantage of living on a small island. It's easy to find people." He paused for a moment. "There's one thing certain," he said. "Mr. Malloy hasn't left Bermuda."

"Certain?" Hamish repeated.

"Yes. No ship sailed today. Not even a small boat."

"Well, whoever imagined that he had left?" asked Hamish. "He wouldn't cable me to come down here to discuss an urgent matter and then go off without a word with me. He certainly wouldn't go away without a word to his wife."

"Mrs. Malloy has her own theory about that," said Jesser.

"Does she think she knows where he is?" asked Hamish, sitting up straighter.

"She's convinced that he's dead," said Jesser. "Murdered."

# CHAPTER FIVE

There was a moment's silence while the words rang in Hamish's ears. It gave him a shock that was like a physical blow, and yet he could instantly accept it and believe it. He could believe that Hector lay dead on a lonely beach with a knife in his back; he could believe in Hector sprawled face downward in a wood, with a bullet through his heart.

Jesser rose.

"Of course there's no evidence to support such a theory," he said. "But women...." He smiled a little and got into his raincoat. "Mrs. Malloy wants her own doctor," he said. "I'll stop at his house on my way home. Good-night, Mr. Grier!"

"Good-night," said Hamish.

The door closed after Jesser, and there was Hamish, somehow in charge. Sergeant Welcome stood outside the door of the room where Raymond lay; behind another closed door was poor Faquita, with only Leah to comfort her.

"What's to be done?" he thought.

He glanced at the sergeant, who was not looking at him or at anything; he simply stood there, erect and solid, with no sign of impatience. After an interval of unhappy hesitation Hamish knocked softly on Faquita's door, and Leah opened it promptly.

"Will you ask Mrs. Malloy if I can do anything for her?" He spoke very low, but Faquita heard him.

"There's really nothing, Hamish," she said, her voice infinitely weary. "You'd better try to get some sleep."

"I'll call you, sir, if there's anything," said Leah, and respectfully closed the door in his face.

Hamish sauntered down the hall toward the sergeant.

"What's the next step?" he asked, nonchalantly.

"Nothing to trouble *you*, sir," said the sergeant, with an air of benevolence. "They'll be here to remove the body, but they'll be quiet about it. Won't disturb you. And I'll be here until I'm relieved tomorrow morning."

He could hardly have told Hamish more plainly that he was not in any way necessary.

"Then I'll get a bit of sleep," said Hamish.

"Right, sir!" said the sergeant, with hearty approval.

So Hamish had to go into his own room and close the door. He knew how it was going to be. He sat on the edge of the bed, hands clasped between his knees, staring at the wall before him and thinking of Hector.

Only now did he fully realize what Hector meant to him. He had lost more than a friend; it was as if all the colour, and stir, and laughter had gone, leaving him a life that lay before him, straight and flat as a railway track.

"I needn't take it for granted that he's dead," he told himself.

But he did take it for granted. For one thing, he had already looked upon death tonight, so that the idea had a stark reality. A man could be alive and, almost in a moment, could be dead.

"And what else could keep him away from Faquita?" he thought. "He wouldn't let her worry like this, if he were alive."

It appalled him to think of Faquita. With Hector gone there was nothing left for her, nothing at all. She had none of the background other women had; she had no home, no circle of family and friends. Hector had found her, forlorn and empty-handed; he had made a life for her, given her everything. She had known romance at its highest, and now she must know a supreme bereavement.

"Perhaps she'll want me to cable to that aunt," he thought. "In Vermont, I think she lived. I could take Faquita there."

The idea was so lamentable that he grew angry.

"Jesser said that there was no evidence," he told himself. "And that's true. Poor Faquita's worn out with worry, she's high-strung and sensitive. Natural for her to get such an idea into her head. But I'm not going to take that for granted."

He took off his shoes and his jacket and lay down on the bed in the dark. He did not think, only lay there with a leaden oppression upon him, and dozed a little. He heard stealthy footsteps and a low voice.

"Easy there, you. Got the sheet? Steady now!"

They were taking Raymond away. The house was very still after that; he could hear the sea lapping softly against the rocks, some tree or bush stirred with a paper-like rustle, a tethered goat bleated. He had just fallen into a light doze when the sound of a galloping horse startled him. It came on with the effect of panic, a carriage rattling behind it.

"Malloy?" thought Hamish, with a surge of hope, or fear, or both.

He got up; he stood in the dark room, waiting. When the carriage stopped before the house he hastened into the hall and opened the front door. The horse stood there breathing so heavily that the carriage shook; a man was just hurrying round the corner of the house. Hamish started after him, when a beam of light shone into the man's black face.

"Now then!" said an official young voice. "What are you up to?"

"Come to see my vife," said the man, apologetically. "Leah, that's my vife. She didn't come home—"

"You can't enter the house," said the other. "That's my orders."

"Just vant to speak to her," said the man, in the same anxious, apologetic voice. "Ve vere worried. Leah didn't come home, and ve heard there vos—"

"She's all right," said the young constable. "But *you're* going to get yourself in trouble, driving like that."

"Horse, he wants to get home," the man explained.

"That you, Sam?" said Leah's voice behind Hamish. "Excuse me, sir." She stood there, fully dressed, neat, composed, severe toward her husband. "Heard you coming," she said, "making enough noise to wake the dead. If you want to speak to me, come around to the window of the mistress's room. She doesn't want me to leave her. Go along!"

She spoke to him like a dog, and he obeyed like a dog. She addressed herself then to the constable, with a sort of austere civility.

"Mistress says will you step into the kitchen and have something to eat?"

"Tell her I'm verra much obliged, but it's against orders."

"I'll make you a sandwich and bring it to you," said Leah.

She went back into the house, but Hamish stood where he was. It was a mild night, but very damp; the floor of the verandah felt wet beneath his feet. But he did not want to go inside; the memory of that wildly galloping horse still excited him; he had a feeling of waiting for something. He tried to talk to the young constable, invisible in the dark, but it was a remarkably pointless conversation.

"It must be tiresome, this patrol duty."

"It's what we have to expect, sir."

"Are you a Bermudian?"

"No, sir, I'm a Scot."

"Want a cigarette?"

"It's against orders to smoke on duty, sir."

It went on like that. The tired horse stood with his head drooping; now and then he shook himself, with a squeak of leather. The sea was lapping at the wall; that paper-like rustle came from the leaves of the banana plants when the breeze stirred them. Nothing was happening.

"Will you come around to the back door?" said Leah, and though her tone was still civil there was no 'sir' or other title for the constable. "I've left a tray on the steps."

"Thanks," said the constable.

But he lingered, embarrassed to walk away from Hamish and eat. So Hamish went back to bed. He looked at his watch—two o'clock.

With his hands clasped behind his head, and his eyes closed, he began to think, very lucidly and easily. And was asleep at once.

As soon as his eyes were open, he was wide awake, as always; his hardy young body and his tough, vigorous mind were without sluggishness. He got up and went to the window, and he was amazed.

He saw a beauty that almost stopped his breath. The calm sea was a glorious blue, beneath a blue sky without a cloud; beside the house was a banana plant with fresh-washed leaves of a glossy green; there was a hedge of hibiscus starred with cream-yellow flowers. A sweet breeze blew, and over everything lay a clear golden light. For a moment he was completely and unthinkingly happy, and then with a stab of pain, he remembered Hector. Hector dead on a day like this?

"Maybe there's been some news," he thought, and was suddenly in a great hurry for the day to begin. His watch showed seven o'clock. He went quietly to the bathroom and had a cold bath; he shaved, and dressed in a clean white suit; and all that took him twenty-five minutes. He then went looking for Sergeant Welcome and found him in the kitchen, drinking tea, with Leah at the stove.

"Good-morning, sir," said the sergeant, rising.

"Anything new?" asked Hamish.

"Not to my knowledge, sir," said the sergeant.

"Mrs. Malloy's doctor come yet?"

"Not yet, sir."

"Shall I serve your breakfast now, sir?" asked Leah.

She was neat, clean, composed as usual; and she and the sergeant between them gave the morning a matter-of-fact, even cheerful air that Hamish found very agreeable. He sat in the gloomy little dining room, and Leah brought him tea, toast, eggs, and bacon.

"How is Mrs. Malloy this morning?" he asked.

"She's sleeping now, sir. She had a very poor night."

"I understood that her doctor had been sent for."

"Yes, sir," said Leah. "But Doctor Leaming don't hurry himself."

"Let me know, will you, whenever Mrs. Malloy wants to see me," said Hamish.

He finished his breakfast, lit a cigarette, and went out on the verandah to wait for something to happen. A policeman came sailing along the road on a bicycle and mounted the steps, and Hamish stood watching him with a quickened heartbeat. But it was only P.C. Duckley, come to relieve the young Scot. He reported to Sergeant Welcome, and the sergeant came out, raincoat over his arm, and rode off on his bicycle. Plenty of people came along the road, on bicycles, on foot, in carriages, in carts; life was going on, this lovely morning.

"Jesser said there wouldn't be much difficulty in finding Hector," thought Hamish. "They've had all night. There ought to be some news."

Then he thought that if there were news, nobody would bother to tell him. Or perhaps he was expected to make inquiries.

"I might ring up the police station," he thought.

He was just about to enter the house for that purpose when a buggy, driven by a little Portuguese boy, stopped before the house. A pale, slim, fair-haired young man descended and came up the steps carrying a bag.

"Mr. Grier?" he said. "I'm Doctor Leaming."

He seemed in no sort of hurry, and his mild and casual air angered Hamish.

"The servant says that Mrs. Malloy had a very poor night," he observed.

"Yes," said Doctor Leaming. "Very disturbing."

"A bit more than that," said Hamish, and his hostility was so marked that the doctor could not ignore it.

"No point in my coming last night," he explained. "Leah makes a very good nurse, and there was nothing I could do."

"I thought that in a case of shock, it was usual to give some sort of sedative," said Hamish, stiffly.

"Well!" said the doctor, with a sigh. "We'll see."

He went into the house, and Hamish remained looking out at the sunny road, more angry than ever.

"That fellow's no good," he thought. "He's simply not interested in Faquita. He doesn't care—"

Another buggy stopped, and Superintendent Jesser got out; he stood in the road for a moment, speaking to his driver, and then he came up the steps.

"Good morning, Mr. Grier!" he said. "How is everything?"

"Doctor Leaming just managed to get here," said Hamish. "Is there any news?"

"No news of Mr. Malloy," said Jesser. "It's dashed odd...." He lit a cigarette and sat down on the rail. "Certainly he didn't leave the island. The whole thing's surprisingly vague. Mrs. Malloy and Leah say that he left the house about eleven o'clock yesterday morning to go to his office on Front Street. You wouldn't think this was possible, but I can't find out whether or not he ever reached his office."

"Nobody saw him?"

"I got hold of his partner, Reggie Cornwall. He was busy somewhere else, and he didn't go to the office until after lunch, so he doesn't know. I made some enquiries. A girl in the china shop next door said she'd seen Mr. Malloy go past sometime in the morning. But after I'd questioned her, she admitted that she wasn't sure she'd seen him that morning. It was simply that he always did go past the shop every morning. There were a couple of other people like that. They were accustomed to seeing Malloy every morning, and they can't swear whether they saw him yesterday or not. All they know is that they usually did see him. No...." He paused. "Of course we'll make more inquiries," he said.

An idea came into Hamish's head, but he did not wish to say it aloud until he had done more thinking.

"Stephanie?" he asked himself. "She was pretty dam' cool about Hector's disappearance. I'm almost sure she had a key to the shed. What if he went to her when he left the house?"

And if he had gone there, where was he now?

"No..." Jesser repeated. "I imagine the boy Raymond is the one who could have given us the information. Something very queer there. His locking you into the shed, just at the time Malloy left.... Doctor Piggott performed an autopsy last night, y'know. Queerer than ever. Boy died of opium poisoning."

"Doctor Piggott said something of that sort."

"Yes. But it rather knocks out Sergeant Welcome's homicide theory."

"Why? I don't see—"

"My dear fellow, how would it be possible to force a quantity of opium down anyone's throat? Especially in broad daylight, with people about. Piggott says the dose was probably administered at five or six in the afternoon. Mrs. Malloy was in the house at that time, and so were you, as well as Leah. I've found out that two tradesmen called. There'd have been some sort of struggle—and no one heard anything. What's more, there are no marks of a struggle on the body. Unless you're willing to believe that someone, somehow, forced the boy to swallow the poison, and after that the boy went about his business for possibly an hour, without mentioning the matter to anyone...."

"You think it's suicide, then?"

"Well, what do *you* think?"

"I'd like to know more...." said Hamish.

Jesser glanced at him quickly and smiled.

"You'd make a good policeman, Mr. Grier," he said. "You like facts better than theories. But suppose you had only the facts I have, and you were expected to construct a theory?"

Hamish had nothing to say.

"It might be helpful," said Jesser, "if we knew exactly why Malloy cabled for you to come down here."

"It might be," Hamish agreed.

"You didn't have any letter that might give a clue?"

"No, none," said Hamish.

He felt fairly certain that Jesser didn't believe him; but that didn't matter much.

"Stephanie..." he kept saying to himself. "That girl knows something. I dare say the police could get it out of her."

But he could not make up his mind to set the police on her. Not yet, anyhow.

"Y'see," said Jesser. "What we lack is information about Malloy. You knew what he was likely to do—where he was likely to go. Mrs. Malloy can't help us. She has what you might call a romantic idea of her husband. She can only insist that nothing but death could keep him away from her. His partner, Cornwall, can only tell us about Malloy as a business man. If we could find someone with a more personal outlook...."

"Stephanie," thought Hamish again.

And there she was, coming up the steps. She wore a blue and white striped cotton dress with a broad red belt about her slim waist; the sun made her fair hair bright. She looked remarkably pretty and remarkably happy. Somehow, it disturbed Hamish to see her coming here so confidently.

"Hello, Hamish!" she said, like an old friend. "Good-morning, Mr. Jesser!"

Her voice was very clear. She looked at Jesser with an expression of innocent candour. And he seemed pleased to see her.

"Good-morning, Miss Rose! How are you?"

"Fine, thanks!" said she. "I saw the doctor's carriage, and I came to see if anyone was ill."

"Mrs. Malloy is—very much upset," said Jesser.

"That's too bad!" said Stephanie, earnestly. "But naturally.... Having someone commit suicide in the house...."

"It's Mr. Malloy's absence that disturbs her," said Jesser.

"Does it?" said Stephanie. "I should think he'd be the last person anyone would worry about. I mean, he does impress you as a man who can look after himself, doesn't he?"

"Oh, undoubtedly!" said Jesser. "But, unfortunately, accidents can happen to anyone."

"But, in a place as small as this, wouldn't you have heard by this time if he'd met with an accident?"

"In a place as small as this, and with a man who was known by sight to so many people, it's difficult to explain Mr. Malloy's disappearance—except by an accident," said Jesser.

She didn't turn a hair.

"I'm sorry Mrs. Malloy's so worried," she said. "Is there anything I can do for her?"

"You're a neighbour, Miss Rose," said Jesser. "Perhaps you can help us a little. When you saw Mr. Malloy yesterday—"

"No, I didn't see him yesterday," she said, with the same air of candour. "I haven't seen him since I got back from New York."

"That's too bad!" said Jesser. "Let's try going back a little. Two weeks ago—the night before you sailed for New York—did you find Mr. Malloy in good spirits?"

"Oh, yes!" said Stephanie. "He stopped in for a minute, to ask if I'd take a package up with me. Mrs. Mapes and I both thought he was just as usual."

This was a duel. Hamish looked on with profound disquiet. It was obvious that Jesser had not overlooked Stephanie, obvious that he had been making enquiries. It was obvious, too, that she was well aware of this, that for all her air of cheerful assurance she was alertly on guard.

And why?

"And you don't think we ought to worry about Mr. Malloy?" asked Jesser.

"Oh, I couldn't say *that!*" said Stephanie, earnest again. "You know lots more about Mr. Malloy than I do. He just seemed to Mrs. Mapes and me like the sort of man who could always look after himself."

"Then—" Jesser began, when Leah came out of the house.

"Excuse me..." she said, with a trace of anxiety. "But Mrs. Malloy sent a note for you, Miss Rose."

She handed Stephanie a folded piece of paper. The girl opened it, and as she saw the contents a wave of colour rose in her cheeks, until they were crimson.

"Well..." she said. "I'll have to get back to my work now. If there's any way I can help you, Mr. Jesser.... Come and see us, Hamish."

The two men stood watching her down the steps, down the road, and out of sight. She went leisurely, very straight, very easy. Yet Hamish knew, and felt sure Jesser knew, that she went away defeated.

# CHAPTER SIX

Jesser turned to Leah who was still standing in the doorway.

"You'll have to attend the inquest this morning," he said. "And I'll want you before that to make a formal identification of the body. Better come along with me, now."

"I can't leave the mistress alone, sir."

"Get someone else to stay with her," said Jesser. "What about the young lady next door, Miss Rose?"

Hamish felt a curious twinge of apprehension. He was sure that Jesser had his reasons for saying that; he was beginning to think that Jesser had a reason, a motive, behind every word he spoke.

"Miss Rose, sir!" said Leah. "The mistress wouldn't have Miss Rose by her if there wasn't nobody else in the whole world."

"Oh, yes, she would!" said Jesser. "Those little disagreements between neighbours are soon forgotten."

Leah's thin fingers were crumpling her apron; she was silent for a moment and then she spoke with an effort, as if she were forced to speak.

"She's a godless woman, sir."

"Miss Rose?" asked Jesser, as if shocked.

"I speak the truth, sir. It is a godless household, drink and drugs and all manner of wickedness."

"It's a wonder to me that you'd repeat gossip," said Jesser very gravely.

"It's not gossip, sir. I've seen drinking going on there with my own eyes. Out on the gallery where anyone could see them. Even Mrs. Mapes with her white hairs, she drinks and she smokes."

"Does she take drugs?" said Jesser, lowering his voice.

"Yes, sir. She's forever taking drugs for headaches and neuralgia. The Lord meant us to be afflicted, and we got to stand pain."

"Where does she get the drugs?"

"She goes into the drug-store and buys them, sir."

"Openly?"

"Got no shame about it, sir. She wanted *me* to take one of her pills, the time my back was wrenched."

"Did you see the name of it?"

"Yes, sir," said Leah, and repeated the name of a well-known anodyne.

"Mrs. Mapes took an interest in your mistress, then," said Jesser. "I suppose the three ladies saw a great deal of each other."

"No, sir! When they came here they wanted their cocktails and their cigarettes, and the mistress didn't like that. And she didn't go over there. She doesn't go out. Likes her own home."

"I see!" said Jesser. "By the way, I hear Sam came to see you last night."

The light went out of her black eyes; it was as if her spirit retreated.

"Yes, Sir. Came like he always does. That's my cross to bear."

"I suppose Mrs. Malloy was annoyed at being waked—"

"No, sir; she wasn't asleep. She had a talk with Sam through the window, while I was in the kitchen. But it's no use. Isn't anything anyone can say to Sam."

"What did he want?"

"Wanted money, sir. Like he always does."

"Well!" said Jesser, rising. "Get your hat, Leah, and come along."

"But who's to stay with the mistress, sir?"

"I'll speak to Doctor Leaming," said Jesser. "See if it's all right to leave her alone for a bit."

"Doctor Leaming—" Leah began, and stopped.

"You think that possibly he minimizes Mrs. Malloy's illness?" asked Jesser, in a low, confidential tone. "I mean you think perhaps he doesn't realize how ill she is?"

"Yes, sir, he *does* minimize!" said Leah, seizing upon the word. "I've seen it again and again. The mistress isn't one to complain, and when she doesn't say anything he minimizes."

"I'll bear that in mind," said Jesser. "I think he's coming out now."

The house door opened, and Leaming came out, his pale young face serious and fatigued.

"Morning, doctor!" said Jesser. "Leah here is worried, because she's got to go down to the inquest to identify the body. She doesn't like to leave her mistress."

"Mrs. Malloy will do very well for an hour or two," said Leaming. "As long as there's someone within call."

"We might send a nurse," said Jesser.

"Yes," said Leaming. "I'll see to it at once. Good-morning!"

The shadow of a smile flitted across his face, and he went down the steps.

"Now then!" said Jesser. "Mr. Grier, we shan't want you until eleven o'clock. I'll send a carriage for you. In the meantime, if you'd be kind enough to step in the house, within call, in case Mrs. Malloy wants anything... A nurse will be here very shortly. Come, Leah!"

Leah went into the house, and Jesser looked at Hamish, a steady, smiling regard. And Hamish looked back at him, very much troubled, very much at a loss. He was a little angry, too; it seemed to him that both Jesser and Doctor Leaming were curiously indifferent, even heartless toward Faquita.

"The thing is," said Jesser, answering his unspoken thought, "that in a case like this there's nothing anyone can do. No cure. No one can give Mrs. Malloy any reassurance. Her husband has gone. That's the one undeniable fact. I'm not as unfeeling as you might imagine. Only tragedy's what you might call my daily bread. Not so much here. Bermuda's a law-abiding spot. But I've been in London.... Other places.... You see things, y'know. Things that simply have to be endured."

While Hamish was trying to decipher a hidden meaning in this speech, Leah came out to them.

"The mistress says she doesn't wish a nurse, sir," she said to Jesser. "She's dressing now, and she'll sit in the parlour with Mr. Grier."

"That's better!" said Jesser. "Is there any friend or neighbour she'd like sent for?"

"No, sir," said Leah. "I'm ready, sir."

She had a shiny black straw hat set very straight on her head; she had taken off her apron; she followed Jesser down the steps and crowded into the buggy. Hamish saw her drive off, sitting very straight.

And he was panic-stricken.

"What can I *say* to Faquita?" he thought. "If she asks me questions about Hector.... Suppose she breaks down? My God! I don't know...."

He did not know whether he ought to assume a hopeful, cheery attitude, or whether he should be sympathetic. He was appalled at the thought of facing that poor girl; his hands were cold. He lit a cigarette and tried to prepare himself.

"Hamish?" said her soft voice.

He flung away the cigarette and entered the house. She was in the sitting room, lying back in a chair, white as a ghost, and so beautiful.

"How are you feeling?" he asked.

She didn't answer that.

"Hamish," she said, "what did Stephanie say?"

"Nothing much," he answered. "Asked if there were anything she could do."

"Hamish, what do you think of her?"

"Well, I don't know..." he said, and that was true enough.

"I'm afraid I've been unkind," she said. "Unkind—and perhaps unfair. But when I heard her voice out there I couldn't stand it." Her eyes filled with tears, but her voice was steady. "I—almost hate her. And I don't want to hate anyone. I want to try to understand—if I can. Maybe you can help me, Hamish...."

"I'll do anything I can."

"I sent her a note. I suppose she told you?"

"No," said Hamish. "She didn't say anything."

"It was a cruel note. I wish I hadn't written it. I asked her to go away and never come again. I should have remembered that she's very unhappy, too."

"Unhappy? Is she?" thought Hamish. "She disguises it pretty well."

"You see, she loved Hector," Faquita went on. "And she.... It's so hard for me to understand. I've been brought up to see things so differently. Of course, I've read about people like Stephanie, in books, but they didn't seem real. She never made any secret about what she was doing. She wanted Hector, and she tried her best to get him away from me."

Hamish was embarrassed; to cover it he lit a cigarette.

"Oh, sorry!" he said.

"Please smoke, Hamish. I don't mind at all. Hector never saw through her. I was glad he didn't. She used to ring him up all the time and ask him to come to the cottage. She played for him; she lent him books; she even used to go to his office. She has that cool, offhand way with her. Hector thought she was just friendly."

"But are you sure—it wasn't that?" asked Hamish.

She did not answer for a time.

"I'm very sure," she said. "I was sure all the time. And then, you see, Mrs. Mapes came to see me. She's devoted to Stephanie, and she was worried. She asked me if I wouldn't speak to Hector—ask him not to go there any more. She couldn't see anything but Stephanie's interests. She said that Hector's being married didn't mean anything to Stephanie. She said that all young people were like that in these days. Is that true, Hamish?"

"No!" he answered, briefly.

He fell silent, thinking of Stephanie. Easy to see how a man like Hector would appeal to her; easy to believe that she could be pretty resolute in getting what she wanted. And he was unaccountably sorry about the whole thing—sorry to think of Stephanie deliberately trying to wreck another woman's happiness, sorry she had those ideas. He remembered her walking away in the sunshine, so straight, so nonchalant, yet with that burning colour in her cheeks.

"She's young," he thought. "Maybe she didn't realize...."

Someone had come up on the verandah; it was a constable in uniform, come to escort Hamish to the inquest.

"I don't like to leave you alone, Faquita," he said, troubled. "But the nurse will soon—"

"I don't want a nurse, Hamish," she said. "I don't mind being alone."

Poor, lovely, desolate girl! He had to leave her there, lying back in her chair, white and spent. Finished. There was nothing ahead of her, with Hector gone.

"Stephanie didn't love Hector," he thought. "She's not really unhappy, but worried. I don't think she could love anyone. Too self-sufficing."

He went to his room to get his hat. And as he entered, someone rapped on the top of the open window. He crossed the room and saw a Negro there, a big man, neatly dressed, with loosely hanging hands and an anxious face.

"Boss," he said in a whisper, "can I have a vord vith you?"

"What do you want?" asked Hamish. "I'm in a hurry."

"Boss, I got information for you."

"What d'you mean?"

"I got something to tell you, boss."

"Tell it!" said Hamish.

"Vant to tell it *vith* the documents, sir. If you'll spare me jest a few minutes—"

"Are you Sam?" asked Hamish.

"Yes, sir, I'm Sam."

"I suppose you want money."

"Before God, I don't vant no money, sir!" said the other, passionately. "Vants to see justice done, and no more. Boss!" He came as close to the screen as he could. "Boss, I got information about how it vas Raymond come to die."

Hamish's immediate reaction was to reject this touch of melodrama; he would not be rushed. He wouldn't believe anything until he had a chance to think.

"Why don't you take your information to the police?" he asked.

"Police ain't no friends of mine, sir. I vant to give my information to a gentleman, sir."

The constable, waiting in the hall near the front door, coughed.

"I've got to go to the inquest now," said Hamish. "If you have anything genuine to tell me, you'll have to be quick."

"Couldn't be quick, sir. These things got to be explained. I can tell you how it vas Raymond came to die, sir. And *who done it.*"

In spite of himself, Hamish was startled.

"Tell me as much as you can—quick," he said. "I can't be late to the inquest."

"I'll vait till you come back, boss. If you'll just put me some place, where there won't nobody see me."

"I'll meet you somewhere."

"Can I slip into your room, sir? I can come in through the vindow and vait for you. Needn't be afraid to trust *me*, sir. I got the name of a honest man all over this island, sir."

"No," said Hamish. He couldn't let a stranger into Faquita's house. The constable scraped his feet and coughed again. "Wait!" said Hamish, and hastened through the kitchen, out of the back door, and round the house to where the man waited.

"You can wait in the shed, if it's open."

"Key hanging right in the kitchen, sir," said the Negro. "I'll lock the door, so there can't nobody get in."

"I'll lock it on the outside, if you like," said Hamish.

For a moment, the man hesitated.

"Hurry up!" said Hamish. "I've got to go."

"All right, sir. Lock me in," said the other. "Got the uttermost confidence in you, sir. If you lock me in, sir, you'll let me out."

Hamish found the key hanging on a nail, let the man into the shed, locked him in, and hurried to join the constable. There was a surrey waiting; the constable got in front with the driver, and Hamish sat alone in the back seat. They went fast, along the hard white road; on the high bank two little kids played with silly, enchanting grace, and behind them Hamish had a glimpse of that blue, blue sea, glittering in the sun. A beautiful day.

"Sort of day Hector would have liked," he thought, with a stab of pain.

He was very apprehensive about the inquest. The police, he thought, had probably found out new things, perhaps terrible things. He would have to sit there and listen. He would be asked questions about Hector....

The inquest was held in the Town Hall with a lack of formality that surprised him. The coroner and his jury were already there, and the proceedings began at once. Sergeant Welcome in a loud and monotonous voice told the exact minute at which Hamish's call had reached the police station, the exact moment at which he had reached the house, find what he had found there. Leah Delaine was called next; with melancholy composure she attested that the body she had viewed was that of Raymond Prout, employed as house boy by Mr. Hector Malloy.

Mr. Hamish Grier was next, and Mr. Grier was questioned very briefly. He had noticed the lid of the chest partly open; he had raised it and found the body in it. He had removed the body, and as soon as he decided that life was extinct, he had telephoned to the police. That was all; Mr. Grier might stand down. Doctor Piggott next. Doctor Piggott had performed an autopsy, and in his opinion deceased had died from opium in liquid form.

Then Superintendent Jesser rose and requested an adjournment of two weeks to enable the police to communicate with the authorities in Trinidad. The coroner assented at once, and everyone began to leave. Hamish stepped out into the street with a curiously flat feeling. Nothing had happened. Hector's disappearance had not been mentioned. He was going toward the surrey when Jesser stopped him.

"Oh, by the way, Mr. Grier," he said. "While you're here in town I wonder if you'd be kind enough to send a cable to New York and ask someone there to send down all your correspondence with Mr. Malloy."

"We never had any correspondence. He sent me a postcard now and then."

"I see! If you'll get me the postcard, then, that refers to the business Mr. Malloy wanted to discuss with you—"

"He never wrote me anything about that," said Hamish. "I thought I'd told you before that I don't know what he wanted to discuss."

"Oh, yes," said Jesser. "You did tell me that. I quite understand that you know nothing definite about this business, Mr. Grier. But if we go over his letters—postcard, I mean—more carefully, we might be able to find some clue."

"I've only had one letter from him in my life," said Hamish. "And that was just a note, to tell me he'd settled here."

"If you'd let us see this letter—"

"Sorry, but I don't keep letters," said Hamish, briefly.

He was quite certain that Jesser did not believe him; and he resented that ardently.

"Y'know," said Jesser, with a confidential air that failed to soothe Hamish, "we haven't found any trace of Mr. Malloy yet. Extraordinary! You see, of course, that we're obliged to get all the information we can as to his plans and so on."

"You said he couldn't possibly have left the island."

"I should have qualified that statement," said Jesser, and was silent for a moment. "I should have put it this way—Mr. Malloy couldn't have left the island alive."

"I mustn't be—such a damned fool," said Hamish to himself. "There's nothing new in that idea. I've been thinking enough about it."

Only, coming from Jesser, there was a bleak reality in the idea of Hector's death which had not been there before.

"Then you've given up hope of finding him?" he asked.

"No," said Jesser, quietly. "We may find him, or the tide may bring him in."

"You agree with Mrs. Malloy? You think he was murdered?"

That was a strange word to use, in the sunny street, with people coming and going. A butcher's boy went past on a bicycle, whistling the latest hit from New York; he saw a friend and called out to him with the characteristic accent of the island.

"Hello, Villie! Vere you going?"

Two little girls in sailor blouses came leisurely along. Life was going on. Murder didn't cast a shadow.

"There's always the possibility of an accident," said Jesser. "Malloy might have been taking a walk, might have slipped and fallen into the sea."

"He's a remarkably strong swimmer."

"Might have struck his head on a rock."

Hamish lit a cigarette and was annoyed to find that his hand was not quite steady.

"You think that Raymond's death has some connection with Malloy's disappearance?" he asked.

"Well, don't you?" said Jesser. "Otherwise it's a striking coincidence, to say the least."

"Do you still think that Raymond committed suicide?"

"I still can't imagine how anyone could have forced him to take a dose of poison in the middle of the afternoon."

"Couldn't it be disguised in tea—something of the sort?"

"Doctor Piggott tells me that opium is not tasteless."

"Perhaps I'll find out something about that," thought Hamish. "Good-morning, superintendent!"

"Good-morning!" said Jesser. "And perhaps if you think it over a bit, Mr. Grier, you'll remember some letter or postcard from Mr. Malloy that you've forgotten. Let me know if you do, will you?"

Hamish got into the surrey and rode back to the bungalow, oblivious now of the beautiful day. He felt a hot anger against Jesser, and a very great impatience to hear what the Negro had to tell him.

"It may be nothing at all," he said to himself. "I don't expect to hear anything important."

But he did. Leah opened the door for him, still wearing her hat, and he was not pleased to see her.

"The mistress is lying down in her room, sir," she said. "She wants me to stay with her for a while. But I'll have your lunch ready by one o'clock, sir."

"All right, thanks!" said Hamish.

He went down the hall to his room, and waited until he saw Leah safely shut in with Faquita. Then he went out by the back door and unlocked the shed.

It was empty.

# CHAPTER SEVEN

amish went into the shed; he examined the windows and found the bars immovable. He was certain that he had locked the man in here and taken away the key, as he was equally certain that someone had let him out.

"Leah?" he thought.

Leah could not have got back here much before him; he recalled that she had still been wearing her hat. Nevertheless, she seemed to him the obvious suspect. Sam was her husband. She was likely to know where another key was, if one existed. He started toward the back door and checked himself.

"I can't ask her point blank," he thought. "If she did let him out, she'd probably deny it."

And what did one do in the face of a denial?

"I'm not Jesser," he thought. "I haven't the experience...."

He began to realize, a little, how excellent Jesser's technique was; he was reluctantly obliged to admit that he would not know how to get the truth from Leah.

"And if she didn't do it," he thought, "if she didn't know that Sam had come here, I don't want to give him away. He was damned anxious for secrecy. I'll have to go slow with this."

He sat down at Hector's desk to reflect.

"Sam came here to tell me something. Well, why me? How did he know anything about me? Was the whole thing a hoax? So that he could get into the shed?"

It was improbable, if not impossible. It had been Hamish's own suggestion that the man should wait in the shed.

"Yes. But did he work around to it?" thought Hamish. "Did he somehow get me to suggest it?"

He tried to remember the exact words of the brief talk they had had, but he could not.

"I can tell you how it was Raymond came to die. And *who done it.*"

He remembered that, well enough. He remembered the fellow's mention of documents, too. All a hoax, a pretext for getting in here?

"Anything valuable in here?" he asked himself. "Not likely."

Then he remembered that Raymond used to sleep in here, and a curious excitement rose in him.

"Raymond may have left a note," he thought. "There's no harm in looking."

He decided to begin with the desk. It was not only the most likely place, but it was the one possible place in this bare room where anything could be hidden. He pulled open a drawer and found in it a jumbled assortment of objects—a pipe, a harmonica, a nickel watch, a clean, folded handkerchief, three pencils, things which might have belonged to Hector as well as to Raymond. He opened another drawer, and found a few letters, business letters from England, dealing with Hector's various agencies.

And sorrow came over him in a tide; the excitement of the search vanished. After all, this wasn't a game. He didn't care how or why the man had left the shed; he was not even much concerned with Raymond's death. The one stark fact was that Hector had gone. Here, in this hot, bare little room he had read these letters. On this blue and gold island he had lived, had been happy and successful. And now he was gone.

Hamish closed the drawer and rose.

"The police probably searched this place, anyhow," he thought. "I'm just making a fool of myself. The amateur detective—I suppose I ought to feel like that. I ought to want vengeance, the mystery solved. But what the hell does it matter, if he's dead?"

As he pushed back the chair he trod on something, and stooping to look, he saw a little collection of things on the floor—some pennies and ha'pennies, a sprinkling of loose tobacco, a packet of matches, and a folded paper. He picked up the paper and opened it.

Things can't possibly go on like this, Reggie. It's really a desperate situation. You've got to help me. I know how you feel about it, but you'll just have to forget your scruples. Come tonight. I'll get rid of Mapes by eleven.

Steve.

He read this with surprise and dismay. And anger. At every turn of the case that girl appeared, and always in an unfavourable light. And when he looked back upon it he realized that he was always ignoring her connection with the tragedy. He didn't exactly make excuses for her; he simply dismissed the thought of her, as if she couldn't possibly be involved.

There was every reason to believe that she was involved. She had unlocked the shed, and she had lied about it. She had done her best to delay him from going to the police.

"Faquita said..." he thought.

He didn't like to recall what Faquita had said.

"What's the matter with me?" he asked himself, indignantly. "Being chivalrous? Or just being a fool, because she's young and pretty? She's in this thing up to the neck. Faquita told me she was in love with Hector and that she was trying to get him away from his wife. That's a thing I certainly haven't much sympathy for. 'A desperate situation,' is it? And she writes to Cornwall. Tells him he's got to help her. Help her to do what?"

"...You'll just have to forget your scruples...."

"That's a dam' queer thing to say to a man," thought Hamish.

He admitted that she was very pretty, but he had thought her too cool, too matter-of-fact to be alluring. It occurred to him now that he might have been wrong about that. Perhaps she wasn't always cool and matter-of-fact. And without that manner, she might be attractive. So attractive that Cornwall had been willing to forget his scruples and help her—in God knew what?

"No!" he said to himself. "That's nonsense. She couldn't have had anything to do with Hector's death."

And why couldn't she? Why did he so obstinately rule her out, always? She wouldn't be the first young and pretty girl to be involved in a crime.

"If she did love Hector.... And he didn't love her?..."

There was no crime more common than that. The *crime passionel*.... The sudden impulse of a desperate, jealous heart....

"No!" he said again, remembering his last glimpse of her, walking down the path, so straight and proud, with that hot colour in her cheeks. "No! She may have some pretty advanced ideas about things, but she wouldn't commit a murder and be perfectly cool about it. If she had done a thing like that—on impulse, by accident—she'd probably tell the police herself. She might be reckless, but she'd never be artful."

He remembered her on the ship, so friendly, so good-humoured.

"She's only a kid. She simply imagined she was in love with Hector. If she had been, she wouldn't take it like this. Naturally, it would seem more serious to Faquita than—"

The door opened and Sergeant Welcome entered.

"Beg your pardon, sir," he said. "I didn't know there was anyone in here."

"That's all right," said Hamish. "I'm just leaving."

"Excuse me, sir," said the sergeant, standing solidly in the doorway. "But would you mind telling me how you got in? The door was locked this morning."

"I—took the key from the kitchen," said Hamish with growing disquiet.

"I'm afraid I'll have to trouble you for that key, sir. My orders are not to let anyone in here during Mr. Malloy's absence."

With an air of nonchalance, very far from genuine, Hamish gave him the key. For a moment he contemplated giving some bogus explanation of his presence, but he decided against that. It looked queer, and nothing he could say would make it less queer.

"Mr. Malloy's partner has got permission to take over his papers," said the sergeant. "He'll be here this afternoon. Beg your pardon, sir, but if you've—" He hesitated for a moment. "If you've come across anything, sir, it will have to be replaced."

"I looked in the drawers, that's all," said Hamish. "I haven't taken any of Mr. Malloy's papers."

"Quite, sir," said the sergeant. "But any sort of document—"

It occurred to Hamish that the sergeant might have been watching him through the window, might have seen him pick up the note, read it, and put it in his pocket.

"I tell you I have nothing of Mr. Malloy's," he said.

"Even if you chanced to pick up something, sir, that wasn't Mr. Malloy's, it ought to be left for the superintendent to see."

"He knows, all right," thought Hamish. "But I don't think he has any authority to make me give it to him."

Anyhow, he decided to take the chance.

"If I should find anything that the superintendent ought to see, I'll show it to him," he said.

"Excuse me, sir, but I'll have to ask you for that bit of paper that you picked up."

"That?" said Hamish. "It happened to be a letter of my own that I dropped, and I don't intend to show it to you. Let me out, will you? It's damned hot in here."

"I'll have to report this to the superintendent, sir," said Sergeant Welcome, and not pleasantly.

"Report until you're blue in the face," said Hamish. "I'm not going to hand over my personal letters to you."

"Very good, sir," said the sergeant, and stepped aside.

"Now what have I done?" thought Hamish. "Jesser won't let this stop here. He's made up his mind already that I'm lying about that precious correspondence with Hector. This will just about put the lid on. I'll have to get rid of the note, quick."

When he entered the kitchen, he found Leah there at the stove and he looked at her sharply.

"You?" he thought. "Did you let Sam out of the shed?"

He stood still, unable to make up his mind whether or not it would be better to question her. If she hadn't done it, what was the use of putting ideas into her head?

"She was away from the house, too," he thought. "Someone else may have opened the shed while we were both away."

As someone else had opened the shed before.

"No," he said to himself, with a frown, "she wouldn't have *two* keys."

"Sir?" said Leah.

She was looking at him anxiously; and he realized that he had been staring at her in silence for some time.

"Nothing," he said, and turned toward the door leading into the hall just as a coloured boy came pelting up the back steps with such extreme consternation on his face that Hamish stood still.

"Mis' Delaine!" he cried. "They vant you home quick! Mr. Delaine, he took sick."

"What's the matter with him?" asked Leah, with a certain coldness.

"Couldn't tell you, ma'am. Miss Ronnie, she told me to get you right away."

"I've heard that before," said Leah. "You tell Miss Ronnie I'll try and get down this evening—"

"Miss Ronnie says he very low! They got Doctor Leaming, Mis' Delaine! Miss Ronnie, she tell me to break it to you, Miss Delaine!"

"Every time Sam gets a bottle of rum down his throat, thinks he's dying," said Leah, angrily. "Sam ain't goin' to die that easy."

The boy's face was contorted with distress. A hobbledehoy of fourteen or so, in knickerbockers and a white shirt with red dots.

"Mis' Delaine! Miss Ronnie she vouldn't send for you, less'n it wasn't serious. She know you got trouble here."

"You hold your tongue, Gilbert!" said Leah, sternly. "You go and tell Miss Ronnie, can't leave the mistress. Isn't anybody here to look after her."

"Mr. Delaine goin' *die!*"

"Not him!" said Leah, scornfully. "And if he was, I couldn't save him. Been drinking that rum too long. Drinking and gambling and all manner of wickedness.... There is no health in him.... The wicked bound to perish."

Gilbert seemed impressed. "Yes, ma'am..." he said. "O'ny Miss Ronnie, she say she can't look after Mr. Delaine all by herself."

"I'll come down after I got the dinner cleared away this evening," said the inflexible Leah. "You stop by and tell Merla to come here and sit with the mistress. Now don't you bother me any more, Gilbert! I got my work to do, and I'm *not* coming now."

"Yes, ma'am," said Gilbert, and hurried away.

Hamish went toward his own room, faintly amused by Gilbert's dramatic intensity and Leah's unwifely coldness. But the thing had another aspect, not at all amusing. This was a singularly unfortunate time for Sam to fall ill.

"Unless he's doing it on purpose. He may have some object...."

Sam could be thought about later; his immediate concern was with this note.

"I'll burn the damned thing," he thought, as he shut himself into his room.

But with the note in his hand, he hesitated, filled with an uneasy sense of guilt.

"I have no right to destroy it," he thought. "It might be important."

But if Jesser got hold of it? He didn't know whether or not Jesser was legally entitled to demand the note, perhaps to search him, and take it. If he saw it, he would certainly question Stephanie.

"That wouldn't hurt her," he said to himself. "Unless it's something she can't explain satisfactorily. Unless.... Well, suppose she and Cornwall are in love with each other? I mean, it's hard on a girl to have to answer questions about a thing like that. To have her note read by a lot of people."

He had a vision of Stephanie confronted by Jesser, Stephanie being cool and nonchalant but with that hot colour in her cheeks.

"I don't think that Faquita understands that a lot of girls talk as if they hadn't any standards, when it doesn't mean a thing," he thought. "It's possible that Stephanie wasn't really sincere about Hector...."

He looked at the note again.

"Anyhow," he said to himself, "she ought to have a chance. I could ask her to explain it myself. I could—"

Leah knocked at his door to summon him to lunch, and he ate alone in the gloomy little dining room.

"How is Mrs. Malloy?" he asked.

"She's very downcast, sir," answered Leah gravely. "She's taken to her bed."

"What about the nurse?"

"The mistress sent her away, soon as she came, sir. Says she wants me and nobody else," said Leah.

"How long is this going to last?" Hamish asked himself in a sort of wonder. "What am I waiting for?"

Was he waiting for news of Hector? There might never be any. Perhaps no one would ever know what had happened to him. Or ever know the truth about Raymond.

"Sam may come back with his information," he thought. "I wish to Heaven he would. If he doesn't, I ought to go after him."

The difficulties of such an enterprise were appalling. Sergeant Welcome and Jesser would certainly not allow him to visit Sam unquestioned ; even the initial step of asking anybody where Sam lived would be highly suspicious.

"How do these amateur detectives in books manage?" he thought. "They go around questioning people...."

"I'll have to let Sam wait," he thought.

And he was not good at waiting. He finished his lunch and smoked a cigarette; and then he set out to do what he had made up his mind to do. He left the house with a casual air; he strolled up and down the verandah for a moment before he went down the steps. But in his heart was a sense of haste and alarm that made it very difficult to keep a leisurely pace.

"I wonder if Jesser has anybody watching me?" he thought.

It seemed very likely. There was no one to be seen in the little garden; no one in the road except passers-by going about their business. The sun was high; there was a cheerful tranquillity in this hot and brilliant world. Yet he had the feeling of being watched, a feeling of dread. At any moment he expected to be stopped and the note demanded of him. He wished now that he had destroyed it; halfway along to the cottage, he stopped.

"I'll tear it up," he decided. "I don't need to have it with me. I can just as well tell her I've read it."

Too late. If there was someone watching him he would be seen tearing it up; the fragments would be collected. He had to go on. He mounted the steep bank, and he saw the cottage before him, neat and bright as a doll's house, white curtains at the windows, a flower-bed before the verandah where cool little flowers, pale pink and white, stirred in the light air; two dark cedars shaded it. It had, he thought, a curiously northern air, incongruous here, yet pleasing.

He went up on the verandah, and he was just about to ring the bell when he heard Stephanie's voice inside.

"I'll never, *never* forgive myself!"

"Don't be such an ass, my dear girl!" said Cornwall. "You couldn't possibly know...."

"I ought to have known! It's all my fault! I don't think I can stand it, Reggie. I think I'll have to go to the police."

"Look here!" Cornwall interrupted. "You'll ruin your life, d'you realize that? And for no purpose. It won't bring him back."

Hamish rang the bell, suddenly and loudly. He wanted to hear no more. There was a moment of complete silence; then Cornwall opened the door.

"Oh, hello, Grier!" he said, in a serious, confidential way. "Come in, won't you? I'll tell Steve. She's—upset, y'know.... I mean Malloy disappearing. Next door neighbour and all that...."

He left Hamish alone in the sitting room for a moment; then he returned.

"Steve will be with you directly," he said. "Sorry, but I'll have to push off. The police are after me all the time. Every time I go into the office, either the sergeant or the superintendent is there. They ask me questions. Lord! I'm beginning to believe I've committed every crime in the calendar. If they ask me the same question a second time, I know dam' well I answer it differently."

His manner remained quiet and cheerful as ever, but his face betrayed his strained fatigue. He took up his white helmet from the table and went off with his springy gait, and almost at once Stephanie came into the room.

Hamish was struck by the sight of her. Her face was stained with tears, her eyes reddened; her white linen dress was rumpled; her fair hair was tied back from her forehead with a narrow black ribbon. She looked so desperately unhappy, and so very young.

"Hamish!" she said with a sob. "You've got—some news?"

"No," he answered. "I'm sorry—"

"Haven't they *found* Hector?"

"I'm sorry," he said again.

She caught one of his hands in both her own. "Oh, *you're* from home!" she said. "You're the only one!"

She buried her face on his shoulder, sobbing forlornly. He had to put his arm around her. And she was pliant and clinging.

"Steve!" he said. "Don't, please don't!"

She sprang away from him as the door-bell rang and ran to the window. "It's that dam' superintendent," she whispered.

Hamish whisked the bit of paper out of his pocket.

"Get rid of this, quick!" he whispered back.

# CHAPTER EIGHT

He thought that she would hurry away with the note, but she did-n't even look to see what it was. She slipped it into a book that lay on the table, and went at once to admit Jesser.

"Ah, Miss Rose! Good afternoon!" he said. "And Mr. Grier. Beautiful weather!"

"It's no use," said Stephanie. "You can't put me at my ease. I'm terrified of you."

Hamish observed her with amazement. A moment before she had been weeping in his arms; her face was still tear-stained and pale, her lashes wet. But she had a smile for Jesser, half-friendly, half-provocative; a new note in her voice, to which he responded with gallant readiness.

"That's very gratifying," he said. "I try to inspire awe. But it's not your turn—yet. I just came for a few words with Mrs. Mapes."

"Mrs. Mapes?" she repeated with dismay. "Oh, but why do you want to see poor Mrs. Mapes?"

"Just a few routine questions," said Jesser, soothingly.

"She's gone to the movies. But I'll do just as well, won't I? Mapes can't tell you anything that I couldn't tell you."

"How do you know?" asked Jesser. "She may have all sorts of secrets. She may be deep, Miss Rose. Very deep."

His playful manner filled Hamish with alarm. In spite of her remarkably quick recovery, her self-possession, Stephanie seemed like a child beside Jesser; a kid, with that black ribbon in her hair.

"Really, I wish you wouldn't talk to Mrs. Mapes," she said. "She's very hostile to the police. She had some sort of trouble with them in Barbados."

"Ah-ha!" said Jesser. "So she's been in trouble with the police—already. *That's* interesting!" He was smiling down at the girl, and she smiled at him, reluctantly.

"Something was stolen from her," she explained. "Poor Mapesie was sure she knew who the thief was, and she told the police, and they wouldn't pay any attention to her. There was a long investigation—and in the end, after questioning her and bothering her for ages, it turned out that she'd been right. She's never got over it. She thought they should have apolo-gized. She thinks she was persecuted. Do let Mapesie alone, Mr. Jesser! Ask *me* the routine questions!"

"Keep quiet!" cried Hamish in his heart. "Don't you see what you're doing?"

"Oh, I'll come back to you, later on," said Jesser. "And I'll put Mr. Grier through it, too." His smile was for Hamish now. "What time d'you expect Mrs. Mapes back, Miss Rose?"

"I don't know," she answered. "But she'll probably be late. Anyhow, do give me a chance to prepare the poor thing. Let her have her dinner in peace, won't you?"

"I shan't use the third degree," said Jesser. "Don't worry, Miss Rose. I'll handle Mrs. Mapes with care. What picture did she go to see, d'you know?"

"I don't. She goes to all of them."

There was a moment's silence.

"Is there any news yet?" asked Stephanie.

"About Mr. Malloy? No," said Jesser.

"What do you think?"

"I try not to think," said Jesser. "I try to find out facts."

"You must have a theory."

"One theory is as good as another," said Jesser. "Tell me yours. It might help me. Remember Mrs. Mapes's experience. How she was right and the police were wrong."

Again there was a little silence. When Stephanie spoke, her tone had changed; there was no lightness in it now.

"I was very fond of Hector Malloy," she said. "He used to come here in the evenings. He liked to hear me play. We were really friends. But in a little place like this where there's so much gossip, we had to be ridiculously secret about it."

"One does," Jesser agreed, seriously.

This was, thought Hamish, pathetically transparent.

"She knows he's either found out already about Hector's coming here," he thought, "or that he will find out from Mrs. Mapes. So she's trying to get in her own version. If I can see through it, certainly Jesser can. She's making things worse and worse. I wish to Heaven she'd keep quiet."

But she would go on.

"I think I knew Hector as well as anyone did," she said. "I think perhaps I could tell you—tell you more about him than anyone else."

She had grown still whiter, her glance fixed upon Jesser's face had a desperate intensity.

"Don't be such an ass, my dear girl!... You'll ruin your life...."

That was what Cornwall had said to her. And was she mustering the courage now to speak the words that would be ruin to her?

"I'm afraid I'm due for trouble, myself," said Hamish. "Sergeant Welcome found me in the shed, in very suspicious circumstances."

"He reported that," said Jesser.

The thing was to hold Jesser's attention, to give the girl a chance to think. He could only hope that if she did think, she would realize the dangerous folly of her course.

"I dropped a letter out of my pocket," Hamish went on, "and I picked it up. The sergeant seemed to think it was an important document, and he wanted to see it. I'm sorry I was so pig-headed. He was only doing his duty, and if I'd shown him the thing—"

"It would have been wiser," Jesser agreed.

"I've still got it," said Hamish. "It wasn't anything of the least importance." He was improvising now, rapidly but cautiously; he was trying to remember just what he was carrying in his waistcoat pocket. It must be something without an envelope, in case Welcome had noticed. "It was a receipt from the steamship company," he said.

"Too bad you didn't show it to the sergeant," said Jesser. "He'd have been quite satisfied. But Americans have a rather different attitude toward the police, haven't they?"

"Well, here it is!" said Hamish, taking everything out of his pocket. A folding chequebook, two or three letters. And Stephanie's note.

He recognized it at once. He had given her the company's receipt. Jesser stood there, waiting....

"I haven't got it, after all," said Hamish. "I must have left it in my room...."

Jesser stood there, waiting....

"I'll look for it," said Hamish.

He saw Stephanie, behind Jesser's back, take the folded paper out of the book and drop it on the floor. Their eyes met.

"Is this it?" she asked.

Jesser turned and picked it up.

"That's it!" he said. "Thanks! I shan't keep you any longer just now, Mr. Grier. I'll show this to Sergeant Welcome and explain your attitude. I suppose I can reach you at Mr. Malloy's if anything turns up?"

"I don't know," answered Hamish, suddenly aware of a new aspect of the situation. "As soon as I've had a talk with Mrs. Malloy, I think I'll move to one of the hotels."

Because he wasn't Hector's guest now. No use waiting for Hector to return.

"I'll let you know where I go," he said.

"Oh, we'll find you, Mr. Grier," said Jesser. "This is a small place. Don't bother about us! Well, good-day!"

He had to go and leave that girl alone with Jesser. He held out his hand to her, and she took it.

"Be careful what you say to the superintendent!" he said. "He's a dangerous man."

He knew well enough that his attempt at a playful tone was a conspicuous failure. He knew that Jesser was watching them, that he saw the glance they exchanged, perhaps saw how his fingers tightened on her warm, sturdy little hand.

"I'm a fool," he thought, as he left the house. "God, what a fool! I've made things worse. I don't see...."

What he did see was Mrs. Mapes coming along the path, somewhat out of breath from climbing the bank.

"*How* is poor, sweet little Mrs. Malloy?" she asked presently.

"She—I believe she's resting," said Hamish, rather at a loss.

"I'll come over this evening," said Mrs. Mapes. "Perhaps she'll want to see me."

"Superintendent Jesser is in the cottage," said Hamish, abruptly.

"What ever is *he* doing there?" demanded Mrs. Mapes, with indignation.

"He said he came to see you," said Hamish. "I think—" He paused. "In a case like this..." he went on. "The police will dig up everything. They'll want to know just how often Malloy came to see Miss Rose—and you." He paused again, looking at Mrs. Mapes with a sort of despair. Her face, flushed with exertion, was not reassuring; she didn't look notably intelligent. "They might easily make a scandal out of it," he said, and hoped with all his heart that she would understand.

She opened her round eyes wide, in a look of affronted amazement.

"What!" she exclaimed. "They'll try to drag Stephanie into this? Very well! *I'll* know how to manage your Superintendent Jesser!"

She tried to pass Hamish, but he stood in her way.

"Mrs. Mapes.... It's important to be very careful—"

"Leave it to me!" said she. "I've had experience with the police. They won't believe you when you tell them the truth. Very well! *I'll* tell them that Hector Malloy never set foot in the cottage!'"

"No! Don't!" cried Hamish. "He knows—"

"Leave it to me!" said she, and stepping off the path passed him and went toward the cottage, a little unsteady on her high heels, but how resolute. Resolute to tell Jesser what he would know to be a lie; what would make a bad situation infinitely worse.

"Don't!" he said again. "If you'll let me talk to you for a moment—"

"Leave it to me!" said Mrs. Mapes.

He had to go on his way, with all his sense of failure, and dread, and misery weighing upon him.

"I don't know what Steve has done," he thought. "But there's no doubt that she's in a spot. She said I came from home. That I was the only one who could understand. Well, I don't understand; but I'm sorry for her."

And when the bungalow was in sight, he remembered Faquita and was sorry for her, too.

"I must have a talk with her," he thought. "I can't stay alone in the house with her. Wouldn't do. But I can't simply walk off, without seeing her. She'd better let me cable to that aunt in Vermont. Even if she doesn't care much for her, she ought to have someone of her own."

He was startled when Faquita herself opened the door for him. She was wearing a black dress that made her look slighter than ever; she looked ill and alarmingly agitated.

"Hamish!" she cried. "Leah's *gone!*"

"Her husband was ill," he said. "Probably—"

"I know! That's what she wrote in the note she left for me. She went while I was asleep, and when I waked up I was all alone in the house!"

"I'm sorry, Faquita. I just stepped out. Sit down and try not to be so upset, won't you?"

She sank into a chair on the verandah, and he sat on the rail beside her.

"Look here, Faquita!" he said, gently. "Let me get someone to stay with you. Someone you like, some friend—"

"I have no friends!" she said. "I never wanted anyone but Hector."

"Your aunt?"

"No! No! The only person I want with me is Leah. She's kind, and good, and faithful. I'd rather be alone until she comes back."

"But, you see," said Hamish. "I'll have to leave you, Faquita."

"You?" she cried. "You're going to leave *now*, Hamish? Now? In this dreadful time?"

"I shan't go far. Just to a hotel."

"But why? Oh, why, Hamish?"

"It's.... You have to think of the conventions," he said, and thought it the most priggish speech a man had ever made to a beautiful and grief-stricken woman.

But to his surprise, she took it seriously.

"I hadn't thought of that," she said. "I suppose you're right. I owe it to Hector to think of things like that."

The sun had moved into the west; the quiet, leisurely feeling of mid-afternoon was in the air. He sat staring at the floor and trying to solve Faquita's problem.

"Well, what about a nurse?" he asked.

"I'm not ill, Hamish. I'm as well as I'll ever be again. And I don't like nurses."

There was a dreadful resignation about her which he did not know how to combat. He knew it was a wrong, an atrocious thing, that anyone so lovely should think of life as a thing finished, already in the past; she had no plans, she wanted nothing, cared about nothing.

"Faquita," he said, cautiously, "why don't you get away for a while? A little trip, perhaps."

Her dark eyes met his. "Then you've given up hope, too?" she said. "You don't think Hector will ever come back?"

He did not know how to answer; he could not decide whether it was better to encourage her to hope when Jesser, when Stephanie, when his own heart denied such hope; or whether it would serve her better to be candid.

"I'm not going away, Hamish," she said. "I'm going to stay here, always, in the house that Hector chose for me. And I'm going to see that the guilty person is punished."

He didn't like the way she said that. Without passion, quietly, and inexorably.

"I was happy," she went on. "I don't think anyone was ever so happy. And now...."

He waited a moment.

"You make it harder for yourself," he said. "Staying on here—alone."

"I really couldn't bear anyone near me but Leah. I'm used to her. I'd rather be alone until she comes back."

"You can't be alone," said Hamish. "I'll stay—"

"No! That would cause gossip."

"Nobody would gossip about you—now," he said. "I'd like to know when Leah expects to come back."

"That will depend upon how her husband gets on, of course," said Faquita. "He's a terrible trial to her, but she has a sense of duty toward him. If he's really seriously ill, she may feel that she's got to stay with him."

"Tell me where she lives, and I'll go and find out."

"And, Hamish.... Will you do one other thing, too?"

"Anything, Faquita."

"It's—difficult," she said, looking down at her clasped hands. "But if you'd stop and see Reggie Cornwall.... If you'd ask him about the business—if there's any money.... You see, I haven't a penny."

"Look here, Faquita! Let me—"

"No!" she said, vehemently. "I couldn't! I'm sure there's plenty. Reggie will know."

She telephoned for a carriage for Hamish; she wrote down Leah's address on a piece of paper, and Cornwall's.

"I'll be back soon," he said.

"To dinner?"

"Certainly! But see here. What will you do about dinner, and so on, Faquita?"

"I can cook," she said.

He hated to go off and leave her alone in that house; he hated to sit alone in the back seat of the surrey and be obliged to think. All his thoughts had the confusion, the oppression, of a nightmare; he had that nightmare feeling that something horrible was going to happen very soon.

"If that fool of a Mrs. Mapes has told Jesser what she said she'd tell him... Stephanie's badly involved in the thing, anyhow. Jesser may know things that I don't know. Stephanie's done something that she's sorry for. All right! It's not murder. It's impossible to think of her...."

Why was it? Because she was young and pretty? Because she had wept in his arms? Was he being one of those fatuous dupes such as he had read about in books?

"Nope!" he said to himself. "It's her character. She's not capable of anything criminal."

Why was he so sure of that?

"Well, damn it! I am sure!" he told himself, angrily. "And I don't believe she tried to get Hector away from his wife, either. May have flirted with him a little, that's all."

"I don't think I can stand it, Reggie." He had heard her say that.

Can't stand it.... White and tear-stained, making disastrous blunders in dealing with Jesser....

"Her precious Reggie doesn't seem to be helping her much," he thought. "He's pretty much of a lightweight, anyhow."

He felt a curious hostility toward Cornwall.

"Why didn't he take charge of the situation?" he thought. "He was the obvious person. Hector's partner. He should have looked after Faquita, made arrangements for her. And he hasn't even come back to see if he could do anything. He's failed her, and he's failed Stephanie. All the advice he could give her was to say nothing. About what? He knows."

The sun was setting now. That homeward flight had begun again: the swift rush of bicycles, the carts, a trolley rattling along toward the stable, the Portuguese workmen in chattering groups. The surrey seemed unreasonably light, bounding over every inequality of the road. It was a long time since he had ridden in carriages, and suddenly he found it irksome, longed for the speed of a car. He longed for New York, where he knew his way about, where he had friends, where he belonged. The horse jogged steadily along, forever.... Now and then he caught a flash of colour: a scarlet hibiscus, a blue house, a window dazzlingly bright where the sun struck upon it. But he was no longer interested; he looked about him for one purpose only. He wanted to find a spot where he might safely tear up that note and scatter the fragments, and there was none. There was always a house, or a passer-by.

The surrey turned into a street at the foot of a hill, a street of poor little houses, neat, and somehow melancholy; it stopped before a cottage of white coral stone, with all the shutters closed.

"Must be Sam is very bad," said the driver, with alert interest. He waited. "This Mis' Delaine's house, sir."

"Yes," said Hamish, not moving. It didn't seem decent to knock at that door and ask Leah when she would return to her service.

"I don't think I'll bother them."

"I'll jest ask Miss Ronnie, sir," said the driver. "Horse he'll stand, sir."

Filled with eagerness, he got out; as he opened the gate a woman came out of the house, an elderly black woman, very like Leah in her neat austerity. She and the driver spoke together in a low tone; then they both approached the carriage.

"I'm Ronnie, sir," said the woman. "Leah's auntie. Would you wish to step in, sir, to speak to Leah?"

Reluctantly Hamish descended, and all three of them went to the house. Ronnie opened the door and stood aside, and Hamish stepped into a room rammed with furniture. Among the tables, rocking chairs, plants in pots, there was incongruously a big brass bed. An oil lamp, blue with pink roses painted on it, shed a mild light on the figure lying there.

"He looks stricken terrible bad, Miss Ronnie," said the driver.

"I'm doing my bestest for him," said Ronnie.

Sam lay on his back, neatly covered to the chin with a white sheet; his face was calm and blank.

"Is he—dead?" asked Hamish.

"No, sir," said Ronnie.

"What's wrong with him?"

"It's a judgement, sir," said Ronnie.

# CHAPTER NINE

Hamish couldn't take his eyes off that dark, inscrutable face. This was the man who had come to give him information, and now he was 'stricken.' The coincidence was too striking. Hamish's mind rejected it.

"What does the doctor say?"

"*Doctor* say he got a stroke, sir," said Ronnie, with marked emphasis.

"You don't agree with the doctor?"

"Doctor got to know his own business, sir," said Ronnie.

"Doctor Leaming, wasn't it? Does he think Sam is going—to be better, soon?"

"No, sir."

"Then Leah won't want to leave, of course."

"Leah say she'll go back to her mistress this night, sir. Say she got to cook her mistress dinner. Say, if Sam going to die, he going to die."

Leah came in then from another room.

"I'll he back at six o'clock, sir," she said. "Time to cook the dinner."

Neither she nor her aunt nor the driver showed the least concern for the silent figure on the bed. If he were dying, his death would cause little enough grief.

"Is Sam getting any sort of treatment?" Hamish asked, with a trace of sternness.

"Isn't no one can look after the sick like my auntie, sir," said Leah, and the driver upheld her.

"Ain't no one like Miss Ronnie for the sick, sir, *and* the dead," he said. "Miss Ronnie, she lay out my wife, the best I ever saw."

"Did the doctor give you any medicine—any directions?" Hamish intervened.

"Yes, sir," said Ronnie. "Doctor leave medicine, but Sam can't swallow."

There was something in this scene that profoundly disturbed Hamish. There was not a voice lowered. The two women didn't even look at Sam, and the driver's glance at him had a ghoulish sort of admiration in it.

"I don't believe the man's getting any proper care," he thought; and aloud, "Well," he said, "I hope he'll improve."

He hoped that, not only on account of humanity, but because of that 'information.'

"Dam' queer," he thought as he left the house.

"How did he get out of the shed, and why?"

He climbed into the surrey again.

"D'you know where Doctor Leaming's office is?" he asked.

The driver did know and took him there, but the young girl in charge told him the doctor would not be in until eight in the evening.

"Now, d'you know the Maple Leaf House?" he asked the driver.

"Yes, *sir!*"

The Maple Leaf House stood on a corner, a square building of sober aspect; Hamish entered a dim little lobby and asked the clerk for Mr. Cornwall. The clerk touched a bell, and a coloured boy hastened forward.

"Go into the bar and tell Mr. Cornwall there's a gentleman to see him," said the clerk.

Promptly enough Reggie Cornwall came into the lobby.

"Oh, Grier !" he said, holding out his hand. "Come and have a drink."

"No, thanks," answered Hamish, and there was an awkward moment of silence. "What's the matter with the fellow?" Hamish thought. "Is he drunk?"

There was an odd look about Cornwall. He was very neat in a white linen suit with a jacket that stood out squarely from his lean body; but his sandy hair was ruffled, and there were faint lines visible about his eyes, a look of strain that made him seem considerably older.

"Care to come up to my room?" he asked.

"Yes, thanks," said Hamish.

They got into a lift of remarkable slowness; it mounted upward with a wheezy, laborious effort, and at the third floor they got out and entered a bedroom of the old school, thin red carpet on the floor, starched white lace curtains at the windows, a washstand with jug and basin of white and gold. Cornwall sat down on the bed, and Hamish took a varnished rocking chair, and there they sat. The sun was gone now; a clear pale brightness filled the sky, and inside the room dusk was beginning to gather.

"Oh! Will you smoke?" asked Cornwall, rising in his springy way. He put an ash tray on the table beside Hamish; he offered him cigarettes.

"Thanks, but I'll stick to my own," said Hamish.

When he took a package out of his pocket, he noticed that what Cornwall had held out to him was the same brand. It was embarrassing; it was too obvious, he thought, that he didn't want to accept anything from Cornwall.

"Mrs. Malloy asked me to see you," he began. "She—she'd like to know what the financial situation is."

"Oh! That?" said Reggie. "Yes, naturally. The trouble is that I can't be very definite just yet. I mean to say—there are certain books and papers that I haven't got. Y'see, our partnership was a bit informal. Never down in black and white. We—" he paused, and stroked the back of his head, "we got on very well," he said.

"I see!" said Hamish. "But Mrs. Malloy is worried about finances. She's short of cash."

"Oh! That?" said Reggie. "I'll arrange that tomorrow morning, as soon as the bank opens. Anything she wants."

Hamish didn't like this at all. This was no way to conduct a business matter.

"Did you and Malloy have a joint account?" he asked.

"No. But I'll draw on my own account, until we've straightened things out."

"Mrs. Malloy won't want it that way," said Hamish. There was something wrong here, something very wrong, and it was his duty to protect Faquita. "She wants to know how she stands. You can give me a rough statement, can't you, of Malloy's assets?"

"Well.... Just at the moment I can't," said Reggie. "Everything's in the devil of a mess."

"Why?" asked Hamish.

He was perhaps ten years younger than Cornwall; he was considerably less expert in the ways of the world, yet he had the upper hand now. In the fading light he looked dark, stubborn, even grim, sitting straight and still in the rocking chair, his steady narrow glance fixed upon Cornwall. And Cornwall looked away from him, shifted restlessly.

"Obvious, isn't it?" he said. "I mean to say—Malloy disappearing naturally upsets things."

"That doesn't follow. A man can disappear, without leaving his business in such a condition that his own partner doesn't know anything about it. You kept some sort of books, didn't you?"

"Look here!" said Reggie. "Are you representing Frances—Mrs. Malloy?"

"Not officially," he said, at last. "If you like you can say that I'm representing Malloy. He was my friend. I'm going to look after things for him."

"Were you—much attached to Malloy?" asked Cornwall.

It was an unexpected question, and he asked it in a new tone, with a sort of brusqueness.

"Yes," answered Hamish.

"Very good, then!" said Cornwall. "I'll tell you something. I wanted to keep it quiet, and I hope you'll say nothing, unless you're obliged to. Malloy was getting ready to leave Bermuda."

"Why?" asked Hamish.

"That's not my affair—or yours either. He intended to go, and go quietly. We were on the point of settling our business together when he disappeared."

"And that's why you haven't got the books, and so on?" asked Hamish.

He didn't believe a word of this; he thought it as clumsy a lie as ever he had heard.

"That's why," Cornwall assented. "He took the books away from the office with him. Took all his papers out of the safe—his will—everything."

"When did he intend to go?"

"To-morrow," said Cornwall. "He must have wanted to see you first."

"D'you know where he was going? How long he expected to stay?"

"No," said Cornwall.

"He was going to wind up your business?"

"Yes, he was," said Cornwall, with a sort of exasperation. "I was quite willing to leave the whole thing to him."

"I got down here yesterday," said Hamish. "That was Monday. You say Malloy was planning to go away, for an indefinite time, on Wednesday. No signs of any packing up in his house. Do you mean that he was simply going to leave everything?"

"He knew I'd look after matters."

Hamish struck a match, and the little flame suddenly showed him how dark the room had become. Cornwall's face was scarcely distinguishable.

"You mean that Malloy was going *without telling his wife?*" he asked.

"I don't know what Malloy intended to tell his wife!" cried Cornwall, vehemently. "I don't much care for this cross-examination, Grier. I've told you something—in confidence—but I thought you were a friend of Malloy's. I thought you'd understand."

"Understand what?" asked Hamish. He waited, and no answer came. "You want me to understand that Malloy had some good reason for running away? Trying to imply that there was something damned wrong? Well, I don't understand anything of the sort."

"My God! Steve was right!" said Reggie, springing to his feet. "She said we'd have trouble with you."

"You will!" said Hamish.

There was a silence between them.

"Look here," Cornwall began, in a far more conciliatory tone. "You can't—"

A knock at the door stopped him; he crossed the room and opened the door, and Jesser entered.

"Am I making a nuisance of myself?" he asked. "Purely unofficial visit; and if you don't want me, say so."

"Not at all!" said Reggie. "Come in!" He turned a switch, and a chandelier in the ceiling came alight, throwing a harsh brightness upon the room. "Sit down and have a smoke, Jesser. Grier and I were talking over the financial situation. Mrs. Malloy wants to know."

"Rather peculiar," said Jesser, lighting a cigarette for himself. "Malloy's bank account shows a balance of sixteen hundred pounds—about five times his average. He deposited a draft on a Canadian bank on Saturday. If Mrs. Malloy actually needs anything, I think we can get a court order."

"I can look after things for a time," said Cornwall.

"I think Mrs. Malloy would prefer a court order," said Hamish.

"I'll ask her," said Jesser, affably. "Well! We've made a thorough search of that shed Malloy used as an office. We've made inquiries at his bank, to see if he'd left any papers there. And no trace of the missing books, or the will."

"Not much use in a will, just now, is there?" asked Hamish.

"Always useful," said Jesser. "We could learn something of what Mr. Malloy had in mind, for one thing. For another, we might find out the name of his lawyer and how much of an estate he had. There's no information available here. I've cabled to Quebec, to the bank from which he got that draft. But here's Cornwall, Mr. Malloy's partner. *He* doesn't know who handled Mr. Malloy's affairs, or even where the lawyer is to be found. And here's Mr. Grier, urgently sent for—and he doesn't know anything either."

He smiled, ruefully, as if he simply regretted their peculiar situation.

"I'm afraid I'll have to go on being a nuisance," he said. "Asking questions, right and left.... You've no news for me, Cornwall? Haven't come across anything? Not even some little memorandum?"

"Not a thing!" said Cornwall. "Not so much as a scrap of paper."

"A scrap of paper..." Hamish said to himself.

It was dark enough now. He could tear up that note in the street and scatter it so that it would be practically impossible to retrieve the scraps.

"If you don't need me any longer, superintendent," he said, "I'll be getting back to Mrs. Malloy. I left her alone in the house."

"I saw a carriage waiting, didn't I?" said Jesser. "I wonder if you'd be good enough to let me come along?"

"Very glad!" said Hamish.

Jesser rose, smiling, and Hamish fancied he saw something sinister in that smile.

"Suppose I'm arrested as soon as I leave here?" he thought. "Searched? For all I know it may have been illegal to pick up that note and keep it. Obstructing the police.... Well, if they find the thing now, it'll seem twice as important." He turned to Cornwall, and his dark face had a look of invincible stubbornness, his eyes narrowed, his lower lip a little outthrust. "Have you a bathroom here, Cornwall?" he asked.

"I'll show you where it is," said Jesser. "Down the hall, a bit. I know this place! I stopped here when I first came to Bermuda."

Hamish was not going to leave the room in Jesser's company, with the note in his pocket.

"That fool girl's already got herself into plenty of trouble," he thought.

On the table was one of those glass ash trays with a matchstand in the centre. Hamish looked at it for a moment, while he made up his mind. Then he struck one of the wooden matches and, taking the note out of his pocket, held the flame to one corner. It caught at once, and he held it in his finger tips.

No one said a word. No one stirred. He was forced at last to drop the blazing fragment into the ash tray; he poked at it until nothing remained but a black, charred dust.

"Ready?" he asked Jesser.

"Whenever *you* are," said Jesser, politely.

Cornwall went out to the elevator with them. They all said good-night to one another, in cheerful, ordinary voices.

"Will there be a policeman waiting for me downstairs?" thought Hamish. "All right! Nobody can possibly know what it was I burnt. Nobody can make me tell. They can't have anything definite against me, anyhow. Nothing but suspicion."

There was no policeman in the lobby; no one stopped them as they crossed the pavement and got into the surrey. Before they reached the corner the street lights came on, and the driver got out to light his lamps.

"I hear you went to take a look at Sam Delaine," said the superintendent.

"Hardly. Mrs. Malloy wanted to know when Leah would be coming back."

The carriage rattled along through the streets that had a new aspect now. The lighted windows of the houses in their walled gardens indicated a life Hamish couldn't imagine; there was a faint, sweet fragrance in the night breeze.

"Mr. Grier," said Jesser, "I've been told that Americans have very little regard for the law. I was willing to believe that, in regard to certain elements of your population. But I didn't believe that a man like yourself—a man of good family and position—would deliberately hamper an attempt to investigate a serious crime. Especially when the crime involved the disappearance of a friend."

Hamish had nothing to say to that.

"I don't understand your point of view," Jesser continued, his voice quiet and stern in the dark. "You're willing to assist Mrs. Malloy apparently, in a good many ways; but not to end her anxiety. Not to discover the truth about her husband."

"You admitted that there was the possibility of an accident," said Hamish. "It seems to me that everything points to it."

"For instance?" asked Jesser. And waited. "What facts seem to you to point to an accident, Mr. Grier?"

"Well," said Hamish, "what motive would there be for anything else? For—murder?"

"That's quite another thing," said Jesser. "What I want to know now is your theory to account for an accident. An accident to a very vigorous, level-headed man, on a perfectly bright morning. Where do you think Malloy went to have an accident, after he left his house?"

"Very well. Who could murder a vigorous, level-headed man on a bright morning, in a densely populated place?"

"That looks very much easier to *me*," said Jesser. "I'm able to imagine Malloy getting a message—a note perhaps." He paused. "A message of some sort, which he accepted in good faith, and which induced him to go where his murderer wanted him."

"Yes, it's possible," said Hamish, with growing uneasiness.

"The suicide theory is one I'm frankly unable to consider," Jesser went on. "I don't pretend to be a psychologist, but I have learned to size up a man more or less. And I'd say that Malloy was the last man on earth to kill himself. Of course I only knew him superficially—met him at the club, and so on. You knew him better, Mr. Grier. He was your friend. Would you consider it likely that he's committed suicide?"

"No," said Hamish, briefly.

"Then d'you think he's merely lost? On a small island, for two days and a night? Bermuda is one of the most densely populated spots on the globe. D'you still think that Malloy is lost, or hiding somewhere?"

"No," said Hamish again.

"If he didn't meet with an accident, if he didn't commit suicide, if we're agreed that he's not deliberately hiding—then what, Mr. Grier?"

The horse's hoofs beat rhythmically on the hard road; the carriage swung round a corner, and Hamish, swaying, touched Jesser's shoulder, very solid, in the dark.

"The circumstances don't point to an accident," said Jesser. "They point to murder, Mr. Grier. The murder of a man you called your friend. I suggest, sir, that for his wife's sake—and for your own, you provide me with the explanation I need."

"What do you think I can explain?"

"First," said Jesser, "you can tell me the contents of the note you picked up in the shed and burned just now."

"That was—a personal note. Nothing to do with Malloy's murder," said Hamish, his face grown hot.

"You can tell me what your business was with Mr. Malloy."

"I've told you already," said Hamish. "I don't *know* why he sent for me."

"Very well, Mr. Grier," said Jesser. "There's not much point in continuing. I'll ask you a third question, merely as a matter of form. You're not obliged to answer any of my questions." He paused a moment. "As a matter of form, Mr. Grier, why did you think it expedient not to mention that Mr. Malloy had arranged to go to New York tomorrow, using the cabin reserved for you?"

"I—didn't know that," said Hamish.

"Mr. Malloy told Breckley, the steamship agent, that he had your consent to this arrangement. Is there anything you can say to that, Mr. Grier?"

"No," said Hamish.

# CHAPTER TEN

Because there was nothing he *could* say. He could only continue to deny all knowledge of this move of Hector's, and he was perfectly aware that his denials were unconvincing.

"I don't blame Jesser for not believing me," he thought. "He's sure now that I know a lot more than I've told. I suppose he'd be justified in arresting me."

A fatalistic calm filled him. He couldn't help it if he were suspected and arrested, and he didn't even care very much. He was not physically tired, but he was tired in some other way entirely unfamiliar to him. There was no place to go where he could feel secure and calm; there was no one to whom he could speak freely.

"Well!" said Jesser. "Here we are! You're stopping here indefinitely, Mr. Grier?"

"No," Hamish answered. "If Leah has come back, and if she's going to stay, I'll get a room at a hotel."

"Quite!" said Jesser. "I'd like to suggest one thing. It's not possible to conceal Mr. Malloy's absence any longer. There have been plenty of rumours floating about already, and now the truth will have to come out. You may be approached by the newspaper people. Other people may ask you. The less you say, the better, Mr. Grier."

Jesser got nimbly out of the carriage, leaving Hamish to settle with the driver for a sum surprisingly large.

"Legal rate, sir," said the driver.

The windows of the bungalow were lighted. Leah came to open the door; there was a sort of doll-like coziness in the place.

"Where's Superintendent Jesser?" he asked.

"Gone into the mistress's room, sir," said Leah. "They won't let her alone. All the trouble and sorrow she has, brought down upon her by the wickedness of others.... Won't give her any peace."

"Yes," said Hamish, and went into the sitting room, leaving Leah still talking in a low, bitter monotone. It did seem barbarous to question Faquita, but probably it was necessary. Anyhow, nobody cared. The law had been set in motion, a machine, a Juggernaut that nothing could stop.

"Burning up that note won't do any good," he thought. "Jesser will find out whatever it is that Stephanie knows. She's no match for him. Perhaps it was a mistake. I don't exactly see...."

He couldn't see exactly why he had done it. He was certain that Stephanie was not guilty of any crime; he did not believe she was in danger of being accused of anything serious.

"You don't like to think of a girl being mixed up in a thing like that," he said to himself. "It'll have to come, but I don't want to be the one who starts it."

He thought about Stephanie with that infantile ribbon in her hair, thought of her crying, with his arm about her.

"Not so darn matter-of-fact, after all," he thought. "She must have been fond of Hector. But not the way Faquita thinks."

How did he know that? Well, he did, that was all. He simply knew that Stephanie would not scheme to take a man away from his wife.

"She doesn't care for Cornwall, either," he thought. "She may like him. They may be friends. But that's all. That's obvious. The way they talked...."

She had not turned to Cornwall in her grief, her tears, but to him. And he had accepted her trust. She had asked him to help her, and he would. He would stand by her now, for ever and ever, because that was the way he was made.

"I'm going to see her before here," he decided. "I'm going to advise her to tell Jesser the truth. I don't think she will, though. She's—stubborn."

With his dark face blank, his underlip stubbornly outthrust, Hamish thought about that girl's stubbornness. And in the background of his mind was his aching regret for the loss of his friend. He was sitting here, in Hector's house, and Hector was gone. All this dark trouble existed because Hector had gone, like some demigod who had given light and warmth and laughter to his little world.

A step in the hall made Hamish rise; he thought it was Jesser, and he preferred to face him standing. But it was Doctor Leaming who came out of Faquita's room, bag in hand.

"Oh! Good-evening!" he said.

"Good-evening!" Hamish answered. "May I have a word with you?"

The young doctor was very polite; he entered the sitting room, and Hamish closed the door.

"I've been trying to persuade Mrs. Malloy to send for some relation or friend," he began at once.

"Is she ill?"

"That's a difficult question to answer," said Leaming, with a sigh. "Brooding, sleeplessness, extreme nervous tension will often produce a functional disorder. If she continues to shut herself up in her room, with nobody but the coloured woman.... She was completely wrapped up in her husband. No life apart from him. I've never seen such a devoted couple. Always together. We used to notice, at the club. He'd never stay after nine o'clock."

There was a look on his thin, fatigued face, as if he were dreaming.

"A beautiful thing," he said. "Malloy was the most considerate, devoted husband. But, of course, that makes it worse for her now."

To Hamish, this did not seem a 'beautiful thing' at all.

"Abnormal," he thought. "But I suppose that when a man like Hector does settle down, he's more settled than anyone else." He looked up. "I stopped at your office this afternoon," he said. "D'you mind telling me a bit about Delaine's illness?"

Leaming sighed again, and sat down on the arm of a chair.

"I got my training in London," he said, "but I was born and brought up in Trinidad. I've seen that sort of thing before. It's almost incredible—but it happens. Sam will die, because he's made up his mind that he must. There's nothing much wrong with him, physically. He's a heavy drinker— but he'd have been good for another ten years."

"You mean he didn't have a stroke?"

"I've got to call it something," said Leaming. "In a way, it is a stroke. A stroke of fear. He's literally dying of fright."

"What's he afraid of?"

"God knows!" said Leaming. "And his wife and Ronnie know. I don't. When they called me in, he was breathing with difficulty, his face was congested, heart irregular. I applied restoratives, and he came to, for half a minute. 'Death coming on me, boss,' he said. When I left, his heart action and breathing were normal, but he was unconscious. Genuinely so. He didn't react to any stimulus, even touching the conjunctiva. He'll simply lie there and die."

"D'you mean to say there's no physical cause?"

"Fright produces very definite physical reactions."

"But, don't you think—" said the incorrigibly skeptic Hamish, "that this Ronnie may be dosing him?"

Leaming shook his head.

"I'd know that," he said. "That's the first thing I thought of. She's been in trouble about that before. Giving her herbs, and God knows what, to the whole neighborhood. She's highly regarded as a witch. I think she's put a spell on Sam."

"Can't you do anything about it?"

"Oh, I'll keep on trying," said Leaming. "I'm going to insist on his going to the hospital tomorrow. But he'll die."

Hamish was shocked. He did not believe in any of this.

"Learning simply doesn't know what's wrong with the man," he thought. "And he won't admit it."

He very much wanted Sam cured and able to give his 'information'; he was not going to stand by and let the man die, because of Leaming's fatalistic indifference. The only way he could see to prevent this was by telling Jesser the whole tale. It was an extremely unpleasant prospect. Jesser could say, with perfect justice, that Hamish had seriously hampered the police by his delay in telling them. He could call Hamish an ass, a menace.

"About Mrs. Malloy..." said Leaming. "She tells me you're leaving here to-night." He paused. "You're more or less in charge here, Mr. Grier. I don't know anyone else to approach. I'm very uneasy about Mrs. Malloy."

"I thought you said she isn't seriously ill."

"It's her nervous condition," said Leaming. "She refuses any sort of sedative—anything that might tend to relax her extreme nervous tension. She—" he paused. "I'm extremely interested in psychotherapy. I attended Doctor Cawling's clinic, you know. I think you might be of assistance."

"I don't know anything about psychotherapy," said Hamish.

"If you could induce Mrs. Malloy to talk freely.... It doesn't matter what she talks about. And if you could make notes of her conversation, afterward...."

"Sorry, but I couldn't," said Hamish. The very idea of taking notes of a personal conversation affronted him.

"Well!" said Leaming. "We'll have to see what's to be done. If she could be persuaded to travel.... Or to engage—some cheerful companion...."

He went off, and Hamish stood in the hall for a minute.

"I never heard such a lot of dam' nonsense," he thought. "Sam making himself die—psychologically. Poor Faquita isn't allowed just to grieve for Hector. She's got to be psychological, too."

He was angry. He felt as if he were enveloped in cobwebs. There was nothing real, nothing definite—only suspicion, fear.... Raymond dead, Sam dying, Hector gone. A sound from the kitchen sent him in that direction to speak to Leah.

"You'll be staying here until the morning?" he asked her.

"Yes, sir," said Leah. "Got to go see Sam to-morrow. Got to do so, because of evil tongues."

"Don't you want to go?" asked Hamish.

"No, sir," said Leah. "If I was to say I was grieved I'd be telling a lie. Sam didn't have no righteousness in his heart whatever. Broke his marriage vows, time and again. Money he ought to give to his lawful wife, he spent and squandered on them trashy girls."

"What did he do for a living?"

"Own his own horse and carriage, sir. He could make good money, unless'n he was too drunk to hold the reins. Be days and days when he never made a penny, and then he'd come to me and try to take what I earned with my honest work."

"I bet he didn't get any," said Hamish. He wanted her to go on talking about Sam, in the hope of some revealing word.

"Time and again I give Sam money," said Leah, somberly. "Obliged to do so. If a man hasn't got no money, he'll get himself some money, and he don't care how. I didn't want to lose my good name, 'count of my lawful husband getting himself in trouble."

"It must have been a great shock," said Hamish, watching her sidelong. "A strong, healthy man—"

"No, sir. Wasn't no shock, sir," said Leah. A pot on the stove boiled over, and she took off the lid. "The wicked is exposed to destruction," she observed. "Would it suit you to have your dinner a little early, sir?"

"Any time," said Hamish. He glanced at his watch. "I'll be back in about half an hour," he said.

He had decided to see Stephanie. He wanted to know how she had got on with Jesser—and he wanted to give her some advice. He felt that what Jesser didn't know already he would find out before long, and he wished to advise Stephanie to be entirely candid. He admitted that he had not been so, himself, but that was different. That was really the girl's own fault.

"If she'd told me the truth—" he thought, "if I'd understood what the note meant, I shouldn't have had to burn it up."

He was certain that there was a rational and innocent explanation for the note, and for all of Stephanie's conduct. He went toward the cottage with a sort of eagerness.

"You're from home," Stephanie had said.

He understood what she had meant; he felt that way himself. Faquita and Jesser and Cornwall; Leaming and the sergeant and Leah—they were all alien to him. Only Stephanie was a girl from home, and he could talk to her.

"I like her," he thought, and a calm, brotherly affection filled him. She had behaved foolishly, but she would explain all that now; they would talk the thing over, he would help her.

She opened the door for him.

"Hello, Hamish!" she said. "What do *you* want?"

It was not a friendly tone. She didn't look friendly, either, or touchingly young and forlorn. She had put on a black chiffon dress with long sleeves and a long skirt; her hair was arranged in smooth waves close to her head. She looked taller; she looked cool, assured, and a little annoyed.

"I want to speak to you," he said. "It's important."

"I haven't much time," said she. "Mapesie has to have this cold compress changed all the time."

"What's wrong with Mapesie?"

"You told her that Superintendent Jesser was here. I don't know what else you told her, but you frightened her dreadfully. She tried to hurry too much, and she was wearing high heels. She fell on the steps and hurt her ankle, poor dear!"

"And that's my fault?" demanded Hamish, outraged by this extraordinary injustice.

"You frightened her," said Stephanie. "She has a lot of pain now, and she's worrying herself into a fever."

"Too bad," said Hamish, stiffly. He was still standing on the verandah. She had not asked him to come in and had not even smiled once. He felt inclined to walk off and leave her. But it was not his habit to do as he felt inclined; he was not easily deflected from a chosen course.

"Anything I can do?" he asked.

"No, thanks. I got Doctor Leaming. He says she'll be laid up for some time."

There was a silence. They stood facing each other, both of them tall, and straight, and inflexible. Hamish spoke first, because he thought it was his duty.

"I had a nice little talk with Jesser," he said. "He knows that Hector meant to leave Bermuda. I suppose you knew that, too."

"Yes," she said. "Come in, Hamish."

That was one step forward. But when they were in the cool, lamplit room she remained standing and did not ask him to be seated.

"Did you tell Jesser?" he asked.

"I did not. I didn't tell him anything," she said, calmly and somewhat boastfully.

"You're making a mistake," said Hamish.

"I know what I'm doing," said Stephanie. "I have nothing to tell Superintendent Jesser that could help him one bit. I don't know *anything* about Hector's disappearance."

"Don't you?" said Hamish. "Would it have bothered you at all to explain to Jesser about the note you wrote to Cornwall? The note that said you were 'almost desperate' and that he'd have to forget his scruples and help you?"

"Has the superintendent got *that?*" she asked.

"No," said Hamish. "He never will, either. I burnt it up."

"If he knows you did that—"

"Knows! He saw me. I did it under his nose."

"You're an idiot!" she cried.

"I believe I am," said Hamish. "That's not the point, though. I came here to give you some advice. I advise you to tell Jesser everything you know. Even if it means trouble for you. Because, if you don't tell him, he'll find out for himself, and that'll mean very much more trouble."

"Then, if you're so devoted to candour," said she, "why didn't you show him that note?"

"Because," said Hamish, "as you said, I'm an idiot. Good-night!"

"Good-night!" she answered. "And *I'm* not an idiot. And I'm not afraid of your superintendent or your sergeants. And I'm *not* impressed by your advice."

Hamish returned to the bungalow and sat down to a solitary dinner. It was a good dinner, and he ate it, but without relish. A hot anger against the girl had risen in him, but it had died down almost at once. He wasn't angry now; he was sorry. And he was filled with a heavy apprehension. Trouble was on the way—trouble for himself, trouble for that boastful, head-strong girl.

"It's worse for a girl," he thought. "Once her name is coupled with Hector's, it'll be damnable. Even now it's probably too late to do anything. Probably all the time she thought she was being so clever she was giving herself away to Jesser. He's nobody's fool."

He looked up at Leah.

"Ask Mrs. Malloy if I can see her, just for a moment, will you?" he asked.

Leah went away and returned promptly.

"Mistress say she hopes to see you for luncheon to-morrow, sir."

"Women are—they're hopeless!" thought Hamish, in a sort of despair.

He telephoned for a carriage, and when it came he drove off to a hotel in the town. He was very exacting about a room; he found faults with the rates, with everything. He was unreasonable, and he knew it. But that was the way he felt. The hardest thing for him to endure was vagueness. He could confront anything that was clear and definite; he could stand anything as long as there was a chance to act. But now he could not act; he could not understand; he could not see his way. Trouble was coming, and he didn't know in what form.

He drove back to the bungalow to get his bag, and to try once more, and more resolutely, to see Faquita. He did not want to leave the house without seeing her. When he had last spoken to her she had seemed ill, exhausted, but admirably in control of herself; he wanted to see with his own eyes whether she were still like that; or whether Leaming's idea of her had any foundation. She was the woman Hector had loved, and she was most pitiably alone now.

As he got out of the carriage he was surprised to see the bungalow blazing with lights, the verandah, every window bright. This disturbed him; everything had become disturbing. He ran up the steps, and before he reached the door, it was opened by Leah.

"We been robbed, sir!" she cried.

# CHAPTER ELEVEN

"**W**hat d'you mean?" he demanded.

"The master's things gone, sir. All the pearls—"

"Pearls?" Hamish repeated.

"Yes, sir. Master had a little bag of pearls he got from some heathen land. Had a gold case for cigarettes, had a watch, had papers—"

"Where were these things?"

"In his room, sir. In the chest of drawers."

"When did you miss them?"

"Just this moment, sir. Mistress tell me to bring her the master's things. Say she want to look at them. So I went to get them—and there wasn't one of them left."

"When did you last see them there in the drawer?"

"This morning, sir. It was on my mind, sir, all the time. The pearls.... I used to look all the time, see if they were all right. Didn't want to ask the mistress to put them away, because I knew how she'd feel. Master was going to get a necklace made for her when he got three, four more. Knew how much she valued them."

"Have you telephoned the police?"

"No, sir. No, sir, I haven't."

"I'll do so at once."

"Police can't do nothing, sir. Just worry the mistress. Seems like they better wait till morning."

"No. That won't do. You've told Mrs. Malloy?"

"Couldn't help doing so, sir. She asked me to bring her the things, and—"

"Yes, I see. Tell Mrs. Malloy, will you, that I want to speak to her?"

This time Faquita was ready to see him, and he entered her room. A dim little rose-shaded lamp burned, making a circle of light about the head of the bed where she lay, flat and white; beyond the light loomed the shape of heavy and sombre objects, an enormous clothes-press, a clumsy bureau with a square mirror, a peculiar sort of dressing-table decked out with lace over pink silk. She looked so pitiable, so young and frail, surrounded by this pompous ugliness. Hamish realized, as never before, how alien she was, how out of harmony with the modern world.

"Leah's so frightened," she said. "I wish you'd try to reassure her, Hamish."

"I will. But I think we ought to notify the police at once."

"Perhaps," she said with a sigh. "If only they'd let me alone. I can't tell them anything. I haven't heard anything while I've been lying here, Hamish. I wish I were dead."

"Don't talk like that, Faquita. I know how bad it is for you, but—"

"You couldn't know. I loved Hector too much. It's a sin to love another human being so much. A sin. And I'm being punished for it."

Her black eyes looked tragic, her voice was sadder than anything he had ever heard. And his youth, the vigorous life within him, rebelled against this despair.

"Faquita," he said, "you can't go on like this."

"I don't want to go on."

"For Hector's sake..." he said. "He'd want you to go on. He'd—"

"Let's not—talk any more, Hamish, please. Leah said you're leaving. Will you ever come back?"

"Certainly. I shan't go, anyhow, until the police have been here."

"Thank you," she said, and turned away her head, so that he saw her rich black hair spread out over the pillow.

"Leaming was right, in a way," he thought. "She's in a bad state. Something ought to be done."

And whatever was done would have to be done by him. Again he realized his strange and difficult position; again he was in charge. He was obliged to accept this responsibility, because there was no one else. No one, anywhere.

"Cornwall certainly doesn't do much," he thought. "He was Hector's partner...."

He felt a sort of rage against Cornwall; and it was increased when he suddenly remembered the carriage that stood outside waiting for him.

"Am *I never* going to get away from this house?" he asked himself.

He went to the telephone, and when he got the police station asked for Sergeant Welcome.

"There seems to have been a robbery here," he said; said it in a curt, annoyed tone. He was, to tell the truth, very little interested. There were too many other things.

"Very good, sir!" said the sergeant. "I'll be there at once."

Then Hamish paid the driver, and sent hint away, and sat down in the sitting room to wait. It seemed to him that he had been waiting for one thing or another ever since he had arrived here. He decided to give the robbery a little serious thought now; it might be important, might belong with the other things.

But he fell asleep, and so soundly, that Sergeant Welcome had to tap him on the shoulder.

"Sorry, sir!" he said.

Hamish was instantly wide awake.

"All right!" he said, steadily. And he thought "All right! Now it's happened. He's going to arrest me."

"I'll have to ask you a few questions, sir, relative to this alleged robbery."

"Go ahead!" said Hamish.

"Did you, at any time, see this property?"

"Bag of pearls, and so on? No, never."

"When we searched Mr. Malloy's room, on the night when you discovered the death of Raymond, we did not see any such property in the chest of drawers."

"Didn't you?"

"Upon questioning Mrs. Malloy—"

"Did you have to do that?"

"Couldn't be avoided, sir. She's the presumable owner of this property. Upon questioning Mrs. Malloy, I was informed that she saw this property yesterday."

"I wonder," thought Hamish, "whether they suspect me of having stolen the 'property'? A bag of pearls...."

This seemed to him almost comic; but he showed no trace of amusement.

"Mrs. Malloy informs me that yesterday evening the woman Leah brought her the property, at Mrs. Malloy's request. After examining the property, Mrs. Malloy returned the property to Leah. Upon questioning Leah—"

"Did I sleep through all this?" asked Hamish.

"Apparently, sir," said the sergeant. "Leah alleges that last night Mrs. Malloy told her to fetch the property from the chest of drawers in Mr. Malloy's room. She further alleges that she found the property in a top drawer and returned it to the same place, when Mrs. Malloy returned it to her. I believe, sir, that Mrs. Malloy was left alone in the house this morning, while you and Leah were attending the inquest."

"That's right."

"To the best of your knowledge, sir, nobody came to the house during your absence?"

"I couldn't very well know who came while I wasn't here," said Hamish.

"You might have heard something mentioned, in regard to someone being expected. Something of that sort."

"I didn't."

"Did you, at any time, see any suspicious character, or any stranger, in the vicinity of this house, sir?"

Hamish gave a slight start.

"This is the time," he thought.

This was a chance, and probably the very last chance he would have, to tell about Sam's visit. Even now it was going to look bad, very bad. But if he could adopt the right tone.... He frowned, as if in thought.

"I did see someone," he answered. "Just before I went to the inquest, a man came to my window. Leah's husband, Sam. He said he had some information to give me about Raymond's death."

"What was the nature of this information?" asked the sergeant, with a marked change of tone. He was not polite and respectful now.

"I don't know. I never heard it. I had to leave then. Sam said he'd wait until I got back. But he didn't."

"What was your reason for not reporting this matter immediately to the police?"

That would take a good deal of explaining.

"In the first place," Hamish began, "I didn't take the thing very seriously."

"That wasn't for you to judge, sir. There was a constable here in the house. It was your duty to report this matter to him at once."

"I thought I'd wait until I'd heard what Sam had to say."

"When you returned and found that Sam had not waited what steps did you take to secure this information?"

"None. I didn't know where he was, or how to get hold of him."

"Were you looking for Sam when I discovered you in the shed?"

"I was."

"You didn't mention the matter to me. Later in the day, you met Superintendent Jesser. You didn't mention it to him?"

"No. No, I didn't."

"You then went to see Sam?"

"Yes."

"And found him unconscious?"

"Yes."

"What was your reason for withholding this information from the police?"

"I was thinking of something else," said Hamish.

It occurred to him that he had never heard a statement more feeble, more unconvincing than this one, which was absolutely true. He had been thinking of Cornwall's news that Hector intended to leave Bermuda; then, when Jesser had come, he had been thinking first of that wretched note, and later he had been very much concerned with Jesser's suspicion of himself.

"I spoke to Doctor Leaming about it," he said, with a half-apologetic air.

"Do you mean that you informed Doctor Leaming that Sam had come here?"

"Well, no," said Hamish. "I—asked him some questions about Sam's condition."

"*I see!*" said the sergeant. He took out a notebook and wrote something in it and put it back into his pocket. "Very good, sir."

"I've taken a room at the Regal," said Hamish. "Any objection to my leaving here now?"

"I have no instructions to cover that, sir," said the sergeant, stiffly. "In view of Mrs. Malloy's condition, however, it might be advisable not to leave her here alone."

"Leah—"

"Leah is coming along to the station."

"Can't you question her here?"

"I've questioned her," said the sergeant. "And I'm going to charge her."

"She's—you've arrested her?"

"That's so, sir."

"Charge her with what?"

"Grand larceny," said the sergeant.

"You think she stole the pearls?"

"You don't think so?" countered the sergeant. "Well, we'll see. Duckley!"

He scarcely raised his voice, but he made himself heard. Constable Duckley came out of the kitchen, accompanied by Leah with her respectable black hat on her head.

"Mr. Grier, sir," she said, "they call me a thief!"

"Leah," said the sergeant, "I've already warned you that anything you say—"

"They call me a thief," said Leah, addressing Hamish and ignoring the sergeant. "They going to be punished for that, sir. Don't matter to me if my enemies revile and persecute me. Truth going to come out, sir, sure as I stand here. Onliest thing is, I don't like to leave the mistress. It'll be a sore blow to her, when she hears they've carried me off, and cast me into prison. I beg you to be the one that tells her, sir. Isn't nobody else to comfort her in this house of trial."

"We'll attend to that. Carry on, Duckley."

"*Come* along, now!" said Duckley.

"You won't desert the mistress, sir?" cried Leah.

"No, I won't," said Hamish.

Standing by the window, he watched them down the path and down the steps. Leah and Constable Duckley first, and Sergeant Welcome in the rear. And he pictured himself going off like that.

"That's the only way I'll ever get out of this house," he thought.

Again he was left in charge; again he was solely responsible.

"And when I've gone?..." he thought.

Then poor Faquita would be utterly alone.

"Well, if I ask Jesser to come here," he thought. "If I tell him everything, candidly...."

It was too late, he thought, for candour. His story would sound incredible and idiotic. There would be a noticeable gap in it, too, because his candour would not include the contents of that note. He was not going to tell Jesser, or anyone else, that Stephanie had asked Cornwall to forget his scruples.

"I know she didn't mean anything serious by that," he thought. "But other people—"

The girl herself was coming up the path. He opened the door and stood waiting for her.

"Mapesie wants to see you," she said, briefly.

"I can't leave, now."

She came upon the verandah where it was light; she looked tall, proud, scornful, in her long black dress.

"For Heaven's sake, go and see her!" she said. "She imagines she has something important to tell you. And if you won't listen to her, she'll find someone else. Mapesie's efforts to help me are—a little alarming. She means well, poor darling; but she.... Do come!"

"I can't leave Faquita."

"Won't Leah look after her?"

"Leah's been arrested," he said. "For stealing a bag of pearls."

She stared at him for a moment, wide-eyed, and then she laughed.

"Oh, Hamish!" she cried. "It really is funny! For you—of all people!"

There was something in her sweet careless laugh that stirred him to a passionate resentment. Not against her. Against all this sad and sorry tangle, this shadow that hung above her bright head.

"It's not funny, Steve," he said. "Raymond murdered and Hector—"

She laughed again.

"I don't care!" she said. "I'm never going to care about anything, ever again. Life's simply—a horrible, cruel joke."

He took her arm and drew her to the end of the verandah, away from Faquita's room.

"Life isn't a joke," he said. "I don't think it's horrible either, if you face things."

"'Life is re-al, life is earnest,'" she quoted, mockingly.

"All right, my poor kid," he said, gently. "You're upset now, but you'll get over this. You can take it, Steve."

He put his arm around her shoulder, and she made no protest; he felt her trembling as if with a chill.

"I thought—I could," she said. "I thought I was pretty—hard-boiled. But when I think of Hector.... You see... I think Hector was the grandest person."

"Yes."

"And it's my fault—if he's dead."

"No," said Hamish. "It couldn't be."

"You just—don't know.... If it wasn't for me, he'd be here now. But I encouraged him—all I could—to leave Faquita. I made Reggie help me. I kept on and on, until I made Hector promise—to leave her. And then—you *see* what's happened!"

"I see what you mean. But I don't think you're right, Steve. You think he killed himself—"

"I *know* he did! He brought the books from his office and his private papers—the night before I came. He left a note asking me to keep them for a while. He said that at last—he'd made up his mind to go. He'd left everything in order for Faquita. I didn't understand then—where he was going."

"Sit down, Steve!" said Hamish, and when she paid no attention he pushed her down into a chair. "Have a cigarette. It'll do you good. We'll talk this thing over, Steve—"

"Will you please—see Mapesie first," she said, unsteadily. "I know she hasn't anything important to say—but she thinks it is. I don't want her ever to know what harm she's done by telling those pathetic lies to Superintendent Jesser. I've often felt—simply frantic about her. When she *would* talk, while I was trying to work.... She isn't even a good housekeeper—and that's what I brought her down here for. She's silly, and muddled, and tiresome but I'm *fond* of her. And she's—so loyal."

"All right, Steve!" he said. "You'll sit here quietly, like a good kid, until I come back. You'll hear Faquita if she calls. I'll leave you cigarettes and matches."

She caught his hand.

"Hamish! Hamish, you're so sweet!"

He drew away his hand.

"Take it easy, Steve!" he said. "I'll be back in a few moments."

Because it wasn't fair to let her strong little fingers cling to his; it wasn't fair to let her say things now, when she was so upset and unhappy.

"Is the door unlocked?" he asked.

"Just walk right in," she said. "But call out and tell Mapesie who you are, because she's frightfully nervous about the police."

Hamish ran down the steps and went along the road. A soft and faintly scented breeze blew cool in his face; the stars were bright in the sky.

"She didn't realize..." he thought.

It was true then. She really had tried to make Hector leave his wife. She had involved Cornwall in the affair. She had caused irrevocable harm and suffering, and it was just that she should suffer. Yet his heart ached for her.

"Poor little devil! So darn cocksure. Thinking she was so hard-boiled.... I suppose she loved Hector—in her own way. And Hector?... Hector loved her enough to make him kill himself?"

That happened. Love brought men to these desperate expedients. Cornwall too? Had Cornwall forgotten all scruples, all sense of honour, all decency and kindliness, so that he was willing to join in the monstrous betrayal of Faquita, because he loved Stephanie?

"I hope to God I'll never love a woman as much as that," said Hamish to himself.

He climbed the bank and went along the path to the cottage. It was very dark. He stumbled over a root and nearly fell; presently he tripped over a stone and did fall to his knees.

"But there are no lights in the cottage!" he thought, suddenly.

He knew then that something was amiss. He could see the shape of the little cottage in the starlight; he heard the whispering of the quiet sea against the rocks. He mounted the steps and pushed open the door.

"It's Grier, Mrs. Mapes!" he called in the dark.

There was no answer. He felt for a switch and found it, and light sprang up in the little hall. He went into the sitting room, and turned on the lights there.

"Mrs. Mapes?" he called again.

He didn't like to call again. He went into a bedroom that was empty. And then, in the next room, he found Mrs. Mapes. She was lying in bed, and her face was covered by a pillow. He had to take the pillow off....

# CHAPTER TWELVE

It was beyond doubt that she was dead. He did not need to touch her. And he knew the police would want nothing disturbed. But he drew up the sheet to cover her face, and he left the bedside lamp burning. He gave one quick glance about the neat, peaceful room; there was no obvious sign of any disorder, and he had no inclination to linger here. He felt sick; physically sick.

"By God! I'd like to meet the man who did that," he said to himself.

He would have to notify the police promptly, but he must tell Steve first. The girl must have a few moments to pull herself together before the new inquiry began.

He left the lights on in the cottage, and that illumined his path for a way. He wished with all his soul that he might meet the man who had done that. He had no theories now, no least idea who this killer was. He wasn't even trying to think it out. Someone had murdered that white-haired woman. Had smothered her with a pillow.

"How shall I tell Steve?" he thought. "How can you tell a thing like that?"

He had to, though; he had left the girl trying to calm herself, and now he had to come to her with this news; to overwhelm her, utterly.

"I'll have to break it carefully," he thought. "Very carefully. Thank God, she didn't *see*...."

He slackened his hurrying steps; he went up the path at a leisurely gait, lighting a cigarette on the way. She sat where he had left her, at the end of the verandah, she was leaning back in her chair, but she did not look in any way relaxed.

"Well, did you—" she began, and stopped. "Hamish!" she said sharply. "What's the matter?"

"Come inside," he said, in terror that Faquita would hear something.

"Tell me, quick!"

"Now, look here!" said Hamish. "You've got to behave yourself. Come inside!"

She followed him into the hall, and then he hesitated for a moment. The sitting room was entirely too near Faquita.

"Here!" he whispered, opening the dining-room door. He closed it after them. "Sit down, Steve!" he said.

"*What—is—it?*" she asked, with a sort of ferocity.

"Something's happened. Brace up!"

"Stop trying to be tactful!" she cried. "Tell me!"

"Mrs. Mapes is—dead," he said.

"No!" she said. "She's *asleep....*"

"Here! Where are you going?"

"I'm going to see for myself! I don't believe—"

"You've got to believe it," he said, holding her fast by the arm. "She's dead, Steve."

"*You're* not a doctor! You wouldn't know."

"I know this all right! She's dead."

"I tell you she couldn't be! She was in pain when I left her, but she was perfectly well. She couldn't... *Hamish!*"

"Not so loud."

"I *will* go!"

"Look here," he said. "It wasn't a natural death."

"What?" she said, frowning, staring at him. His meaning began to dawn upon her. "You don't mean—you *can't* mean—that somebody *killed* Mapesie?"

"Try to be calm."

"It's... I don't believe it! How?"

"We can talk about it later—"

"How?" she repeated, seizing him by the shoulder.

"She was—smothered with a pillow."

The girl didn't faint, didn't scream. Only she kept looking at him.

"I'm going to telephone to Jesser, now," he said.

"Stop! Just a minute, Hamish. Let me think."

"Not a good idea, to delay," he said. "Jesser's got a pretty long score against me already. I'd better show a little cooperation this time."

"That's just it," she said. "I'm thinking of how this will look. For you."

"I don't care."

"I do. Hamish, let's go to the cottage together and discover poor Mapesie."

"That wouldn't work. Jesser would find out."

"He couldn't!" she said, impatiently. "You seem to think he's supernatural. He only knows what people tell him, or what he can see for himself. We'll go over there together. We'll find exactly what you found, only there'll be two of us."

"No," said Hamish.

"It's just impossible to talk to you!" she said. "You're so pig-headed, and stupid, and irritating. Don't you see how it will look to the superintendent? He's been at me about you, already. When I met you on the ship. Did you mention what business you had with Hector? Did I gain any impression as to the nature of this business? And so on. I told him that you'd never said any thing about anything. But I don't think he believed me. And then the way you behaved about that note... Things are bad enough already, you—you chump! If you go to him now with a story that you 'discovered' Mapesie— Well, don't you *see?*"

"You're exaggerating everything," said Hamish. "He may think I've been a pest—getting in his way. But he doesn't think, and he won't think, that I'm a murderer. Why should he? What possible motive could I have for coming down here and bumping off people I'd never heard of before?"

"Hasn't it dawned on you yet what your motive for everything is supposed to be?"

"It has not!"

"Mapesie knew," she said. "She told me. And she's probably told Jesser, without realizing that she'd told him. It's because you're in love with Faquita."

"Mapesie told you *that?*" said Hamish, astounded.

"Yes. And she believed it, too. She said that you were so infatuated with Faquita that there was nothing you wouldn't do for her."

"But what the devil put that into her head?"

"You did," said Stephanie. "It would come into anybody's head. You always speak of Faquita with a hushed reverence. You hang around, waiting to see what you can do for her. Of course, you knew her before—"

"All right!" said Hamish. "Now I'm going to ring up Jesser."

"We're both going to tell the truth, are we? Mapesie knew your secret. She sent for you. Alone. You come back and say you found her dead. Hamish.... Was it.... Is that a dreadful way to die?"

"Very easy," said Hamish. "Quick and painless."

And he was more than ever determined that Stephanie should not see poor Mapesie and know the truth. It hadn't been quick. She had obviously struggled.

"Hamish," said Stephanie, very quietly, "listen to me, for once, and try to show a little bit of common sense. We've got to make that discovery together. We'll say that I came over here and that you walked home with me—"

"No!"

"Is it really going to help your future career to be arrested for murder?" she asked. "Or is it just your idea of good, clean fun?"

"Thing's impossible," said Hamish.

She was looking straight into his face, and he returned the look steadily. And, in the complete silence, someone knocked at the door of the house.

"I'll go," said Stephanie.

Hamish put her aside and went to the door himself. It was Jesser.

"Sorry to disturb you," said Jesser. "But there are one or two things...."

"Come in!" said Hamish, in a low voice. "Better come into the dining room, so that we won't disturb Mrs. Malloy."

Jesser followed him, walking quietly. And the dining room was empty.

A sort of rage came over Hamish. Where had that girl gone, and what was she up to? Had she gone back to the cottage? Was she going to reappear with some story that would contradict his own straightforward account? And make matters worse—worse for everyone.

"Mr. Grier," said Jesser, standing with his back against the closed door. "I've made a good many concessions for you. I can't make any more. I've given you the benefit of every possible doubt, because I've ascertained, through your consul, that you and your family are people of standing in New York. I've come here now, after considerable hesitation—to give you one final opportunity to explain yourself."

"Who's that?" asked Hamish, startled by the sound of footsteps in the hall.

"Some of my people," answered Jesser. "And we've brought Leah back. That's not to the point, however. Mr. Grier, it is my duty to inform you that you are not obliged to answer any of my questions. And that anything that you do say may be used in evidence against you. I am simply giving you an opportunity to make a voluntary statement, in case you believe that such a statement would benefit you."

No trace of friendliness in Jesser now; his face was impassive and very tired.

"Is there a charge against me?" asked Hamish.

"I have a warrant here for your arrest, Mr. Grier. On the charge of willfully destroying and concealing material evidence. Other, and very much more serious charges may be brought, subsequently. You are legally entitled to demand the services of a lawyer and to refuse to answer any questions."

So things like this did happen. Murder happened. Not the murder of unknown people, read about in a newspaper, but ordinary people like Mrs. Mapes. Violence and tragedy happened. And injustice. If it was possible for Mrs. Mapes to be murdered in her bed, then it was possible for Hamish Grier to be arrested and tried for a crime he had not committed. And sentenced and hanged. He contemplated that in silence for a time.

"If I can convince you that I haven't destroyed any material evidence," he said, "will that be good enough?"

"If you can convince me of that," said Jesser, "the warrant made out for your arrest will not be executed."

"But there'd be other warrants?"

"That question is not in order, sir. We have to deal now only with the charge already made against you."

"Well! Let's hear it," said Hamish.

"I'll read you the warrant presently. But first—if you like—I can tell you in more detail just what we have against you that needs explaining. I am stretching a point in your favour, sir. I'm not sure that I'm not exceeding my authority in giving you this opportunity. I am doing this at the earnest request of your consul, who has been in communication by cable with your father."

"My father?" Hamish repeated. He had a sudden vision of his father, tall, thin, serious. "A little like Jesser himself," he thought.

His father, that man of courteous pride and reserve, beyond measure kindly and loyal toward his son.... His cheerful, pretty mother.... He could imagine them, in the familiar little drawing room of the old house in the East Seventies—a couple of friends with them, perhaps—everything so orderly and quiet. And a cable arriving....

"What did the consul tell my father?" he asked.

"The consul will tell you presently, in person," said Jesser. "I haven't much time, Mr. Grier. I'll state the case briefly. Sergeant Welcome deposes that he saw you pick up a folded paper from the floor of the shed on Mr. Malloy's premises. He further deposes that you refused to allow him to examine this paper, when he requested you to do so in the performance of his duty. You informed me, later, that this paper was a receipt from the steamship line. Upon my request to be shown this receipt, you produced it with the connivance of Miss Rose—"

"Connivance?"

"The paper which Miss Rose picked up from the floor was not on the floor when I entered that room, sir."

"Very likely not," said Hamish. "It probably dropped out of my pocket while I was talking to you."

"We shan't get very far if you continue to make statements of that sort," said Jesser, with a sort of faint distaste, which made Hamish flush. "I suggest, sir, that the original paper you were seen to pick up in the shed was not the company's receipt. I suggest that the paper you picked up remained in your possession and that you burned it in my presence in Mr. Cornwall's room."

He waited.

"I suggest that this paper was material evidence, essential to our investigation into Mr. Malloy's disappearance—"

"Well, it wasn't," said Hamish. "I'll admit that I didn't want it to get into your hands. But it was a—purely personal matter."

"Are you prepared to tell me the contents of that paper, Mr. Grier?"

"Sorry, but I'm not."

"Are you prepared to state under oath that this paper contained no reference whatsoever to Mr. Malloy?"

"Oh, God!" thought Hamish. "How can I get out of this? If I tell him the truth now—after I've made the thing so dam' important by destroying it, it will look bad for Steve. Especially now, when he knows that she tried to fool him about that receipt. Where is she now? What the hell is she doing? Making things worse.... If Jesser finds her in the cottage...." His throat felt dry.

"I'm prepared to swear that there was nothing important in that note," he said. "It—it referred to Malloy's leaving Bermuda."

"I'm not attempting to trap you, Mr. Grier. I point out for your own protection that you have already admitted that this paper you stated was a receipt was not a receipt. You have admitted that this paper contained a reference to Mr. Malloy. Do you wish to state by whom the note was written?"

"I.... No!" said Hamish.

"Was it addressed to yourself, sir?"

"It wasn't addressed to anyone."

Jesser did not speak for a moment and did not look at Hamish. He didn't need to. Hamish was well enough aware of the impression he was making.

"Mr. Grier, did you admit the man Sam Delaine to the shed? You are not obliged to answer."

"I don't mind answering. I did let him in there. He said he had information to give me about Raymond's death. Your constable was waiting to take me to the inquest, so I put Sam in the shed, to wait until I came back."

"You stated to Sergeant Welcome that Sam was not in the shed when you returned?"

"I did."

"Had you locked the shed on the outside?"

"Yes."

"What did you think, Mr. Grier, when you found the man gone?"

"I thought that someone had let him out, of course."

"You didn't see fit to inform the police of this?"

"I meant to do so. I should have done so in a little while."

"You knew that this man became ill, very shortly after he had volunteered to give you certain information?"

"Yes."

"Even then, you didn't think it necessary to inform the police?"

"I did inform Sergeant Welcome."

"According to Sergeant Welcome's statement, your information could not be called a voluntary statement, but was elicited by the sergeant's questions."

"All right," said Hamish.

"Mr. Grier," said Jesser. "I suggest that the paper you found in the shed was left there for you by Sam Delaine and that it was a part, or possibly, all of the information he proposed to give you."

"I don't know how it got into the shed. But I'll swear as much as you like that it had no connection with Raymond's death."

"You consider yourself qualified to make such a statement, Mr. Grier?"

"Certainly."

"You believe, then, that you know the cause and the motive for Raymond's death? So that you can confidently state that a note, which you tell me referred to Mr. Malloy's leaving Bermuda, had no connection whatever with Raymond's death? You're convinced, Mr. Grier, that Raymond's death and Mr. Malloy's disappearance are in no way related?"

Hamish took out a cigarette and struck a match. And regretted it. His hand was unsteady; he was sweating in a queer sort of torment. The torment of being trapped, of being helpless. A great temptation assailed him—to give up, to shrug his shoulders and to let Jesser have his way. Anything to end this questioning.

But it wasn't his way to give up. He was aware of a change in Jesser, a new light in his grey eyes, a new tone in his voice. The gloves were off. In spite of the American Consul, in spite of that family of good standing in New York, Jesser was no longer disposed to give him the benefit of the doubt. He had had his chance to explain, and he had not explained.

"I don't know the reason for Malloy's disappearance," he said.

"I understand that you questioned Doctor Leaming closely as to Sam's illness. Have you any reason for suspecting that this illness was not due to natural causes?"

"No. No reason. Except that it seemed rather a striking coincidence for a man to be taken ill so soon after he had volunteered some information."

"You didn't think it necessary to mention this coincidence to the police?"

"I've just pointed it out."

"Mr. Grier, you're still unwilling to state the purpose of your visit to Bermuda?"

"I've stated that very definitely. I came because I had a cable from Malloy. He asked me to come down. He didn't explain why. I don't know why. I haven't even any theory as to why he asked me."

"Mr. Grier, are you willing to make any statement in regard to your letters to Mrs. Malloy?"

"My letters—to *Mrs.* Malloy?" said Hamish. "I never wrote her a word in my life!"

"Mr. Grier, I have received information from a trustworthy source that you wrote several letters to Mrs. Malloy."

"Am I allowed to ask who the 'trustworthy source' is?"

Jesser paused for a moment.

"In the circumstances," he said, "I don't see any objection to letting you know. I received this information about your letters to Mrs. Malloy from Mrs. Mapes."

# CHAPTER THIRTEEN

Hamish felt no indignation, no fine warm anger; he felt stunned by an accusation so utterly unfounded.

"In view of Mrs. Mape's statement, do you wish to reconsider your answer, Mr. Grier?"

"No," said Hamish. "I never in my life wrote one word to Mrs. Malloy. She will tell you that herself."

"Mr. Grier," said Jesser. "I advise you to get in touch with a lawyer at once. I shall be obliged to question you about a very much more serious matter, and you should not answer without advice."

"I'll waive that," said Hamish. "I suppose you're going to arrest me?"

"You've left me no alternative, Mr. Grier. You've given me no acceptable explanation of your conduct."

"All right!" said Hamish. A fatalistic calm filled him. He was confused and tired; the thing he wanted most was to be let alone.

"I can give you the names of two or three lawyers—"

"To-morrow, thanks," said Hamish.

"These questions will not wait until to-morrow, Mr. Grier."

"All right; ask them now!" said Hamish, impatiently. "Let's get them over."

"You voluntarily agree to answer my questions, without advice of counsel?"

"Yes, go ahead!"

Jesser took out a notebook and looked at something in it.

"At what time did you return here this evening, Mr. Grier?"

"You ought to know. You were with me."

"I mean, at what time did you return here after seeing Mrs. Mapes?"

"That's a trap!" thought Hamish, suddenly alert again; and the meaning of the trap began to dawn upon him.

"So, I suppose I killed Mrs. Mapes," he thought, "to keep her from talking any more. Things are working out very nicely."

It was dawning upon him, little by little. They might find his finger-prints in the cottage on the electric light switch, on door knobs, all over the place.

"At what time did you return here, after seeing Mrs. Mapes, Mr. Grier?" asked Jesser, again.

"I haven't spoken to Mrs. Mapes this evening," said Hamish.

Jesser was silent, looking into his little book. A bad silence.

"A murder charge," thought Hamish. "They'll cable home, 'Your son held on charge of murder.'"

"Mr. Grier—" Jesser began, and stopped, frowning at the sound of a door banging.

"No, I won't!" said Stephanie's voice, clear and imperious. "It's just silly. I'm going to see Superintendent Jesser."

"You can't see him now, miss," said Sergeant Welcome's voice.

"I can!" said Stephanie. "I'm not going to be shut up here. I want to go home. Mrs. Mapes will be worrying about me."

Hamish glanced quickly at Jesser and was relieved to find him looking toward the door. Then perhaps he hadn't seen Hamish's violent start.

"She means me to hear that," he thought. "She hasn't said anything."

The door opened, and Stephanie appeared; but Sergeant Welcome pulled her out by the arm. Jesser strode across the room, and reopened the door.

"What's this, Miss Rose?" he asked.

"I want to go home," said Stephanie. "And why shouldn't I? I left poor Mapesie in bed with a sprained ankle. She can't get up to wait on herself, and I've got to go back. I just ran over here to talk to Hamish. I saw him come driving up in a carriage with you, and as soon as you'd gone, I darted over. Naturally, I was frightfully curious, and—"

"Very well, Miss Rose. I'll see you presently. I'm sorry to keep you waiting."

She came forward so that Hamish could see her now. But she didn't look at him; she was looking at Jesser with an expression of honest indignation that amazed Hamish, that even shocked him a little. Never had he seen such perfect acting.

"Is Hamish still being chivalrous?" she asked.

"I'll see you presently, Miss Rose—"

"*I told* Hamish to tell you the truth!" said she. "About that note—"

"I must ask you to leave—"

"All right!" said Stephanie. "But if Hamish hasn't told you yet, I'll have to. The note was one I'd written to Reggie Cornwall. It did sound very incriminating, and I believe poor Hamish thinks I've committed a crime. I didn't much want you to see it, but it can't be kept secret now."

"What was the content of the note, Miss Rose?"

"I'll write it down, as well as I can remember it," said Stephanie. "And Hamish can do the same. Then you can see if they tally. And then I'll explain—to both of you—what it meant. It's not so bad as it seems. Don't be worried, Hamish. Put down everything—the scruples and everything. Can Sergeant Welcome let go of my arm now, Superintendent Jesser? I'm going to be good and tell all—if you'll let me."

"All right, Welcome," said the Superintendent. "Wait outside! Here's a pencil, Miss Rose. You have a pen, Mr. Grier?"

They both wrote—Stephanie much more rapidly.

"But if they're exactly alike," she said, "you'll think we fixed it up together, won't you?"

"Let's see," said Jesser.

He glanced at the two notes and put them into his pocket.

"Mr. Grier," he said, "are you willing to declare on oath that what you have written here is a duplicate of the paper you picked up in the shed and later destroyed in my presence?"

"Yes. As well as I can remember," said Hamish. "I may have a word or two wrong."

"But, to the best of your knowledge and belief, what you have written here is a duplicate of that paper?"

"It is."

"Why did you refuse information?"

"He did that out of niceness," said Stephanie.

"One moment, please, Miss Rose. I must ask you not to interfere."

"Please let me interfere for just one moment. Hamish can't tell you much, because he doesn't know. I can explain, because I do know. I wrote that note to Reggie, because I was worried about Hector. I wanted Reggie to help me."

"Help you in what way, Miss Rose?"

"Oh! In arranging for Hector to get away."

"You wished Mr. Malloy to leave Bermuda?"

"I thought he needed a change."

"Did this change you desired for Mr. Malloy include abandoning his wife?"

She was silent for a moment.

"I—just thought he needed a change," she said, again.

"You believe that Mr. Malloy was planning to leave the island?"

"I know he was. That's why I didn't worry, at first. I thought he'd managed to slip away somehow. I knew he was only waiting for Hamish."

"How did you know that, Miss Rose?"

"Hector said he was expecting a friend. He said he felt sure this friend would understand the situation and take charge of things here."

"You didn't consider it necessary to tell Mrs. Malloy anything about this, even in her great anxiety?"

"No," said Stephanie.

"Was Mr. Cornwall aware of the proposed departure of Mr. Malloy?"

"Yes," she said. "But Reggie wasn't much help. He didn't want Hector to go. Reggie is terribly conservative. That's what I wrote to him about."

"Were you also planning to leave Bermuda, Miss Rose?"

"Do you mean, was I going to run away with Hector?" she asked, her glance steady, no tremour in her voice, for all the hot colour in her cheeks. "No, Superintendent Jesser, I wasn't. In the first place, I'm a little too conservative myself for that sort of thing. And in the second place, I didn't love Hector. I was—very fond of him. I admired him—more than I could say. That's all."

"You no longer believe that Mr. Malloy left the island on Monday?"

"You said it was impossible."

"But you think I may be mistaken?"

"No," she answered. "Not now." She was silent for a moment. "Not any more..." she said. "Hector wouldn't—just run away without a word. Without arranging things for Frances, or saying good-by to me."

"How could you account for his disappearance, Miss Rose?"

"He killed himself. I'm sure that's what has happened."

"You think he'd do that, without arranging matters for his wife or saying good-by to you?"

"No. I think he *did* arrange things. I think he left a letter for Hamish."

"You suggest that Mr. Grier is withholding—"

"No, I don't! Hamish is absolutely honourable and trustworthy! I don't believe he ever got that letter. Can't you see for yourself? Hector wouldn't send for Hamish and then—then go without explaining."

"Where would you suggest looking for this letter, Miss Rose?"

It was a long time before she answered; the colour drained from her cheeks. When she spoke it was reluctantly, in a low tone.

"I think Frances has that letter."

"Mrs. Malloy? Have you any grounds for thinking so, Miss Rose?"

"Nothing—except that it would be typical of her."

Jesser put the little notebook into his pocket.

"You say you left Mrs. Mapes ill in bed?" he asked. "Nothing serious, I hope?"

"Oh, no! You remember how she fell and hurt her ankle when she came in. But Doctor Leaming says on account of her age she'll be laid up for some time."

"How can she do it?" thought Hamish. "I couldn't."

He could not have answered questions about Mrs. Mapes with that complete naturalness.

"I wish you'd come and talk to her, Superintendent," Stephanie went on. "I think I've persuaded her to tell you the truth now. She thought she was protecting my reputation by saying Hector had never come to the cottage. But I told her you knew he'd come. She's rather worried now and very anxious to see you. Could you possibly come now?"

"Miss Rose.... You say you came here directly you saw me leave."

"Yes. I told you so."

"You've been in this house ever since?"

"Why, yes."

"You remained here alone, when Mr. Grier went out?"

"Hamish didn't go out."

"Don't!" cried Hamish in his heart. "Someone may have seen me. They'll find out that I went there. And that'll get you into trouble."

"I mean the time he stepped out for a few moments—"

"He didn't step out for one moment. We were here together every moment."

"Here, in the dining room?"

"You're rather terrifying," said Stephanie with a rueful smile. "I suppose you saw the light go on in Hamish's room. Well, we did go in there—"

"We didn't!" said Hamish. "I—"

"Hamish!" she cried. "It's insulting for you to act as if it were anything to be ashamed of! Why shouldn't I go into your room? I don't really need quite such a lot of protecting. All that chivalry about the note only made things worse. That's finished, though, isn't it? You don't suspect Hamish of any sinister intentions about that, do you?"

"The explanation seems quite reasonable," said Jesser.

"Then shall we go over to the cottage, Superintendent?"

"Miss Rose," he said. "I'm very sorry to tell you that—there's been an accident."

He was watching her, Hamish saw that. But she did not betray herself by even the slightest sign.

"What sort of accident?" she demanded.

"Mrs. Mapes is in a serious condition," said Jesser. He was still watching her.

"But how? In what way? She wasn't ill when I left her."

"I'm sorry, Miss Rose...."

Was that compassion in his face, or was he simply experimenting? Acting, as she was?

"Please tell me, Superintendent."

"Mrs. Mapes is dead, Miss Rose."

She looked into Jesser's face with a sort of blankness, and then, before Hamish could stir, she fell forward in a heap.

"Let her alone, Mr. Grier," said Jesser, as he knelt beside the girl. "Don't try to pick her up." He shifted her limp body so that she lay on her back. Her face was blanched; her eyes closed.

"How could she make herself do that?" thought Hamish, overwhelmed. And aloud: "I'll get some water," he said. "Or some whiskey."

"Better let her alone," said Jesser, with his fingers on her pulse. "Fainting isn't serious, as a rule. Most of the measures people take are quite unnecessary. You might fetch Leah."

"Where is she?"

"With Mrs. Malloy.... But never mind! She's coming to. Easy now, Miss Rose! Feeling better? Glass of water, Grier, if you please!"

Hamish hurried to the kitchen, where he found Constable Duckley sitting on a chair. When he returned with a glass of water, Stephanie was sitting up, leaning against Jesser's shoulder, and crying. She swallowed the water between sobs; tears were raining down her cheeks.

"What can I do? What can I do?" she cried.

"Nothing, Miss Rose," said Jesser. "Try to take it quietly." He helped her to her feet; he got her settled on a sofa. "If you can think of anything— anything at all that might help us.... If you know of anyone who might have a motive for injuring Mrs. Mapes—"

"No, I don't! I can't think of anyone—who'd want to kill Mapesie."

Hamish caught his breath and glanced at Jesser. He saw on Jesser's face the flicker of something like a smile.

"Jesser didn't miss that," he thought with a sinking heart.

There had been no mention of murder—yet Stephanie admitted the knowledge. After all her gallant, her brilliant, performance, she had betrayed herself now, at the last moment.

"Sit here and rest for a bit," said Jesser, in a kind, sympathetic tone. "I'll be back presently."

Hamish could say nothing for a moment; could only look at the girl, pale, woebegone, tears still running slowly down her cheeks.

"I don't think she knows she's given herself away," he thought.

And that made him inordinately sorry for her.

"Stephanie..." he said. "Look here! I don't know how to thank you.... I was in a spot. If it hadn't been for you...."

"You were stupid about the note," she said. "But—it was sweet of you."

"You certainly weren't stupid," he said. "I never saw anything like it. If you hadn't given me the clue, I'd have been in jail now, and probably charged with murder."

"I know," she said, drying her eyes. "I was getting desperate when you were shut up here so long with Jesser. I didn't know *what* you'd be saying. If Jesser made you think he suspected me, you'd probably have confessed that you'd done—everything."

"I don't want to see you in any sort of trouble," muttered Hamish.

Something strange was taking place within him. She had defended him, undoubtedly she had saved him, and he felt a sort of delight in her courage and resourcefulness. But it was her defeat that made her so dear to him.

She didn't know, yet, how she had given herself away. It was unbearable to think that she must know.

He sat down on the sofa beside her, and she turned to him with that lovely smile again.

"Steve," he said, "you're wonderful."

"It was a strain," she admitted. "I could just hold out. I talked about my poor Mapesie in that cheerful way, when I knew.... And then, when he *said* it—I crashed."

"Did you really faint?"

"Certainly!" she answered, a little affronted.

"Steve," he said, "what you did for me was—so wonderful. Will you marry me?"

She looked straight at him. He thought she was astonished by his words, and so was he.

"You're simply unbelievable!" she said, in a tone that made him wince. "You're the most chivalrous, noble young man that ever *lived*. I help you out, and you're willing to marry me to repay my devotion. Well, you won't need to make the supreme sacrifice, my poor lad. I didn't do it because I was in love with you. I did it because you were a boy from home, and because Hector liked you. I do not expect you to marry me. I think you the most unbearably conceited, obstinate *prig* in the world."

Hamish rose. "Anything I can do for you?" he asked politely.

"No!" she answered, and reluctantly added, "thanks."

# CHAPTER FOURTEEN

As Hamish came out of the dining room, he found Sergeant Welcome in the hall, just standing there, very solid and straight. They stared at each other and said nothing. With his hands in his pockets, Hamish strolled down the hall toward the front door; he wanted to get out into the air, to be alone and quiet, while he thought over the situation.

"Sorry, sir," said the sergeant. "I'll have to ask you to remain in the house, for the present."

"Superintendent still here?"

"He is, sir. But I have orders not to disturb him. He's in the kitchen, examining a witness."

"What witness?"

"Leah," said the sergeant.

"I thought she'd been released."

"That is so, sir."

The sergeant's tone made it obvious that he was not eager to give information, and Hamish went past him into his own room and closed the door.

"I've got to do some thinking," he said to himself.

Sitting on the edge of the bed, he did think—about Stephanie.

"I've never heard of such a bad-tempered, utterly unreasonable girl," he thought. "I didn't say that to be 'noble.' I said it—I don't know why. I expect to get married, some day, and she seemed a nice girl. It's of no importance, anyhow. Lord knows I've got enough to think of, without that."

But he went on thinking of that.

"All right! I'll admit that I—lost my head, for a moment. This situation's been a strain. I *like* her, but, naturally, I don't—love her."

He had no intention of falling in love in any such hasty, ill-considered way. Marriage was a serious matter, needing deliberation.

"This isn't love," he thought. "Can't be. I only met the girl four days ago, on the ship."

And love was a joyous, rhapsodic emotion. He knew that. Impossible to love a girl and be so angry at her.

"Absolutely unreasonable and unjust," he thought. "'Unbearably conceited, obstinate prig,' she called me. Very well. I may be obstinate. But if she thinks I'm conceited—"

It would be difficult, he thought, to find anyone on earth less conceited, less pleased with himself, than he felt at this moment.

"I've failed in everything," he thought. "Every dam' thing I've done has been wrong. I was a fool about the note. I was a fool not to tell Jesser about Sam at once. I was a fool not to ring him up from the cottage, as soon as I saw what had happened."

He remembered Mrs. Mapes. And he remembered all the other things he had forgotten, and he was ashamed that he could have been, even for a moment, preoccupied with his personal affairs.

"I'm not free," he thought. "I'm not allowed to leave the house. I may be arrested any moment. No time to waste."

He knew what he had to do. He had to see Faquita.

"Stephanie's prejudiced against her," he thought. "I don't think it's at all likely that Faquita would keep any note Hector had left for me. I don't think he did leave a note, because I don't believe he even thought of suicide. But I've got to see her before I go—to the hotel, or to jail. For one thing, I've got to make some financial arrangement for her. And I'm going to tell her about those letters. She ought to know, before Jesser springs it on her."

He took off his jacket and poured water from the jug into the china basin; he washed and then went to comb his hair before the mirror. He disliked the image he saw there; this young man in a wrinkled white suit, with a dark, gloomy face.

"I've got to do better than this," he thought. "I've got to keep my head clear. The trouble is it's been going on so long. There's certainly no suggestion of any third degree methods about Jesser. It's simply being asked such a lot of questions—and your answers not believed. I can see how people get rattled. There's no way of making anyone believe you when you're telling the truth. It doesn't show in your face. Jesser doesn't believe that I don't know why Hector sent for me—"

He thought of Mrs. Mapes again. She, too, had sent for him.

"She wanted to tell me something. So did Sam. So did Hector."

Three people had tried to tell him something and had been silenced. Effectively silenced.

"But who did it?" he cried to himself.

He knew of five people who had been in and out of this house. Faquita, Stephanie, Leah, Cornwall, and Doctor Leaming. The doctor, Stephanie, and Cornwall had also been in Mrs. Mapes's cottage, to his knowledge. Which one of these five had murdered Raymond and Mrs. Mapes?

"None of them," he said to himself. "I can't possibly suspect any one of them, and that's flat. But there may be any number of outside people I've never even heard of. After all, I've only been here two days. Only two days?"

A feeling was growing upon him that somehow he was responsible. He was the one to whom these people who were silent now had tried to speak. It was his duty to learn what they had wanted of him.

"If Hector didn't leave me a note..." he thought. "If Faquita had some reason of her own for keeping quiet about it...."

He was willing to admit that women could have reasons entirely incomprehensible to him. He still didn't think there was such a note; but he would have to find out if he could.

"I'll try Jesser's method," he thought, with a sigh.

He was tired, but he didn't know it, didn't recognize this tenseness as fatigue. He straightened his tie, and opened the door, and looked for Sergeant Welcome. It worried him not to see the sergeant. There were so many closed doors; the bungalow was very quiet. Yet, he thought, it was filled with a secret life; things were going on of which he knew nothing. Was Steve still in the dining room? Was Jesser still in the kitchen, asking Leah his questions? Where was Constable Duckley?

"They may not let me speak to Faquita," he thought, and at once felt certain of that. Felt certain that he was going to be arrested directly he stepped out of his room. He did step out, though, scornful of his sense of apprehension and haste; he went down the hall and not in a hurry; he knocked at Faquita's door.

But when there was no answer, something like panic rose in him. If she wasn't quick, he would not be able to speak to her or help her. He knocked again, louder than he meant; and the front door of the house opened, and the sergeant entered.

"Oh, it's you, sir?" he said, and went out again.

Hamish knocked again; and now he heard a key turn in the lock, and Faquita opened the door.

"*Hamish!*" she said. Her lip trembled, her eyes filled with tears. "I was asleep," she said. "I haven't been able to sleep for such a long time."

"I'm sorry, Faquita. But I've got to see you for a few moments."

"I can't talk now," she said. "I'm worn out. You can't think what it is like—not to sleep. Doctor Leaming was always wanting me to take drugs. But I never would. I never *touched* the stuff he left."

"I'm sorry," he said again. "But—may I come in, Faquita?"

"No. I'll come out—if you must talk to me now."

"We'd better talk in here. It's quieter. There are—some other people in the house."

"What other people?"

"Oh, Superintendent Jesser—"

"Why is he here—again? Can't they let me alone? Come in, then, Hamish."

She closed the door and locked it; then she sat down on the edge of her bed. She had tied a thin black scarf over the lamp shade, so that the room was very dimly lit; she wore a black silk dressing gown with a cape, and her rich, black hair in two braids. The room and the poor girl herself were extraordinarily depressing; it was hard to maintain his feeling of resolution here, hard not to feel that nothing mattered any more, that everything was finished.

"Sit down, won't you, Hamish?" she asked, politely.

"No, thanks. I haven't much time. There are one or two things.... Faquita, if you need money—"

"I don't, thank you," she said, very definitely.

He hesitated for a moment.

"I don't like to bother you now," he went on. "But I'm afraid I'll have to. Jesser will surely ask you about this. You'd better know beforehand. You see, Faquita, Mrs. Mapes told him that you'd been getting letters from me."

"Well?" she asked. "Would anyone pay attention to that ridiculous woman?"

"Jesser might."

"Not at all," she said with a trace of haughtiness. "Mr. Jesser was a good friend of Hector's. He knows me very well. He'll believe what I say."

"I'm afraid it's not like that, Faquita. In a matter like this, friendship wouldn't count. Jesser will ask you—"

"Then I'll tell him the truth. That the whole story is one of Stephanie's lies."

"Stephanie wouldn't—"

"Hamish," she said, "I tried to warn you about that girl. But you wouldn't believe me. And now you're infatuated with her. Now you won't—you *can't* see her as she really is. She's—very clever. She got hold of Reggie some time ago. Now she's got you. She hates me. She's made up her mind to take everyone, everything, away from me. But she couldn't get Hector. She's killed him."

"Faquita! Look here!"

She looked steadily at him.

"Hamish, do you believe that Hector killed himself?"

"No," said Hamish. "No... I don't."

"You're the only one who knows, Hamish. You came to our wedding. You saw.... You saw how Hector loved me. Do you believe that Hector would have left me of his own free will? Just left me—alone and disgraced?"

"Disgraced?" Hamish repeated.

"Is there in this world a more bitter disgrace than for a woman to be deserted by the man she loves?"

There was something indefinitely foreign in her speech, not an accent, some shade to make Hamish remember that she had spent almost all her life in Latin countries. She wasn't modern, she wasn't like an American. She had another sort of pride. He glanced at her uneasily, saw the sorrowful and delicate beauty of her face.

"Would Hector do such a thing?" he thought. "Leave her? Isn't it possible that Stephanie and Cornwall were mistaken?"

A curious sort of mistake. A mistake supported by so many positive statements.

"If it was a mistake, Cornwall made Stephanie believe it," said Hamish to himself.

Stephanie had said that Hector himself had talked to her about going away. Very well, she had misunderstood him. He was incapable of deserting Faquita. Stephanie had said that she wanted Hector to go away, that she had been willing to help him. Very well; then she didn't realize what this meant.

"Because Stephanie's O.K.," he said to himself. "She may be a bit impulsive—a little reckless. But she's so honest and straightforward—"

And what about the magnificent performance she had put on for Jesser? When she had talked about Mrs. Mapes so easily, so naturally, knowing her to be dead?

"Dam' it! She did that for me!" he cried in his heart. "If she hadn't said and done just what she did, I'd be in jail now. I *know* Stephanie's all right!"

"Hamish," said Faquita, "can you leave me now? I am so tired."

He glanced at her with infinite pity.

"I'm afraid you'll be asked more questions," he said.

"Oh, why?" she said, wearily. "About these letters you were supposed to have written to me?"

"Yes," said Hamish.

And other matters. Other questions. It made no difference how tired she was, how desolate.

"Can't you see Mr. Jesser, Hamish, and tell him I've talked to you? Can't you ask him not to bother me until to-morrow?"

"I'm afraid not. I think he's waiting—"

"What's he doing?"

"He was questioning Leah."

"*Again?* But they let her go, Hamish! There was no evidence against her. And everyone in the place knows how honest and good she is. Why don't they let her alone?"

"Nobody's going to be let alone," said Hamish, half to himself.

"I'll see Mr. Jesser now," said Faquita. "Tell him please, Hamish, that I'll see him in the sitting room, at once."

She spoke with the imperiousness he had noticed in her before.

"Poor girl!" he thought. "She doesn't know what she's in for...."

"I want to finish with this," she went on. "So that I can rest. Let him hear what *I* have to say about these letters; and then he can listen to that malicious, troublesome old woman, Mrs. Mapes, and see which one to believe."

"Should I tell her about Mrs. Mapes?" thought Hamish.

But when he looked at her, he could not. In that dim light her face looked so worn; she was so fragile and so utterly alone.

"I'll speak to Jesser," he said, gently.

He had his own ideas as to what he would say to Jesser. He intended to ask him not to see Faquita. Not to-night. He went out into the hall, and there was Sergeant Welcome.

"Sergeant," said Hamish, "will you ask the superintendent if he'll see me for a minute?"

"Sorry, sir, but my orders are not to disturb the superintendent unless it's an urgent matter."

Hamish hesitated for a moment.

"It's more or less urgent," he said. "I'll take the responsibility for disturbing him."

"I'll give him your message, sir," said the sergeant, and went off down the hall.

Hamish waited for Jesser with a grim resignation. He doubted very much whether Jesser would consider Faquita's rest as an urgent matter.

"I'll try, though," he thought. "She has no one else."

There was no one else to protect her, to care what happened to her.

"Cornwall was Hector's partner," he thought. "You'd imagine he'd want to do something."

And Stephanie? Stephanie couldn't show any mercy to another woman, and a woman so bereaved.

"She's too young to understand," thought Hamish.

He wondered if she were still in the dining room. Or had she gone back to the cottage? Had they made her go there, and see—what he had seen?

The sergeant was coming back along the hall.

"The superintendent says will you step into the kitchen, if you please, sir," he said.

As he opened the kitchen door, Hamish was surprised by the curious calm of the scene before him. The room was brightly lit, perfectly neat. Jesser sat on the edge of the table with a sort of negligent grace; Constable Duckley sat in a chair, feet planted squarely before him and a notebook on his knees; Leah sat in another, erect, thin, her hands clasped loosely in her lap. No trace of agitation, of haste.

"Come in, Mr. Grier," said Jesser. "Close the door, will you? This may interest you...."

Constable Duckley had risen, and Jesser waved Hamish to his vacant chair.

"We've cleared up one little point," he said. "You'll be pleased to hear that your statement is corroborated. In one respect. Leah Delaine, having been duly cautioned, made a voluntary statement. Care to repeat this for Mr. Grier, Leah? In your own words."

"I don't mind, sir," said Leah. "Haven't done nothing contrary to the law and order."

"Leah let Sam out of the shed," said Jesser. "She says Sam told her you'd locked him in there. Just as you stated. Go ahead, Leah."

"When I came home from the inkvest," said Leah, with perfect composure, "I went down in the yard to take up some napkins I left spread on the bushes to bleach. When I pass by the shed first thing I see is Sam's ugly face, looking outen the window. I ask him what he doing, and he don't want to tell me. So I went to the kitchen and got the key, and I opened the door, and I told him to go along home."

"You had a little trouble with him, didn't you, Leah?"

"Yes, sir," answered Leah. "Never had nothing *but* trouble with that man."

"D'you mind telling Mr. Grier how you dealt with Sam?"

"No, sir," said Leah. "I don't mind. The power is not mine nor the glory thereof. Couldn't have done it, without it was willed to be so. Sam, he said he wouldn't go. I knowed he come to make trouble. That's the onliest thing he ever did. He say he won't go, and I told him what was going to happen to him. 'Cause that moment I saw it as clear as I see you, sir. I said, 'Sam, you got death written on your brow, and you got the seeds of death in you.' I say, 'You going to die within two days, and you better go home and die in your bed.' He knowed it was true, and he went."

"But—what was the matter with him?" asked Hamish.

"Jest his own wickedness, sir," said Leah. "Says in the Book the wicked shall perish, and it is so. Sam, he came here to cause trouble, and he was bound to die."

"You have strange powers, haven't you, Leah?" asked Jesser.

"Yes, sir," said Leah. "Me and Ronnie both has. Runs in the family. My grandma, she had it, too."

"Look here!" said Hamish. "You can't—"

The door was opened by Sergeant Welcome, but before he could speak Faquita had swept past him. She still wore the dark dressing gown with a cape; it was made of taffeta and stood out about her slight body, rustling over the floor. She had pinned up her heavy braids; she looked very beautiful and, thought Hamish, very ill.

"I'm sorry, Mr. Jesser," she said. "But can't I get this over with, and rest?"

"Sit down, Mrs. Malloy," said Jesser, rising, as did Hamish and Leah.

"No, thank you," she said politely. "I thought that if I just made a statement.... Hamish says that Mrs. Mapes told you some preposterous story about my having got letters from him. I want to deny it."

"Better sit down, Mrs. Malloy...."

"That's all I can say, Mr. Jesser. I can only deny it. It's my word against Mrs. Mapes's. If she keeps on with that lie—"

"Sit down, Mrs. Malloy," said Jesser, and very gently forced her down into the chair. "Mrs. Mapes is—ill."

"I know. Her ankle—"

"More serious than that, Mrs. Malloy."

"What do you mean?"

"Mrs. Mapes is dead," said Jesser.

"Dead!" said Faquita, her great black eyes widening. "She can't be! *That* couldn't have killed her!"

"What!" cried Hamish.

Jesser gave him a deadly look.

"You mean that you didn't mean to injure her seriously, Mrs. Malloy?" he asked, in a pleasant, quiet tone.

"Of course I didn't," said Faquita.

# CHAPTER FIFTEEN

Hamish stepped backward, until he felt the wall behind him.

"Faquita!" he said. "Don't say anything!"

"I think Mrs. Malloy would prefer to explain," said Jesser. "You understand, Mrs. Malloy, that you're not obliged to answer any questions, or to make any statement, and that anything you say may be used in evidence against you."

"Yes, I understand," she said. "But I've done nothing. It was an accident. That couldn't really have killed her."

"Faquita!" cried Hamish. "For God's sake, don't talk!"

"I want to, Hamish," she said. "I want to get this over with. Nobody could really blame me. I think she must have died of something else. Heart failure perhaps, or a stroke. She couldn't have died so quickly and so easily— just from that."

"I want you to understand the situation, Mrs. Malloy. You will be charged with having brought about the death of Mrs. Mapes, by means of suffocation."

"That's nonsense!" said Faquita. "People don't die like that. When I was little, I had a nurse who always did that when I was naughty and began to scream. She'd put a pillow over my face—" She stopped and turned her head as Hamish struck a match. He looked away from her and lit a cigarette. Too late to help her now.

"One time, when I kept on fighting and struggling, Juana kept the pillow over my mouth too long and I fainted," Faquita went on. "But she gave me something to drink—some herb—and I was soon perfectly well again. Why don't you ask Leah to give Mrs. Mapes something? Leah's wonderful with herbs."

"Mrs. Mapes is dead, Mrs. Malloy."

"It's not so easy to be sure of that," said Faquita. She crossed one knee over the other, and Hamish saw her slim ankles, her slender little bare feet in straw sandals. "I saw something, years ago, in Trinidad. There was a Hindu.... I saw this *myself,* and I talked to the man. They put him into a coffin, and buried him, for a week. And when they dug him up he was perfectly all right."

"Amen!" said Leah.

"He said that hundreds—thousands—of people we think are dead aren't really dead at all. If only we knew how to call them back—"

Hamish inhaled his cigarette, tried to breathe quietly, tried to fight down the sick horror that rose in him.

"Send for a lawyer, Faquita!" he said. "Don't go on...."

"But Mr. Jesser knows that I didn't do anything. Mrs. Mapes was old. Perhaps she was ready to die."

"You left your room by the window, didn't you, Mrs. Malloy?"

"Yes. I didn't want anyone to see me."

"Will you tell us why you went to see Mrs. Mapes?"

For the first time she hesitated, looked uneasy.

"It was—something private," she said.

"You wanted to secure a certain letter, which you believed to be in Mrs. Mapes's possession, didn't you, Mrs. Malloy?"

She was silent, her lashes lowered, black and soft against her white cheeks. She was beautiful, but Hamish saw in her beauty no gentleness, no romance, but a dreadful vacancy. And it had always been so. He realized that now. He realized that he had never heard her say anything intelligent, or interesting; that he had never seen the least evidence in her of those qualities he had believed her to possess. No warmth, no spirit, only that beauty of line and texture, and colour.

"Wouldn't you rather tell me, Mrs. Malloy?" said Jesser. "Would you prefer to talk to me alone?"

"No, thank you," she said. "There wasn't any letter."

"I have the letter, Mrs. Malloy."

She looked up quickly at Jesser and then down again.

"It was—a joke," she said.

"You mean you wrote it as a joke?"

Then she looked at Hamish with those beautiful soft, dark eyes. It was a look of appeal. She was growing frightened.

"No. Hamish wrote it," she said. *"Didn't* you, Hamish?"

He had to moisten his dry lips to answer.

"You see, Faquita... I don't know what letter you mean."

"The one you wrote me—before you came down here. You do—remember, don't you, Hamish?"

"If I could have a look at it?"

"Sorry, but I can't hand it over," said Jesser. "I'll read it to you, if you wish. That may refresh your memory, Mr. Grier. Would you like me to clear the room?"

"Never mind," said Hamish.

Jesser took a paper from his wallet.

My beloved Faquita [he read, with no expression], To think that I shall actually see you again! All these months I have so longed for the moment. Only my joy in the thought of seeing you is poisoned by the jealousy that consumes me. I feel sometimes that I must kill the man who dares to call you his own. Terrible thoughts haunt me.

Yours—in love and despair<br>Hamish

Hamish went on smoking.

"Do you recall having written this letter, Mr. Grier?" asked Jesser.

Their eyes met.

"I—prefer not to answer," said Hamish.

But it made no difference whether he answered or not. Jesser knew he hadn't written that letter.

"Hamish!" said Faquita. "You *did!* You did—"

"A handwriting expert will be able to settle the matter, Mrs. Malloy."

She was afraid. She glanced from Hamish to Jesser and dropped her eyes.

"I wrote it," she said. "But it was—a joke. Mrs. Mapes was such a hateful, meddlesome, old woman. She went all around, telling lies. Lies! She came here and told me a lie. She said she'd heard Hector talking to Stephanie—about going away. About leaving *me!* You know, Mr. Jesser... You've seen, often enough, how wonderful Hector was to me. You know he wouldn't leave me of his own free will!"

There was terror in her voice now.

"Can't this—wait?" said Hamish in a low voice to Jesser, and Jesser shook his head.

"Did Mrs. Mapes understand that this letter was a joke, Mrs. Malloy?"

"How did I know what she understood? She was very stupid. You see, she said she heard Hector tell Stephanie that he had sent for Hamish—to look after me when he had gone. That Hamish would be kinder to me than anyone else he knew. I couldn't let her go telling that lie to other people. So I said that Hamish was coming to see me, not Hector. I showed her that letter. I did not know until later that the stupid old woman had kept the letter and taken it home with her. I had to get it back. I didn't want Hamish to turn against me."

Hamish dropped his cigarette on the clean-scrubbed floor, and trod on it, and at once lit another. She was afraid. She was trapped now. Too late to help her.

"You didn't intend Raymond to die either, did you, Mrs. Malloy?"

"No. I didn't."

"Jesser!" said Hamish. "This is—brutal! Can't you—"

"This is a case of murder, Mr. Grier," said Jesser, quietly. "Mrs. Malloy is not obliged to answer. She has been cautioned. It is to Mrs. Malloy's advantage to answer me fully and frankly now. If you don't like it—I suggest that you step outside."

"Please don't go, Hamish!" said Faquita. "Please don't believe Mr. Jesser. It's *not* murder. We only gave Raymond the medicine Doctor Leaming gave me."

"We?"

"It was me gave it to Raymond, sir," said Leah. "Gave him more than what the mistress told me. She say give him one pill, and I give him five, six."

Faquita rose and then sat down again, her eyes fixed upon Leah; Leah in her clean dress and apron, a strange look on her thin black face.

"How did you induce Raymond to take these pills?"

"Raymond had the greatest confidence in my powers, sir," said Leah. "I give him medicine before that. These people from Trinidad, they got the fever, lots of them. There isn't anyone can treat the fever like Ronnie. Times he felt the shivering coming on, or a headache, he'd come to me, and I'd give him some of the herb tea what Ronnie gave me. That morning, I said to Raymond seemed to me like he looked poorly. He was like most folks, white *and* coloured. Say they looks poorly, and they begins to feel poorly. Told him I had some fine new medicine from Ronnie. And he took what I gave him."

"Where did you get these pills?"

"Mistress give me one, sir, and I go fetch the others, sir."

"Where did you fetch them from?"

"From—the bathroom, sir."

"They were in a blue bottle, weren't they?"

"Yes, sir."

She must have read from Jesser's face that she had made a mistake.

"Not sure about that blue bottle, sir," she said. "Might have been—another bottle. Might have been a box—"

"Never mind," said Jesser. "You state that Mrs. Malloy gave you a tablet for Raymond. Why?"

"She think it going to help him, sir. Make him well. Medicine what the doctor give *her.*"

"I see!" said Jesser. "That's all, Leah. You'll have to go with Sergeant Welcome, now."

"To the jail, sir?"

"Yes," said Jesser. "You'll be charged with the willful murder of Raymond."

Her hands went to the pin at the neck of her dress, a huge pin, made like a basket filled with pink flowers. But she said nothing, and she did not look at her mistress.

"You're quite sure Mrs. Malloy gave you only one tablet?"

"Yes, sir."

"No!" said Faquita. "I—it may have been more. I—I think it was—two. I'm quite sure it was two. Leah only did as I told her. It's—you really *can't*—take her away! I... I can't go on, all alone...."

"You gave Leah these tablets to cure Raymond? Cure him of what, Mrs. Malloy?"

"I.... Not exactly to—to cure him, Mr. Jesser.... Doctor Leaming said they'd make me sleep. I—really wanted Raymond to—sleep."

"What directions did Doctor Leaming give you in regard to those tablets?"

"I don't remember. I never took any of them."

"I'll get Doctor Leaming on the telephone."

"No. He told me—to take one."

"And no more than one?"

"Yes."

"You gave Raymond five or six?"

"Maybe," she said.

Hamish looked at Leah, and she still stood there, with that strange look on her face; a look of austere resignation.

"It didn't occur to you, Mrs. Malloy, that you were taking a risk?"

"No, it didn't!" she said sharply. "Raymond was no good, anyhow. I'd asked Hector to get rid of him, time after time. But Hector simply wouldn't see how good-for-nothing that boy was."

"How long did you want Raymond to sleep, Mrs. Malloy?"

"Oh, I don't know!" she cried impatiently. "What does it matter?"

"But he died, Mrs. Malloy."

"Yes."

"You put him into that chest?"

"I?" she said. "I wouldn't have *touched* him for anything!"

"Was me did that, sir," said Leah. "I didn't want anybody should find him."

"You thought that nobody would ever find him there?"

"No, sir!" said Leah. "I ain't a fool. I told Sam how it was, and how he'd have to come back late that night and get Raymond out of the house. Only it was appointed that Mr. Grier'd find him. Then it seems Sam got troubled in his conscience. Never had no trouble with his conscience when he was drinking, and gambling, and committing adultery. Just had this troubled conscience about Raymond, and he come here to tell Mr. Grier. 'Spect he thought he'd get money from Mr. Grier."

"Did Raymond leave the house on Monday morning?"

Leah's eyes were fixed on Jesser's face, trying to read the meaning of this question.

"No, sir," she said reluctantly. "Didn't see him do so."

"Mr. Grier! Raymond came to you on Monday morning and told you that Mr. Malloy wished to see you at once, in the shed?"

"Yes."

"Did you go with the boy immediately?"

"I think so. I can't remember delaying."

"Mr. Malloy was not in the shed?"

"No."

"Did you gain the impression, from Raymond's manner, that he believed Mr. Malloy to be in the shed?"

"Yes, I did."

"Did Raymond state definitely that he had seen Mr. Malloy in the shed?"

"Yes," said Hamish, slowly. "I think... I'm pretty sure the boy said Malloy was waiting for me."

"You questioned the boy later? What did he say?"

"He said he didn't hear any sound of voices, and he thought the shed was empty."

"Did you gain the impression that the boy was lying?"

"No."

"Did you think at the time that Mr. Malloy had been having a little joke with you? That he sent for you and then went away?"

"No."

"Do you believe that he sent for you?"

"It occurred to me that possibly someone else had got me into the shed."

"Who else?"

"I don't know."

"Why?"

"I don't know."

"Mr. Grier, did this possibility ever occur to you? That Mr. Malloy was waiting for you in the shed, and that he was induced to leave there on some pretext?"

"It's—possible," said Hamish.

What in God's name was coming now?

"You consider that possible? Do you believe this—that if Mr. Malloy knew you were waiting for him he would have gone away for any length of time without a word?"

"Hector got a telephone call from his office," said Faquita.

"From whom?"

"I don't know. Raymond answered the telephone."

"Did Mr. Malloy employ a secretary or an assistant in his office?"

"It might have been Reggie Cornwall."

"It wasn't, Mrs. Malloy. Mr. Cornwall was not in the office at that time."

"Anyone could have gone in there."

"The office was locked in the absence of both partners."

"Then perhaps the call wasn't really from his office. Perhaps Raymond made that up. Perhaps he wanted to get Hector out of the house, and Hamish locked in the shed, so that he could steal—"

"No, mistress," said Leah. "Raymond wasn't no thief."

"Keep quiet, Leah!"

"I got to bear witness to the truth, mistress. I know Raymond wasn't no thief. He's dead now, can't defend himself. I got to say that."

"Mr. Grier, has it occurred to you that possibly Mr. Malloy didn't go very far?"

"I don't get you," said Hamish.

"Doesn't it seem to you likely that as Mr. Malloy had sent for you he would not have left the shed—except to return to the house?"

"I understood that he had returned to the house, to answer a telephone call."

"Who summoned him?"

"I—don't know," said Hamish with a great dread rising in him.

"Did it ever occur to you, Mr. Grier, that Mr. Malloy returned to the house—and never left it alive?"

# CHAPTER SIXTEEN

Hamish could not answer. The question came with the force of a blow.

"Duckley," said Jesser, "call the sergeant!"

Sergeant Welcome appeared at once.

"How many men did you leave at the cottage?" asked Jesser. "Two? Telephone them, and tell one of them—Verrill, I'd say—tell him to report here. I want you to make a thorough search of these premises. I have a warrant. And ask Doctor Piggott to come."

"Very good, sir," said the sergeant, saluting.

"Mr. Superintendent, sir," said Leah. "Mistress got to get dressed before these men come in."

"Give Constable Duckley the key of the door, then," said Jesser. "And please take no longer than is necessary, Mrs. Malloy."

"Have I got to see these men?" asked Faquita.

"Not if you object, Mrs. Malloy. But they must have access to your room."

"No!" she cried. "I won't let policemen come into my room! I won't—"

"Come, mistress!" said Leah, and as Faquita did not move, she took her hand. "Come, mistress!"

Faquita rose and went off with her, without another word. Constable Duckley followed them.

"Look here!" said Hamish. "You—you're not serious about this, are you?"

"Not serious?" Jesser repeated.

"I mean—" said Hamish, "you don't think Malloy is—here? In the house?"

"Doesn't seem very probable, does it?" said Jesser. "But we may come across some bit of evidence. You realize, of course, Mr. Grier, that so far we've had nothing. Not one scrap of evidence that Mr. Malloy ever left here. Mrs. Malloy states that he left the house, telling her that he had been summoned to the office. I've considered the possibility that this call was a false and misleading message, designed to get Mr. Malloy out of the house. But in this place where he was known by sight to a large number of persons, and in broad daylight, we could find no one who had seen him. Further investigation, with the cooperation of the telephone company, proved that there had been no telephone call to this house on Monday morning."

"Did you think of this before?' Hamish asked. "That he hadn't left the house?"

"It was the first thing I thought of," said Jesser. "Suppose I state the case as it would appear to an outsider? A man disappears. At the same time, the books and papers pertaining to his business disappear. This man's partner asserts that he was preparing to leave the island; and the assertion is corroborated by a young woman who was apparently on friendly terms with the missing man. The facts support the theory that the disappearance is voluntary. They lead to the conclusion that the disappearance could not possibly have been accomplished without connivance. There was one person whose connivance seemed obvious."

"Who?"

"You, Mr. Grier," said Jesser. "Mr. Malloy disappeared as soon as you arrived. You never made any satisfactory explanation for coming here. You deliberately withheld information. If Mr. Malloy were hiding in the house, you seemed to be the most likely person to be assisting in the concealment. You caused us considerable trouble, Mr. Grier."

"D'you still think I've been conniving?"

"No, I don't. And I don't think any longer that Mr. Malloy's disappearance was voluntary."

"You—suggested that he never left the house alive?"

"I'm obliged to think so. The fact that he was not seen leaving, not seen at all, is very convincing."

"You think he's—here now?" asked Hamish, his voice unsteady.

"I don't know, Mr. Grier. We have made more than one cursory examination of the premises, and it seems—I can only say 'seems'—impossible that he could be here—alive."

"Dead, then?"

"That seems still more impossible. Concealment of a body in a climate like this—for three days...."

"Then why are you searching the house?"

"In the hope of securing some evidence. It's difficult to commit a murder without leaving some trace."

"You've been in and out of the place often enough...."

"There's one room we haven't searched yet, Mr. Grier."

Hamish was silent, and Jesser sat down on the table again.

"I made an inexcusable mistake," he said, and the look on his face startled Hamish, a look of profound melancholy. He had not imagined that Jesser was susceptible to any such emotion. A decent fellow, courteous, patient, very likable, but not altogether human, Hamish had thought.

"From the first," Jesser went on, "I considered the possibility of Mrs. Malloy's being involved. She was the one who asserted that Malloy had left the house. She was the first one to voice the theory of murder. But I allowed my reasonable and logical suspicions to be overruled by—personal bias. That's the supreme sin, for a policeman."

"You mean, you didn't think she was capable of anything—criminal?"

"Oh, no!" said Jesser. "It wasn't that." He was silent for a moment. "My error was that I didn't realize how stupid she was."

"Hmmm," said Hamish, half-aloud.

"Not an uncommon error," Jesser went on. "Men very seldom form a just estimate of a beautiful woman. Certain conclusions in regard to Raymond, and to other matters, naturally occurred to me. But I dismissed them as impossible. I couldn't believe that Mrs. Malloy was so stupid."

"When you began questioning her this evening, didn't you have any suspicion?"

"Oh, I knew enough then," said Jesser with a sigh. "The evidence in the cottage was unmistakable, and almost unbelievable. We found everything! Black hairpins on the floor by Mrs. Mapes's bed. A handkerchief with the initials F.M. A complete set of footprints outside Mrs. Malloy's window. It was so obvious, that it looked like what you people call a 'plant.' But I knew it wasn't. Only one person had motive. You see, Mrs. Mapes had given me the letter purporting to be written by you. She believed it was written by you, and she was very much alarmed. Mrs. Malloy had told her of your passion, Mr. Grier, and she imagined that you were trying to throw Mr. Malloy and Miss Rose together. That you were working to persuade them to run away, so that you could marry Mrs. Malloy. When she sent for you, I fancy she was going to plead with you, or perhaps to threaten you. Poor woman!"

"She didn't show any remarkable intelligence, either," observed Hamish.

"No. But she was always *understandable*, Mr. Grier. She acted from motives which we can all comprehend. She was devoted to Miss Rose, and she wanted to protect her from what she believed to be a disastrous entanglement with Mr. Malloy. Her point of view was in no way unusual. Whereas, Mrs. Malloy—" He paused. "Mrs. Malloy's point of view took me by surprise. And I have no right to be taken by surprise."

"But you can't.... Good God! You can't think that *she*...? Whatever else she may have done, she'd never hurt him. She's utterly devoted to him."

"Undoubtedly," said Jesser. "Mr. Grier, you've been in Mrs. Malloy's room, and I haven't. Did you notice any cupboard, or any article of furniture there, that might lend itself to the concealment of—evidence?"

Hamish remembered the towering clothes press in the dim room, and his spine prickled.

"Yes," he said.

"There's one more question, Mr. Grier. It's rather personal. Don't answer, if you'd rather not. But it would he helpful, if you could give me some idea of the relations between Mr. and Mrs. Malloy."

Suddenly Hamish remembered the day he had gone to see them off to Persia; the wedding day of that romantic, ideal couple. He had been as wrong as he could be about the beautiful dark-eyed bride. She was not tender, gentle, touching. She was stupid; she had the monstrous callousness of a creature without imagination. And Hector must have discovered that long ago. He must have—

"Hello, Hamish!" said Stephanie from the doorway.

She was pale, and heavy-eyed; but she gave him that smile he liked better than any other in the world.

"You look a little like a street cleaner who's been knocked down by a truck," she said.

"That's about how I feel," said Hamish.

"May I come in, Mr. Jesser?" she asked. "Or is Hamish getting the third degree?"

"No," said Jesser. "He's had that. Come in, Miss Rose."

She entered and sat down on the chair where Faquita had sat.

"I went to sleep," she said. "With my head on the dining-room table. My neck's dislocated, and I think my back's broken, but otherwise the nap did me good. May I have a cigarette, Mr. Jesser? Thanks."

She smoked for a moment, and the two men were content to watch her. Her presence somehow changed everything. In this unhappy house she was young, and strong, and sane; looking at her, they could realize that life was going on, like a clear stream beneath a mass of dark and tangled weeds.

"May I go home, Mr. Jesser?" she asked, not quite steadily.

"Not yet, Miss Rose. I'm sorry."

"I don't mind—if Mapesie's still there," she said. "I was fond of her before—and she hasn't changed—to me. We're—still friends."

"I'm sorry," said Jesser again. "But there's a routine to be gone through."

"Have you found out anything yet? Have you any idea who could have done a thing like that?"

"I think we'll have to postpone any discussion of that for the time," said Jesser. "My men are going to make a search of these premises in a few moments, Miss Rose. I suggest that you go to a hotel for the night, or what's left of the night."

"What are you going to search for?" she demanded, sitting up straight.

"Matter of routine," said Jesser. "And, as you can see, the fewer people—" He glanced at his watch and rose. "Time Mrs. Malloy came out of there," he said.

"Hamish," said Steve. "I don't honestly think you're conceited."

"Or—obstinate?"

"We-ell...."

Someone was knocking on a door. Hamish got up and saw the superintendent outside of Faquita's room.

"Are you ready, Mrs. Malloy?"

"No, sir!" called Leah's voice, on a curious high note. "Mistress ain't quite ready yet!"

"Miss Rose!" called Jesser, and the girl came running. "Miss Rose, would you object to going in there to see what's going on?"

She looked up at him.

"Mrs. Malloy is dressing," Jesser explained. "But she's been rather long about it. Duckley, unlock the door."

The constable turned the key in the lock, but something held the door. He pushed vigorously, and it opened, almost throwing Leah to the ground. She recovered herself and stood aside, and they all saw Faquita lying in the bed. Her eyes were closed, she looked white, sorrowful, lovely. Jesser strode across the room and lifted her hand; he raised her eyelid.

"Get hold of Doctor Piggott!" he said to Duckley.

"Can I help?" asked Stephanie.

Sergeant Welcome was in the doorway; his arm barred the girl from entering.

"Is she dead?" asked Stephanie.

"Not yet," Jesser answered.

"Ain't nothing can save her now, sir," said Leah.

"Well, Leah?" said Jesser.

"Worldly justice been done, sir," she said. "But the justice of Heaven is still to come."

"Tell me exactly what happened."

"Mistress drank death, sir."

"What did she take? Be quick!"

"No name for it, sir. Made from the death-berries."

"Where did she get it?"

"She make it herself, sir. Little berries she brought with her from one of those foreign lands. She boil it up in a tea, one day, and put it in a bottle. 'That's sure death,' she tell me. 'It's something the Indians have, and there isn't no white doctor in the world can cure you if you drink this.'"

"Show me the bottle."

Leah handed him a little bottle, empty now.

"You let her drink this? You made no attempt to stop her or to call for help?"

"She want to go before the Throne of God," said Leah. "Wasn't for me to hold her back."

"Is this what you gave Sam?"

"Never gave nothing to Sam, sir. Isn't a doctor in the world can find anything wrong with Sam. Just the wickedness in his own heart is working on him."

"I'm going to take you to the station," said Jesser. "You'll be charged—"

"Yes, sir," said Leah. "I know that's worldly justice. But I'd like to say—"

"Anything you say will be taken down and may be used as evidence against you."

"I don't mind that, sir."

"Take this down, sergeant."

"I'd like to say this, sir, before all these witnesses and enemies of the mistress, that she only wished to carry out heavenly justice. Raymond offended against her seventy times seven with his impudence, and she forgave him. She wouldn't have hurt a hair of his head, 'cept she was driven to it."

"Do you wish to make a voluntary statement as to Raymond's death?"

"I don't want to keep nothing back—now, sir," said Leah with a sigh. "Tell you everything, if you'll just let me hold the mistress's hand. She asked me to do so, sir."

"Very well," said Jesser, as Leah moved to the bedside; she lifted one of Faquita's hands and held it in both of hers.

"Raymond gave too much trouble, sir. Say he was going down to see you, and tell you the master never leave the house. Mistress, she said give him some of those pills, to keep him quiet. They were the pills what Doctor Leaming gave her, sir, just to make her sleep."

"Did you see the box these pills were in?"

"Yes, sir. Say 'one pill.' But the mistress say that was for a delicate lady like herself, and we have to give Raymond more. I just scrunched them up in water, and tell Raymond it was a new herb of my auntie's."

"What time did you give him this?"

"After lunch was cleared away, sir. And there didn't nothing happen for a while. Mistress, she kept thinking of things to keep him busy, and he couldn't get to see you, sir, and then I see his eyes begin to get queer. He told me he was so sleepy he didn't see how he'd serve the cocktails. But he did, and then he said he'd have to go to his bed. I led him into the master's room, sir. He didn't know what he was doing then. I tumbled him into the chest, and I left the lid up a little. I kept coming back to see if he was still asleep. And one time, I found he was dead." She paused. "I felt very bad," she said. "I didn't mean to kill him."

"Exactly what did Raymond know, that made it necessary to keep him quiet?"

"Didn't *know* nothing, sir. But he suspicioned. Didn't have a thought for anyone but the master, and he suspicioned."

"What happened to your master?"

Doctor Piggott came hurrying into the room, and Leah moved away. The doctor bent over the bed for a brief moment; then he drew the blue silk spread over Faquita's face.

"Gone?" asked Jesser.

"Yes," said Piggott, irritably. "What's going on?"

"Any idea as to the cause of death?"

"Poison of some sort. I can't tell until I've made a P.M. What's going *on?*"

"Presently," said Jesser. "Go on, Leah. What happened to your master?"

"I got to bear witness, sir!" she said, with a sort of restrained vehemence. "Mr. Malloy he was always very kind to me, sir. But I got to bear witness for the mistress. Truth got to prevail, sir. Mrs. Mapes, she come here and tell the mistress that the master is planning to leave her. Going to leave his lawful wife, sir. Mistress wouldn't believe it—only when Mr. Grier came, she was worried. Then I heard Raymond go tell Mr. Grier that Mr. Malloy want him in the shed. Then I tell the mistress, and she say to tell Mr. Malloy quick to come to her, that she's got a heart attack. And when he came in...."

"Yes?"

"She knowed he wasn't telling her the truth, sir. Could read on his brow he wasn't telling the truth. He was her lawful, wedded husband, sir. Couldn't expect the mistress to let him break his vows and go off with a strange woman."

"How did she stop him?"

For the first time Leah hesitated.

"Tried to reason with him, sir. Said she wanted to tell him about Mr. Grier, before they had a talk. Told him how Mr. Grier been writing her love letters. But the master just laughed. And then he was took sick—"

"Why?"

"Mistress had a drink ready for him, sir. Whiskey, it was. And there wasn't no time of the day or night the master wouldn't take a drink."

"The drink had poison in it?"

"No, sir. Wasn't poison. It was only a charm."

"What sort of charm?"

"A love charm, sir. To make it so he *couldn't* leave her."

"Where did Mrs. Malloy get this 'charm'?"

Leah was silent.

"Did you give it to her?"

"Yes, sir."

"Where did you get it?"

"From an old West India man. He's gone home now."

"Did you get the stuff from Ronnie?"

"No, sir!" said Leah, but her composure was shaken now. "My auntie don't use anything but the best herbs there is. Wouldn't make nobody sick."

"In what way was Mr. Malloy taken sick?"

"Got up, sir, and glared around like a bull. And then fell down on the floor."

"And then?"

"Then the mistress say we got to keep this secret for a while. I got a clothes line, and we tie him up."

"He was unconscious?"

"Yes, sir."

"And then, when you had him tied up?"

"Then we roll him along to the clothes press, sir."

"How did you get him out of there?"

"He's in there now, sir," said Leah.

# CHAPTER SEVENTEEN

He lay on the floor of the wardrobe, with a row of garments on hangers above him; a long black dress with silver sequins trailed across his shoulders. He was trussed like a bale, arms fastened to his sides with clumsy coils of rope, his ankles tied together. Jesser and Hamish lifted him out and laid him on the floor. There was a bluish tinge to his lips, his eyes were closed, his face had a strange and dreadful expression of anguished effort.

"God! What a way to die!" cried Hamish.

"Steady on, Mr. Grier!" said Jesser. "Keep back, please, Miss Rose!"

Piggott was kneeling beside the trussed figure.

"Cut these ropes!" he said, and Sergeant Welcome bent over with a knife and sawed through them. "My bag!" said Piggott.

He broke a capsule under Malloy's nose, and Hamish saw him stir, a slight motion like a shudder.

"Any chance?" asked Hamish, but Doctor Piggott had taken a stethoscope out of his pocket. He listened; he felt Malloy over carefully.

"Sergeant, give me a hand. We'll carry him into his own room."

"Can't you tell me anything?" Hamish demanded.

"No, I can't!" said Piggott.

Malloy was a heavy man; Jesser helped the doctor to lift his shoulders. As they shuffled along toward the door, Hamish followed.

"Stop where you are, please," said Jesser. "Duckley!"

"Sir?"

"No one's to leave the room."

"Are we—arrested?" asked Stephanie, with a little laugh that sounded very wrong.

The constable made no answer, and Stephanie strolled over to the window, stood there with her back to the room. Leah had returned to the bedside again. The whistling frogs outside were piping, shrill, and sweet, and desperate; the sea was running in gently against the rocks.

The constable stood aside to admit Sergeant Welcome.

"The superintendent wishes to see everyone in the dining room, if you please," he said to nobody.

"Who's going to stay with the mistress?" asked Leah.

"The constable will remain here on duty," said Sergeant Welcome.

He went with them to the dining room, which was empty; he went in with them and stood near the door.

And presently Jesser entered, slim and erect, so very pleasant.

"Sorry to keep you waiting," he said. "Sit down."

"Is Malloy dead or alive?" said Hamish, bluntly.

"Oh.... Alive. Doctor Piggott says he's coming around splendidly. Magnificent constitution...."

"He needed it," said Hamish.

"Quite! Piggott says it's almost incredible that he's come out practically unscathed. Half-starved, half-suffocated—"

"Mistress didn't believe no one could smother, sir," said Leah. "Had that fixed in her mind ever since she was a child. She say to me, the master ain't going to smother in there. But I know people *can* smother. I saw a young infant what was smothered to death, when the poor mother overlaid it in her sleep."

"But you stood by and let Mr. Malloy take his chance?" said Jesser.

"No, sir. I got a gimlet we have in the kitchen, and while the mistress was taking a bath I made all the holes I could in the side of the press. Even if the master was worldly, I didn't want him to die. Next day, I made more holes. Didn't want him to stand before the Throne, without he had a chance to repent."

"Did you ever take the trouble to see if he was dead or alive?"

"Yes, sir. Many times. The mistress, too. Many times the mistress kneel down and hold a glass of water to his lips."

"That was very kind," said Jesser.

Leah glanced at him; she had not missed the irony.

"She never intended to do the master harm," she said. "It was only fear took possession of her."

"What was the plan? How long did she mean to leave her husband there?"

"Wasn't any plan, sir. She was waiting on Providence. She was waiting until Mr. Grier went away. He was the one that frightened her. That's why she put the master into the press. 'If Mr. Grier comes back to the house, and sees him so,' she said, 'he'll be terrible stubborn. He's worse than the police,' mistress said."

Jesser did not look at Hamish.

"Do you know how long Mr. Malloy remained unconscious, after he drank the charm?"

"It wasn't long, sir. We looked in the press, and he opened his eyes, and he said 'whiskey.' She gave him some in a spoon, and then he could talk. He asked if she had poisoned him. He was very angry, sir, and the mistress tied up his mouth. She was afraid to let him out, when he was so angry.

She tell me, wait till Mr. Grier and the police went away, and then she would manage him. She thought maybe the charm would begin to work, and he wouldn't want to leave her."

"Was the charm meant to make him unconscious?"

"No, sir. Never see it do that before. Must be he was resisting it."

"Yes," said Jesser. "Didn't you realize that your master was in a serious condition?"

She was silent for a moment.

"I was very anxious, sir," she said. "I told the mistress that if she'd let him out, I'd tell everyone it was me that gave him the charm. Wouldn't be no blame on her. But she thought he was so angry, he'd leave her as soon as she set him free."

"You were worried, but you let this go on?"

"Yes, sir."

"You weren't very much worried, then?"

"Knew how it was with the mistress, sir. The master was kind to her. Isn't nobody can deny that. But he didn't love her. I knew that the first day I came here to work. He was restless, never wanted to sit down and be peaceful in his own house. Always asking the mistress if she wouldn't go out with him somewhere. And she didn't like to go out. Liked her own home best. She'd never had a home before. She was an orphan, and she didn't have a soul in the world but the master."

Jesser waited a moment.

"That idea of the pearls?" he said.

"Mistress said it would get the police away from the house, sir. I thought she meant she'd let the master free, but—there was another thing in her mind." She paused. "Isn't anybody here but me know what she suffered. The night Sam came—"

"You'd sent for him?"

"Yes, sir. I sent a message to him, and I was going to make him take Raymond away. But he didn't know that. Mistress wished to speak to him and give him a note for my auntie, so I gave some food to the policeman that was here. I got him sitting on the back steps, where he couldn't see nor hear. But Sam, he ran away, and the mistress told me why. Time Sam was standing up close to the window, the master took a sort of fit of struggling. Knocking and banging around in the press, and Sam, he thought it was ghosts. He was so scared, his knees were knocking together."

"How did you quiet Mr. Malloy?"

"Mistress see to that, sir."

"And you did your share by murdering Sam, eh?"

"Sam ain't dead, sir."

"You tried to kill him. You gave him something—"

"Before God, sir!" said Leah, with a trace of impatience. "I never gave Sam nothing. Never laid a hand on him. It was just like I told you. When I saw his ugly face looking out the window of the shed, I knew what he was after. Knew he'd been thinking about those ghosts and came to get some money out of Mr. Grier. Told him he going to die in two days."

"And he will?"

"Unless I forgive him," said Leah.

"I'll give you a chance," said Jesser. "You've enough to answer for without Sam's death as well. Sergeant, take Leah to the station. Hold her as a material witness. And, on the way, stop at her house and let her—forgive her husband."

The door closed after them.

"Weren't you pretty hard on her, Mr. Jesser?" asked Stephanie. "I thought she was rather—grand."

"Rather grand, eh?" said Jesser. "Perhaps. But now we'll have one of these infernal affairs. She'll have to stand trial for Raymond's murder. I imagine she'll be acquitted of intent to kill, but the whole thing will have to come out. All this hocus-pocus. Love charms, death berries.... It'll reach the New York and London newspapers; you can imagine what they'll make of it. Witchcraft, police baffled, sensationalism...."

He was agitated, as Hamish had never imagined he could be; he walked up and down the room with his hands clasped behind his back; his fine profile looked stern, even fierce.

"Sensational..." he said. "That's what the newspapers will call the case."

"But it is, isn't it?" asked Stephanie, with a sort of wonder.

He gave her a sidelong glance as he paced by her.

"It needn't be," he said. "If it could be handled properly.... If this hocus-pocus could be kept out...."

"But isn't the hocus-pocus the most important part if it, Mr. Jesser? I mean, if Hector hadn't been given a love philter—"

"Ha!" he said, with a frown. "I suppose you realize that you'll be called as a witness—inevitably? You won't like *that.*"

"I don't know..." said she. "I think I shall like it."

"You don't understand," he said, curtly.

"I do! But I'm just not timid and shrinking."

He glanced at her again.

"Possibly not," he said. "This is quite unofficial, Miss Rose. Don't answer if you find it—disagreeable. But have you any idea why Malloy was determined to leave his wife?"

"Yes. It had nothing to do with me. We were friends—really friends. That's all. He'd have been just as determined to get away, if he'd never set eyes on me."

"Why?"

"He was so *bored!*" she cried. "You can't imagine! Faquita was the most boring person who ever lived. And she made him stay home, and be bored with her. She didn't have any energy or life in her. She didn't want to see anything, or do anything, or know anything. She wanted to keep him shut up in this horrid little house, and he couldn't stand it. He'd have left her plenty of money. He'd bought the house for her. He'd sent for Hamish to reason with her—"

"Why me?" asked Hamish, coldly.

"Because—" she began, and stopped for a moment. "Because you're so chivalrous," she said.

There was a silence in the room.

"D'you think I could see Malloy?" asked Hamish. "Just look in on him?"

"You can try," said Jesser. "Piggott's still in there." He stopped his pacing and held out his hand with a smile that brought lines at the corners of his eyes, a tired, and singularly attractive smile. Hamish took the outstretched hand in a firm grip; they said nothing. Then Hamish went out in search of his friend. He knocked at the door, and Piggott opened it.

Hector lay in bed, long and straight, and neat. The bluish tinge had left his lips; his eyes were open; he looked debonair again, with his straw-coloured moustache.

"Hello, Grier!" he said, heartily.

"No talking," said Piggott. "No excitement. No visitors until the morning."

"If I could have a small—"

"No stimulants," said Piggott.

Hector sighed.

"Till to-morrow..." he said to Hamish.

"Till to-morrow..." Hamish repeated.

He wanted to get away from this house for a few moments. He opened the door and stepped outside, and he was startled to see that the dawn was coming. The sky was still pale, a blue so delicate that it was scarcely a colour at all, with clouds like white smoke drifting across it in the fresh wind. A chorus of passionate ecstasy rose all about him—birds, and insects, and little whistling frogs, all wild with joy because the sun was coming again. He saw Stephanie standing at the edge of the cliff, and he joined her.

"Hello!" he said.

"Hello!" she answered. "Look!"

The sun was coming up, a disk of copper just showing above the horizon. The sky was growing brighter, a deeper blue; sparkles of gold glittered on the sea that was beginning to glow like a sapphire.

She reached out and took his hand. He glanced quickly at her, but she was looking steadfastly out over the water. So he said nothing; he was glad enough to be silent like this.

THE END

# TOO MANY BOTTLES

*Dedication*

*for*

**DOCTOR HARRY B. HOGGINS, III**

WHO HAS HELPED ME WITH THIS BOOK, AS FEW
WRITERS CAN EVER BEFORE HAVE BEEN HELPED,
BOTH BY HIS EXHAUSTIVE RESEARCH IN THE FIELD
OF GALACTICS, AND BY HIS VAST KNOWLEDGE OF
BOTTLES, AND THEIR CONTENTS.

# *CHAPTER ONE*

This party is the pay-off, James Brophy said to himself, as he began to shave. The buzz of the electric razor seemed to him unusually loud this afternoon, like an angry bee shut into the stifling bathroom with him. The afternoon sun made the opaque window blaze like a diamond; the mirror was misted from the hot water he had run, distorting his image a little.

God! he thought. It's hot in here. But the damn window won't open, and if I open the door, Lulu will come in. She'll sit on the edge of the bathtub—"perch" is what she'll say. And she does "perch." On railings, on the arms of chairs. She'll want to talk about this party, and it will be a damn mistake. It's the pay-off. That would make a good title. The Party Was the Pay-Off. This woman would be giving a cocktail party, and somehow she asks the one person in the world she's afraid of. Blackmailer? No. Someone who wants to murder her?

He was growing interested in the idea, almost excited. Someone brings this fellow, he went on. She's been hiding from him—changed her name. Thinks— Oh, Lord! Here she comes! Lulu!

A door had opened, along the hall; he heard the sharp tap of high heels. She always sounds as if she were walking very fast, he thought. But she isn't. She's like a little wooden horse, prancing up and down in the same spot.

The knob turned; she was trying to open the door. "Let me in, Jimmy—Jim," she called.

"Can't right now, Lulu."

"Yes, now! I want to get some medicine."

She rattled the knob hard, and that was a thing that irritated him.

"In a moment," he said.

"Now!" she cried, rattling the knob again. "I want to take my medicine before the people come!"

"In a moment," he answered. "You have plenty of time."

That made her very angry. Once more she rattled the knob, she gave the door a kick, and then he heard her sharp heels prancing away. Couldn't let her in, he thought. Couldn't have her opening the medicine cabinet right in my face while I'm shaving. Lord, what a lot of medicine she takes!

He was not angry at her, or even seriously annoyed. That's married life for you, he thought, and that was his custom. The things that wearied and exasperated him he blamed married life for, and not Lulu in particular. His parents had been forever bickering; he had married friends who were like that; you saw and heard such couples on the radio, in the movies, in comic strips—the wife stamping her foot, ordering her husband to mow the lawn; the husband cringing up the stairs, shoes in hand, after a poker game with the boys. He had never wanted to marry, and to this day he could not quite understand why he had done it.

He had met Lulu on a West Indies cruise, the first time he had ever been aboard a ship. She was a pretty little woman, and very popular; he was flattered that she should single him out. And he had thought then that she was sophisticated, a woman of the world. She had lived in Paris and in London; she knew people in New York, well-known, even famous people; writers, artists, musicians. Yet she had shown so great an interest in his work.

"But I'm no celebrity," he had explained. "So far, I've worked mostly for the pulps. I'm just beginning to break into the slicks."

She had wanted to know what the pulps were, and what the slicks; she had wanted to know what he was working on then; she had listened with an interest he had never before encountered.

"I think artists ought to be taken care of," she had said.

Brophy believed that he was a pretty good writer, and that someday he would be a very much better one, but he was not inclined to think of himself as an artist.

"I want you out for a week-end," Lulu had said. "You'll have a room and bath to yourself, and the sun-porch, to work in, and *absolute* peace and quiet. My sister Norma will be there, for a chaperone."

Well, he had come out here, to this very house, and it had been as Lulu promised, peace and quiet for his work, and, in addition, the company of the two pretty, gay sisters, wonderful meals, sweet, sunny spring weather.

He had gone home to his gloomy little hotel room in New York, and, as soon as he had enough money, he had called up Lulu and invited her to dinner and a show.

"Oh, that's awfully *nice* of you!" she had said. "But I'm simply morbid about coming in to New York in the summer. Couldn't I get you to come out here again? Come Friday, and make it a nice, long week-end."

"Well, but...."

"Do come!" she had said. "We'd love it."

He had accepted, and it had even been better than the first time; the peace and quiet for his work, the delicious meals, the good drinks, the cheerful companionship of two young and pretty women. Norma was the younger and the prettier of the two, a slender girl, with chestnut hair and beautiful dark eyes; she was very quiet, with a slow and gentle smile, and she played the piano in a way that seemed to his uncritical ear remarkable and charming. There had been a time when he had thought he was more attracted to Norma. But not for long. She was too hard to talk with; indeed, if he had not been so fond of her, he would have called her a first-class bore.

And Lulu had never bored him. She would tell him little incidents from her former life, about trips she had made with the husband she had divorced. He had been pleased that she never said a word against the man, never complained of him; she would just mention him casually. When Mel and I were in Rome—something like that. She did not use his name, and Brophy did not know what it was, or care.

There had been days when she had been pale and fatigued. I couldn't sleep, she would say, or it's this migraine. I'm no good to anyone. Then she would not try to talk; she would sit in the garden with him, in the living-room, and turn the pages of a magazine; sometimes she would lie back, with her eyes closed, and he knew he could either stay with her, or stroll off to find Norma. She never bothers you, he had thought. She's too independent.

They had had very little company; only now and then a few local people in for cocktails. I like to entertain, she had told him; dinners, everything. But two women alone, two sisters.... It's rather ridiculous. Anyhow, I can take people, or leave them.

"You're pretty independent, altogether, aren't you?" he had asked.

"Thank God my father left me so that I could be," she had said.

Well, he had learned now, after a year of marriage, that she was not "independent," but desperately clinging. He had learned that she had no scruples about complaining of her former husband. And he had learned how she really felt about people, about entertaining; he knew now of her almost frantic desire to be "popular."

"I *used* to be!" she had cried. "I don't know what's the *matter* now. Maybe it's because I've been dragging Norma everywhere with me. Or—"

"Or if it's me?" he had asked, and she had made no answer to that.

Brophy himself had never thought about being popular; he had friends, old and greatly valued friends; there had been girls who had certainly shown no aversion to him. When he wanted company, he could always find it. But for the greater part of his time he was alone, and had to be alone, to do his writing. In the beginning, he had thought Lulu exaggerated the situation; he could see no reason why people shouldn't like them. But little by little, he had to face the truth. They almost never got an invitation; they were left out of things; Lulu would read the little local newspaper and point out to him that this neighbor or that one had given a garden party, a dinner, a Sunday lunch at the Country Club. And not asked the Brophys.

What really and sharply brought it home to him was the episode at Mrs.

Wylie's garden party, to which they had been invited. Two girls had been standing on the lawn, facing the house; they had not seen or heard him coming up behind them.

"Oh, Lord!" one of them had said. "Isn't that the awful Brophy's car parked there?"

"Yes," the other said, and he knew her: Biddy Hamilton. "But I haven't seen the gorilla around, have you?"

He had moved away then, in haste, to prevent Lulu coming any nearer and hearing anything like that. But he could not forget.

He unplugged the razor and dried his face, and for a moment stood contemplating his image in the mirror. He was stripped to the waist, a sturdy young man of thirty-five, his broad chest tattooed with a green and blue mermaid. Such a hateful, vulgar thing, Lulu called it, from time to time, but he was rather fond of that mermaid; it reminded him of his three war years in the Merchant Marine. He was of a good enough height, five feet ten; he was straight, strongly built, only his arms were too long. He had, naturally, known since he was a kid that they were long, but it seemed to him now that they were—grotesque. He looked at his face, and it seemed different, almost unfamiliar. The map of Ireland, one girl had called it. But now—he didn't know.... The dark, curly hair that grew low on his forehead, the deep-set dark-blue eyes, the long upper lip... gorilla?

Biddy Hamilton was one of the people Lulu had invited, sending out bright little cards. "Cocktails—6-8. Don't bother to answer. Just come!" She sent out over forty of these, many to New York; she had liquor enough for thirty-five, canapés of all kinds from a caterer, an extra maid.

I wish to God she hadn't done this, he thought. She'll be badly upset, miserable, if only a handful of people come. Now, in this story, the Party Is the Pay-Off, the hostess will be very popular. Has to be. Woman of the world. She's happy, pleased with herself. *Until* she sees this man arrive, brought by somebody else. She's been trying to avoid him, changed her name, and so on. He's a blackmailer? No.... I don't like that.

He unlocked the bathroom door and stepped out into the bedroom. Lulu was sitting at the dressing-table, putting on her make-up by the special light over the mirror, a fierce, white light, very unflattering. It's meant to be, she had told him. It shows up even the tiniest blemish.

"Hurry up and dress, Jim," she said, frowning. "Someone might come early."

"I will," he said.

Not a blackmailer..., he thought. No! No, look here! It's not a man that comes in, to make all the trouble. It's a girl. I'll make her very nice, pretty. And the man the hostess thinks she's got hooked has been looking for this girl for a year. He's in love with her.

"There!" cried Lulu. "The doorbell! Fix my medicine for me, Jim, quick!"

"What medicine?"

"It's a new bottle that hasn't been opened, quite a small one."

"What color?"

"Oh, it *hasn't* any color! *Do* hurry up! It takes a little while to act, and I *need* it. I feel wretched today."

"I'm sorry, Lulu."

"A tablespoon in half a glass of water," she said.

He found the unopened bottle in the bathroom cabinet, and the spoon she kept there; he measured out the dose and brought it to her.

"Just put it down here on the dressing-table. I can't stop now...."

She was darkening her lashes, one eye tightly closed, as if in a painful squint; he watched her while he dressed.

"I'll go down now," he said. "Don't hurry too much, Lulu. I'll look after things, if there's anyone there."

"It's very likely someone you don't know."

"Well, even at that...," he said, smiling a little.

"Try not to be too Bohemian," she said, and picked up the glass of medicine.

That was a word she used often, and it irritated him; when she had first begun calling him "Bohemian" he had protested forcibly. But not any more. There's never going to be another quarrel, he had said to himself, long ago, and he had held to it. The quarrels they had had, in the early days together, had been intolerable to him. She would become hysterical, screaming at him in a voice that rang in his ears long after; twice she had rushed at him, pounding his broad chest with her fists, calling him anything, everything. I hate you! I hate you! Get out of my house!

But she did not hate him, and certainly she did not want him to leave her. He knew that. She could not master these frantic outbursts. He had heard her screeching at Norma, and a colored maid; sometimes when she was driving the car, some other driver would do something that enraged her; her olive-skinned face would flush darkly; she would begin to drive recklessly, until he had to take over the wheel. She would go on and on about that other driver, calling him—or her—the ugliest names she knew. Then, in time, the fury would ebb away, leaving her exhausted, pale, yet somehow relieved.

He had realized, months ago, that this was a most unhappy and unfortunate marriage for him. The "peace and quiet for your writing" that she had used to promise was lost; he had trouble enough to get any time alone. He never asked a friend of his to come here; he very seldom went in to New York. But he had his work, after all; he saw his old friends when he did get to the city; he was healthy, unexacting, and he had, in his mind, an unreasoned hope that some how, at some time, things would get better.

As he stepped out into the hall, he saw that the door of "his" room was open. It was not his any longer; it was the one he had used to have, when he had come here as a guest; his own bathroom opening out of it, a little balcony. Norma was in there now, arranging flowers in a vase.

"This is the Ladies' Powder Room," she said, and smiled a little. "There's going to be a maid in a uniform. Does it look nice, Jimmy?"

"Very. And so do you."

He did not entirely mean that. She was always pretty, with her fair skin, the sweet color in her cheeks, her shining chestnut hair; she was well-made, too, with a fine, proud bosom and long legs. But he did not admire her clothes; nor the rose-pink dress she was wearing now, with a flowered silk sash in a big bow at one side, fancy short sleeves, fancy low neckline in scallops, a white bead necklace and a bracelet to match. Too fancy. She had nothing of Lulu's style and taste, poor girl. Always looks like a hick, he thought, a village maiden.

"Come in and have a cigarette," she said.

"I'd better go downstairs," he said. "Lulu thought she heard the doorbell."

"It's not quite six yet," said Norma. "But maybe you'd better go and just see...."

He went on down, and in the big living-room he saw Biddy Hamilton sitting in a chair, all alone. Now, why did she come, he thought. You wouldn't think she'd want to visit the Awful Brophys. The gorilla.

She was, he thought, a remarkably attractive girl, very tall, with red hair that she wore brushed flatly back from her thin face and done in a funny little knob at the back of her neck; long blue eyes under straight sandy brows, and an air of almost insolent assurance.

"Hello!" she said. "I didn't mean to be so early. My watch was slow."

"You couldn't be too early," said Brophy. "I'll get you a drink."

"Two different maids brought me drinks," said Biddy. "But I refused. I didn't think it would be mannerly to sit here drinking alone."

"My presence makes it absolutely correct," he said. "Cigarette?"

While he was lighting it for her, a maid came in with a tray of cocktails, followed by another maid with canapés.

"Ah... !" said Biddy. "How beautiful!"

She helped herself to four canapés, and at once bit in two something like a tiny pie.

"Ho!" she said, with pleasure.

The girl in my Party story could be her type, more or less, thought Brophy, sitting on the arm of a chair and watching her. She's been avoiding the man the hostess wants, but she loves him. Why has she been running away from him? Because she thinks he's guilty of—something? No. That's the pulp touch. It's got to be more psychological. No. She thinks—

The doorbell rang, and a maid ushered in a couple Brophy had not seen before, a stout blonde woman in a tailored black linen suit, and with her a dark man, black eyes popping out of his head, a half-open, astonished mouth.

"Are you possibly Lulu's husband?" cried the blonde. "My dear, I'm thrilled! A real, live author, Froggy! I'm Billie de Paul, and this is my little playmate, Jack Lord."

Her exuberance was agreeable to Brophy. Cocktail in hand, she walked all round the room, looking at the pictures, her long, white jade necklace bouncing up and down on her plump bosom.

"I'm crazy about Art," she explained. "Whenever I go into a strange room, I can't settle down until I've looked at the pictures on the walls. Oh, isn't that utterly charming! Froggy, come here and look!"

"Later," said Froggy, in a deep mournful voice.

Then in came Mrs. Wylie and one of her daughters; the young man who ran the lending library in the village came, an old, old couple from the neighborhood, a lively young girl, escorted by a boy, a tall, bony woman in a black hat with a peaked brim that almost touched the bridge of her nose, a fattish young man in a short-sleeved yellow shirt and no jacket.

One, two, three, four, five, six, seven, eight, nine, ten, eleven, twelve, Brophy counted. Well, that's something, anyhow. Only, what's the matter with Lulu? Why doesn't she come down? And where's Norma? The party was getting on very well, making a good, cheerful noise; nobody was left out, or sitting in a corner; plenty to eat and drink. But he was uneasy at Lulu's absence.

"Where is Lulu?" Billie asked him, three or four times, and, a little later: "Suppose I just scamper upstairs and *drag* her down?"

"No!" said Brophy, hastily. "It's—probably a long-distance call. She'll be along in a few moments."

She was coming now; he could hear the sharp tap of her heels on the stairs; she was coming fast, too, faster than he ever heard her come. She almost plunged into the room.

"Billie!" she cried, in a sort of scream. "And *Froggy*!"

She snatched a cocktail from the maid's tray, and swallowed it, and hurried forward, both hands outstretched.

"It's been such ages!" she said, in that same high, loud voice. "Tell me everything—about everybody. Maid!"

She took another cocktail, and stood there between Billie and Froggy, and Brophy thought she had never looked better, never had been more chic. She wore a new dress, of thin black material, with narrow white ribbons threaded in and out round the neck; sandals of crossed black ribbons;

her shining black hair was waved close to her fine little head; her dark eyes were brilliant.

He waited, reluctant to interrupt her talk, but at last he felt obliged to go to her side, and touch her arm.

"Better say hello to Mrs. Wylie and the others," he murmured.

"The hell with them!" she said aloud, and did not move, or even turn her head.

"Lulu.... The Jobsons are here—"

"Let me alone!" she cried. "You go and talk to them. These are the only people *I* want to see."

She staggered a little, and caught Froggy's arm to steady herself.

"Jimmy...," said Norma's voice at his side, very low. "Perhaps you'd better—let her alone."

He turned, and at the sight of Norma's face his brows drew together.

"What's the matter?"

"I don't quite know.... But she's—so keyed up.... If you could just get her not to drink any more, Jimmy."

"She never drinks much. You know that, Norma."

"Yes. But.... She had a bottle—an opened bottle of whiskey on her dressing-table, Jimmy. I saw it when I went to tell her to hurry."

"She was pretty nervous about this party," he said. "Maybe...."

Mrs. Wylie had come up to Lulu.

"Good-night, Mrs. Brophy," she said, very distinctly and very frigidly. And no wonder, thought Brophy. Lulu had not spoken to her, or even once glanced at her.

"Don't go *now!*" she said, loudly. "There'll be a crowd of people coming out from New York any moment, and I want you to be here."

"I'm sorry," said Mrs. Wylie, "but we really can't stay. Good-night!"

"All right then!" cried Lulu. "Get out, and stay out!"

The elderly Jobsons now approached, obviously nervous.

"I'm afraid—," Mrs. Jobson began.

"*No!*" said Lulu. "I don't want you to go now."

"But I'm afraid—"

"No!" cried Lulu. "Go and sit down and have another drink. I want you to wait."

They retreated to a corner, where Mrs. Jobson sat in a big, high-backed chair, and her husband stood beside her; they shook their heads when drinks or appetizers were offered to them.

"We might sit down ourselves," said Lulu. "Come on, Billie and Froggy."

She started across the room, glass in hand, and no one could fail to see how she staggered. She half-fell onto the sofa where Biddy Hamilton was sitting.

"Move, will you?" said Lulu. "Sit somewhere else. I want my friends here."

"All right!" said Biddy, amiably, and picked up a glass from the coffee table.

"That's *my* glass!" said Lulu. "Put it down!"

"All right," said Biddy again, and taking the other glass from the table she moved leisurely away, followed by the fattish young man in the sports shirt.

"She's a bitch," said Lulu for anyone to hear. "Look at her! If she can't get *a real* man, she'll take—"

"Lulu!" said Brophy.

"Shut up!" she shouted and kicked him on the shin, hard.

He stepped back, out of reach, and tried to think of a way to end this. I can't carry her away, he thought, and I'm not going to leave her here. I don't know.... My God! I don't know what to do.

A maid came up to her.

"New York on the telephone, madam," she said.

"I'll take it!" cried Lulu. "Tell them—I'm coming!"

She could not get up until Froggy helped her; when she tried to cross the room, Brophy took her arm. She pulled away from him, and fell on her knees.

"Get out!" she screamed. "Let me alone!"

Biddy Hamilton took one of her arms and Brophy the other; they got her on her feet, and out into the hall. Norma was waiting there.

"My call! My New York call!" she shouted. "Let me *go!*"

"Take the call in your room, Lulu," said Norma, and in a whisper, "Can you carry her up, Jimmy?"

She struggled frantically in his arms; she screamed and swore at him; she began to claw his face, and he hitched her up over his shoulder and began to mount the stairs.

He wondered if Biddy were still in the hall; maybe there were other people, too, watching.

"Lulu...," he kept saying to her, in a whisper. "Take it easy, Lulu."

# *CHAPTER TWO*

He carried her into the bedroom, and when Norma had followed them inside, and shut the door, he set Lulu down and turned the key in the lock. She rushed at him, and he dropped the key into his pocket.

"Don't," he said, absently, watching Norma take the bottle of whiskey from the dressing-table and lock it in the closet.

Lulu stood turning her head, her eyes glaring; then she ran lurching over to the telephone, and, trying to lift the transmitter, she knocked the instrument to the floor.

Norma picked it up, and Brophy caught his wife as she reached an open window.

"Norma," he said, "call Doctor Griffin."

"Oh. Jimmy, no! Let's not get anyone *else* into this. Its bad enough."

"She ought to have a sedative, something. She's.... Maybe it's the D.T.'s."

"People don't get D.T.'s unless they've been drinking a long time, Jimmy."

And has she been drinking a long time? he thought. Was that the cause of her hysterical outbursts? He had never seen a whiskey bottle in their room before; he had never noticed any smell of liquor about her; he had never known her to take anything more than two cocktails before dinner, or at a party. But he had heard about the slyness of secret drinkers.

"Get Doctor Griffin, Norma," he said. "This might be serious."

He and Norma had both become curiously numb to Lulu's screams and struggles. Brophy held both wrists in one hand; she tried to kick him, but she could not, and he no longer heard anything that she screamed at him.

"Jimmy, no! Jimmy, let's wait, and see if she doesn't quiet down."

"No. Call him now, Norma. She'll exhaust herself—to the danger point—like this."

"Jimmy, please! Jimmy.... He might—send her away."

"What d'you mean?"

"She's been so—so queer, lately. Oh, Jimmy. Give her a chance! She's had—so much trouble in her life."

"What d' you mean?" he asked, again.

"Just wait, Jimmy, and see if she doesn't—quiet down."

"Norma," he said, holding fast to the struggling, screaming creature, "she needs medical attention She's—"

There was a violent drag on his hand; Lulu had sunk to her knees. He raised her, and she was limp, her eyes half-open.

"You see!" cried Norma. "She'll go to sleep now, Jimmy. This is all she needs."

He laid her on the bed, and stood looking down at her.

"I don't know...," he said. "She looks—I don't like her color. I'd rather call in Griffin."

"Oh, Jimmy, don't, please! She'd hate it so. I can look after her now. I've done it before."

"You've—seen her like this before?"

"She just needs to be let alone for a while, Jimmy. She'll wake up in two or three hours, and I'll give her a glass of milk, and two pills."

"What pills?"

"Sedatives. Then she'll go to sleep again, and it'll be a good, restful sleep."

"Norma, d'you mean that she—she often...?"

"Not often," said Norma. "Leave her with me now, Jimmy. Hadn't you better go downstairs and see—if everyone's gone?"

He stood silent at the bedside for a time. I can't do it, he thought. But he had to do it. Perhaps they were all still there; perhaps more people had come, and they would all be eating and drinking and laughing, and whispering about Lulu.

Lulu's got allergic to alcohol, he thought. That's what I'll say. Just within the last few weeks. Can't touch it without bringing on one of these attacks. The thing is, that she couldn't quite believe it, and this afternoon, she was so pleased to see everyone....

That was the best he could think of; he unlocked the door and went slowly along the hall, elaborating his story. She'll probably be laid up now for two or three days, after just those two cocktails. The lucky part is, she won't remember a thing. If anyone calls her up tomorrow, say what a— good time they had....

If I say that, he thought, then maybe some of them will call her up. That would help her. But maybe she will remember. Some of it, anyhow. Poor girl! Poor devil!

As he went down the stairs, he heard no sound of voices; when he came to the doorway, he found the living-room empty. The windows were open, and the flowers in bowls and vases stirred in the light summer wind. Everything was in order; the plates and glasses removed, the ash-trays emptied; each chair and table in its proper place. The party's over, he said to himself, with a sigh of relief.

The Party Is the Pay-Off, he thought. I'll have to have a scene at the end of that, of course. Dramatic.

But I'm going to keep it a little understated. It'll all be there, hatred, violence, shock—

Why, shut up! he cried to his own mind. This is no time to think about your damn story. The real thing that's happened here is a tragedy. That's no exaggeration. I don't know how Lulu'll get over it, poor girl. Maybe other people came—

Their own housemaid, Regina, had come up behind him.

"Excuse me, sir, but will there be anybody extra for dinner?"

"No...," he answered. "Mrs. Brophy's not well. You might take a tray up to her room for Miss Crockett."

"Then there'll be just yourself at the table, sir?"

"Only me," he said.

He went upstairs to knock at Lulu's door.

"Just a moment!" Norma answered; and presently when she said, "All right, now, Jimmy," he found that she had got Lulu undressed and into a pale-blue nightdress and bed jacket. She lay back against the pillows, her lashes inky-black, in contrast to her dreadful pallor, her mouth still a vivid red from her lipstick.

She doesn't look right, he thought. She doesn't look—real. He went over to her, and laid his hand on her chest, and he was glad to feel the very gentle rise and fall of her breathing.

"But anyone who's been drinking generally breathes heavily," he said.

"Not everyone, Jimmy. Try not to worry."

"Regina's bringing you a tray. After dinner I'll come up and stay with her, Norma, and you can get some rest."

"I'd rather stay with her tonight, Jimmy. You see, I—well, I've done this before, and I understand just what to do."

"Stay here all night?"

"Yes. You can sleep in your old room, Jimmy. If I should need you, I can get you in a moment."

"Thanks, Norma, but I'd rather stay with her."

The gold-shaded bedside lamp was turned on, but Norma stood outside its orbit of light.

"Jimmy," she said, in her quiet, even voice, "we've got to think of Lulu. And when she wakes up, I'm sure she'd rather—find *me* here."

You never knew about women, he thought. Never! Maybe when she wakes up, she'll be sick—wouldn't want me to see her. God knows.

"Suppose we just get Griffin to take a look at her," he said. "See if her—breathing is all right, and so on."

"Oh, think how she'd hate that! Jimmy, let's wait. We can call him first thing in the morning, if she isn't all right."

"You've seen her like this before?" he said. "I mean—so pale. I mean—this shallow breathing?"

"Yes."

"More than once?"

"Yes, Jimmy. More than once."

Of course, he thought, Norma could be wrong. Lulu might want it to be me here when she wakes up. But then she'll send Norma for me.

He went down to the dining-room and sat at the place that was laid for him. The dinner was excellent—bluefish, baked with anchovies—and he was a little ashamed that he had so good an appetite. Lulu never seems busy, he thought. You'd never know she lifted a finger. But she runs the house perfectly; all the meals are fine, and served on the dot; everything is clean and comfortable. Well, could she do that if she was a "secret tippler"? "More than once..." Norma had said. A bottle of whiskey in the bedroom; those hysterical scenes....

All right! he thought. *If* it is that way, something can be done for her. Maybe she and I could go away for a while, take a trip. Or move out of this neighborhood altogether and start all over again, somewhere else. That would be the best thing. She'll never be happy here again.

If she remembers. She's sure to know that something went wrong, and she'll want to know who was here. That would be of paramount importance to Lulu, sick or well. Out of the more than forty people she had invited, how many had come? Twelve.

Unless there were some more later, who went away when they heard something was wrong. She'd like to know if anyone else—especially those New York friends—had come. It would make her feel better, poor girl.

He did not like to ask the maid; nor the Jobsons. The affronted Mrs. Wylie had left while he was there; the scholarly library owner was out of the question, and he did not know the names of the lively girl and her escort, or the fellow in the sports shirt. He would not have wanted to ask them, anyhow. There was nobody but Biddy Hamilton, and somehow it seemed easy and simple to ask her.

He went, after dinner, to the telephone in the small library and looked up the number listed under her father's name. President of the local bank, Slowe Hamilton was, a benign and portly man with a handsome wife, two pretty daughters, and a handsome son. Brophy knew their house very well—from the outside; an old-fashioned sandstone house, like a little castle with two turrets, set well back from the street behind a wide lawn. Driving past it in the afternoon, he had seen people on the terrace that was decorated with massive stone jars filled with trailing ivy, or sitting out on the lawn in deck-chairs; one time, driving past it in the evening, he had heard someone playing a piano inside, had seen the ground-floor windows lighted, a light in one of the turrets. He imagined a family life going on in there, old-fashioned, the mother taking the daughters shopping, two sisters on the window-seat in a bedroom, talking secrets, the father coming home to a hearty dinner, young men in the evening, old-fashioned beaux, bringing a bunch of flowers, a box of chocolates. There was certainly nothing in any way old-fashioned about Biddy, but that was the way he chose to imagine the Hamiltons' life.

A maid answered the telephone.

"Will you ask Miss Biddy, please, if she can speak to Mr. Brophy for a moment?" he asked, and Biddy came, promptly.

"Sorry to disturb you—," he said.

"You're not," she said. "Anything but. Somebody *else* has just dropped in to teach me to play canasta. I don't know why I feel I have to keep on trying. I hate card games, all of them."

"I can play Bingo," he said.

It was so easy to talk to that girl, who was so easy herself, so casual.

"I mustn't keep you from your lesson," he said. "I only wanted to ask if you'd happened to notice anyone else...? I mean, any more—guests, after I—went upstairs."

"No, I didn't," she answered. "But, you see, I left, almost right away. I asked the whole crowd over to my place. Some of them came, and some didn't, but anyhow we all went flocking out together."

"Thank you," he said, and after a pause, "thank you."

"Well.... Au revoir!" she said.

He went upstairs then, and knocked at Lulu's door. Norma opened it.

"Sound asleep!" she whispered. "Get a good night's rest, Jimmy dear."

He turned away, to the room where he had used to sleep, and he found the bed turned down, pajamas and dressing-gown laid out, slippers side by side. There were magazines and books on the bedside table, a thermos jug of ice-water, cigarettes, matches, an ash-tray. Norma must have done all this, he thought. The way Lulu used to do. Very kind of her.... But the comfort and peace of the room had no appeal for him now; he sat down in an armchair and lit a cigarette, and a black cloud of anguish came down upon him. Lulu will sleep it off, he told himself. She'll be all right tomorrow. Tomorrow and tomorrow and tomorrow.... There's some poem like that, isn't there?

His easy-going optimism had left him; he could no longer think, This will pass, things will get better. If what Norma implied were true, if Lulu was, in fact, a secret drinker, things would, inevitably, grow worse. There would be more and more "scenes." I can't help her, he thought. I couldn't make her happy. I—couldn't even pretend....

He could never again, he thought, take her in his arms without remembering the screeching, clawing hell-cat he had carried up the stairs. He put his hand to his cheek, and when he withdrew it, there was a little blood on his fingers.

All right, he thought. She wasn't herself. She didn't realize.... You've got to be decent. You've got to have pity....

After a time, he went back to her room again, and again Norma opened the door. She was still wearing the fancy pink dress, but she had taken off her shoes, and her rich chestnut hair was disheveled.

"Still sleeping, Jimmy," she said. "Do try to get some rest."

She kissed him on the cheek, as she had done often before, a thistledown kiss. He patted her shoulder and went off, back to his room. He undressed and got into bed, he turned out the light and fell asleep at once.


The sun was up when he opened his eyes, and Norma had her hand on his shoulder.

"Jimmy!"

Her quiet voice seemed to him ominous.

"Is it—Lulu?" he asked.

"Yes, I'm afraid—"

"She's worse?"

"I'm afraid—"

He got up and put on his dressing-gown and slippers; he was in a hurry to get out, but Norma caught his sleeve.

"Jimmy, dear, before you go... Jimmy, she's—gone."

"Gone?" he repeated, and frowned. "Where?"

"She's dead, Jimmy."

That made him angry.

"I don't believe it," he said. "It's impossible."

"Jimmy, the doctor's here."

His frown deepened; he looked at Norma with a sort of stupid amazement. He felt stupid; not able to understand the words he heard.

"The doctor? You sent for the doctor—without calling me?"

"Jimmy, I wasn't sure. I thought perhaps I was."

"She got worse? But you didn't let me know?"

There were tears running down Norma's cheeks, but they did not move him at all.

"Why didn't you call me when she got worse?"

"You see—it wasn't like that. I went to look at her every hour or so— and the last time I looked—" A sob made her pause. "I was—afraid. So I called up the doctor."

"And not me. Why didn't you tell *me*?"

"I thought that if it wasn't—serious, after all—"

"All right!" he said, curtly. "Let me go, Norma. I want to see..."

The bedroom door was open, and standing by the window was a man he had never seen before, a tall, thin, black-haired young fellow with his hands in his pockets. He took them out as Brophy entered; he put on a grave expression, like a transparent mask over his cheerful, blunt-nosed face.

"Mr. Brophy? I'm Doctor Binder. I'm looking after Doctor Griffin's patients while he's away at the convention. This is a very sad thing, Mr. Brophy."

Brophy went over to the bed and looked down at Lulu. She's gone, Norma had said, and that was the right word. She was not greatly changed in appearance, but you could see that she had gone.

"Why should she be dead?" he demanded.

"Well, that's a question we can't answer, Mr. Brophy," said the young doctor. "Very sad thing, at her age. She came to see me twice, you know, about what she believed were heart symptoms. I strongly advised a cardiogram, but she wanted to postpone it for a while. My examination, in the office, didn't point to anything very serious, but these cases—"

"She died of a heart attack?" Brophy interrupted.

He was being rude, and he meant to be. He didn't like this doctor; he didn't like anybody. He was hostile, and angry.

"And all that alcohol was the worst thing possible," said Doctor Binder.

"What d'you mean by "all that alcohol"? *You* don't know...."

He bent over, and, as he had done before, he laid his hand on Lulu's chest. Her skin was cold. And there was a reek of liquor about her.

But it wasn't like that before, he thought, startled. Did Norma give her anything more to drink? He straightened up and looked at Norma, and he was angry at her, too. One of the shoulder-pads in the pink dress had slipped down her back, giving her a hunched, lopsided look; her thick hair stood out in a bush; her face was mottled by tears. He turned toward the doctor.

"Well?" he demanded. "What are you going to do about it?"

The doctor was somewhat disconcerted.

"I'm afraid there's nothing further I can do, Mr. Brophy," he said. "I'll make out a certificate, and—"

And that was all. He was going to walk off and leave Lulu—like that.

"Have you *tried* anything? Done anything to—to revive her?"

"Jimmy...!" said Norma. "Jimmy, dear...."

"The patient had ceased breathing before I arrived," said the young doctor, stiffly. "About two hours ago, I should say."

Brophy drew the sheet up over Lulu's face, and stood back, leaning against the wall with his arms folded, while Norma and the doctor went out of the room. She's dead, he said to himself. She died, and no one told me. They were in here together, those two, like two damn buzzing flies, and they didn't tell me. If I'd known.... If we'd got a doctor earlier.... A different doctor....

It seemed to him that this death was his fault; the guilt of it made his heart like lead. If I'd stayed with her, myself..., he thought. Not left it all to Norma.

He heard Norma coming back along the hall, shuffling in her mules.

"I called Regina," she said. "If you'll get dressed now, Jimmy, we'll have breakfast."

"What? Just leave her here?"

"I've—made arrangements, Jimmy. The undertaker will be here at ten, to talk to you. And Doctor de Peyster, from St. Andrew's, a little later."

He was silent for a moment.

"Norma, look here...!" he said. "I—if you wouldn't mind—I wish you'd—put some perfume on her."

"Perfume, Jimmy?"

"Yes. Sort of—sprinkle it around. The thing is—" He paused. "There's such a damn strong smell of—liquor."

"I didn't notice it, Jimmy. But anyhow it would evaporate, dear."

With an effort, he went over to the bed and drew down the sheet; he bent over the rigid little doll that lay there, all in blue silk and satin and lace.

"No!" he said. "It's enough to knock you over."

"But I don't think perfume—" Norma began. "I think that would be worse."

He went to the dressing-table. There was an empty atomizer there and beside it a tiny bottle labeled Amour du Diable. He took out the stopper and sniffed it, and it seemed to him overpowering and horrible. But Lulu knew about those things; she always bought the best. He filled the atomizer and brought it to the bedside; he sprayed her hair, her neck, her nightdress, the pillow.

"Jimmy!" cried Norma. "Oh, don't! No more!"

The whole room was filled with the intolerable perfume; it was like a mist, like the smoke of some ancient erotic incense. A wave of nausea swept over him; he put his hands into his dressing gown pocket, so that Norma should not see them clenched.

She drew the sheet over Lulu again.

"Jimmy, you'd really better get dressed now," she said, and for the first time since he had known her there was a kind of coldness in her tone.

All right! he said to himself. All right! I don't like the idea of this—undertaker fellow finding the room like this any more than she does. But it's better than the other.

He went out of the room reluctantly, and in his dazed mind was a feeling that some monstrous wrong had been done to Lulu. Why *should* she be dead? he kept asking himself.

# CHAPTER THREE

He had breakfast alone with Norma, and Regina waited on them, sniffling, giving a suppressed sob from time to time.

"She must have been fond of Lulu," Brophy said, when the girl was out of the room.

"I don't think so," said Norma. "It's just a servant-girl theatricalness."

Brophy did not agree. Thin and flat-bosomed, with pale, dust-colored hair, a pale face with a big bony nose, Regina seemed a creature without age; you could, thought Brophy, easily imagine her going off to school, in a middy blouse and dark skirt, and long black stockings, with this same face and figure and hair. But she had always seemed to him entirely honest and guileless. When she broke anything, she had come to him, or to Lulu, weeping, making no excuses. I dropped it. I knocked it off the table.

She was fond of Lulu, he thought. And who else?

"We ought to send telegrams," he said.

"I telephoned a notice to the New York papers," she said, "and the local paper."

Her chestnut hair was smooth now; she was pretty again, in a black cotton dress with a white embroidered collar.

"Thank you," he said. "But aren't there any relatives?"

"No," Norma answered. "None that she'd want here. And her friends will see the notice in the newspapers."

She was distrait this morning, exhausted and hollow-eyed; she was strange, as everything else was strange, and unreal. She went off to the kitchen after breakfast, and Brophy did not know where to go, or what to do with himself. He had put on a dark suit, too heavy for the warm weather, and a black tie, left over from a war-time funeral; he felt clumsy and foolish, entirely at a loss. It didn't seem right, he thought, to read the newspaper; he walked up and down the sun-porch, hands clasped behind his back, until the undertaker came.

Caulish, his name was, and he was a very decent fellow, quiet, serious, with none of the maudlin sympathy Brophy had dreaded.

"Miss Crockett tells me that Mrs. Brophy wished to be cremated," he said.

"Well...," Brophy said. "I don't know. We never discussed it."

"I suppose her sister would know."

"Yes...," Brophy said.

"At three o'clock tomorrow afternoon, isn't it?"

"Tomorrow? Too soon," said Brophy.

"I understand that's what will be in the newspapers, Mr. Brophy."

Norma's taken too damn much on herself, Brophy thought, with a flash of annoyance. But it passed off at once, and he felt a little ashamed of it. After all, he thought, *I* didn't do a thing, didn't make a move. And somebody had to take charge.

"Miss Crockett tells me you want everything very simple, quiet," Caulish went on. "She mentioned a sum.... I don't like to mention it now, but it's always better, Mr. Brophy. Better for the family to know exactly—"

"What sum?" Brophy asked.

"Miss Crockett said five hundred dollars."

Brophy had no idea whether that was a high price, or a low one, or simply average. Better leave it to Norma, he thought.

"Yes," he said.

Then, for the first time, he began to think about money. He did not like it; it seemed a sort of cruelty to Lulu. He knew, of course, she had an ample income; the house was in a good neighborhood, there were always two servants, the food and the liquor were of the best quality; she had plenty of money for clothes, anything she wanted. He had known, from the beginning, that she had much more than he had ever earned, and he had been glad of that; indeed, he would never have asked her to marry him otherwise. She couldn't have lived on his average of four thousand a year. Whenever he sold a story, he gave her a check, keeping out enough for his taxes, his clothes; his small personal expenses.

"Someday you'll make a fortune!" she used to say. "You'll write a best-seller."

She had, he thought, been extraordinarily tactful and decent about money matters. No matter what "scenes" they had had, they had never been in an way connected with finances. He had never asked her for money; he had had enough of his own to buy what he needed, and he had felt independent. Only now, after Caulish had gone, did he face the situation squarely.

She supported me, he said to himself. My God! And she's probably left me money—a lot, maybe. I can't take it. I've been.... My God! A kept man.

And why did I ever get married, anyhow? I didn't mean to. I'd made up my mind I never would. I suppose that was because of my parents. They didn't give me a very rosy view of—domestic life....

His father had been a captain in the Merchant Marine, on the South American run; he had been away eight weeks at a time. His mother had been a stylist in a department store, a tall, handsome, full-bosomed woman; she had made a good salary, she had a lot of friends. They had both been kind to him, and interested in him, nice people; he still didn't know why they had not liked each other, why they had lived apart and never seen each other.

Well, it didn't matter any more. Only that now, when he tried seriously and honestly to examine his own marriage, he could understand it. He had found Lulu attractive, but not more so than a dozen other women; he would never have thought of marrying her if he had not come here for those week-ends.

And that, he had thought, was Home. The order, the grace, the quiet, the companionship—when he wanted it—of the two pretty, cheerful women.

If she's left me enough money, he thought, I could keep this place on; I could work here; I could ask Matthews to stay here. No!

He walked up and down the sun-porch, up and down, sweating in his heavy suit, trying to think things out, trying, in his fashion, to think out himself. Some writers, as he well knew, were autobiographical; they could look inside themselves and dredge out a passion, a grief, a joy; the heroes in their books were themselves, and the villains but another facet of themselves.

But Brophy knew little or nothing about himself. He was purely and simply an observer. He was interested in other people; he noticed how they acted, how they talked; in his writing, his characters had an excellent appearance of being real. But they haven't any insides, Matthews had told him. You've never even tried to understand what makes people tick.

It's true, he thought. I never understood Lulu. Did she—love me? And did I love her? Ever?

Regina came to the doorway.

"Doctor de Peyster's here, sir, and Mr. Jones."

Oh, Lord! thought Brophy, in a panic. Doctor de Peyster was the clergyman who had performed the marriage service for Lulu and himself; he had made little impression then upon the nervous bridegroom, and he had, since then, become obliterated. I don't know how to talk to a clergyman, he thought. He'll—I suppose he'll try to comfort me, and all that.

He felt obliged to go into the living-room, though, and there he found two clergymen, standing side by side, one small and elderly, with a thin and fine-cut face, the other taller, a weedy young fellow.

"Mr. Brophy," said the older man, "this is my curate, Mr. Jones."

Mr. Jones took Brophy's outstretched hand in a limp grip.

"Miss Crockett telephoned me this morning," Doctor de Peyster went on. "She asked me to conduct your wife's funeral service, and, naturally, I assented. I did not know, at that time, that it was to be a cremation."

"I see...," said Brophy.

"I am sincerely anxious to avoid bigotry in any form, Mr. Brophy, and I can assure you I have given the matter long and serious study. I can come to but one conclusion. The burial service established by the Episcopal Church is not and cannot be adapted to cremation. Moreover, a conscientious reading of the Scriptures confirms my view. I cannot officiate at this cremation, Mr. Brophy."

"I'm sorry," said Brophy. "We can change it, then, to—"

"Miss Crockett assures me her sister was very strongly in favor of cremation. Very strongly. She had, in fact, exacted a promise from Miss Crockett to see that this wish was carried out. Had she—expressed this wish to you, Mr. Brophy?"

"We never talked about it," said Brophy.

"No? That's rather unusual, I think. Most of us, I think, take an interest in deciding upon our final resting-place."

He went on, and Brophy tried to listen.

"My young colleague, however," said Doctor de Peyster, "doesn't see eye to eye with me in this matter, and he will, if you wish, conduct the services tomorrow afternoon."

"Oh, thanks!" said Brophy.

"I wanted, however, to come and explain in person to you and to Miss Crockett my reasons for not fulfilling her request. If you'll extend her my deepest sympathy...?"

"Oh, I will!" said Brophy, and shook hands with him and with Mr. Jones. As he went to the door with them, he realized that he had not asked them to sit down; the serious conversation had been conducted standing. Damned oafish! he called himself, displeased.

He and his mother had always lived in second-rate hotels; he had gone to boarding-school at an early age, and to summer camps; he seemed out of place in a house, a home. Mine? he thought. Well, I don't want it. I'll sell it.

They took Lulu away; he heard the men go upstairs, and then he went into the library and shut the door; he heard them come down again, slowly. Poor girl! If I'd stayed with her, if I'd got a doctor earlier....

There was a knock at the door, and he opened it. "Jimmy," Norma said, "do you mind having lunch alone, dear? Because I—think I'll take a nap."

"Of course!" he said. "Only—"

She gave him a smile, and turned away, but he put his hand on her shoulder and turned her back. "Norma...," he said. He found no right words in his mind; he used what came naturally. "Norma, you look like hell."

"I'm tired," she said.

She looked as if grief had clamped a brutal hand against her face, bruising her healthy and delicate skin; there were deep purplish rings under her eyes, the lids were discolored and half-closed, her lips were parted as if it were difficult to breathe.

"You shouldn't stay alone," he said.

"I want to. I must."

"Norma... Doctor de Peyster told me to give you his—deepest sympathy. Norma, d'you want him to come back and—talk to you?"

"No. Nobody. Please."

He let her go then, but without knowing whether this was right or wrong. Her face haunted him; he closed the library door and lit a cigarette, and he felt ashamed of this. His chief and overwhelming emotion was this miserable shame; he was ashamed that he did not feel more grief, more sense of loss, ashamed that he enjoyed his cigarette, that he felt a certain hunger for his lunch.

Above all, he felt ashamed that he should profit by Lulu's death. I hope to God she's left everything to Norma, he thought. But he knew it couldn't be so; the husband had some sort of legal right or share. I don't want anything! he cried to himself. As soon as I can, I'm going to get out of here. Out of this house; out of this town. I don't want anything, not a damn cent.

Little as he liked to face it, he knew why. It was because he had not loved the dead woman. He had never understood her, or tried to do so; even his lovemaking had had a casual quality. Like a sailor in a strange port, he thought. Sometimes when he sat here, in this very room, reading, she would come down the stairs in a gauzy negligee; she would put her arms round his neck, there would be the scent of some new perfume....

Perfume...! he thought. I hope that perfume I used on her did the trick, so that the undertaker and his men didn't notice—that other. But I can't understand it. When I left her, when she was asleep, there wasn't that smell of alcohol on her. I know that, I could swear to it. But when I came back, she was reeking of it.

All right! She got something more to drink, after that time I saw her asleep. It's got to mean that. Well, how? Maybe she got up when Norma was asleep and found the bottle in the closet. That could happen. Or maybe Norma left her for a few moments, went to get something from her own room. However it was, however it happened, she got some liquor. And maybe that was the last straw. Maybe that was the pay-off.

The Party Was the Pay-Off. Shut up! Never mind about your damn story now. The thing is, if I ought to tell the doctor? All right; why? Lulu's dead. *Any* sense in suggesting that Norma slept through her getting up, or left her for a while? When Norma did—what I ought to have done. Stayed with her. And I went to bed, and slept. Like a hog.

A gorilla, Biddy Hamilton had called him.

"Lunch, sir," said Regina, with a sort of scratch at the door.

It disturbed him to see the table spread with a linen cloth, a bowl of flowers in the center, the usual silver service at this place. These were Lulu's things, she had provided them; it seemed to him wrong and petty to be using them; to be sitting here alone in luxury, gross to have an appetite for the meal before him.

"Mr. Melton's here, sir," said Regina, in a whisper.

"Who's that?" he asked.

Her eyes filled with tears of embarrassment and distress. "It's him—it's Mrs. Brophy's—first, sir," she answered.

"Oh, yes!" said Brophy, as embarrassed as she was. He knew the name, of course, he had heard it often, had seen it written in books and so on. But Lulu had resumed her maiden name after the divorce; he had never heard her called Mrs. Melton, never had thought of her so. I don't want to talk about him or about our three miserable years of marriage. It was a mistake; we ought to have known from the first time we met that we could never, never get on together.

Norma had been more talkative. Just the sight of them together was enough, she had told Brophy. Gilbert was so gross-looking and Lulu was so delicate. No, I never liked Gilbert. He was always trying to "kid" me as he called it, and I—wasn't amused.

What's he come out here for, Brophy asked himself. It seemed to him that politeness, or correctness, required that he should go out to meet this unwelcome guest in the living-room and not eat lunch in his presence, or invite him to partake. He had not finished his meal; with great reluctance, he pushed back his chair and rose.

I don't think the fellow's "gross-looking," he told himself with a certain surprise. On the contrary, he thought Melton remarkably handsome, tall, a little heavy about the chest and shoulders, with neat silver hair and a ruddy face. Type I'd use for a millionaire yachtsman. I'd make him the trustworthy type; a gentleman.

"Mr. Melton?" he said.

"And you're Brophy? I've heard about you—read some of your stories."

Certainly there seemed nothing in the least hostile about Melton, no sign of the jealousy he might have shown toward a man considerably younger than himself, who had supplanted him with a possibly much regretted woman.

"If you have no objection, Brophy," he said, "I'd very much like to— attend the ceremony tomorrow."

"Well, you see," said Brophy, rather at a loss, "I've left things pretty well in Norma's hands.... I mean to say—"

"Oh, *she* won't want me," said Melton. "But she'll be reasonable, Brophy. And if *you* don't object—"

"No—," said Brophy.

He was not entirely sure how he felt about this. It might, he thought, be a little unseemly, even ludicrous, to see two husbands at Lulu's funeral....

"And now that we're alone, for the moment...," said Melton, lowering his voice, "I'd like to speak about the financial set-up, Brophy."

"I don't know anything about it," said Brophy. "I don't know what Lulu had, or how she's disposing of it."

"She didn't have anything but her alimony—"

*"Alimony!"* cried Brophy.

Melton paused a moment, obviously ill-at-ease.

"She—well, she certainly gave me to understand that you—well, understood the situation. I mean to say, legally, of course, the—the alimony would stop when she remarried. But she asked me—she explained the situation.... She said you intended to pay back every penny, when the book came out."

"No," said Brophy, and walked over to the window, stood there looking out over the smooth lawn, at the road where cars went by in a stream, at the tree-shaded street that ended before the red-brick public library. I've been living on this fellow's money, he thought. That's the hardest thing to take....

"Lulu wrote about you, several times," Melton went on. "Said you were very generous to her with whatever you did make. And she seemed to feel sure that this book you're writing would make a fortune."

"What book?"

"Afraid I don't know the details, Brophy. But some new book you're writing."

"I don't write books," said Brophy. "Just serials and shorts, mostly for the pulps."

"Pulps.... Ah, yes!" said Melton, obviously entirely at sea. "Very interesting, Brophy. In the meantime, I'd be glad to—to share the—extra expenses—"

"No, thank you," said Brophy in a louder tone than he was accustomed to using. He had never felt so utterly sunk and depressed.

"No...," he said. "As soon as the funeral's over, I'll leave here. Tomorrow."

"But, my dear fellow! You'll need to see about subletting the house. And moving out Lulu's things."

"I'll find someone to arrange all that."

"Tell you what," said Melton. "Billie de Paul's very good at that sort of thing. If she's still here in the house—"

"No. She went home yesterday, after the—party."

"She was here this morning. Called me up from here."

"Not here. Not in this house."

"Well, she said so. Called me at some unearthly hour before it was daylight. She was the one who told me about the—tragedy. Said she was calling from your house."

"She wasn't," said Brophy.

"Told me she came back after the party. Said she was worried about Lulu, wanted to talk to you. But she said she found you—sort of tied up with some girl, so she waited out on the sun-porch, and presently she fell asleep, and when she waked, you'd gone upstairs. She said she didn't feel in any shape to drive herself back to New York that night, so she went into the kitchen and got herself a snack, and went back to sleep until this morning."

"She says she was here in the house all night, and no one saw her or heard her? The doctor coming in and out, and Regina— That's hard to believe."

"It's been done, Brophy."

"Yes. I've used things like that in stories. But this girl she says I was 'tied up with'.... Does she mean Norma?"

"Lord, no! If she'd meant Norma, she'd have said so. No.... Billie's one of the best; very fond of her. But she's certainly outspoken. Maybe a little too much so. Well...." He paused, and glanced at Brophy sidelong, a glance Brophy could not read. Was it reproach, or was it a sort of pity? "Want the picture in Billie's own words?" he asked. "A snooty red-headed bitch—"

"All right!" said Brophy curtly. "I wasn't 'tied up' with anyone, and I don't believe the de Paul woman was here all night. It doesn't matter, anyhow."

"You're right!" said Melton, earnestly. "It doesn't matter. Well, Brophy, I'll shove off now. And with your permission, I'll see you tomorrow at the—"

"The ceremony," said Brophy. "You'd better get in touch with Norma about the details."

"I'll do that, Brophy. And later, perhaps, we can discuss... eh?"

"Thanks," said Brophy.

From the open doorway he watched Melton climb into a fabulous roadster, with a chauffeur at the wheel, and go spinning down the drive. I've been living on his money. Alimony....

He went to the telephone and called Matthews' number. An understanding sort of fellow, Matthews was, an old and greatly valued friend, a commercial artist.

"Find me a room—a cheap one—for the day after tomorrow," he said. "Or, if you can't, let me stay with you while I look around."

"Sure," said Matthews. "But—anything wrong Jimmy?"

"Plenty," Brophy answered. "I've got to get out of here."

# *CHAPTER FOUR*

Norma came down to dinner, and it was an ordeal. She made an effort to talk; Brophy made an effort to respond. But he could not endure the sight of her stricken tear-stained face.

"I thought we'd have the service here, Jimmy, instead of in the church," she said. "I was sure you wouldn't mind—and I think Lulu would like it better."

"Oh, yes! Certainly!" he said.

"It'll be at half-past two," she went on. "They'll bring Lulu here at one—so that everyone—can see her."

"Norma...," he said. "Try to take it a little easy, dear."

She tried to smother her sobs with her napkin.

"I want—I want everything—to be as lovely—as possible. For L-Lulu."

"I know it, dear."

"There are a few people—from New York. I've asked them—to an early lunch—so that they—can see Lulu...."

"That's—very nice. Very thoughtful."

"And Gilbert. You don't mind, Jimmy?"

"No. Only, who's Gilbert?"

"Gilbert Melton. Oh, Jimmy, I haven't hurt you, have I? *Have* I, Jimmy?"

"No, no!" he protested. "No, Norma, you haven't."

But she was sobbing so desperately that he got up and went round the table to her; he put his hand on her shoulder and she laid her cheek, wet with tears, against it.

"Jimmy...," she said. "Did you *love* Lulu—*very* much?"

"Look here!" he said. "I don't think this sort of talk is good for either of us, Norma."

"But I—I *must* know that. If you—loved her—very much."

"Certainly," he said.

And what is love? he asked himself. I don't know. I don't know. I don't know why I married her. I was attracted by her; I liked her. But—all right. What really got me was her way of living. I liked coming here more than I'd ever liked anything. The peace and quiet that I had for working. Then; not afterward. The house seemed to me the way a home ought to be. Everything cheerful and cozy, everything running so smoothly. I thought it was what I'd been wanting, all my life.

Yah! Poor, lonely young fellow, weren't you?

Wanted a home, and probably kiddies, did you? So you married a woman who certainly wasn't likely to have kiddies, and you lived in a home that was paid for by another man's money. And you didn't do this wonderful work you thought about. Three stories to the slicks, in two years. Otherwise, the good old pulp stuff. "Death Shakes the Dice." "Murder Wears a Muffler." All done on alimony. O God...!

"Jimmy... I ordered flowers. Beautiful flowers...."

"Norma, let's not talk any more. I—let's not. Have you got anything that will help you to sleep?"

"I don't want to sleep, Jimmy. I want to give this night—to Lulu."

"Norma, that's—I mean, it can't do poor Lulu any good and—"

"How do you know it can't?" she asked, raising her head. "How do you know she's not here with us *now*?"

He had a hard time to get her up to her room. Then he went to the bathroom he had shared with Lulu, and opened the cabinet, to look for some kind of sedative. He had opened that cabinet at least once, and usually twice every day for over two years, but always casually, to get out his toothpaste, shaving lotion, iodine for a cut, perhaps. He had never before really looked at it. And now, when he did, he felt a slight shock. The four glass shelves held row after row of bottles, liquids and pills of varied colors, vivid greens, ruby red, bright-yellow capsules and bright-blue ones. Almost all of them had prescription numbers, from Larsen in the village; many of them had blue stickers. This prescription cannot be repeated, or a copy given. He saw labels that read: One teaspoon at bedtime. One capsule at bedtime. Sleeping stuff, he said to himself, in deep distress.

He had friends, fellow-writers, who took goof-balls, got them in the black market at fantastic cost. He had often enough argued with them. Those things slow you down, he would say. Better to stay awake all night. Maybe you're all right now, but in the end, they'll catch up with you. Sure as fate.

He looked at all those bottles. He remembered the nights when he had stayed downstairs to work, and then come up, never very late, to find her sleeping; so soundly she did not hear him when he came in, did not stir when he got into bed beside her.

Dick Johansen committed suicide with those damn pills, he thought. And Alice Baker.... They saved her, the first time she tried, but the second time she brought it off. I don't know why. She was a pretty girl, with lots of friends; she made plenty of money; she had Charlton waiting to marry her.... I don't understand these things. Taking drugs, killing yourself. I couldn't write a psychological novel. I wouldn't know how to motivate my people. I'm too healthy. Or maybe too dumb.

He closed the cabinet. Nothing there for Norma, he thought. Well, I'm sorry. I didn't realize how much she cared for Lulu. He went downstairs and poured himself a moderate drink of whiskey; then he went up again, to that old room he had used to have; he undressed and got into bed. All those damn bottles... he thought. If Lulu had kept away from doctors, and drugs....

Had she—taken something, last night? Or was it just liquor? The doctor would have known. Almost every drug has pretty definite symptoms. I know that. I've used a lot of them in stories. I've looked them up. Poor girl! Poor Lulu! I never knew she had a bad heart. I thought—well, to be frank, I thought she was pretty much of a hypochondriac. I didn't listen very carefully to all her—symptoms....

He waked at seven, which was his habit, and went down to breakfast, served to him promptly by the still red-eyed Regina. I want to finish that story quick, he thought. I'll need the money.

He felt it would be improper to work in the sun-porch, where he could be seen; he sat in that guest-room, and so well did the writing go that the time flew past.

"Lunch is served, sir," said Regina, knocking at the door.

He made haste to wash and comb his hair, and go downstairs. And what he saw dismayed him. The two big living-rooms were filled with white flowers, masses of them; he had never seen so many. At one end of the front room was a sort of bower, and there she would lie, he thought.

Norma was there, in a sheer black dress; Melton was there, and two people he didn't know.

"Mr. and Mrs. Revell, Jimmy," Norma said. "Old friends of Lulu's."

Mrs. Revell was a thin woman with a blotched face and fair hair worn very long; her husband was big and burly and bald, and the marks of dissipation were on them both. They all followed Norma into the dining-room; they sat at the table in pompous silence, and the air was heavy, almost sickening with the perfume of the white flowers. I suppose it's the heat, Brophy thought. Even if I don't pay the rent. But not a word came into his head. Melton and Norma were the ones who carried the burden. Melton said it was a sultry day; Norma said the farmers need rain.

"What do they grow around here?" Melton asked.

A car was coming up the drive; in a moment the doorbell rang, and Regina went to answer it. She came to Brophy's side, and leaning down, she whispered:

"It's the police, sir."

Brophy pushed back his chair and rose.

"Excuse me just a moment...," he said, and went into the front living-room.

Doctor Griffin, whom he knew well enough, was there; a portly little

man with a high crest of gray hair, like a cockatoo, and somewhat the figure of one, with his chest thrust out, his short legs and in-turned toes.

"Here's Lieutenant Levy," he said, in his irascible way. "Horton County
Police. We've come to stop this funeral, Brophy."

"Now, just a moment...," said the man with him, a tall and lean young
man, black-haired, with a big nose, big ears, big hands and feet. He was,
Brophy thought, like an Egyptian monarch in some ancient frieze, but his
long, dark eyes were gentle, his voice was mild. "We're very sorry to
intrude just now, Mr. Brophy, but Doctor Griffin has lodged an objection
against Doctor Binder's—certificate and we're obliged to investigate."

Doctor Griffin had lost every trace of bedside manner; he was bristling.

"Binder certified that Mrs. Brophy died of endocarditis. I—" He checked
himself, with an effort. "I have no wish to—belittle a colleague, but I am
sure Binder was misled. The day before I left for the convention—that is,
exactly nine days ago—I completed a thorough check-up of Mrs. Brophy.
There were no symptoms of endocarditis. A cardiogram showed nothing
wrong with the heart. The circulation, blood pressure and so on were
excellent. As soon as I learned of this certificate, I went immediately to the
police."

"Doctor Griffin's our County Medical Officer," said Lieutenant Levy.

"I demanded an autopsy, before this woman was hurried off to be cremated. In my examination of her, exactly nine days ago, I found nothing,
nothing whatever that might cause this extraordinarily sudden death. I
make no claim, mind you, to being one of your heart specialists. But neither is Binder. And I'd had Mrs. Brophy under my care for nearly four
years. I know her condition."

"Then what do you think caused her death?" Brophy asked.

"Poison."

"What?" said Brophy. "What? Yon think someone—*poisoned* her?"

"Not necessarily," said Doctor Griffin, irritably. "She might very well have
done it herself."

"Suicide?" cried Brophy.

"*No!*" said Doctor Griffin, angry now. "It's simply that Mrs. Brophy was
very indiscriminate, very rash in her use of drugs. I've always been aware
that, instead of keeping to the prescriptions I gave her, she was in the habit
of visiting other doctors, quacks, charlatans, buying patent medicines. I
don't know what she'd taken before this party—"

"I gave her some medicine," said Brophy. "She asked me for it."

"What medicine?"

"I don't know. A new bottle she told me to open."

"Let me see it."

"I wouldn't know it now from the others, now it's been opened."

"Let me see all the bottles you have."

"You're welcome to go upstairs and look in the medicine cabinet," said Brophy, curtly. "You know the way."

"You'll accompany me," said the doctor.

"No," said Brophy.

"We'd better all go," said the Lieutenant, amiably.

The doorbell rang, and Regina came hastening to open it; she admitted two women, all in black, and led them at once into the library. Brophy saw them standing there, surrounded by all the white flowers; he saw Norma come out of the dining-room to meet them.

"All right!" he said, quickly.

Half-way up the stairs he stopped Levy with a hand on his sleeve.

"Look here!" he said. "What am I going to tell all these people? What in God's name can I tell my sister-in-law? She'll be—I don't know how she'll stand this."

"I'll tell her, Mr. Brophy," said the Lieutenant.

"Couldn't we just have the ceremony—and then you could take her away?"

"I'm sorry, Mr. Brophy, very sorry. But the deceased has already been removed to the hospital, and we couldn't take her out until after the P.M."

"This is a damned brutal thing for Griffin to do."

"It's no more than his duty, Mr. Brophy. Mrs. Brophy was his patient, and if he had reason to believe that the certificate issued was incorrect—"

"Brophy!" called Doctor Griffin.

He was standing before the open medicine cabinet, looking at the incredible bottles.

"Be good enough to identify the bottle from which you poured medicine for Mrs. Brophy," he said.

"I told you I couldn't," said Brophy.

"No wonder," said Levy. "Now, if you just have some recollection of the size of the bottle, the color of the liquid in it, anything like that, it might help us."

"It was colorless—like water...," Brophy answered, trying to concentrate. "At least, I think it was. What I do remember is, that it had a screw top—black—and I had to whack it against the basin a few times to make it turn."

Then he remembered something else.

"I chipped it!" he said. "If that's any help. I knocked a little piece out of that top."

Doctor Griffin was already examining the bottles, taking down one or two and setting them on the basin.

"Levy," he said, "I'll want all this trash—everything, without exception—taken down to the laboratory and analyzed."

"I'll see to it, Doctor."

Brophy looked at the Lieutenant with a certain exasperation. He's a booby, he said to himself. Nice fellow, very civil and all that, but he's letting that pompous ass of a Griffin run the whole show. It's Griffin that stopped the funeral, Griffin that says it's poison; Griffin gives the orders.

"I'll be off now," said the doctor. "Calls to make. See you later, Levy."

He gave Brophy a curt nod, and went past them, down the stairs.

"My sister-in-law will have to be told," Brophy said. "And all the rest of them. It's—"

"It is," said Levy. "I'll do it for you, if you want."

"But—how will you do it?"

"I'll find someone with authority, some sort of standing, and I'll tell him to get everyone out, quietly. I'll tell him the doctors have disagreed about Mrs. Brophy's heart condition, and that has to be settled before a certificate's issued. I'll make it very medical. Big words. Coronary occlusion. And nothing about poison."

"Thank you," said Brophy, after a long moment. "But I think I ought to do it myself."

"I see! I'd advise you, Mr. Brophy, I'd strongly advise you to say nothing—to anyone at all—about the theory that Mrs. Brophy may have taken something injurious."

"Why not?"

"That's my advice, Mr. Brophy."

"All right."

"And just a moment. Before you go downstairs, will you give me a list, or a partial list, of the people at the cocktail party?"

"The local people, yes."

Levy wrote down the names in a little book.

"Anyone else. Mr. Brophy?"

"There were two people from New York, but I don't know where they live."

"Their names, please?"

"There was a woman called Billie de Paul, and a man called—" He thought a moment. "Jack Lord."

"Thank you," said Levy, putting away his little book.

"When will you know about—my wife?" Brophy asked.

"Sorry, but I can't tell you. We might get a full report tomorrow, and it might be a week or more, if Doctor Griffin makes them analyze every tablet in an aspirin bottle."

"He's a damn bad-tempered pest," said Brophy. "What does it matter if the poor girl took some medicines that didn't belong together, or something of the sort? He might think a little about the living—about her sister, for instance."

"Mr. Brophy," said Levy, "everyone in a community can be thankful for a doctor who is vigilant."

There was a dignity in the Lieutenant that impressed Brophy, against his will.

"Sorry, but I'm not thankful for this fellow's interference," he said. "Well, I'll be going now...."

As he began to descend the stairs, it seemed to him that he *could not* do this, that it was beyond him. Find somebody with some authority and standing, to go around and tell people....?

It occurred to him that Melton would be very good for this, but he dismissed the idea, a little shocked at himself. The perfume of the flowers reached him now; he heard a rustling and murmuring, as if from an enormous crowd. My God! he thought. If there is a big crowd—come to her funeral.... And when she was alive, and wanted a crowd, at her party....

The Party Was the Pay-Off.... What made me think of *that* for a title?

He had come to the foot of the stairs now, and from the hall he could look into the living-room. There was not a big crowd, as he had imagined, but there were certainly twice, probably three times as many people as had come to her party. Some of them were seated, but most of them were standing in small groups, talking in low voices, or whispering. Susurrant..., he said to himself. That's a word I like. Only not good for pulp stories....

The young clergyman stood with a group of ladies around him, Norma among them; a rather weedy young man he was, with a thin neck rising from his clerical collar, and he wore pince-nez. All right! Brophy thought. He may not be much good at it, but he's the one.

As Brophy crossed the room, people drew a little aside; he looked neither to right nor left, feeling this to be correct; he touched the clergyman's sleeve.

"Excuse me...," he said. "Just a moment, please."

They moved back into a corner, almost on top of the white flowers, and Brophy began his tale. The doctors had disagreed about Lulu's heart condition, the permit had been withdrawn. Endocarditis, one of them said. Coronary occlusion, said the other.

"Shocking!" said the young clergyman. "Shocking! Then the ceremony will not be performed today?"

"No. And I thought that if you'd let them know.... Get them out of the house."

"My dear Mr. Brophy, I'll do anything—anything at all that might help you in this most distressing situation."

"*If* you'll just get them all *out* of here."

"At once," said the young clergyman.

He stepped forward, and cleared his throat.

"My good friends," he said, "if I may have your attention for a moment, please...."

His voice was resonant; he had exactly the right air of authority, of leadership. After all, thought Brophy, he's been trained. Trained to take charge, when there's trouble, trained to handle people.... Levy's been trained; Griffin's been trained. They know what to do. Only not me.

"You will all understand what an ordeal this is for the family," the young clergyman was saying. "Let us all join in a brief prayer, and then leave them, to be sustained...."

"Heart condition, my eye!" said a whisper near Brophy. "I know what killed her."

Brophy turned his head, and it was Billie de Paul.

"Hush!" whispered Melton, standing beside her.

# CHAPTER FIVE

They were all going away, all facing the open door by which the first couple had departed. They went very slowly, in a sort of polite herd; grave faces, black gloves. But when they get home...! thought Brophy. My dear, there *wasn't* any funeral. It's been postponed. Something about Lulu's *heart,* they *said.* But, my *dear...!*

She never said anything about her heart, he thought. Her migraine, her sinuses, her allergies, her chest, her eyes, her strep throat.... Now, shut up. Don't think about her like that, poor girl. She must have been sick, to die that way.

The young clergyman came and took his hand.

"If you want me, Mr. Brophy," he said, "day or night...."

Everyone had gone now. Except Melton, and Billie de Paul, and Biddy. Billie de Paul, he thought, was the type to hang around; Melton, he thought, might feel he had some right to wait for further information.

But Biddy.... He looked at her; their eyes met, and she came straight across the room to him.

"Look here!" she said. "Shall I take the flowers to the hospital? Now? The chauffeur's outside with the station-wagon, and we could take them. All of them."

"Yes!" said Brophy.

She went out of the front door, and returned in a moment with the chauffeur. He began taking up the big wooden tubs, Biddy filled her arms with the pots, and they moved toward the door.

"What are they doing?" cried Billie. "Taking away Lulu's flowers...!"

"To the hospital," said Brophy. He found it curiously hard to speak a word; he stood leaning against the doorway into the hall, and did not want to move.

"Well, I want some of them!" said Billie, beginning to cry. "For a—souvenir—of my sweet Lulu...."

She picked up two pots of white flowers, and held them against her heart.

"Isn't she going to *have* any funeral?" she demanded. "Ever?"

"Hush!" said Melton. "I'll take you to the station—"

"When I go," she said, "I'm going to the *police* station."

"Oh, hush!" said Melton. "Keep quiet, Billie."

Norma had come in through the dining-room.

"What does she mean?" she asked Melton.

"Nothing," he answered. "Don't pay any attention. Hysterical."

"I'm not! I'm not! Last night, when I was in that sun-porch I *saw* a woman, in the garden. I saw who it was, and I saw what she was doing. She was *burying* something, and I know just where, and I fully intend to tell the police. Because I know what it was. It was the *weapon.*"

"What weapon?" asked Brophy, with a sort of idiot interest.

"*Hush!*" said Melton, in something like a shout. "Don't encourage her, Brophy. She's—"

"But, dear...!" she said, her blue eyes swimming in tears, looking at Brophy over the flowers she held. "Dear, *you* know and *I* know, don't we? It was a *murder.*"

"*Hush!*" said Melton, and this time he gave her a hard shake that made her drop one of the flower-pots, to smash on the floor.

"Oh, it's an omen!" she screamed.

Biddy and the chauffeur were working quietly and quickly, without a turn of the head or a glance at what went on about them. Billie rushed at the chauffeur and tried to seize a tub he was carrying, but it was too heavy for her; she ran to Biddy and snatched at a pot of white carnations. Biddy relinquished it at once, and went off to get another.

I ought to do—something, Brophy thought. I shouldn't just stand here, like this. Only—it isn't real. It's—

"Come, Billie!" Melton was saying, trying to push her toward the front door.

"I don't think she's really fit to go, just now," said Norma, quietly. "Billie, wouldn't you like to go upstairs and lie down for a while?"

"Yes, I would!" said Billie. "You're a sweet, sweet girl, Norma. You always were."

"Good-bye!" said Biddy, standing in the doorway. "I guess we've finished now."

"Thank you!" said Brophy and Melton, and she went out, followed by the chauffeur.

"There's a bitch, if you like," said Billie, so loudly that it must have been heard outside.

"Hush!" said Melton.

"I wish you'd stop saying that, Mel," said Billie. "That's all I hear. Hush, hush, hush. But there's one thing I want to know, and I'm going to know. Did anybody else see what she did at poor Lulu's party?"

"What she did?"

"She changed glasses with Lulu! I saw her!"

"That was nothing, Billie. Everyone saw that. And they changed back."

"Doesn't *anyone else* see what that girl's up to?" Billie demanded. "She's hell-bent on getting Jimmy. Even before poor Lulu—"

"Come on, Billie!" said Norma, soothingly, and taking her arm, she led Billie, still clasping the flowerpots, up the stairs.

"Drinking..." Brophy said.

"Oh, yes. But it's hard to tell, with her. She's the most flighty, irresponsible creature.... As soon as she says something, she believes it."

"She could start a hell of a scandal, in a small place like this."

"Not about a girl like that. You can see that girl is—well, I mean to say—"

"Yeah," said Brophy, because Melton made him feel like that. "Quite. But if she goes to the police—"

"My *dear* fellow! What in God's name has she got to tell the police? She looks out at the garden—in the dark—and she sees a woman trying to hide the murder weapon! When there's been no murder. Then she says the girl changed glasses with poor Lulu—when there's been no question of anything wrong with any of the drinks. No... I'll give you the clue to the whole thing, my dear fellow. Billie's all right, except for one thing. She's— well, I don't have to tell you that she's—not quite out of the top drawer. And she's inclined to be resentful toward any women who are."

The top drawer, no less, thought Brophy. Now, my bottom drawer is good. Nice folded pajamas, and shorts, and sweat-shirts, and so on. But my top drawer.... A bottle of pills some doctor gave me, a lot of loose paper clips, a lot of bills, some old socks that don't match, newspaper clippings, a fancy comb a girl gave me....

"She's all right with Norma," he said.

"Yes, but.... But, of course, you know, Norma and Lulu—poor Lulu— charming girls.... But their father was a dentist."

"My God!" said Brophy.

He wished he could laugh; he wished he had someone to laugh with him. But maybe he was never going to laugh any more.

"I think I'll push off now, old chap," said Melton. "What about your coming to the Inn for dinner tonight? I'm stopping, you know, until—"

"Thanks," said Brophy, "but I don't like to leave Norma alone."

"Quite!" said Melton. "Well.... Keep in touch, eh?"

"Quite!" said Brophy.

When Melton had gone, he went out on the sun-porch, and sat down before the long table Lulu had put there for him. I've *got* to work, he thought. I've *got* to make some money. He looked for the pages he had written of The Party Was the Pay-Off but he could not find them, and, anyhow, he did not want them. I'll do a serial, he thought. More money. Mystery. Allison said they were in the market for spy stuff, but I can't do it. They like the hero to be a spy—super-spy—and I don't like spies. You make friends with a beautiful blonde, or a swarthy man with a black mustache, or a fishy-eyed Komissar, just to turn them in. No.... I'd rather be a Bad Man in a Western, stamping up and down the street with a gun in each hand. Then everyone knows what you're up to. No.... A mystery.... Beautiful blonde? No. Tragic brunette. She's saving her brother—or she thinks she is, only he never done it....

"Excuse me, sir," said Regina, "but cook says, would you mind an early dinner, because her grandson's got a virus, and he's only four, and she wants to get home."

"I don't mind. But did you ask Miss Crockett?"

"Yes, sir. She doesn't mind...."

And whose house is this, anyhow? he thought. Who's paying the rent now? All right. All right. Let it go. I can't leave tomorrow, the way I told Matthews. I suppose there'll be another funeral. More flowers. Thank God, Biddy took those away. I don't know how I could have sat down to dinner, with the place like that.... What a girl! You couldn't use her in a story, very well. Couldn't get her across. She's beautiful—but it's in a quiet way. It's— thank you, Mr. Melton—it's aristocratic. Of course, you could get in the good old touches. How the lamplight made her hair a red-gold glory. How she stretched out her delicate hand....

She stands by; that's the wonderful thing. She sees the thing you want most, and she gets it done. She's quiet....

Norma was coming down the stairs now. She was quiet, too, but he was aware of the tide of pain that ran beneath the surface, that some most trivial thing could force into a wave that almost engulfed her.

"I hope I didn't commit a sin," she said. "I gave Billie some soup and sandwiches this afternoon—and then, just now, I let her have some more drinks. She certainly didn't need them, only I wanted her to go to sleep— and shut up."

"Never heard of a better idea," said Brophy. "I can't understand her popularity."

"She's kind-hearted," said Norma.

Not about Biddy, she isn't. "That girl is hell-bent on getting Jimmy...." God! I'd nearly forgotten that garden party, when she told the other girl I was a gorilla.... Very, very tame gorilla.... In the jungle, they beat on their chests, make a big boom-boom. Maybe it's a love-call—but maybe it's just showing off.

"You don't mind if—I go upstairs now, Jimmy?" Norma asked, her dessert untouched before her. "I'm—rather tired."

"It's the best thing you could do, poor girl," he said.

He went to the foot of the stairs with her, and patted her shoulder.

"Try to sleep," he said.

He went back to the sun-porch then, and standing by the window, he saw the cook coming round the house from the back door. Dora was her name, a middle-aged woman, and very stout; her sparse, pale hair was pulled back into a tiny knot; as she went waddling away, it seemed to him that even her walk was cross and aggressive. She didn't live in the house; she came in after breakfast, and if she were late, the lunch was late; everything in the household was disrupted. But nothing could be said to her; she was too temperamental.

A cook, and a maid, and a gardener three times a week... he thought. *But, when I lived in that stinking little hotel, it was, really, the same thing. Somebody made my bed and tidied my room; somebody cooked the food I ate; somebody saw that there was hot water and steam heat. Somebody, somewhere, makes my shoes and my suits, and my hats. Very good. And my job is to amuse these people—if they ever read anything. There have always been people like me. The minnesingers, standing outside of castles, with the songs they made up, and long before that, long before, there was old Homer, blind. He'd strike his lyre; he gave them the* Iliad, *and the* Odyssey. *And how many listened? I can't get the scene. I've never been in Greece. A hillside, maybe, in the dusk. There'd be couples making love. There'd be people who had too much dinner, too much wine; they'd be dozing. There'd be politicians, thinking of their next speech; generals and admirals, thinking about the next war.*

*But there was someone, maybe a professor, with a gray beard, maybe some kid who wanted to make stories. Anyhow, somebody cared; somebody wrote it down. Any time you write anything, maybe it hits someone....*

He wrote until late; then he went up to that guestroom, and thought about the next day's work until he fell asleep. You could do that, often, and in the morning you could start to work as soon as you opened your eyes.

It was raining when he waked, a wild wind, the trees tossing. He liked that. He got up and took a shower and began to dress, and then in an instant, without warning, all the pain and dread and dismay came down on him.

*Will there be another funeral today?* he thought. *My God! I'll have to see Caulish. He can't charge double, because yesterday.... But he'll charge more, and I've got so damn little in the bank.... I'll have to tell Norma I can't afford so many flowers.... Poor Norma.... Poor Lulu....*

When he went downstairs, Norma was at the table.

"Regina overslept," she said. "But I made some coffee, Jimmy."

"Fine!" he said.

It was the worst coffee he had ever tasted, weak, horrible. He drank a little, and lit a cigarette.

"I knocked and knocked at Billie's door," she said, "but she didn't answer. So I thought I'd better let her alone."

"Much better," he said.

Regina came in, with a fresh pot of coffee; she brought orange juice, and toast, bacon and eggs.

"You're not eating anything, Norma," Brophy said.

"I can't," she said. "It doesn't matter."

It made him a little ashamed to be hungry, but he ate, and she sat with him.

"There's a car coming up the drive!" she cried.

He could understand how she felt. Everything that happened now, the ring of the telephone, or the doorbell, the sound of a footstep, everything could mean shock and distress.

"I suppose...," Norma said, "they'll bring her home?"

"Oh... I suppose so...," Brophy answered.

He had not thought about that, and it was another embarrassment. Things like that shouldn't be embarrassing, he thought. They ought to be tragic. But—well, it's me. I don't have the right feelings.

"It's Lieutenant Levy, sir," said Regina. "And he says if you haven't finished your breakfast, not to hurry, because he can wait."

They both rose at once, and went into the front living-room. The Lieutenant was in uniform this morning, and it did not suit him; it seemed, Brophy thought, too big for him, giving him somehow a helpless look; his black leather belt with a holster sagged, his dark hair bushed out a little behind his large ears. Maybe he's not much good as a policeman, Brophy thought, and that worried him.

With him was Doctor Griffin, the bristling cockatoo, all alive, neat as a pin.

"Well, sir!" he said. "We worked all night, the County Medical Examiner and his staff and myself. We're prepared to state definitely—*definitely*—the cause of Mrs. Brophy's death. She died, sir, by atropine poisoning!"

"Well," said Brophy, unstartled, "you told me yourself, some time ago, you thought she'd taken too much of some of her medicines."

"She didn't *have* any atropine!" said the doctor, with an air of triumph. "Not prescribed by me, or by Doctor Binder. And she couldn't get it without a prescription. This was no mistake, Mr. Brophy!"

# CHAPTER SIX

"Hold on!" said Levy. "Not so fast, Doctor. We don't know—yet—anything about how Mrs. Brophy obtained this medicine, and we're not making any unsupported statements."

"I state," said the doctor, "and I shall continue to state that atropine is not a constituent of any medicine prescribed by me or by Doctor Binder, nor is it a constituent of any patent medicine known to me. With the exception of certain preparations for the eye."

"Do you use eye-drops, Mr. Brophy?"

"Why, no," said Brophy. "I had some stuff once—boric acid, that was it."

"And you, Miss Crockett?"

She did not answer.

"Miss Crockett," asked Levy, "do you use any sort of eye-drops or lotion?"

Brophy turned, in surprise, to look at her, in her strange silence, and he was frightened by her look.

Her cheeks were sucked in, her eyes were staring; she was white as never before.

"Norma!" he cried, springing to his feet.

"Sit down, Mr. Brophy," said Levy, curtly. "Let her alone, please."

"She's going to faint."

"No. Take your time, Miss Crockett."

"Do you—want to see them—the drops—the bottle?" she asked, falteringly.

"Presently, Miss Crockett. Where is this bottle?"

"In—my bathroom, I think. Has that got—has *that* got—the poison in it?"

"We'll look into it, Miss Crockett."

"But—I didn't know.... I didn't know—"

"If you're upset, Miss Crockett, we'll wait," said Levy. "Perhaps you'd like to lie down for a while?"

"No," she said. "No, thank you. Only.... You see I didn't know...."

"We'll wait, Miss Crockett," said Levy.

He did not look now like a paternal Egyptian ruler; he looked, thought Brophy, like a policeman, cold, and steady, and inhumanly patient.

"I—didn't know...," Norma said.

"Yes, Miss Crockett."

"It was the day—the day...."

"The day of the party," said Levy.

"Yes!" Norma said, as if relieved.

"And that day, Miss Crockett?"

"My sister came to my room. She said—her eyes hurt. She asked me—if I had anything...."

"And did you?"

"Yes!" Norma answered, with a sort of fury. "I had some eye-drops—Doctor Griffin prescribed."

"Had you yourself used these drops?"

"Yes. Once. Anyhow, I thought they'd be perfectly safe to give to Lulu."

"Did she take them, Miss Crockett?"

"Well, yes."

"Did you see her use them?"

"No... I gave her the bottle—and then I went to speak to the cook. But I told her. It's one or two drops in each eye. I told her...."

"You still have this bottle, Miss Crockett?"

"Well, I—I think so. I mean—I didn't see it—in the room. I—I think Lulu would naturally have put it back in the bathroom."

"Suppose we just take a look?" said Levy.

They went up the stairs and into Norma's room; Brophy stayed there while the others went into the bathroom. But almost at once she gave a cry.

"The bottle's *empty!*"

"How often had you used it?" the doctor asked.

"Once. Just once. And Lulu used it once."

"Was there enough in that bottle...?" Levy asked the doctor. "Lethal dose?"

"There was," said the doctor. "You'll notice the label. Marked Poison. For External Use Only."

"But Lulu wouldn't—!" cried Norma. "I know Lulu wouldn't—"

"I understand that Mrs. Brophy was in a very nervous state, just before this party," said Levy. "Very much agitated—"

"Hold on!" said Brophy, in a sudden burst of anger. Things are bad enough as they are, he thought. The party was such a damn disappointment to the poor girl.... And if they're going to hint now that she killed herself.... "If you're trying to insinuate—," he began.

"No, sir," said Levy, at his mildest. "I'm not insinuating anything at all, Mr. Brophy. I don't need to, you know." He paused for a moment, after this gentle but unmistakable reminder of his authority. "A maid may have upset the bottle and put it back without saying anything about it. Or Mrs. Brophy herself might easily have upset it, especially if she was nervous and apprehensive—"

"Why should she be 'apprehensive'?" Brophy interrupted.

"Worried," said Levy. "Some people get like that, when they're giving a party. Too anxious for everything to be exactly right."

"Well...," said Brophy. "Yes. But I don't want it suggested that my wife was in any sort of—abnormal state of agitation, or whatever you want to call it." He remembered Lulu coming down to her party, remembered her wild, even insensate behavior, and a violent pity seized him, and shook him. "She was—a little nervous, that's all. Absolutely all."

"Then you don't think she could have taken that stuff by accident?" asked the doctor.

"No. I do not," Brophy answered. "Lulu wasn't insane, and she wasn't a fool. She wouldn't have drunk a bottle of eye-drops."

"So!" said the doctor, and his eyes looked brilliant in his white-crested cockatoo's face. "So! If you rule out accident, rule out suicide, then what have you got left?"

They all stood silent in Norma's tranquil and orderly room.

"All right!" said Brophy. "Amen. That's it."

"No!" cried Norma. "I don't—I won't.... Anyhow, in any case, whatever happened—*I'm* responsible. I gave—poor Lulu—the eye-drops."

"Why don't you try to get a little rest, Miss Crockett?" asked Levy. "Perhaps you could sleep for a while, or if not, you could lie down and read a nice book...?"

What's a Nice Book? thought Brophy. It's not the same as a Good Book; that I know. When a customer in a lending library asks for a Good Book, the librarian knows just what's expected. But you hear plenty of people ask, What's a Nice Book for me to take to the country this week-end? What's a Nice Book for my husband? He's laid up with a cold. Well, the librarians seem to know the answer. I wish I did. Maybe I could make a good living, by writing Nice Books.

Levy seemed to be having some trouble with Norma. She was in tears again, and she had got hold of the empty little blue bottle and held it in both hands, against her breast.

"I'll have to have that bottle, Miss Crockett," Levy was saying, patiently.

All right; let them carry on for a while, thought Brophy. I'm sorry for Norma. I'm sorry for Lulu. Maybe I'm sorry for everybody, for all of us, poor naked worms that we are.

Suddenly Norma held out the bottle to Levy.

"Fine!" said Doctor Griffin. "A fine lot of fingerprints you'll get from that *now,* Lieutenant."

"I'll manage," said Levy. "Thanks, Miss Crockett. Now, if you please, I'd like to see Miss de Paul."

"I'm sorry," said Norma, "but she's not up yet."

"It's after ten. I'm afraid we'll have to disturb her."

"I did knock on her door, but she didn't answer," Norma said. "So I thought.... You see, she had quite a lot of drinks last night...."

"Let her alone! Let her alone, Levy," said the doctor. "Nothing more hopeless, nothing worse than an intoxicated female."

"Sometimes it's a help," said Levy, musingly. "Well! I'm afraid I'll have to see Miss de Paul, Miss Crockett, even if she's not feeling very fit. Y'see, she sent for me."

"What!" cried Norma.

"She telephoned me twice last night. Asked me to come first thing this morning."

"Last night? But why?"

"She said she had important information to give me."

"But—about what?"

"I'll have to see Miss de Paul."

"But—I told you. She'd been drinking, Lieutenant."

"That was pretty obvious, on the telephone."

"I wouldn't have thought she was *able* to telephone," said Norma. "Not when I left her."

"She managed," said Levy. "Twice. The first time around midnight, and the second time she got me at home, at three o'clock this morning."

Why are people so keen about telephoning, when they've got a load on? Brophy thought. Is it because they feel lonely? Probably. The same thing that makes them insist on talking so damn much in bars and so on. She may have forgotten all about her crazy story now, the woman running through the garden, to hide the "murder weapon." About Biddy changing the glasses.... I only hope to God Biddy doesn't get dragged into this. Or even be mentioned.

"Miss Crockett," said Levy, "will you ask Miss de Paul if she'll see me now?"

With obvious reluctance Norma moved away, but not toward the hall. She opened a door at the side, and went through it, closing it after her.

"What's that?" Levy asked.

"Bathroom," Brophy answered. "Between this and the guest-room. There! You can hear her knocking now."

For a moment the muffled sound of knocking went on, then it stopped. Levy went out into the hall, sauntered a few steps, and halted by Miss de Paul's door.

"My God!" said Billie's voice, hoarse and wretched. "Am I sick!"

"I'll help you," said Norma. "If I run a nice tepid bath for you...?"

"All right!" said Billie, dolefully.

The sound of running water drowned their voices; there was only a low murmur.

"Lieutenant," said the doctor, sharply, "do you want me to stay, and straighten out your customer? If I can."

"No, thanks," Levy answered. "I like her the way she is. She'll be feeling remorseful this morning, guilty. Just right."

"If you believe a word you hear from a woman in that condition, Levy—"

"Lies are just as good," said Levy. "Sometimes even better. That could be a maxim for one of these famous sleuths. Encourage your man—or woman—to lie. Pretend to accept what you hear. Because once you find out what a man lies about, you know what he's afraid of, and when you know *that*—"

"Pish and tush," said the doctor. "When my patients start lying, I pin 'em down. Well, I'll be off, then. By the way, we'll get the burial permit by tomorrow morning, Mr. Brophy. So you can make your—arrangements for the afternoon."

"What were the findings?" asked Brophy.

"What I expected. Atropine poisoning. No organic heart trouble. And— you might be interested to know—a very small trace of alcohol. Your wife had not been drinking heavily, Mr. Brophy."

"I.... She never had," said Brophy.

"The very strong smell of whiskey about her I explain in this way," the doctor continued. "I think that, in her extremity, Mrs. Brophy attempted to give herself a drink, in the hope that it might relieve her condition. Her tremor, however, caused her to spill the liquor from the bottle, drench herself with it."

"Yes...," Brophy said. "That's how it must have been." And, after a moment: "Thanks," he said.

He believed that the doctor was trying to be reassuring and friendly, and he was grateful for this. "You can make your arrangements," he had said.

He must mean another funeral, Brophy thought.

The doctor was going down the stairs now, and Levy stood in the hall, with his wonderful patience. His big hands hung easily at his sides; he never shifted his feet, never made any sort of restless gesture. The bathwater had long ago stopped running, but there was no sound of voices from the room.

The door opened suddenly, and Norma came out into the hall.

"Oh, *dear!*" she cried. "Now she's *gone back!*"

"What d'you mean, Norma?" Brophy asked.

"I'd just got her clothes together—they were scattered all over—and she said she'd have to take a hair of the dog, before she took her bath. Lots of people think that's a good idea. Anyhow, I couldn't get her out of bed without it. So I poured her out just a medium drink, and I left her there sipping it while I went into the bathroom to collect the things she'd left there. Of course, she *might* have got up and poured herself more, but I don't know. She was still lying in bed when I came back, and she had her eyes closed. I reminded her that you were waiting, Lieutenant, and she kept on saying, 'Just a moment. Just a moment.' At last I told her she'd *have* to get up, and she didn't answer at all. I spoke to her again. I shook her. But I can't—I *cannot* wake her up."

"I'll just step in...," said Levy.

"No...!" Norma protested. "The room isn't done, and Billie—"

He went past her into the bedroom, and Norma followed him, with Brophy behind her. Miss de Paul lay on her back, breathing heavily, her lips parted. She wore a dainty white bed jacket tied with a pink ribbon, but that did not help her; she looked years older, and, Brophy thought, pitiably helpless, without that bouncing vitality like a light within her. The blonde hair straggling over the pillow was very sparse; there were lines at the corners of her eyes, and the lids were wrinkled; with her mouth open, her double chin was obvious; her rosy skin was unbecomingly flushed.

"Miss de Paul?" said Levy, and then, more loudly: "Miss de Paul!"

She did not stir.

"See if you can catch the doctor," Levy said to Brophy. "Quick!"

Brophy ran down the stairs and out of the house. The doctor was already in his car, sitting behind the wheel and studying a little memo book.

"The Lieutenant wants you to come back, Doctor!" Brophy called.

The doctor came, without a word; he went stamping up the stairs, and into the bedroom.

"Everybody out," he said, curtly.

But Levy remained; they were shut in there together for a few moments; then they came out into the hall. The doctor went down the stairs again, still without a word. Levy closed the bedroom door, and stood leaning against it.

"Out like a light," he said, sighing a little. "The doctor's sending for the ambulance—"

"Oh, why?" cried Norma.

"They can straighten her out quicker, in the hospital."

"No!" said Norma. "After all, she's our guest, and I don't see why she should be—disgraced. No! I really couldn't allow her to be taken to the hospital."

"There won't be any disgrace about it, Miss Crockett."

"She'd hate to have strangers see her like this. No! Do let the poor thing alone, to sleep it off."

Levy lowered his glance, displaying long, thick black lashes that gave his bony face a modest and demure expression.

"Well, you see," he said. "the doctor thinks she's taken something."

"Taken *what,* for God's sake?" Brophy demanded, in a sort of exasperation.

"He thought he smelled chloral hydrate," Levy answered.

"And what's that?"

"'Used as a sleeping medicine," said Levy. "Also used in a Mickey Finn."

"What's that?" Norma asked. "A—Mickey Finn?"

"Knockout drops," Levy explained. "If you take it along with alcohol, it knocks you unconscious."

"I don't believe it," said Norma, flatly. "I don't believe she took any-thing—except too much whiskey. I think your nasty old Doctor Griffin's simply obsessed with the idea of everybody taking something."

"Could be," said Levy, rather absently. "We'll know, later." He smiled at her and it was an absent smile, without meaning. "I'll be going now, Miss Crockett. You'll let me know if you want to see me, at any time?"

"Thank you," said Norma.

"Mr. Brophy, if you'll come downstairs with me...?"

It's a funny thing, Brophy said to himself, as he followed the Lieutenant down the stairs, but Levy's got me bothered. Very much bothered. You can't tell what he thinks, about anything. You can't tell who he likes, or who he doesn't like. He thinks there's been a murder committed here, in this house, but he doesn't ask any of us a lot of questions, he doesn't seem to do any snooping. Well, is that because he's not much interested? Or because he thinks he knows already? I know who committed the murder! Billie had said. Murder.... You can't realize it. You can't believe in murder.

"I'm sorry to trouble you," said the polite Levy, "but I'd be much obliged if you'd just show me where Miss Crockett's garden is."

"Don't understand you," said Brophy, puzzled. "I suppose you could call the whole place hers—in a way."

"Can you think of some spot that Miss Crockett's particularly fond of? Some flower-bed, for instance, that she looks after?"

"Oh, there's the rock garden!" said Brophy. "I know Norma designed that, bought all the plants for it, goes to look after it all the time."

"If you'll point it out to me...."

A uniformed policeman jumped out of the police car that stood in the driveway; Levy made some sort of loose-wristed gesture, and the man saluted, and stayed where he was.

"If you'll just give me directions, Mr. Brophy...?"

"I'll take you there."

"No need for you to bother, Mr. Brophy. This isn't a big place. Just tell me."

"Oh, no!" said Brophy. "I'll take you there."

Because he wanted to see for himself.

It was a long time since he had seen the rock garden; not since his first visit here, before his marriage. Norma had taken him there, proudly, and he had expressed a warm admiration for it, because the poor girl had obviously taken so much trouble with it. It was a pile of rocks, heaped loosely in a corner of the back wall; there was cactus growing there, and snake-plant, and others he did not know, small things, growing close to the ground, and, he had thought, all ugly and a little sinister. Half-way up the rocky hill was a miniature bridge, lacquered black, and in it stood two tiny Chinese figures, mandarins, in blue and yellow robes. She had bent down, to turn on the tap of a pipe, and in a moment a trickle of water began, running from the top of the rocks and down, under the bridge, to the grass below.

It was just as he remembered it, even uglier in the blazing midday sun. There was a big green china frog now, squatting under a tuft of pulpy leaves, and a cowboy on horseback, carved out of wood, so small that the desert plants towered above him; he looked like some struggling human on a strange planet.

Levy stood contemplating this display, hands clasped behind his back; after a moment, he walked round to one side of it, and bent down. He remained so for some time, hands on his knees; then he stood erect.

"Mr. Brophy," he said, "will you be good enough to speak to all the members of your household, and tell them not to come here until further notice? Better not come to this part of the grounds at all."

"I will!" said Brophy.

But I'm going to see whatever it was you saw, he said to himself. He passed quickly behind Levy, and bent over, where Levy had been.

There was a sort of tunnel there, where the water-pipe ran; the sun struck through the loosely piled rocks, giving what lay there a diamond glitter. There were dozens of empty beer bottles, bits of broken, jagged glass, and nothing else. Nothing that he could see.

When he straightened up, he found Levy looking at him, with a dark, unwavering glance he could not read.

"I'll station one of my men here," he said.

# CHAPTER SEVEN

What did he mean by that? thought Brophy. That he doesn't trust me to keep myself and the members of my household away from the rock garden? Who are they, anyhow? Norma, of course, and Regina, and What's-her-Name, the cook. What's there, anyhow? All I saw was a lot of beer bottles and broken glass. Did Levy see—something else there? Or did those bottles mean something to him?

But, when you come to think about it, it's a bit peculiar. Because who drinks beer in our house? Lulu never would touch it; she thought it would make her fat. Norma doesn't like it, and neither do I. Regina, and the cook? Could be. I've never noticed Regina smelling of beer when she was waiting on the table.

But, my God! What do I notice, anyhow? Practically nothing. If I were more observant, I'd write better. Far better. Now, about Levy? He doesn't *look* like any gimlet-eyed sleuth. To be frank, he looks like a dope. *Nice* dope; I like him. But what did he see there behind the rock garden that I didn't see?

If I were going to do a story about it...? he asked himself, and an idea came, like a flash. The sun is shining on a heap of broken glass, he thought; it's glittering, dazzling. The other people in the story won't see anything else, but my detective-hero will, all right. He'll see the missing diamond necklace, glittering like the broken glass. That ought to give me a good tag-line. *He smiled, quietly. You'll find diamonds in the broken glass of a good many lives, he said.* No! Too corny. But I can do something with that.

He went slowly up the steps and opened the front door that was left unlocked during the daytime. And as soon as he stepped into the hall, he faced extremely unpleasant reality. Norma was standing in the living-room, speaking in a low voice to Caulish, the undertaker, who stood before her. She turned her head at the sound of the door closing.

"Mr. Caulish is just leaving," she said. "We've made all the arrangements, Jimmy...."

"This is a terrible ordeal for you, Mr. Brophy," said Caulish, in a tone of grave, manly sympathy. "I can well understand—"

"Yes, I don't doubt it," said Brophy, and went past the room and up the stairs. In a moment, Norma came running up after him.

"Oh, Jimmy!" she cried. "You mustn't mind, dear—"

"I do mind that damn ghoul prowling around here. He could have waited until I sent for him."

"But, Jimmy, I sent for him. I thought if I could just take *that* off your shoulders—"

"No," he said. "I'm sorry, Norma, but I'll have to do the arranging."

Because I'll have to do the paying, he thought. He thought of funerals at sea, and resolutely put that out of his head. He thought of his mother's funeral, and a familiar guilt and remorse came over him. He had done his best to play the part of a stricken son, and it had been false. He had not loved her or his father, or anyone but friends he had known, in school, in the war, in his writing life. He thought of a pulp magazine editor he had known, and he knew, very well, that he had respected and admired the man far more than his father; that this man had advised and helped him as his father never had. And I didn't love Lulu, he thought. I admit it now, to myself.

"I thought—," Norma said, "that you'd be relieved, Jimmy."

"Well, I'm not," he said. "I'll call up that ghoul. We'll have it in a funeral parlor, or temple, or whatever they call it."

"Jimmy, no! Lulu has to come here, to come *home!*"

"Here? Again? No!" he said. "I won't have it that way."

"Jimmy.... You want it to be—the way Lulu would want it, don't you?"

"Have you had a telegram from Lulu?" he asked. "Or a dream? Or a vision, where she told you what she wanted?"

"I'm her *sister!*"

"All right. I'm her widower."

"Jimmy!" Norma said, and tears were running down her face. "I only wanted to—help you. And to do—" A sob interrupted her. "To do—what Lulu wants. And I know. I *know* she'd want her funeral here, in her own home."

"Look here!" said Brophy. "This isn't the old homestead, where she was born and reared. It's just a rented house she had for—what is it?—three or four years. We can't have—all that, over again!"

"All what?"

"All those—those flowers!" he cried. "The whole thing. It's nothing but sentimentality. A quiet, decent little service, in one of those chapels, or whatever they call them, that's what we'll have."

"No!" said Norma. "She's coming here. Coming home."

"I say *no.*"

"You can't keep her out of her own home!"

"It's not her own home," said Brophy. "I'm going in to town presently, to see Caulish—"

"Jimmy, you can't! When I've talked to him and made all the arrangements.... I've thought and thought—just what Lulu would want—every detail—"

"Oh, hell! All right, then," said Brophy.

He turned to the window and stood there until he heard Norma go out; he waited, and heard her door close. Then he went, very quietly and cautiously, along the hall and down the stairs to the sun-parlor. I'm going to work, he told himself. I've damn well got to. With these two funerals to pay for. Utter nonsense. Criminal nonsense. It's— I don't know how I can go through it again.

Very well! I didn't have to give in to Norma. But I always do. I always gave in to Lulu, too. And to Mother. Women get so noisy, and so clamorous, and you know they're never going to stop till they get their own way. They keep on.... My God! All of them!... He thought of girls he had known before he was married. Nice girls, some of them. But there was always that chance of a scene, tears, foot-stamping, clamor.

He sighed, and went over to his table. There, beside the typewriter, lay the few pages he had done on that story. The Party Was the Pay-Off. No, he thought. I can't work on that. I'll start another pulp serial, and maybe I can get an advance.

He leaned back, put his feet up on the desk, and lit a cigarette. And that thing started inside his mind.

He could never have explained it, even to himself; it was some extraordinary mechanism that would start working when he needed it, and deliver what he ordered. I want an idea for—a short-short, he would think; an idea for a one-shot, about twenty-five thousand words. No, he thought, I want about forty thousand words. A mystery. A murder. A diamond necklace in with a pile of broken glass. It belongs to the one who gets murdered, and who's she? A rich dowager? Well, no. A blonde. A sort of floozie. She lives on men. She's poison to men. There's the title, I think. Elaine Was Poison. No, not Elaine. No... Angela Was Poison. That's—

The doorbell rang, kept on, in an insistent, annoying way. Oh, shut up! Brophy said, half-aloud. Who are you? We'd like you to try our laundry service.... I'm working for a college scholarship, selling subscriptions to your favorite magazines....

He could hear Regina hurrying through the living-room. She was thin, but, as Lulu used to say, she tramped like an elephant; she walked bent forward from the waist, her bony face contorted by a frown of desperate anxiety. Take it easy! he had often told her. But that she couldn't do.

She opened the door.

"Tell Mr. Brophy I want to see him," said Doctor Griffin's imperious voice.

Brophy got up in haste and went out into the hall.

Everything had become disturbing now; he had a feeling of uneasiness, even dread, of what might happen, what he might hear.

"Mr. Brophy," said the doctor, "I'd like to take a look at your late guest's room."

"Mean Miss de Paul?"

"Yes. She's gone, y'know."

"Gone where?"

"I'm not prepared to say," said the doctor, with a thin smile. "She died five minutes after she reached the hospital."

I don't want to hear any more about this, Brophy thought. I want to— be let alone.

"Not surprised?" the doctor asked.

"I'm not surprised to hear that people die," said Brophy. "I don't know anything about Miss de Paul. For all I know, she might have had any sort of serious disease."

"We're doing an autopsy," said the doctor. "But I can tell you here and now, what killed her."

He waited, for an exclamation, for a question. But Brophy was silent, standing before him, big and stalwart in his tan shirt and brown slacks, looking over the doctor's shoulder at the wall beyond.

"You'll be hearing from the police soon enough," said the doctor. "Your guest was poisoned, Brophy."

"I knew you were going to say that," said Brophy. "Eye-drops?" he asked, politely.

"Not this time. No. A massive dose of chloral hydrate, combined with an excessive amount of alcoholic liquor."

"Doctor!" came Norma's voice from a distance.

She was leaning over the staircase railing, on the floor above; as the two men looked up, she moved, and was about to descend.

"Stay where you are, please!" said the doctor. "I'm coming up."

"Just a moment!" said Brophy. "After all, you're not the police. And I don't know whether you're entitled to the free run of my house."

"Legally, no, I'm not," said the doctor. "You can make a complaint about me, if you like. Later on. But I just about broke my neck to get here before Levy, and unless you've got your own reasons for not wanting the case solved, you won't object to my taking a look at that room."

"I do object," said Brophy. "I'm going to leave the solving to Levy."

"Jimmy, why not let the doctor come up?" Norma asked.

"No," said Brophy. "If he tries it, I'll pull him back by the coat-tails. And if he keeps on bothering me, who knows? I might get annoyed."

"But, Jimmy, dear! Don't you see how it's going to look, if—"

"I don't care how it looks," said Brophy, "or how it smells. I never obstruct the police in the performance of their duties, but I don't mind obstructing doctors, especially when they're not minding their own damn business."

"You'll regret this, Brophy," said the doctor, running his finger round the inside of his collar, as if he were choking. "Your wife was my patient, and as I see it, my obligation is still to her, and to no one else. Her death is officially recorded as 'death by misadventure.' Levy advanced his remarkable theory. He suggested that Mrs. Brophy had had a few drinks, that she was highly nervous about the party, and that, without realization of what she was doing, she poured the contents of the eye-drops bottle into the drink she had there. I attempted to point out the fantastic improbability of this, but he countered by saying—and, mind you, he said it with the purpose of discrediting me—he said that Mrs. Brophy had been so habituated to taking pills, liquids, all sorts of medication, that it was natural for her to swallow anything in a druggist's bottle."

"Could be," said Brophy.

"A physician sometimes has a patient who benefits, psychologically, by medication. I deny that I ever gave Mrs. Brophy, or any other patient, a placebo. I prescribed certain drugs which were undoubtedly beneficial to her, and at times I prescribed half to be put up in liquid form, and half in tablets or capsules. I would order one to be taken before meals and one after, and the two combined made the dose I considered indicated. But, as we saw in examining that medicine cabinet, in addition to the medicines prescribed by me, she had bought herself a lot of rubbishy, dangerous patent medicines. She was a very nervous, high-strung patient, and quite unduly worried about her health. But she was *not a* fool, who'd drink the contents of a bottle labeled 'Poison,' and I am convinced, I am entirely convinced that she was *not* suicidal. However, they got this man from Albany for the P.M., and—"

The doorbell rang, and Brophy went to answer it. It was Lieutenant Levy, and two policemen in uniform..

"Sorry to disturb you," he said, and his face and his voice made this convincing. "But, of course, we've got to make the routine inquiries. Hello, Doctor!"

"Good-day," said Griffin.

"Found any clues?" Levy asked.

"I have plenty of what you'd call 'clues,'" the doctor answered. "But I don't feel disposed to present them to you and your colleagues. You brush aside all my experience, all my knowledge and understanding of the persons involved. You—"

"Never meant to, Doctor," said Levy. "Suppose you make the rounds with me?"

He started up the stairs, and Brophy could not object to Griffin's following him; after a moment, in spite of his secret rebellion, he went after them. Norma was waiting for them; they all went into the room Billie had occupied. Levy glanced around it, with a slow, mild gaze, but the doctor went over to the chest of drawers, opened a bottle of toilet water and sniffed it, stooped to look under the bed. The room was in perfect order now, with a bare look.

"Miss Crockett," said Levy, "did Miss de Paul ask you to give her any sleeping medicine?"

"Why, no, Lieutenant. I thought she went to sleep almost as soon as I'd left. I heard her go into the bathroom once, but after that there wasn't a sound."

"Have you any chloral hydrate, Miss Crockett?"

"I'm sorry," she said, "but I don't know what that is."

"It's a sleeping medicine, Miss Crockett, a liquid; it's colorless, like water."

"Yes, I did have something like that," she said, with a sort of eagerness. "I've had it for ages. I only took it once, because I have a sort of horror of drugs. Doctor Griffin prescribed it," she added.

"What!" said the doctor. "Oh, yes. Yes. You came to my office, said you couldn't sleep, couldn't eat, couldn't rest. This was at the time of your sister's wedding, I believe."

"Yes. They'd gone away, on their honeymoon, and I was here alone. I'd never been all alone before, and I'm afraid I was very silly about it."

"I'd like to see the bottle, Miss Crockett."

"Oh, I'm so sorry! But I threw it away months ago."

"When you threw the bottle away, was it almost full?"

"Oh, no!" she answered, shocked. "I'd never do that. I always empty bottles before I throw them away. I rinse them, too; even polish remover and things like that."

"Very sensible. Now, Miss de Paul had a lethal dose of chloral hydrate last night, Miss Crockett."

"Yes. I heard you telling Jimmy."

"Can you suggest any way in which she might have got it?"

"Well.... Yes," Norma answered. "She could have had it with her."

"You think that's likely, Miss Crockett?"

"Well.... Of course, it's not a crime, only I do think it's dangerous, and—rather dreadful. But poor Billie always took some sort of sleeping medicine. Even years ago. She used to have capsules in her purse, red ones, and yellow, and green. Then when she couldn't buy them any more without a doctor's prescription, she got them in some sort of black market, and she had to pay a simply fabulous price. Why, she told me—"

"That's the way it goes," said Levy. "Miss Crockett, will you send for the maid who did this room today?"

"Regina? I'll run down—"

"I'll get her," said Brophy.

He found Regina and the cook sitting at the kitchen table, each eating half a cantaloupe. He felt a sudden and acute desire for a good, ripe melon himself, but he banished it.

"Regina," he said, "Lieutenant Levy wants to see you, upstairs."

"Ah...! The policeman?" she cried, standing with her hand on the back of her chair. The cook, by the way, had not risen; the only concession she made was to stop eating and lay down her spoon.

"There's no call to mind the police," she said. "They're public servants, is what I say, and I've told them so, to their faces, more than once."

"They put words into your mouth," said Regina, unsteadily.

"That they can't do," said the cook, "for nothing is any good at all to them till it's been done on a typewriter, and you've read and signed it your own self."

"There's nothing to worry about," said Brophy. "But come along, Regina. He's waiting."

She came tramping along behind him; going up the stairs, she was breathing hard.

"Don't be nervous," said Brophy, sorry for her.

"Ah.... But the police is the terror of the world," she said. "Haven't I heard my grandmother tell how it was in Ireland, in the old days? And in the movies—"

"It won't be that way, Regina," he said, and took the frightened girl's arm to lead her into the bedroom.

The three in there were all standing, and close together, and Norma was speaking.

"I didn't *want* her to tell me. I tried to stop her—"

"We'd better wait a bit," said Levy, and turned to Regina.

"Thanks for coming," he said. "I hope I didn't interrupt your schedule?"

"No, sir."

"You tidied up this room, after Miss de Paul was taken to the hospital?"

"I did, sir," she said, and looked about her fearfully, to see if she had done anything strange and shocking.

"Empty the waste-paper basket?"

"I did, sir."

"Were there any bottles in it? Any medicine bottles?"

"No, sir, there was none."

"You're sure you'd remember?"

"I would, sir, the way we put bottles separate from the papers, for there is an old man comes to buy paper."

"Did you see any bottles in the room?"

She looked anxiously at Norma.

"Tell Lieutenant Levy everything, Regina," Norma said. "Even if you don't like to."

"There was a bottle, sir," said Regina. "Only it was a whiskey bottle, and it was standing on the floor by the bed."

"Partly full?"

"Empty, sir. I didn't mean any harm, but I took it downstairs, the way I didn't think it looked—good."

"Quite right," said Levy. "Now, can you remember if there were any medicine bottles in any of the waste-baskets you emptied this morning?"

"There was not, sir."

"If you come across any medicine bottle, in some hole, or corner, or any unusual place, pick it up carefully, with a cloth, keep it safely, and call me up, will you?"

"I will, sir."

"That's all, then, and thanks," said Levy, and she went out of the room, stumbling a little. They were all silent for a time, and Brophy said to himself, They're thinking what I'm thinking. About that missing bottle and all that it implies.

# CHAPTER EIGHT

If there was no medicine bottle in the room, it implied that Billie had brought none with her. Then where did she get the stuff? Brophy thought. Norma? Norma admitted she'd once had a bottle of it. But she wouldn't have volunteered that, if she'd used it. No.... But who else, in God's name? There's no one else in the house but me. And Regina. There's the cook, of course, but she never comes upstairs. And why would she want to murder Billie, anyhow?

"Yes," he heard Norma say, "she had an overnight case."

She opened the closet door, and brought out a bag. Levy looked through it.

"Any purse, pocketbook?" he asked.

Norma brought him a big handbag of blonde leather, and he looked through that.

"But there are still lots of places to look!" she said.

"Oh, yes!" Levy agreed, politely. "But I shan't bother with that, just now. It doesn't seem very likely that Miss de Paul would take a lot of trouble to hide the bottle, especially after a dose like that."

"But she must have brought it with her!"

"We can go into all that later," said Levy. "Now I'd like to hear your account of your talk with Miss de Paul. Are you willing to make a statement of it, Miss Crockett, to be taken down, and later read and signed by you?"

He's changed, Brophy thought. He's more formal, less friendly. And why?

"Well, yes...," said Norma. "Only it seems—I don't know—sort of terrifying."

"I have a man here who'll take it down," said Levy. "If there's some room where we can be alone...?"

"Couldn't I tell you with Jimmy and Doctor Griffin here?" she asked. "I mean, I'd feel so much—easier. I mean—"

"Very well, if you'd rather," said Levy. "But it's to be understood that there's to be no interruption of any sort, no comment from them. Agreed?"

"Yes," said Brophy.

"You scarcely need to ask *me* that," said Doctor Griffin. "You know that I'm familiar with police procedure, Lieutenant."

Levy said nothing to this. He went out into the hall, and he called, in a loud, ringing voice, surprisingly different from his usual mild tone. "Kalinsky! Up here!"

Kalinsky came running up the stairs, a fresh-faced young policeman, with light hair slicked down on his head as if painted; with his staring china-blue eyes and his pursed mouth, he looked owlishly surprised, but happy.

"Sit down," said Levy. "Take Miss Crockett's statement."

Name. Norma Crockett. Age. Twenty-six. Residence.

"Well, here, I guess. I don't know where I'll go next."

"Here," said Levy. "Continue, please, Miss Crockett."

"Well... I went in to see Billie last night—to see if she wanted anything. And she started talking about calling the police. I—well, I couldn't *help* knowing she'd been drinking, and I didn't pay much attention."

"You didn't know that she called me twice, in the night and then early this morning?" Levy asked.

"No, I didn't. She told me first about seeing Biddy Hamilton change cocktail glasses with Lulu. I didn't want to hear any more. I tried to stop her, to get her quiet. But I couldn't. She told me how she'd stayed here, slept in the sun-porch, the night of—of—of—"

"Don't hurry," said Levy.

"The night of—my sister's death. She said she saw a woman run along the path—toward the back of the house. She had a lamp turned on, and she said—"

"Yes?" said Levy.

"She said she could see—who it was."

"Yes? Who was it she thought she saw?"

"Oh, I *don't* want to say it."

"It's necessary, Miss Crockett."

"She said—it was Biddy Hamilton. She recognized the red hair, the dress, everything."

"Did she have any theory to account for Miss Hamilton's running around your garden at that hour?"

"But—that isn't evidence, is it, Lieutenant?"

"No, Miss Crockett. It isn't. But I'd like to hear it."

"She thought—she's always thought—that that Hamilton girl—poisoned Lulu. I don't *want* to tell you. What poor Billie *thought* couldn't be important."

"I want to hear it, Miss Crockett."

"Well, she thought—the Hamilton girl wanted to get rid of—of my sister. So that she could marry Jimmy."

"Did she adduce—bring forward any reason for this suspicion?"

"Oh, I don't want to tell you! It's only what Billie said. I didn't believe it."

"We won't put this into the statement, Miss Crockett. Don't take this, Kalinsky. If you'll just tell me, Miss Crockett. It's not official."

"She said she saw them—"

"Who, Miss Crockett?"

"Jimmy and that Hamilton girl. She said she saw them one night in New York, going into one of those horrible little midtown hotels—and they both had bags. She said she saw them here, the day before—my sister's party. They were in a little lane, off the main road—and she was in his arms. I tried to make her keep quiet, but she insisted she was going to the police. And she said—"

"Yes, Miss Crockett? Go on."

"She said—she'd called up Lulu—the morning before the party—and told her."

So that's what slander is, thought Brophy. Someone starts a lie about you, without any truth in it at all, and the people that hear it believe it. And what can you do? You simply say it's a lie, and that doesn't convince anyone. If I was accused of this in court, what would I say? It's a lie. I never met Biddy in New York, or in any lane. No? Well, So-and-So *says* she saw you.... This one thought you looked at each other in a certain way.

"What did Miss de Paul say she was going to tell the police? Take this, Kalinsky."

"I don't *want* to."

"It may be helpful to us, Miss Crockett. Even if it's not true."

"She said—Biddy Hamilton poured something into Lulu's cocktail. She said she saw her do it. But I don't believe it."

"Would Miss de Paul have had any particular reasons to make trouble for Miss Hamilton?"

"I don't know."

"What reason did she think Miss Hamilton would have for going through your garden late at night?"

"Billie thought she was going to the side door, and up the back stairs, to—"

She stopped, and Levy did not ask her to continue.

"And she said—Billie said—she'd told Mel—Mr. Melton, that is, my sister's former husband. She said she told Mel, and he was furious. He said she'd driven my sister to suicide, by that story. But then he's—"

"Thank you," said Levy. "I'll be in touch with you, Miss Crockett. Good-afternoon. Afternoon, Mr. Brophy."

He went out of the room, followed by Kalinsky, and it seemed to Brophy that he had left everything unfinished. Why didn't he ask me any questions? he thought. Why didn't he give me a chance to tell him that tale about meeting Biddy was a lie?

I'll tell him now! he thought, and went quickly into the hall. But an immense depression came over him there, a despair, a lethargy that kept him motionless. If I tell Levy that, he thought, he'll only think I'm trying to protect Biddy. That I'm in love with her.

He went along the hall to the room he now occupied, and, closing the door, he sat down by the window. I can't protect Biddy, he thought. I can't help her. Anything I try to do will make things worse. No. I'll just clear out, and not see her again. And never see her again. I'd like to clear out now, he thought.

He didn't care where he went. He could not imagine any sort of future. It would be enough, he thought, simply to leave this house, walk along the road, any road. Forget it! he told himself. You've got to be at the funeral tomorrow. Lulu's second funeral. And you've got to pay for both of them.

It was dusk now. I ought to think about Billie a little, he told himself. When people are dead, you ought to do that, ought to give them a little time. Poor devil, I'm sorry about her. I don't know why she told those lies about Biddy and me, but maybe she's one of those people. They make up fantastic lies, and after they've told them a few times, they believe them. Aunt Alma was like that. *Don't* deny it, James! I *saw* you picking at that cake. And she believed she had.

It was queer, he thought, that he felt little or no resentment against Billie, but a great irritation toward Norma. If she'd only kept quiet..., he thought. Of course, she's so damn conscientious, she'd think she had to tell the whole thing, but, after all, what was it? Nothing but lies, malicious lies and tittle-tattle. It might do Biddy a lot of harm. The gossip about her, I mean. I don't think there's any chance of her being accused, or even suspected, of murder.

If this was a story I was writing, who'd be the murderer? He thought about that for a while. Me, of course, I'd have motive, and opportunity. I kill my wife, so I'll be free to marry Biddy. Then I hear that Billie's going to tell the police she saw Biddy coming to visit me, and I kill her, to protect Biddy.

Otherwise, if not me, then Norma? I wouldn't choose her type for a criminal. I'd have to change her, a lot, to give her any even half-way plausible motive for killing her own sister. In actual life, with the real Norma, it's impossible. She was genuinely fond of Lulu, and Lulu of her.

But who else? Regina? She'd be very good, for a story. The housemaid who seems so faithful and devoted. She'd have plenty of opportunity, too. I could make her very sinister. But the motive? That would take planning. Of course, in every instance, Billie gets killed so that she can't tell the police something she'd seen, or thought she'd seen. But she wouldn't have motive for killing Lulu. Nobody would.

And probably nobody did. But I don't believe in the suicide verdict. It was a mistake, an accident of some kind. Of course, in a story—

There was a knock at the door, Norma's knock.

"Come in!" he said, with a sigh.

She opened the door, and he saw Regina standing behind her, her white afternoon cap pushed forward on her forehead in a sort of peak. She looked cross, and anxious.

"Jimmy," Norma said, "we ought to find that bottle."

"I'm tired!" he said.

"I'm sorry. But if we all go together to look, no one can say that the one who found it had put it there."

"It's not important," he said. "As long as it wasn't in her room—"

"But maybe it is! I think it is. She couldn't have gone out of the room, to wander around, in the state she was in. And she must have brought the stuff here with her, Jimmy. If we can prove that—"

He was obliged to admit that it would be a good thing to prove.

"But I'm afraid it's too late, Norma. If we do find a bottle of that stuff, who's to know one of us didn't plant it?"

"I *want* to find it!" she said. "I want to *know*.... Regina, you look in the closet, on the floor, on the shelves. I'll take the chest of drawers, and, Jimmy, if you'll look under the mattress—"

"I turned it this morning, ma'am," said Regina.

"We were all so upset...," said Norma. "It's easy to overlook things when you're in that state."

"I wasn't in a state, ma'am, and I cleaned—"

"Well, never mind," said Norma. "We'll just look. Turn on the light in the closet."

"It's out, ma'am. I was going to tell you. I tried it, when I swept in there this morning."

"Take one out of a lamp and put it in there, will you, Jimmy?"

He obeyed her, feeling the same irritation that he imagined Regina felt. It's damned unfair, though, to feel like that, he thought. Norma's trying to do something, take some steps. I suppose we're both under suspicion; we must be. But *I* don't do anything.

When he had screwed in a bulb to light the closet, he went over to a chair upholstered in chintz, and lifted the seat cushion.

"Here's a bottle!" said Regina.

She was on her knees, and she hitched herself round in that position, holding up a bottle half-full of a colorless liquid.

"Put it *down!*" cried Norma, almost in a scream, and Regina, her mouth half-open, let the bottle fall to the floor where it smashed to splinters.

"Oh, you—!" Norma began, and stopped herself. Her breast rose and fell rapidly; for a moment she was silent, while Regina, on her knees, looked stupidly up into her face. "The policeman told you to pick up any bottle you found with a cloth. So that you wouldn't get fingerprints on it. And now—"

"Never mind," said Brophy.

He got a piece of cardboard from his own room, and brushed the glass on to it with a clean towel.

"There's a label," said Norma.

It was the usual sort of label; the name of a pharmacy in New York, a prescription number, the directions, one teaspoon in a little water. Repeat in an hour if necessary. But the name of the patient was given as Mrs. Yaller, and the prescribing physician was Doctor Bones.

"A phony," Brophy observed.

"Yes, I told you.... What a horrible smell!"

"It is pretty strong. Better cover these scraps so that the stuff won't evaporate."

"I'll call up Lieutenant Levy right away," Norma said. "You needn't wait, Regina. Thanks for finding it."

Norma sat down on the bed and took up the telephone from the night table. Brophy stood near the door, listening to Regina's heavy steps descending the stairs. Clumsy? he thought. Startled, when Norma yelled at her?

Or did she do it on purpose?

# CHAPTER NINE

A policeman came promptly and took away the broken glass. At seven o'clock, as usual, Brophy and Norma sat down to dinner, and Regina waited on them. It was a calm, bright evening, a golden sun sinking in a lemon-colored sky, a breeze blowing in at the open window; birds were twittering and rustling in the trees outside. But inside the house, Brophy found no peace. He and Norma talked in fits and starts, and it was an obvious effort for each of them to find any topic.

The telephone rang, and they both looked up, startled and disturbed. A telephone call, a ring of the doorbell, a car coming up the drive, a footstep, anything could mean trouble now.

Regina came back to the dining-room.

"It's for you, Mr. Brophy, sir," she said.

"Who is it, Regina?" Norma asked.

"I don't know, ma'am."

"You must always ask who's calling," said Norma.

"Let her find out first, Jimmy. It might be one of those newspaper people—"

"I'll come," he said, pushing back his chair.

"Brophy speaking," he said.

"Biddy Hamilton answering. I know it's dinner time, but I've been busy with the police until just now."

"Did they—worry you?" he asked.

"They were—rather exhausting," she said. "But they didn't knock me down, or even hit me. I shan't keep you now, Jimmy. I just wanted to ask you this. Tomorrow, after the—ceremony, would you like to come to dinner with us? We thought perhaps it would do you good to get away from the house for a little while."

"Yes!" he said. "I should like to."

"Come any time," she said. "And Mother and Father send their best regards, and their sympathy."

"Oh, thanks!" he said, and was silent. He knew that Norma could hear everything he said.

"Good-night, Jimmy!" she said. "See you tomorrow."

"Yes. Good-night-and thanks," he said.

Norma was sitting at the table, hands in her lap, waiting for him.

"Unexpected bit of luck," he said. "That was Edith Eccles." Because she could find out from Regina that it had been a woman's voice. "She's assistant editor of a pulp I've done a lot of work for. She happened to come out here, on a business matter, and she wants to see me about a story I suggested."

"When?"

"She's going out to Hollywood day after tomorrow, and that might mean something for me, too. She wants me to have dinner with her tomorrow at some little inn she's found."

"Tomorrow?" said Norma.

"Yes. Going back to New York on a late train."

"Tomorrow?" Norma repeated.

"Yes!" he answered, irritated again.

"You didn't mention to this woman that it was the day of your wife's funeral?"

"I did not. This is entirely a business thing, and—"

Norma rose and went out of the room, leaving her dinner half-finished.

Now, why did I go into that song and dance? he asked himself. I'm under no obligation to account to Norma for where I go and what I do. I'm sorry for her, but still.... Funny, how that lie came along so smoothly. I don't often tell lies. I don't like them. But this one.... Edith Eccles, that's a pretty good name. I might use it sometime. A thin, dark woman with spectacles; she has dimples when she smiles; she's pretty then.

Look here! How about an editor doing a murder? Edith Eccles, we'll say. Very good! One day, a young man comes to her office, a kid, nineteen or so. He's been drafted, and he's going to be shipped out to Korea any day. He hasn't time to write this story before he goes, but he wants to ask her if she thinks his idea is any good.

Of course, she gets plenty of this sort of thing, all the time. But, because he's being shipped out, she listens to him. His idea, his plot is a knockout. She's always wanted to write a book, and this idea of his is just what she's been groping for. He goes, leaving her an outline, and eight or ten pages he's written. It's hopeless; he can't write, just has ideas. And she *can* write—or so she thinks—only she doesn't have ideas. So.... She decides to kill him, and use his idea.

He finished his dessert, and took his cup of black coffee into the sun deck. Thrilled by Miss Eccles? That's not bad.

He began that serial at once, with zest; he worked until the zest was gone and it was half-past eleven. He stacked the pages he had done into a neat pile fastened with a paper clip; he put out the lamp and went upstairs, still thinking about Edith Eccles, whom he could now see clearly. She looked a little prim, schoolteacherish, but she dressed very well; she was somehow attractive. Smoldering, he thought.

As he reached the top of the stairs, Norma's door opened; she stood holding the knob; she was wearing a purple flannel dressing-gown with pale-blue lapels and pockets, a cord tied snugly around her neat waist.

"Jimmy," she said, "I'm sorry. I—couldn't go to bed till I'd told you I'm sorry I was—disagreeable."

"My dear girl...," he said, and laid his hand on her shoulder. "I'm the one to apologize. I've been bad-tempered all day. I'm sorry, too."

In haste, as if he were trying to escape, he withdrew his hand and went on, into his room. He locked the door and stood there in the dark, listening—for something. But the enemy was not locked out, but locked in here with him.

I can't just walk out of here tomorrow and leave her, he thought. I'll have to talk to her and find out what plans she has, where she's going, and so on. I'll have to help her pack up here. Lulu's things and so on. There'll be any number of details, little things to settle. It may be days, even weeks, before I can get out.

In his younger days, when his mother had been living, he had had no sense of responsibility about her. Her husband had supported her; she had friends to whom she could tell her troubles; she had in no way needed her son. They had been fond of each other, after their fashion, but curiously independent; during his school days, he had seldom, if ever, known where his mother was in the afternoons, nor had she known his whereabouts. They had not asked each other questions; in fact, they had not been interested. When he had gone into the Merchant Marine, before the United States went to war, she had cried a little. But she would manage; she would get on all right.

He had had little sense of responsibility for Lulu, either. She was, he had thought, a mature woman, experienced, traveled, one marriage already behind her; he had thought that she had plenty of money of her own, plenty of friends. He could certainly earn enough for his own clothes and other expenses, and there was always in the background that hope, strong as a belief, that in time he would do better than that, a lot better. In the meantime, so he had thought, he and Lulu would live a cheerful and interesting life, side by side, but parallel to each other, making no demands upon each other.

He began to see now how greatly he had feared any emotional demands upon him, how, almost instinctively, he had fled from them. He could like a girl, and make love to her, and be happy with her and generous. But if she said, I *need* you, Jimmy, I just couldn't go on without you, then he would find some way to escape her.

Now he was faced with what was for him an inexorable demand, a responsibility he could not deny. I've got to get Norma settled somewhere, he thought. She's always lived with Lulu, never alone. I don't know how much money she has, but I know she's never worked, never had a job. Well, that would be the best thing for her; a nice job. I'll see people about it. She'd make a nice receptionist; she's pretty, nice manners, good education.

He turned on the light, took up a book, and sat down to read. But he was afraid, and he knew it. After I've paid for these funerals, he thought, I'll have damn little left. I'll find out from Caulish how much his bill is; I'll do that first thing in the morning. Then I'll talk to Norma, see what plans she's made....

And if she hadn't made any? If she were just waiting...? I'm not going to brood about it, he told himself, impatiently, and got up to turn on a bath. While the water was running he began to sing, without making a sound, which was his habit while the water ran.

> A wand'ring minstrel I,
> A thing of shreds and patches,
> Of ballads, songs, and snatches
> and dreamy lullaby....

Well, that's me! he thought, surprised. It was a song he liked, but he had never before given it a personal application. I mean, that's what I'd like to be. He went on with it.

> My catalogue is long,
> Through ev'ry passion ranging—

And that's *not* me, he thought. I've never loved anyone—very much. Never hated anyone—very much. Never wanted anything very much, except to write something—something valuable, someday.

After the bath, he turned out the light and went to bed. He had always been a good sleeper, but this night was very poor. He waked, again and again, and always with a start. He thought of things he did not wish to think of, and he could not, as always before, dismiss them. Little things grew and grew to become enormous. He envisaged the new funeral as being exactly like the other, the same people, the same mass of white flowers, and his one overwhelming concern was how he should talk to the young clergyman. And what'll *he* say to *me?* The same thing? Well, no. The first time, he hadn't heard that she'd been declared a suicide. Now that he has heard it, maybe he won't be allowed to take on the funeral. I wouldn't know.... Didn't they use to bury suicides and criminals with a stake through their hearts? Or was that just for gallows-birds? I wouldn't know.

Only she wasn't a suicide. Look at all the things she had planned ahead. And she wasn't the hype.... No! He fell asleep again, and waked again.

Well, how's about getting a bottle of sherry, and giving the clergyman a glass, in private? Or is that wrong?

He waked and dressed in haste, hoping he could get his breakfast, or at least a cup of coffee, before Norma came down. Regina was crying again, with wretched sniffles, as she waited on him. I'm not going to say a word to her, he thought. I won't ask her any questions, because I don't want to hear any of her answers.

But she burst out with her grief, when she had poured his second cup of coffee.

"Oh, Mr. Brophy, sir! If she'd *only* let me come—to the funeral! The other time—I sent a little wreath, white asters, it was, and you'd never know it was there at all, the way it was hid behind them big flowers. This time I got lilies-of-the-valleys. It is a small wreath, but—it was beautiful, and it was tied with a white satin ribbon."

"Did Miss Norma say you weren't to come to the funeral?"

"She did, sir! She told me to leave here before noon, the way she'd only have to pay me for a half a day."

"Leave? You mean—?"

"She fired me, sir."

The doorbell rang, and she went to answer it. Well, that's Norma's business, Brophy thought. Maybe the girl's done something I don't know about. The sound of footsteps in the living-room made him get up to see who was there. And it was the flowers, coming back.

Where d'you want 'em put?" asked one of the men.

"Oh, anywhere...," said Brophy, and went upstairs, to the telephone extension in his room, to call up Mr. Caulish.

"Will you let me know what my bill is—for everything?" he asked.

"There's no hurry about that, Mr. Brophy," said Caulish.

He was shocked; that was plain.

"I hope you'll find everything satisfactory, Mr. Brophy," he said.

"Sure I shall," said Brophy. "But I'd like to know what I owe you."

"We can take that up later, Mr. Brophy, at your convenience."

"I want to know now, please," said Brophy.

"Well..." said the unhappy mortician, "as you know, we were asked to attend to the flowers, and two limousines, to meet the train from New York. And that, with the—other matters.... I understand what an ordeal this is for you, and I've done my best, Mr. Brophy, to keep everything moderate. But there were certain expenses connected with the—the first arrangement—"

"What's the total?"

"I'll mail you a bill tonight, Mr. Brophy."

"For God's sake, come out with it *now!*" cried Brophy.

There was a silence, as if Caulish were not able to speak.

"Twelve hundred dollars," he said, in a moment. "I can itemize—"

"Never mind, thanks," said Brophy, and hung up the telephone.

I've got nine hundred and twelve dollars in the bank, he thought. And I have those Government bonds that girl made me get. Very neat. I ought to be able to keep the twelve dollars. But it did not disturb him much; he had known times when he had had less than twelve dollars. It's enough to get me in to New York, he thought, and pay for a room and food for a couple of days. Then I can borrow from someone until I sell a story.

Norma knocked at his door, and he called, "Come in!"

"Jimmy," she said, in a low tone, "Lulu is coming."

"What!" he cried. "Oh, I see.... Well, I'll go downstairs—"

She came with him; they stood side by side while Caulish's men brought in the casket, and set it down on the black-draped trestles at the end of the room, where it had been before. Not so many flowers this time, Brophy noticed. They left, walking quietly, looking at no one, and now Brophy noticed that the casket was closed. He did not know what to say, what to do, where to go.

The doorbell rang again, and this time he answered it. It was Melton, hat in hand, looking very hot in a dark suit.

"Oh, Norma...?" he said. "Very hard on you.... Try to take it easy. Now, if you don't mind, Norma. I'd like a few words with Brophy."

"Out here," said Brophy, and led him out on to the sun deck.

"First, Brophy," he said, "I'd like the bill for these two—ceremonies—to be sent to me, in my New York office."

"I'm arranging for them," said Brophy.

He spoke curtly, because he didn't like the way Melton spoke. He remembered a time when he had taken a girl out in a canoe, somewhere in Connecticut on the Sound. She was a nice girl, pretty and well-bred; she worked in Macy's. Just a selling job, she had said. But I'm going to rise in the world, Jimmy. They had seen a little crescent-shaped beach with very few people on it, and, on one horn of the crescent a woodland of fine old trees. Perfect! said the girl. Let's stop here for a swim, Jimmy. So he had beached the canoe and they had got out.

They had had a swim in the calm water that was unexpectedly cold; they had come out to sit in the sun, in the blazing sun. A tall, lean man in white flannels had come quickly along the beach, a middle-aged man, deeply sunburnt, rather handsome, with a big nose. He had stopped beside them. Sorry, but are you members of the Mackasenny Yacht Club? When Brophy had answered no, he had looked away, as if the sight of them was intolerable. Sorry, he had said, but this is a private beach, y'know. Sorry, he had said, but I'm afraid I'll have to ask you to leave.

"I'm sorry, myself," Brophy had answered. "I hope we haven't done too much harm. But you could get the beach, and the water, decontaminated. By planes. Department of Agriculture."

"Oh, let's go!" the girl had cried.

The man in flannels had wanted to help Brophy launch the canoe, but Brophy had declined the offer.

"There's a very decent little beach, just around the headland there," the man had said.

"Public?" Brophy had asked. "I'm afraid that wouldn't do. We need a quiet place, y'know; where we can do our plotting, about overthrowing capitalism and private ownership, and the Mackasenny Yacht Club."

It's like that now, he thought.

"I understand, from poor Lulu's letters, that you weren't any too well-fixed, Brophy," said Melton.

"I'm not fixed at all," said Brophy. "I don't want to be."

"Now, look here. Brophy!" said Melton. "I'm offering to help you, because Lulu believed you had—" He paused. "Talent," he said. "She felt that that excused your treatment of her—"

"What 'treatment'? What d'you mean?"

"When the police interviewed me," said Melton, "I felt—you might say, morally obliged, to show them one of her letters."

"About me? Did she write you many letters about me?"

"She wrote me fairly often. She seldom mentioned you, she simply wrote whatever was uppermost in her thoughts, in, you might say, her heart. She knew she could trust me, and, as she used to say, the one thing she couldn't stand was—isolation. In one letter she wrote, in a rather remarkable way.... That's my creed, she wrote. I want to live *with* people, she wrote. I want to *share* with them, all, all my thoughts and feelings."

"Yes," said Brophy. "Is that what you showed the police?"

"It was not," said Melton, obviously nettled. "I showed them a recent letter. I'm sorry they haven't returned it to me, as yet, or I'd have shown it to you. But I remember most, if not all of it. She wrote to me of her loneliness—'desperate loneliness,' she wrote. Said you locked yourself into your room, to write, most of the day and half the night."

"All right. This is where I wrote. When I did write; which was damn seldom. There's no key, and I've never seen a key in those glass doors. She could come in, whenever she wanted. And she did."

"That's beside the point," said Melton. "She knew you *wanted* to be alone. That was what depressed her. Then she said you hadn't made any friends here. Nobody dropped in. No invitations. She felt isolated, and she's by nature very social."

Let it go, Brophy thought. The poor girl is dead. If I think that "isolation" was her fault, I can keep it to myself.

"She wrote," Melton went on, "and I believe I'm quoting her exact words—she wrote: 'Tonight I feel desperate, Mel. I'm sitting here in *our* room, but I'm all alone, and it's raining outside, and the doctor was worried about me this afternoon. As you know, I haven't been well for a long time. My heart isn't at all good; I can't sleep, I can't eat.' She wrote—"

He made one of those pauses which Brophy had grown to think were characteristic of him, and designed to give weight to his words. "She wrote, 'I'm not intellectual, as you very well know, Mel; I can't lose myself in books, or good music on the radio.' Then she wrote a phrase that seemed to me—rather remarkable. She wrote: 'I'm like a butterfly, Mel, with wet wings. I was meant to fly, for my little time out in the sun, among the flowers. But now I'm in a dark, cold place, where there isn't any sun. I shan't last much longer, Mel. I don't want to.'"

Brophy's neck muscles were tense; his feet had a curious feeling of lightness, as if he could rise on his toes and leap. These were signs he knew very well, and distrusted, and wished to repress. He was, in general, amiable, easy-going, a little reserved. But not always. More than once he had been in what his father, that dour and rigidly disciplined man, had called "brawls." His eyes traveled over Melton, calculating his weight, his reach.

"I don't seem to enjoy your coming and telling me all this," he said. "I don't seem to like you. Get out!"

"Brophy!"

"You'd better get out, or I'll heave you out," said Brophy.

"Brophy, I showed the police that letter, for your sake."

"So they'd see what a hell of a fine husband I was, and how happy I made my wife? I see. Now get out."

"Brophy, I was trying to bolster up that suicide theory."

"All right!" Brophy said. "And I'm trying to tear it down. I call it a damn cruel slander against Lulu."

"But don't you know, Brophy, that a good many of the police officials don't agree with the suicide verdict? They say—I'm going to be blunt—they say it's murder, Brophy."

"All right!" said Brophy. "I like that better."

"But, man!" cried Melton. "Don't you realize that *you're* the chief suspect?"

# CHAPTER TEN

"**W**ell, I don't believe it," said Brophy, frowning.

"You can take my word for it. You'd have been in jail before this, Brophy, except that they couldn't find any possible reason why you'd have done—that. They found out that Lulu wasn't leaving you any money; they questioned me about that, too, y'know. In fact, they had to see that you'd be a damn sight *worse* off, financially, without her. Then they tried another angle. Tried to make out that you were insanely jealous of me. But that didn't work. Then the Police Captain—forgotten his name—he began at me. He'd heard—probably from Norma—that Lulu wrote to me and he asked me if she'd ever written anything about your having some other woman. I told him no. He went on and on. Asked if either Lulu or Norma had ever written or said anything about some little red-headed bitch. I told him no. Well, when the Captain came to talk to me this morning, he was as pleased as Punch. Purring. He didn't tell me anything, of course, but I could glean a lot. I mean to say in a business like mine, I learned, long ago, to size people up, to—well—get into their psychology. I could tell that he thought he'd got the hooks into you. That's why I showed him Lulu's letter. Wanted to show him that she *could* have been suicidal, d'you see?"

The tension went out of Brophy's neck, and the lightness out of his feet; he felt heavy as lead, and dull, and tired.

"I see!" he said. "Then you're willing to let that stigma stay—rest—lie. That stigma remain on Lulu's name?"

"Personally," said Melton, "I don't think suicide is a stigma. We didn't ask to be born, Brophy—"

"Maybe we did," said Brophy. "Who knows?"

"Well...," said Melton, a little taken aback.

He's an ass, thought Brophy, and his knowledge of other people's psychology is astounding. He insults you and hurts you like hell; he drives splinters under your fingernails, but it's all meant to make you feel good. He's not cruel, not arrogant; just the fool of the world.

"They can suspect all they like," said Brophy. "They can't prove anything."

"They can prove opportunity, Brophy, and they're pretty sure now they can prove motive. They'll say you wanted to marry this little red-headed bitch."

"No reason to call her that, even if she doesn't exist," said Brophy.

"Sorry," said Melton, "but that's how I feel about a girl who tries to come between husband and wife, Brophy."

"Well, for your information, there's no girl I want to marry, and no girl that wants to marry me."

"Well...," said Melton. "That's not what the police think."

"I don't give a damn what the police think."

"Now, look here, Brophy. You don't know what you're talking about. I had a friend who was indicted for murder. He had this floozie out on his yacht, and she disappeared. And simply because he was a man with money, and social position, they got after him. Called him a 'wealthy playboy,' and so on. I went to his trial, every day. And it was...." He made one of his pauses.

"You simply don't know. The prosecuting attorney brought up everything they found from his past, a college escapade, anything. Made him out in court as—as someone despicable, capable of anything. He was acquitted, but he never got over it. I'll tell you this, Brophy. Nobody gets over it. You're in a pillory, people throwing rotten eggs. You're acquitted, but for the rest of your days, people are buzzing. The police must have had *something*. There must be *something* in it. And in your case, they'll say you married Lulu, so that you could be supported by her. They'll make you out the meanest, lowest cur you ever heard of. You'll be in jail for weeks before you're tried. The whole thing.... Brophy, if you do know this redheaded-girl, don't go near her until everything is settled."

His earnestness made its impression upon Brophy. I shouldn't want to go on trial for murder, he thought. I've done things.... That night watchman I knocked out, on the pier.... It was too dark to see him; I didn't know he was so old, and so frail. Things like that.... The time I missed my ship, in Tunis.... A lot of things.

But I'm going to see Biddy tonight, come hell or high water. I want to talk to her. I want to explain why I can't see her again.

That made him think of Norma, whom he would have to leave.

"About Norma...," he said. "Has she got any family, any relations to go to? Any money?"

"Brophy," said Melton, "I'm not worrying about Norma. She's been nicking me for plenty, ever since Lulu died. Flowers, for the funeral; bills, all sorts of things. If those girls had any relatives, they kept them under wraps. All the time Lulu and I were married, she lived with us, and every now and then Lulu would say, Norma needs a new dress, or hat, or coat, and I came across. *I* don't know how much money she has, but I'll tell you this, Brophy. *I'm* not taking her on." He paused again. "Why should I?" he asked.

"No reason," said Brophy.

"And there's one more thing, Brophy. I'm—not coming to the ceremony, this afternoon. Fact is, I couldn't take it."

"No reason why you should," said Brophy.

"I'll be glad, very glad to pay—"

"No, I'll pay," said Brophy.

"You can call on me, Brophy, any time."

"Thanks," said Brophy.

He opened the front door for Melton, then he closed it, and went back to the sun deck. Can't take it? he thought. But me, I can take it. I can take the quotes from her letter. She was miserable with me, lonely, unhappy. I didn't know it. I thought that was just her disposition.

He could not work, and he wandered idly about, and found Norma in the kitchen, cooking something on the stove.

"I thought we'd better have an early lunch," she said.

"Where's the cook?"

"I let her go," said Norma.

"No servants?"

"Well, I can't pay them," said Norma. "Can you?"

"Norma, have you made any plans?"

"No," she answered. "I'm not thinking of anything but Lulu, just now."

He stood in the doorway for a moment, and then he wandered off, out of the house. He went down toward the rock garden, slowly, looking all the time to see if there was a policeman. But he saw no one, no one stopped him. He leaned to look at the little tunnel behind the stones, and all the broken glass was gone. A cat was sitting there, in a fat and portly attitude, white front paws side by side, a black tail curled neatly around them.

"Hello, pussy!" said Brophy. "Come on out, and I'll give you milk, or sardines, or salmon, whatever you want. I like cats. I'm your friend."

The cat gave him a glance from its clear amber eyes, and turned away its head. Nobody..., he said to himself. There isn't anybody....

He was ashamed of that, of being hurt by a cat, an animal notoriously capricious and independent. He went back into the house, and, as he closed the door, Norma called him.

"Lunch, Jimmy!"

She had made some sort of a casserole dish; he did not relish it at all, but he ate it because his appetite was good. He praised her, too.

"Fine little chef!" he said.

And why hasn't she got married, long ago? he thought. She must be close to thirty. She's pretty, and she's well-bred, and all that; she likes to cook, and she can sew. She'd make a good wife. Why hasn't she got a husband, and a home of her own?

She couldn't make coffee, though; what she gave him was miserably weak.

"I don't want to hurry you, Jimmy, but it begins at two o'clock...."

She carried out the dishes, and when he heard her rattling out in the kitchen, he went to ask if he could help her.

"Oh, no, thank you, Jimmy! I'd really rather do things alone."

It was curious, he thought, how empty and desolate the house seemed, without Regina and the cook. Norma'll have to do everything, he thought. Of course, I'll help her, but....

At two o'clock, the young clergyman came, and the elderly couple from next door, and the librarian.

"If you could possibly wait...?" Norma said to the clergyman. "Until the cars come back from the station with the New York people."

But they never came. Two Helen Hokinson-type women came, stout, in flowered dresses, and all agog. It was plain that they had simply crashed the gate.

The young clergyman did not do more than shake hands, firmly and earnestly, with Brophy. Then, after a half-hour of waiting, he began the service. Our dearly beloved..., he said. Only he didn't know Lulu, thought Brophy. He couldn't have loved her; I don't know if they'd ever seen or spoken to each other.

The clergyman, the elderly couple, and the librarian went away, after shaking hands with Norma, and longer and more fervently with Brophy. Yes, he thought, I'm the chief mourner.

"Now," Caulish said, "I'll drive you out to the crematorium."

"No," Norma said. "I went once, when my mother died. It was.... I can't do it. Don't go, Jimmy."

"We like someone to represent the family, if possible," said Caulish, and Brophy went with him, in his gleaming black limousine.

"Here!" said Brophy, handing the check he had written out for twelve hundred dollars. "Better cash it quick."

This was what he often said about his checks, but he regretted it now. This was not the time.

"Thank you, Mr. Brophy," said Caulish, gravely and a little sternly. "There was no need to hurry with this. I'll send you an itemized bill, receipted."

He had felt dazed, incapable of caring about anything further, not even interested. But it was not so. He was shaken and sick when he got back into Caulish's car.

"An ordeal...," said Caulish. "But they make the ceremony very impressive, I think."

Yes, I'm impressed, all right, Brophy thought. Caulish stopped the car in front of his house, and he got out.

"Thanks," he said.

Norma was waiting for him in the hall, with a look of despairing anxiety.

"Jimmy," she said, "tell me all—"

"No," he said. "D'you want a cocktail, Norma? I'm going to have a drink."

"I'll take one with you," she said, and sat down on the sofa in the living-room.

She looked exhausted, Brophy thought; she looked ill.

"Look here," he said. "Suppose I telephone to Griffin, and get you a sedative?"

"No, thanks, Jimmy; I don't believe in them."

"Just to tide you over this night."

"This night won't be so different from the others that are coming, Jimmy."

He went into the dining-room and unlocked the cellarette. He went into the kitchen for ice, and it was neat and empty. No cook in there now, beginning to get dinner; no Regina.

He mixed a cocktail for Norma, and poured himself a drink of whiskey, a generous one, considerably more than he was in the habit of taking. He had felt bad enough when he came in, depressed, so heavy in spirits that he felt almost unable to speak, and now an idea was forming in his mind that made his outlook much worse, gloomier, more burdensome.

He took in the drinks, and sat in a chair, facing Norma. The flowers were still here, masses of them; the tepid breeze stirred them, wafting that scent he so disliked.

"I was surprised—," Norma said, unsteadily, "that so few people came. Practically nobody. And I telephoned yesterday—to so many...."

"Well, you see, Norma, I suppose most of them came—the first time. And maybe they—couldn't make it."

"There are some flowers," she said. "There's a really beautiful wreath from Mel, and peonies from the Hamiltons."

He took a long swallow of his drink.

"Norma," he said, "I'd like very much to hear what your plans are."

"They're pretty vague, Jimmy."

"Because, you see, I'd like to close this place up in a few days, before we run into another month."

"The autumn is lovely here, Jimmy."

"Yes. I know it is. But, you see, Norma, I couldn't pay the rent here."

"Not for two months, Jimmy? Such a good place for your work."

"Not for one month. I'm broke, Norma."

"But where will *you* go, Jimmy?"

"Back to New York for a while," he answered. "Until I can find a ship."

"Find a ship? I don't understand, Jimmy."

"I want to go to sea again. For a while, anyhow."

"But, Jimmy, your writing!"

"It'll be good for my work, in the long run. But never mind about that. I want to hear your plans. I—if you'd care to give me some idea how you're fixed...?"

"I spoke to Mel," she said, "and he won't help me. He won't do—*anything* for me."

"Well, but after all... I mean...."

"I thought he'd help me—for Lulu's sake."

"So what else have you planned now, Norma?"

"I'll get a job," she said.

"What sort of job? Office work?"

"No. I don't know anything about offices. No. There's an agency I know in New York, it's where I got Regina. It's a Domestic Employment Agency. I don't think I'll have any trouble getting a place as a housemaid."

"But, Norma! That doesn't seem—"

"It will give me a roof over my head," she said, "and three meals a day. And I'll save my salary, all of it, when I can, for the time when I'm too old to work."

He was silent for a time.

"There's another cocktail all ready in the shaker," he said. "How's about it?"

"Thanks. I'd like it."

He poured it out for her, and another whiskey for himself; he stood before her, with a glance at her weary face.

"I'm just going upstairs to telephone," he said. "Be right down." He moved away, with the glass in his hand. "I'm going to call Edith Eccles," he said. "I'm going to put off our date."

"But, Jimmy, if it's important, to your work—"

"That can wait," he said. "Then presently you and I can cook some sort of little dinner for ourselves."

"Oh, Jimmy! Oh, Jimmy! There never was anyone so kind and dear—"

"Pish-tush!" he said.

"Oh, Jimmy! We'll make a little game of it. It'll be *fun.*"

"You bet!" he said, and went upstairs to his room, still carrying his drink. He took a long swallow before he dialed Biddy's number.

"This is the Hamilton residence," said a voice that sounded very familiar.

"Look here!" he said. "You're not—Regina, are you?"

"I am, sir!" she answered, joyously. "They took me on, this very afternoon. There is three in help here, and there's a fine little radio in my own room."

"Good!" said Brophy. "Miss Biddy home?"

"She is, sir! I'll—"

"No! After all—never mind. I'll give you the message. Tell her, will you, that Mr. Brophy is extremely sorry, but he can't come to dinner tonight."

"I will, sir!" said Regina.

"You might say that I—I don't feel that Miss Crockett ought to be left alone, just now."

"I'll tell her that, sir!" said Regina, still so joyous.

That's a happy house, he thought. He had no warrant for thinking that; he had never set foot in it, nor ever met anyone who had described it. But he believed it. A happy house, a happy family, mother and father, two pretty daughters, a boy of fourteen. He imagined it, he saw it, as if it were a scene in a play; all of them sitting at dinner, Biddy facing him.

He finished his drink and went downstairs, to Norma. I couldn't leave her tonight, he thought. And when can I leave her? Soon! he told himself. Damn soon.

# CHAPTER ELEVEN

Norma was gayer than ever Brophy had seen her, while they prepared their dinner. And he tried to be. Like many another man, he
believed that he could scramble eggs in a remarkable way; Norma made
toast and covered it with butter and with anchovy paste.

"I'll start the coffee," she said, but Brophy put a stop to that; he did it
himself.

"I honestly *love* to cook," she said, when they were sitting at the dinner
table. "And I like to sweep and dust and polish, and make a place look really nice. I'd be perfectly happy in a tiny little cottage, without a bathroom,
or running water, or anything. Or I'd be happy in an even tinier apart-
ment, one of those queer walk-ups in Greenwich Village, over a loft."

"There would be rats," he said.

"*I'd* get rid of them!" said Norma. "And I'd go to an Italian market and get
heavenly things for next to nothing!"

Why haven't you got something like that? Brophy thought. Why didn't
you get married, years ago? You're a pretty girl, a nice girl; why haven't you
any beaux?

I don't know... he thought. She's pretty—but she isn't attractive. Don't
ask me why. She's got a good figure—and that isn't attractive, either. It's—
He sought for a word. It's stodgy, he thought. And, of course, she's not
interesting. Never!

It seemed to him wrong to be thinking of her like that, under her very
eyes. He was trying to devise a nice compliment when the telephone rang.

"I'll go!" she cried, springing up.

It doesn't necessarily have to be Biddy, he told himself. Regina won't
have forgotten my message, or garbled it, either. She never did that. And if
it is Biddy, she won't give me away.

"Then do bring her!" he heard Norma say. "In about an hour? Good!
We'll be expecting you."

She came back to the dining-room, smiling, her dark brows raised.

"*Well!*" she said, her hands on her belt. "Better hurry up, Mr. Brophy!
We're going to have company."

"Who?"

"That Hamilton girl asked if she could come, and bring along someone
whose name sounded like Vanderbilt. So I said, why, certainly!"

"But, Norma!" he said, startled. "You seemed.... When you told the police that tale—"

"I only told them what Billie had told me. I didn't say, ever, that I believed it."

"But you—well, you certainly don't like her."

"I asked her for you, Jimmy," she said. "I thought that after we'd had such a very pleasant dinner, it might be nice for someone to drop in. I *like* company, I think it's part of home-making to have people running in and out, don't you?"

He said yes, but he thought no. He had often felt angry and irritated beyond the possibility of concealment when someone, some old and valued friend, even, came knocking at his door, unexpected. Why the hell don't you telephone? I was just finishing a chapter, the work was just going well.... Now and then there had been a girl, obviously thinking he was going to be delighted by her surprise visit. And if he wasn't.... One girl would pout, one would be furious, one would pretend to be indifferent. One, he remembered, said she would come and sit as quiet as a little mouse while he went on writing.

"I couldn't work," he had told her, "if I had a mouse sitting in that chair, watching me. I kill mice. With traps, and the grocer's cat, and with poison."

"Do you want me to go, Jimmy?" she had asked, forlornly, and, as the harm was done now, he had let her stay.

But Norma was never doing anything in particular; she was never even absorbed in reading a book, and Lulu, too, had been like that. Maybe, he thought, that was the chief reason for their frantic desire to be "popular." Tough luck, he thought, because since I've known them, they've been pretty unpopular.

He helped Norma to clear the table; she washed the dishes, and he dried them.

"Now!" she said. "You'd better get out ice cubes, Jimmy, and put them into the thermos bucket, so you'll be ready to mix drinks for them. I'm going to make some little sandwiches."

"Don't bother, Norma. They won't want anything to eat, so soon after dinner."

"But it looks so much more hospitable, Jimmy, for guests to see you've taken a little trouble for them."

"Maybe it does," he said, sorry for her.

She made so many sandwiches, opening little tins of fillings, cutting off the crusts, spreading on softened butter, a big platter heaped with them. He had a vision of Biddy and whoever she was bringing along, both declining them, and it was too painful.

"They look so darn good," he said. "I'm going to steal one."

She was delighted by this, as he had expected. Smiling into his eyes, she began untying her apron.

"Oh, it's got knotted!" she said. "Will you untie it for me, Jimmy?"

It was, he thought, a pathetically old-fashioned little trick. With another girl, he would have gone close to her, face to face, and put both arms around her waist, and pretended to fumble with the quite uncomplicated bow. But not Norma.

"Turn around!" he said, and untied the apron and hung it over a chair.

A burning color had risen in her cheeks; he hoped it was anger at him, and not humiliation at the failure of her coquetry. He was trying to think of some suitable compliment when the doorbell rang, and she went off, quickly.

He stayed in the kitchen for a moment. I don't know if I want to see Biddy, he thought. I've built her up in my own mind to be something wonderful. Heroine, in a story I've made up. But, of course, she's come here to see me. Certainly not Norma. I've got to go in there.

All right. Biddy looked nice. Looked very nice, in a gray skirt and a sleeveless black blouse, so like a princess, with her red hair done high on her proud head. Maybe she was beautiful, with that delicate skin, those long bright-blue eyes, that slender neck.

"Hello, Jimmy!" she said. "Mrs. Vanderbilt, this is James Brophy. Jimmy, Mrs. Vanderbilt."

Mrs. Vanderbilt rose and strode toward him, holding out her hand; a tall and bony woman in a gray suit too big for her, and gray hair pulled tightly back into a bun.

"Vanderbilt by name only," she said, holding his hand in a firm grip. "Nothing Vanderbilt about my bank account."

She laughed, and so did Brophy. She released him and sat down again; she picked up a lighted cigarette from the ash-tray on the table beside her.

"I never knew, until Biddy told me, that we had a real, live author here," she said. "If I *had* known I'd have been after you, long ago! Then she lent me those magazines with your stories in them—your name right on the cover of some of them! I read one last night. 'Beauty Girl's Last Trip,' about that yacht in the Caribbean. Corking!"

"Thanks!" Brophy said. "It's very nice to hear that."

"Corking!" she repeated. "Good, clear storyline, good style, plenty of tension. You certainly know the tricks of the trade, don't you?"

"Well...," said Brophy.

"You're just what I want," she continued. "You've heard of my little enterprise, I suppose? The Vanderbilt Craft-Clinic?"

"Oh, I've *heard* of it," said Brophy, out of politeness, for he never had heard of it. "But no details, you know."

"All we attempt to do," she said, "all we *want* to do is, help people to make a good living. We have courses in typing, and shorthand, and filing and bezeling—"

"What's that?" Brophy asked.

"Mr. Orlo has charge of that," she said, and smiled, a little nervously. "I dare say I don't pronounce it properly. It's some sort of very *fine* work, I do know that. Engraving, or chasing, I think."

Yes'm, Brophy said to himself. Ah'm jes an ole bezeler, always chasn'. Yipee!

"Of course," Mrs. Vanderbilt went on, "*any* work *can* be creative, typing, even filing. But we have a department of what we call Creation."

Oh, come, come! thought Brophy. I knew those ole bezelers were up to no good.

"Painting, both oil and water color, and we're looking for someone to teach drawing. We have a poetry class. Poesy, we call it. And then—" She paused, with her twinkling little eyes fixed upon him. "And then—we have Logos."

"The Word, isn't it?" Brophy asked.

"Yes!" she said, pleased. "We deal with the spoken, *and* the written word. It's my own special method for training people to be writers. *I* think that before a writer *writes* a story, he ought to be able to *talk* it. To *tell* it."

"Oh, they do, some of them," said Brophy. "They do."

"Then you agree with me?"

"I'm sorry, but it wouldn't work for me. I used to do it. I'd hang some faithful old friend up by the toes, and tell him, with great enthusiasm, all about some story I was going to write. But after a while I had to realize that those stories were the ones I didn't write."

"My dear," said Mrs. Vanderbilt, "I know. I know writers who talk themselves out. But that's because they don't understand my method. Now, for instance, a baby has to go through all the stages of development before it is born. It has to be a tadpole, a snake, and a bird—simply all *sorts* of things, and after they're born, they have more and more stages. A baby twenty-four hours old can swim perfectly, you know, for hours—"

"No," said Norma, clearly. "They make swimming motions, but they would drown Very quickly, because their heads are so very heavy for their bodies."

"You may be right, dear," said Mrs. Vanderbilt. "But let's return to our mutton, as the French say. I want to take my writing students all through the history of writing, the minstrels, and Homer, and, you know, Aucassin and Nicolette, and the others. Once a week, each student has to *tell* a story he's created. And once a month he has to hand in a *written* story."

"Have they got on, in the writing world?" Brophy asked.

He was very much entertained by Mrs. Vanderbilt; he wanted her to keep on talking.

"My dear!" she said. "Two of my students—when I was teaching the class myself—two of them had stories in *Mammalia*. You know that mag, don't you?"

"Oh, yes, I once knew a fellow who wrote for it. Thirty-five dollars for a story."

"And one sold a story to *Ecoutez!* That was a wonderful little mag, but it went under."

"He didn't make much out of that, I'll bet," said Brophy.

"They didn't pay for what they published. They *couldn't*. They couldn't compete with the powerful advertising mags. But, to make a long story short, I gave up the class after three years. I saw that what we wanted was a commercial angle. So ever since then, I've had a commercial writer for them. I mean, someone who writes for money."

"You'd be surprised," said Brophy. "All the writers I know—except the ones in the looney-bin, or drying out somewhere—want to pay their rent and taxes; they want something to eat, and cigarettes, and so on."

"My dear, I *know*!" said Mrs. Vanderbilt, seriously. "That's why I gave up the class. Ever since then, I've had commercial, or, I *should* say, writers who have been published. I had Hugh MacHugh for three years. I've had wonderful people. The one I had last semester was Kimberly Isaacson. But then he sold one of his books to the movies, and he resigned. If you can call it 'resigning.' One Monday he didn't turn up, and he didn't come Wednesday. I telephoned the address he'd given me, and a horrible woman told me, in a screech like a parrot, that he'd gone away. And I've never heard another word from him."

"That was pretty low," said Brophy.

"My dear," she said, "it was stinking. *And*. I've advertised my new Creative Writing course, in my catalogue, to start in two weeks."

Now he knew what was coming.

"I bet you could do it, yourself," he said.

"My dear, *no!*" she said. "I've found out that what pupils *want*, is someone who's had things published. They seem to think that *that's* the test. Selling something."

And it isn't? Brophy asked himself. Then what is? I've met plenty of people who'd written a lot of stuff, and never sold any of it. I haven't worked it out, but I'd say that anyone who's written ten short-stories and sent them around, and never sold one of them, had better try for a job in the Department of Sanitation. With books, three would be the absolute limit.

"When Biddy told me about *you*," said Mrs. Vanderbilt, "I knew you were the one. So many writers are weird, remote creatures, who can't teach. But Biddy says you're *very* normal."

"No," Brophy said. "I'm very weird, and very remote."

"Oh, Jimmy!" said Norma. "You're not. You're such a kind, helpful, sweet-tempered person—"

"I knew it," said Mrs. Vanderbilt. "Now then, if you take the class, you're guaranteed five dollars for each class, and that's three times a week. And in addition, you get one dollar each week, for every pupil, after the first three. Isaacson made fifty dollars a week, and, because they're evening classes, he had his whole day free, for his own work. I'm sure you'd get lots more pupils. He was rather old, and he was hideous. Once the girls see *you*, they'll all want to take your course."

"To teach writing?" said Brophy. "I'm sorry, but I don't think it can be done. You could teach grammar—and a lot of writers need that. The latest horror is to use 'fit' instead of 'fitted.' Even newspapers, which, except for the tabloids, are pretty good on grammar, they'll print, 'She had not fit into his life.' There are a lot of things like that. I've seen 'stridden' in a magazine; I've seen 'trodded' in a book."

He had a lot more to say; he would have gone on, only that Mrs. Vanderbilt stopped him, by pointing a long forefinger at him.

"Will you take that class, Mr. Brophy? I'm sure you could make fifty a week, and probably more, I think, when the girls have seen you, we could run up to perhaps seventy-five."

Brophy was silent, looking down at his shoes.

"Will you, Jimmy Brophy?" Mrs. Vanderbilt asked.

"I'm sorry..." he said. "God knows I'd like to get the money, anything steady. But.... Well, you see, I don't think writing can be taught. If you have it in you, you'll teach yourself. And if you haven't—well, better drop it."

"But you know how Flaubert helped de Maupassant."

"De Maupassant would have got on, without any Flaubert. You mean, to describe the corner grocer as a typical corner grocer, and then show how he was different from someone else? All right. De Maupassant just didn't do it."

"Lots of well-known writers have taken courses, even correspondence courses."

"I never met any," said Brophy.

"Now, listen here! I know you could be a lot of help to young people who want to be writers."

"I couldn't," said Brophy. "People keep coming up to me and asking me where do I get my ideas? I don't know. I finish a story. Almost always I've got another started, but if I haven't, I light a cigarette, and I tell myself, I'd better try a one-shot. Thirty-five hundred words, or maybe more. All right; it comes along, and I start it."

"Listen, Jimmy Brophy! All you'll have to do is, tell these kids to write stories, and you'll criticize them. You can do *that*."

"I couldn't," said Brophy, earnestly. "I should puke."

"Well, you think it over, and call me up, or drop in to see me in my office." She rose, and Brophy, too. "*You're* what I want," she said. "I've interviewed lots of writers, but nobody like you. There's just nothing bogus in you." She held out her hand again. "I just love you to death."

"I love you," said Jimmy. "Couldn't you just stay for a drink?"

"Well," she said, "I ought to go down to my office. But a drink.... Oh, baby!"

"Scotch, rye, gin?"

"Rye," she said. "Tall and dark."

"Biddy?" he asked, and she shook her head.

When he came back with the drink, Norma was there, with her great platter of sandwiches.

"No, thanks," Biddy said.

"My dear!" said Mrs. Vanderbilt. "I've *just* finished an *enormous* dinner at the Hamiltons.' I *couldn't* eat."

"I'll have one," said Brophy.

Mrs. Vanderbilt swallowed her long drink very quickly.

"Pure heaven!" she said. "Now I've got to rush. We're registering now, for the fall classes. I'll hear from you, Jimmy Brophy. You'll change your mind. Good-night, Miss Brophy."

"Miss Crockett," said Biddy.

"Oh, I thought you were brother and sister," said Mrs. Vanderbilt. "I just thought you were. Well, I'll see you both soon."

Brophy opened the door for Mrs. Vanderbilt, and she patted his cheek.

"You'd like a nice sixty, or seventy-five a week, up to February," she said. "Call me up."

"I'll call you up," he said. "And I'd like to see you. But I don't like the job."

"Chump!" she said, with a smile like a shark, and went down the drive to her little sedan.

When he went back to the living-room, Biddy was there alone, leaning back comfortably on the sofa and smoking a cigarette.

"Norma's gone upstairs to bed," she said. "She said she had a terrific headache, and asked to be excused. I didn't object. I can't stand her."

"Why?" Brophy asked.

"She's one of those self-righteous busybodies," said Biddy. "She's a terrible liar, and she doesn't even know it. And she's so neurotic. I knew that Billie—" She was silent for a moment. "Poor Billie...," she said. "She was a tramp, but I liked her. I'm sorry.... I'm—awfully sorry about her. Because she liked to be alive, and that—well, that's endearing to me."

"Yes, I like it, too."

"I don't believe she told Norma that tale. About seeing you and me going into a hotel in New York. About seeing us embracing, in a lane. Norma made it up."

"Why would she?"

"Because she knows I want to get you away from her."

"What?"

"She wants to keep you, and marry you."

"That's nonsense, Biddy!"

"It's not. I do want to get you away from her. I thought that maybe Laura's job would be nice for you. But I loved the way you talked about it. You're a swell guy, Jimmy."

"One time, at a garden party," he said, "I heard you tell another girl I was a gorilla."

"I dote on gorillas," she said.

"You do think I'm one?"

"No," she said, looking squarely at him.

He looked back at her; he liked to do so.

"The police came to visit you?" he asked.

"They did not. They sent for me to go to the Chief's office, and I hated him. He said he had a statement that concerned me. He wouldn't say who'd made it, but it was easy to guess. He said it couldn't be used as evidence, because it was second-hand, but it would be to my advantage to answer his questions. He had a policeman there, taking it all down, but I didn't mind. I couldn't imagine what questions he could possibly want to ask me; I thought it would be something about poor Billie, whether I'd heard that she took sleeping pills, something like that.

"What he led off with just about stunned me. How often had I been in your house, without your wife's knowledge? I said never, except at her funeral. But he didn't believe me. He asked me what was my purpose in entering your garden that night? I said I never had. He kept on and on. He asked me if I had frequently used the back stairs to go up to your room. I said *never,* and I'm afraid I began to yell a little then. He warned me not to be hysterical, and I said I wasn't; I was just mad. He kept on, about my going to hotels in New York with you. He asked me, right out, Is Brophy your lover? and I said no, unfortunately."

"You said—what?"

"You heard me," said Biddy. "Anyhow, he didn't mention Billie, or ask any questions about her. He just wasn't interested in her case."

"Then what was he interested in?"

"It's rather hard, to go on from here," she said. "I hope I shan't seem blunt and rude. If I do, please know I don't mean it."

"Yes. I'll know that," he said.

She was looking downward, and her long gingercolored lashes looked, he thought, as soft as feathers.

"I'm not diplomatic," she said. "Father tells me I'd be simply awful, in *any* sort of business. It's—well, I'll do what that nasty Chief said. Just tell me, in your own words, he kept saying. I asked him whose words I could find to use. That made him worse. He wanted an account—in my own words—of Mrs. Brophy's cocktail party. I said it was the ordinary thing, people dropping in, having drinks and nice little canapés. He asked if I'd stayed after Mrs. Brophy had gone upstairs, and the others had left. I said no.

"Then he asked me... Well, I'd better tell you. He asked me if I thought Mrs. Brophy had—drunk too much. I said I was no good at judging that in people. I said she seemed excited about the party."

"Did you think she was drunk?" he asked, curtly.

"Yes," she answered, as brief as he.

"I don't," he said. "I never knew her to drink too much. She—wasn't like that."

"Well, you see, I didn't really know her," Biddy said, and paused for a moment. "Then that—that old goat, the Chief, began some sort of rigamarole, about my changing glasses with Mrs. Brophy. I did sort of vaguely remember picking up her cocktail glass by mistake, but it hadn't made much impression upon me. I told him yes, I thought I had. And then...."

She looked straight at him again, her light brows drawn together in a frown. Like a little lion, he thought. And she's mad, like a lion.

"Then he said," she went on, "you're not obliged to answer this question. But if you did something that turned out to be very much more serious than you had reason to expect, your best policy is frankness. Then he asked me, What did you put into Mrs. Brophy's drink, while you were holding her glass?

"Even then I didn't know what he was getting at. I said I had put nothing into anybody's drink, and he said two persons had seen me empty a little vial or bottle into the liquor before I returned her glass. And that time, I began to understand. Only I couldn't grasp it, I couldn't believe it. I asked him, right out, I said, Are you hinting that I *poisoned* Mrs. Brophy?

"He said he wasn't 'hinting' anything, but that it was simply his duty to collect all the information he could. Then he went into a sort of lecture about how it wasn't essential to establish motives. He said plenty of people were convicted of crimes, where no motive was ever found. But he said that he personally considered motive very important. He said he always asked himself, first thing in a case, *Cooee bony.* That's the way he said it, honestly, and I didn't understand, and I told him so.

"He gave a superior smile, and spelled it for me, and I was silly enough, and I guess pretty rude, to pronounce it for him the way we learned in school. He was good and mad, then. He said he supposed I knew what it meant, and I said yes. All right! he said. I'm going to find out who wanted Mrs. Brophy out of the way. So far, he said.... Then he leaned back and folded his arms and gave me what I'm sure was a piercing look. So far, he said, I've found—just two—possibilities. Well, you know what he meant, Jimmy."

"Well, not exactly...."

"You're pretty dumb," she said, "for someone who writes mystery stories."

"I'm not so dumb," he said. "Rather clever, in fact. Only, in a story everybody has to do what I say. And, of course, in the end, the murderer is, or ought to be, the one person you never suspected."

"It doesn't work," she said. "I can always spot those people. The bedridden old aunt, or the taciturn Scots gardener, or the mousy little schoolteacher."

"Not in my stories, you can't," said Brophy. "Because I always have three or four mice. And you don't know, until the end, about the fifty thousand dollars hidden in the book or Limoges china."

"Oh, yes, I do!" said Biddy. "The moment the scholarly old gent, who's appointed to be murdered, lays his hand lovingly on the book on his desk, I know all about *that*. You have to plant your clues ahead; that book crammed with money can't just pop out at the grand finale. A smart cookie can call all the plays."

"And you're a smart cookie?"

"It's not for me to say."

"Very good!" said Brophy. "I'll dig out some of my best—"

He stopped short. "Go on!" Biddy said.

"I get letters from publishers and editors, and so on," he said. "They say, this is for your files. All right. My 'files' are an old orange-crate someone sent me, long ago. Everything goes in there; tax notices, bills, stories I couldn't finish, letters, everything."

"My God, Jimmy! What a slovenly way to carry on!"

"Mebbe," he said. "When I was a kid, somebody gave me *Slovenly Peter*. It was translated from the German and it had two or three pictures on every page, all in very sickly colors. I loved it, and the moral lessons never worried me.

        "See Slovenly Peter, here he stands
        With his dirty hair and hands,
        See, his nails are never cut,
        They are grimed as black as soot
        And the sloven, I declare—"

"Not once this year has combed his hair," said Biddy. "We had that book, too. But I did think the punishments were pretty severe."

"I liked them," said Brophy. "Remember Augustus? And on the fifth day he was dead."

"I liked 'Old Dog Tray is happy now. He has no time to say bow-wow.' I used to say that to poor Mother. I used to say to her, I have no *time* to say bow-wow."

"Yes, but... Biddy, we've got to talk about this thing."

"I know."

"You understand who his two suspects are?"

"Sure!" she said. "You and me."

"They haven't any evidence against us," he said. "They've only gossip. But we've got to be careful."

"Not me," said Biddy. "I never have been 'careful' in my life, and I never shall be. I hoped you'd like Vanderbilt's job, but if you don't I'll make Father find you something else."

"Thanks, but no. I've always looked after myself, and I'll keep on."

"You'll think," she said, "that to 'protect' me, you'll never come to see me. All right. I'll come to see *you,* practically every minute."

"Biddy, don't!"

"I will!" she said, rising. "Now I'm going home, to cry for a while. But tomorrow morning, I'll be on deck. I took fencing in college, and maybe I'll come out tomorrow, with a sword. I'll fight policemen, and lawyers, and spiteful old maids."

"You can't fight City Hall, Biddy."

"I think I can," she said. "Jimmy...."

"Yes!"

"Jimmy, count on me."

"I do. I'll see you home."

"Nope. The chauffeur's waiting for me. Jimmy?"

"Yes?"

"Well, nothing. Just good-night."

"Good-night, Biddy."

He opened the door for her, and closing it, stood leaning against it.

# CHAPTER TWELVE

There's no proof, he said to himself, over and over. No proof of anything, against either of us. No proof of this love-affair between us. I could love Biddy, all right. I don't, and I'm not going to. But I could.

I'm going away from here, probably tomorrow. The police aren't likely to stop me. It wouldn't make things any better for Biddy if I stayed here. It might very easily make it worse. And I can't help Norma, with my twelve dollars. Less than that after I've paid my fare into New York. She must have an aunt, a cousin, a school friend, somebody she can stay with. Or, if she doesn't like that, there are plenty of little hotels in New York where she can live, even if her income is damn small.

Me, I haven't any income. I write something, and after it's done, I get paid. Except the things that everybody turns down. I haven't done anything like enough work since I got married. I—don't think I ever could do much in this house. I want to get out of here, get to work, earn a living.

"Jimmy!" called Norma's voice, sharp and loud. He looked up, and saw her at the top of the stairs, in the purple flannel robe.

"I'm frightened!" she said. "Jimmy, there's someone here, in the house."

"Couldn't be, Norma. The back door and the side door are locked, and I've had the front door in sight all the time."

She was coming down the stairs now, and he could see that her hands were trembling, her face very white.

"I heard someone walking, up in the attic," she said. "At first I thought it was a rat. They can sound so loud, when they're galloping. But after a while, I got out my umbrella and climbed on a chair, and knocked on my ceiling. And the noise stopped, at once. Rats would have started up again."

"Not necessarily," he said. "I could tell you some very strange things about rats, and how—"

"And then," she said, "when I was in my bathroom, I heard someone go by, along the corridor. The walls always shake a little, when anyone walks just there. Lulu often said she was going to get in a man to fix the floor, or whatever was wrong. Then I heard a door open and close, very quietly, and I heard a key fall on the floor. I'm frightened."

"All right! Here you have Ain't Afraid of Nobody. I'll search the house from top to bottom."

"Jimmy, no! This—this person may be armed—"

"I've got a gun myself," he said.

"But, Jimmy...!"

"You sit here for a little while, and I'll—"

"I'm coming with you," she said.

He felt sure he could not stop her by anything but physical force, and, as he did not believe there was "somebody" in the house, or any danger, he let her have her way.

"I wish you wouldn't," he said. "I could do it much quicker and better without you."

"I'm coming with you," she said.

"All right! We'll start at the top, and work down," he said, with a sigh.

They went up to the attic, which he had not seen before. And he was amazed by the immense accumulation there. He saw, in a first glance, a big and clumsy wooden cradle, he saw wax flowers under glass bells, he saw fine Dresden figures, two fat and leering little boys in blue tailcoats, two fat and simpering little girls with wreaths of flowers; he saw a large cage, equipped with a sort of treadmill, for some luckless animal; he saw trunks, boxes, bags.

"Was this here when you took the house?"

"No," she answered. "It's ours, Lulu's and mine."

"But, Norma.... Do you want all this, want to take it, wherever you go?"

"I do," she said. "I always have."

One other thing he had noticed at his first glance; he did not mention it to her. There were footprints, on the dusty floor, and they were, he felt sure, new ones. Old ones made long ago would have been covered by the sifting dust that had covered everything.

"Come on," he said, and they went down the steep stairs to the floor below.

"Lulu's room is locked," she said.

"I have a key," Brophy said.

They looked in there, in the bathroom, in all the closets.

"Come downstairs, now," he said.

"But I'm not dressed, Jimmy," she said. "If anyone should drop in...."

"That's not likely," he said, and added quickly: "It's too late."

She refused another drink, but she accepted a cigarette, and leaned back on the sofa.

"Norma," he said, "you'll have to make some plans, dear."

"I can't," she said.

"You'll have to, my dear girl. Haven't you some relations, some old friend you could visit? Or who'd come here to stay with you and share expenses?"

"No," she said. "I haven't anyone."

"Norma, I'm going to New York tomorrow and—"

"For how long?"

"I'm going to settle down, try to work."

"And just *leave* me?" she cried. "Leave me here, in this horrible house, alone?"

"There's no reason for you to stay here, Norma. As soon as I get to New York, I'll start looking for some little hotel where you could live very reasonably."

"On what?"

"Well, I don't know how much you have, Norma, but—"

"I have nothing, only two or three dollars in my purse. I have no income, no bank account. I never did have them. I have *nothing*. No money, no place to go."

She took another cigarette from a nearby china box, and he rose, to light it for her. Poor girl! he said to himself. She's in a spot, all right. I'm sorry for her. But he was not. Looking down at her, pale, wretched, bleakly alone, what he truly felt was not pity, but an almost frantic irritation, and a vague fear. And what am I supposed to do about all this? he thought. Why am I the one who's responsible for her?

He went back to his chair, and sat on the arm of it.

"Look, Norma...," he said. "As soon as I get to New York, I'll try to borrow some money for you—if I can. I'll send it to you by wire—"

"No!" she said, her pale face set and implacable. "I won't stay here— alone. This house is haunted. No! You've got to take me with you."

"Norma, I haven't any place to go, myself. No money, either."

"You can find some place to take me."

"It's impossible. I'll have to find some friend who'll take me in."

"You've got to take me with you," she said, evenly.

"Norma, I want to help you. I'll do anything I can but—"

"But you mean to leave me. If I haven't any home or any money, it's *your* fault."

Her fair skin had suddenly become mottled with red patches; she looked ugly, and menacing, as if she had been stricken by a plague.

"Sorry, but I can't see that," he said, briefly.

"You can't?" she said, with a shadow of a smile on her lips. "Haven't you even tried to think this thing out? I know how you hate to face anything, how you always try to run away, or just forget about things you don't like. But, in the beginning, I really thought you didn't know; I thought it was really a mistake that you didn't even know you'd made. That's why I helped you out, without any hesitation. But then, when I happened to see your story, I *knew*."

"Knew what?"

"It was lying there, by your typewriter. You've always made such a silly fuss about how nobody must ever even touch your sacred 'papers,' as if you were Shakespeare.... I suppose you thought no one would ever look at them. But I did! And then I knew."

"Knew what?" he asked her again, not especially interested in this new tale of hers. What astonished and shocked him was the spite, the malice in her words and her tone.

"There was your story," she said. "The Party Was the Pay-Off. The woman giving the party was like Lulu; and the hero was like you. All your heroes are like you, or what you think you're like."

"Norma," he said. "Don't let's go on with this. You're tired, and it's getting late. Why don't you go up—?"

"Oh, no!" she said, with a laugh. "I'm not going to let you out of my sight. If I went upstairs, you'd run away. That's what you want to do, run away and leave me here absolutely destitute. After you've murdered my sister."

"Norma, you're going too far."

"I thought it was a mistake, a criminally careless thing you'd done, but an honest mistake. That's why I switched the bottles when Lulu began to behave so queerly, at her party. As soon as I looked in the bathroom cabinet, I knew what you'd done. The young doctor's tonic had never been opened. You'd opened the big bottle of eye-drops the New York oculist gave her. I saw the whole thing. I saw you pour out a big slopping tablespoon of it for her. And I noticed then that the eye-drops bottle said Poison. For External Use Only."

"That's a lie. I saw the bottle myself, later on. The tonic had been opened, and a dose poured out."

"I did that," said Norma. "I hid the eye-drops, and I poured a tablespoonful out of the other bottle. If I hadn't done that, and done it fast, you'd have gone to jail, my lad, and you'd still be there. But you put on a fine act. I was sure you didn't know you'd killed Lulu, and I hoped you never would know. I thought it would be more than you could stand. I did everything I could, to help you. I poured whiskey on poor Lulu, because I thought that might put that young doctor off the track. I lied, right and left, to everyone. And then, when I saw that story, when I knew you'd done it on purpose.... I don't suppose anyone like you, so heartless, and with no sense of honor, could ever imagine what my struggle was like.... Lying awake at night, saying to myself, Don't you care anything about justice? Are you going to keep on protecting the man who murdered your own sister?"

"You tried to shift the charge to Biddy Hamilton."

"When I realized that you'd killed Lulu deliberately, I kept asking myself why? Why? It wasn't for money, because she had nothing to leave. The only other motive I could think of was some other woman. I thought you wanted to get rid of poor Lulu, so that you could marry someone else. I didn't think of Biddy, at first."

"Then who did you think of?"

"It's none of your damn business!" she cried, and threw her lighted cigarette at him.

It fell far short of him, on the rug, and he stretched out his leg and crushed it under his heel.

"It *was* Biddy," she said. "Probably she asked you to do it, begged you to do it."

"You invented the story of Billie de Paul's, didn't you?"

"No," she answered. "Certainly not."

"Yes," he said. "She didn't see Biddy out in the garden, because Biddy wasn't there. You didn't want Billie to tell the police what she really had seen, so you fixed *that* up. You—"

He stopped short, turning his head to hear better. Something was coming down the stairs, bump, bump, bump. He sprang up, and crossed the room; he turned the switch that sent a glaring flood of light from the ceiling. Half-way down the stairs he saw a grass-green sandal.

"It's Biddy's!" cried Norma, in a scream. "She's been—listening...."

Brophy went running up the stairs. He turned on all the lights, wherever he passed. He had left the door to the attic locked, when they had come down, and it was still locked, with the key on the outside. He went into each of the bedrooms, into the three bathrooms; he opened the door of every closet; he looked under the beds. But he found nobody, saw nothing out of order. He left all the glaring lights on, and went down the back stairs. The side door was not locked. He went through the kitchen and along the hall to the living-room.

"Whoever it was has got away," he said, and sank into a chair.

"I told you who it was!" said Norma. "This is one of Biddy Hamilton's shoes. I remember—in the lending library—Miss Leslie began to rave about Biddy's green shoes in that stupid, gushing way she has. Heavenly! she said. Like little emeralds. Biddy told her she'd got them by mail from some place—Dallas, I think. And when Miss Leslie said, But *do* you mind if I ask how much? Biddy said, Twenty-eight-fifty. I was so disgusted. To pay all that *tremendous* sum—for a thing like *this*. Really, a kind of sports shoe."

She was holding the green shoe on her knees, running one finger up and down the strap; like a mad-woman, he thought, who imagines she's holding a baby.

"I suppose she's got a key to the side door," Norma said, "so she can get in whenever she pleases."

"You suppose wrong," said Brophy.

He sat slouched back, in a sweat that seemed to enervate him; he pushed back the thick hair from his temples.

"It's a hot night," he observed.

"I don't think so," said Norma. "Maybe you're nervous."

"The sweat runnin' off he head like wahtah..." Brophy sang to himself without a sound. That was from a Calypso record he had bought long ago, in the West Indies. "Pam-palam, pam-palam," he sang to himself. "The temperature was so dam' hot, Dat I stop in a rum shop...." But some of the words I never get straight. "So they carry Brother Nickie down to—" Glen Gairy, is it? "He sat up all night cause he wasn't sleepy...." No wonder! "He hang dat mahning.... Pam-palam, pam-palam...."

He forced himself to rise.

"I'm going to call up Levy," he said.

"About this—person that got into the house? I can identify that shoe."

"No," he said. "I don't care about that. No...."

It was very hard for him to speak at all. "Brother Nickie lock up an' he ain' do not'in', Pam-palam, pam-palam." Once it's done and over with, I'll be all right, he thought.

"What are you going to say to Lieutenant Levy?" asked Norma. "I've got to know."

"I think," he said, very slowly and politely, "I think I believe what you told me. I didn't do it purposely; I didn't even know I had done it. But I think I did kill Lulu."

"You mean you thought you'd tell Levy *that?*" She threw the green sandal on the floor. "Don't you realize what it would do to *me?*"

"I don't intend to mention your name."

"Then how are you going to explain about the bottles?"

"If I'm asked, I'll say that as soon as I realized my mistake, I tried to cover. I'll say I hid the bottle of eye-drops, and fixed up the other bottle."

"But why? Why are you going to tell him?"

"I wish to God you'd let me alone!" he said. "I don't—feel like talking— explaining."

"Except to Levy."

"I'll simply tell him that I gave Lulu that poison by mistake."

"Fine! And I saw you, and I protected you. That puts me in a fine position. I'm an accessory after the fact. I've committed perjury. I'll be publicly disgraced—even if I'm not sent to prison. The girl who stood by her own sister's murderer."

"Murderer...," he said, half-aloud.

"Killer, then, if you like it better. Maybe you can get away with that story about its having been just an innocent, absent-minded mistake. That is, of course, if I keep on protecting you. If I don't mention your nice new story.

The Party Was the Pay-Off. You were all wrapped up in your work, and you didn't see that the bottle was labeled 'poison.' Your Honor, I didn't know it was loaded."

"Norma.... The only thing is, to tell the truth. To get the whole thing straightened out—clear. If I did that to Lulu—and I believe I did—it was criminal carelessness. It's no excuse to say I never thought about poison. She had such a lot of medicines.... I never thought any of it was—dangerous."

"So you've decided," said Norma, "that as long as you got rid of one sister, by what you call criminal carelessness, you might just as well kill the other sister, in just about the same way. By criminal carelessness, by neglect. Only, I think Lulu's way of dying was a good deal easier than mine's going to be."

"What d'you mean by that?"

"You can't tell your story to Levy without getting me involved. I'll be questioned, probably in court. I'll be disgraced, despised by everyone for shielding you; I'll be left utterly alone in the world, penniless, homeless.... D'you think I'm going to enjoy that life? No. This case is going to have another bottle in it. A little bottle I've been keeping for quite a while. It's a very easy way out. You just go to sleep, and you don't wake up."

"You're threatening to commit suicide, if I do what I think I ought to do?"

"It's scarcely that," she said.

The mottled look had gone from her face; she was pale again, and handsome.

"Ever since I was a tiny child, I've always dreaded this," she went on. "Dreaded being left all alone. When Father and Mother used to go out in the evening, I'd wait for a while, and then I'd get out of bed and go downstairs, barefoot, to be sure one of the servants was in the kitchen. And one night, the kitchen was empty. I called for Maggie, and for the other girl, and there was no answer. I—what I felt was sheer panic. I went flying up the stairs again, in terror. I thought things were running after me. I went into our room, and I shook Lulu and made her wake up. She said I was like a wild thing. I kept saying, They're *gone!* They're all gone, and left me *alone.* She said, Don't be silly. You've got me. You're not alone."

She was crying now, very quietly; her eyes were closed, and tears clung in her lashes and rained down her checks.

"She said she'd never leave me. But now—she has. Now she's gone."

Yes, Brophy said to himself. And I did it. I don't know.... I used to think Lulu was the temperamental one, and that Norma was placid. But to-night... Good Lord! She's turned on all the stops. Scorn, fury, and misery and loneliness.

I think her story's true. I think I'm responsible for Lulu's death. And then—am I responsible for Norma's being left alone, with no home, no money, no more help from Melton, nothing? If she did commit suicide.... My fault? I don't know.

"Norma," he said, "I—won't telephone to Levy just now. I won't do anything tonight. I'll—sleep on it, and in the morning, we—can discuss it again."

"All right, Jimmy," she said, and rose. She went past him without a glance, tears still running down her cheeks. So tall in her long robe, with her thick hair loose, her face so grief-stricken, she looked, he thought, like someone in a classic drama.

She did so much for me, he thought. She did all she could. *Can* I just leave her flat? Oh, God! *Can't* I get away?

# CHAPTER THIRTEEN

He did not want to go to bed, or to go upstairs. He lay down on the couch, with one ankle on his raised knee; he lit a cigarette, and tried as best he could to think, to reason.

I killed Lulu, he thought. I believe that. I didn't mean to, but I did it. The psychiatrists would say I *did* mean to, unconsciously. They'd say that I did see, or had seen, the label on the bottle, but I blocked it out, because I wanted to get rid of her.

And maybe I did. I was wanting, more and more, to get away from this place, and from Lulu. I wouldn't admit it, but that's how it was. And the—other thing could have been there, too, in my mind, even if I didn't admit it, didn't even know it consciously. The death-wish.

Forget all that! The psychiatrists don't know and can't know all that was in my unconscious mind, and I don't, either. All that matters is the fact, the accomplished fact. The fact that Lulu's dead, and I killed her. I slopped that medicine out of the bottle without even looking at it. If I had cared enough, I'd have seen there was something seriously wrong with her, at the party. Poor girl! That party of hers would have been a flat failure, even if I hadn't done that.

The Party Was the Pay-Off. Norma thinks that's proof that I killed her deliberately. But Norma is not very reasonable. And not very truthful. When you come to think of it, I don't believe anything much that she says. That green sandal, for example.... If she ever got into court, any lawyer, even a stupid one, could make a fool of her. She'd get up on the witness stand, and swear that that was Biddy's shoe. She wouldn't say that it looked to her exactly like one she'd seen Biddy wearing. She'd swear it *was* the one.

I don't want to see her in court, after all she's done for me. She doesn't realize what she's done. She saw me give that stuff to her sister, yet even after she thought I'd done it on purpose, she stood by me. I *can't* walk out on her.

She poured whiskey on poor Lulu, when she was dying or dead.... Maybe I'd better get drunk, and sleep for a while, and forget the whole thing. Lulu, I *didn't* mean it. I *didn't* have a death-wish.

But I have had it. In the war when I was in the Merchant Marine, I was damn pleased if we thought we'd hit a submarine. I didn't care how many Germans were killed, smothered, drowned. Sons, fathers, brothers—okay with me. I was trained to kill "the enemy."

All right. Never mind all that. I've got to think about my own affair, nothing else. Norma said that was Biddy's shoe that came bumping down the stairs. I don't believe it. Biddy wouldn't come here and sneak around, trying to spy, to overhear. Maybe nobody was here. Maybe Norma fixed the shoe some way, to make it fall down the stairs. Norma said she heard someone in the hall, in the attic. There were footprints there, but maybe Norma made them. I don't trust her. I don't *like* her. Only I believe what she said about my killing Lulu. I did it, and I'm ready to pay for it. If the police, and the judge, and the lawyer, and the psychiatrist all decide I did it on purpose, all right. If I die in the chair, all right. I don't care. I don't want to go on living, if I killed Lulu. And I don't want to take on Norma, for ever and ever. And ever. She's a good-looking girl, nice girl. Why hasn't she got married? Why hasn't she got beaux? Why is it *me*, to look after her? Why the hell can't she get a job, and support herself? These two sisters never thought about that. But Lulu managed to get herself married to Melton—and Norma just strung along. Let her get out, and get to work. Or let her find a man. She could. Only not me.

Maybe there was someone here, to drop that shoe. Maybe there was someone who heard Norma tell how I killed Lulu. All right! I don't give a damn. I'm going to tell Levy myself. Norma says she'll be involved in it, if I do. She says she'll kill herself. Well, I'm sorry. But even if I didn't tell Levy, I couldn't take on Norma for the rest of my days.

He closed his eyes and slept for a few moments; he waked with a start, with a new and dreadful thought. But is that what I ought to do for Lulu? The only thing I can do for her now? To look after Norma? Lulu always did that. "You're not alone. I'm here."

He thought of that story with pain and dismay. That's what Lulu would want, he thought. My telling Levy the truth is only for my own sake. It's because I don't want to endure that burden by myself. But if I want to do anything to atone to Lulu, there's only one thing. To look after Norma.

He was growing sleepy again, and, to his surprise, tears came into his eyes and ran down his face. That's nothing, he told himself. I saw plenty of men cry, in the war. Better men than me. I killed my wife—and I can't get away from Norma... "He sat up all night 'cause he wasn't sleepy.... He knew, Brother Nickie did, that he was going to hang in de mahning." Well, that's not going to happen to me. I'm healthy; I might easily live another thirty, even forty years. With Norma. Will I have to marry her? No, by God, I *won't!*

A loud sob startled him. Shut up, he told himself. If she hears you, she'll come down again. To comfort you. To help you. She switched those bottles, hid bottles, she's got a little bottle now, to kill herself. Bottles, and Bottles.... All those bottles behind the rock garden....

The Party Was the Pay-Off, he said to himself. Norma thought that "evidence." Maybe she thinks I write a story about everything I do. I don't know.... Lulu, I'm sorry. Lulu, forgive me—if you can. I'm sorry.

He fell asleep again, with the tears on his face; he waked this time with a jerk that hurt his neck. I thought I heard the doorbell, he told himself, and turned on his side.

But it was the doorbell, a long, loud ring. He got up, and went staggering, only half-awake, to answer it. Levy was standing outside, with two policemen.

"Well...?" Brophy said. "Yes? Well, what...?"

"I'd like to see Miss Crockett," said Levy.

"Gone to bed," said Brophy.

He thought he saw someone else there, in the shadow of the trees. A woman?

"A woman?" he asked.

"Miss Corrigan," said Levy.

"Never heard of her," said Brophy. "Come back tomorrow, will you?"

"I'll have to see Miss Crockett *now*," said Levy.

"You don't want to wake her up, poor girl. What time is it, anyhow?"

"Three o'clock, more or less," said Levy. "She'll have to be waked, Mr. Brophy. I'll do it, if you'd rather."

"No, but—but why?"

"I have a warrant for her arrest, Mr. Brophy."

"For Norma? She hasn't done anything."

"Will you call her, Mr. Brophy, or shall I?"

"I'll call her," said Brophy, "but it's all wrong."

It was, he thought, like a scene under water. In the dazzling headlights of the police car, the grass was arsenic green; some little tree was caught by the light; its branches, growing stiffly at right angles, were the palest green; the three men standing there had, he thought, green faces. And the woman didn't move. A nun, he thought, swathed in black. The Inquisition? he thought. Torture, and death.

"Come back tomorrow morning," he said, and tried to close the door.

"Pull yourself together, Mr. Brophy," said Levy. "This is a serious matter."

Brophy looked at him carefully and decided just where he would hit, to make him fall backward down the steps. Then the smaller and slighter policeman, and then the big guy. When he had them all lying there, in a row, he would lock the door and go to sleep again.

But no, no, no! cried another voice inside him. You've already committed a murder....

"Come in!" he said, opening the door wide.

That threw more light upon the drive, and he saw another police car, with three men in it. This is it, he thought. But what is it?

Levy's mildness had gone; he was curt and cold. "Get Miss Crockett down here," he said. "Or I'll go up and get her."

Brophy went up the stairs and little by little the confusion in his mind was clearing. They've got a warrant—for Norma? he thought. I don't know what for, but I hope to God she'll behave herself. I mean, be quiet, dignified, all that.

He knocked at her door, and she opened it at once. "I heard the bell," she said. "And I wondered—"

"Look, Norma, Levy wants to see you."

"I'll get dressed then—"

"I wouldn't bother about that, Norma. He's—he seems to be in a hurry. Seems to be pretty short-tempered. Norma, be careful what you say. If he asks you a lot of questions, tell him you want to see a lawyer first."

"And just what will I pay a lawyer with?" she asked. "My virtue?"

"We'll arrange it some way. Come along!"

She came down, in her purple flannel dressing-gown, and she was, as Brophy had hoped, quiet, dignified, almost regal.

"Miss Crockett," said Levy, "I have a warrant here for your arrest on a charge of homicide."

"Really?" Norma asked. "And who am I supposed to have killed?"

"That on the evening of August twenty-sixth and again on the morning of August twenty-seventh you did feloniously and with malice afore-thought administer poison to Miss Billie de Paul, causing her death later in the Addison Memorial Hospital."

My God! Brophy cried to himself. I'd forgotten poor old Billie. It was only Lulu I thought about.

"You are not obliged to answer any questions put to you," Levy went on, "and it is my duty to warn you that anything you say may be taken down in writing and later used in evidence against you."

"Heavens!" said Norma. "You didn't say all this before I made that other statement that your policeman wrote down."

"In the first place," said Levy, "you had not been charged at that time. In the second place, the statement then made could not be offered in evi-dence against you. It was merely an unsupported account of an alleged conversation with a person already deceased."

"Heavens!" Norma said again. "You make me sound so—sinister. Is it all right for me to smoke, Lieutenant?"

"Certainly!" he said, and Brophy struck a match for her.

She's overdoing it, he thought, in dismay. Her air of faint amusement, of nonchalance, was not convincing, and not at all attractive. She might, he thought, show some trace of regret for Billie, some surprise or anger at the charges made against her. And the word she had used in irony about herself could, he thought, be well applied to Levy. *He's* sinister, all right, Brophy said to himself. Entirely different. He's on the job now; he means business. When he sits there like that, with his hands spread out on his knees, he looks like—which one was it? Osiris, judging the dead?

Judging.... I've never admired that. Finding out a few facts about a man or a woman, and then pronouncing them good or bad, damned or blessed.

"Do tell me why I killed poor Billie de Paul?" Norma asked. "I'm dying of curiosity."

"It's not requisite for the police to establish motive," said Levy. "It's always very much more satisfactory, though, if it can be done, and I'm prepared to suggest a motive. Miss de Paul had sent for me, to make a statement. I suggest that you didn't want her to make this statement."

"But I told you all those things she'd meant to tell you!"

"What you told me, Miss Crockett, was not supported by evidence or corroboration of any sort."

"So you think it was all a lie?"

"I haven't said that, Miss Crockett."

It was a lie, Brophy thought. She was trying to fasten suspicion on Biddy, because she hates her. Or...? No! Norma didn't do—that to Billie. She *couldn't*—she's not—

"You saw the bottle we found in poor Billie's room?"

"Yes. The fragments were examined, and traces of chloral hydrate were found, but in an extremely diluted form. One of our men interviewed the pharmacist at the address printed on the label. He said, and he is willing to support this by the records, that they have never had a customer with the name written on the label."

"Billie told me she never used her right name when she got these drugs in the black market."

"This pharmacy is entirely reputable. Not a 'black market.' The pharmacist also said they had never issued a prescription bearing that number, or ever received one from a doctor by that name."

"And what has all this rigamarole got to do with me?"

"It would have been possible for you to have written that label, Miss Crockett. And to have planted that bottle where it was later found."

"Certainly it would have been possible," she said. "For me—and for other people, too."

"For instance—"

"I can't tell you," she said. "Billie's door wasn't locked. Anyone could have got in. Anyone could have given her that—whatever it is—that poison, and left the phony bottle there."

"Can you suggest anyone who would have had the opportunity to do this, Miss Crockett?"

"I could," she said. "But I'm not going to."

"I understand," Levy went on, "that chloral hydrate has a very strong and unpleasant odor. Burns the mouth, throat, and stomach unless it is properly diluted."

"People who are drinking a lot don't care. They don't even notice. Look at the way those girls in bars give a man a Mickey Finn, and he just swallows it down."

She pretended before that she didn't know, Brophy thought. She asked Levy what a Mickey Finn was. Maybe he won't remember that—but I don't think he misses much. If she'd only stop lying.... She'll get snarled up in her lies. It's dangerous.

"In your former statement," said Levy, "you said Miss de Paul told you she'd seen a woman go past a window downstairs, carrying a bottle. We found an extraordinary number of broken glass bottles there. We've had the whole lot examined and tested, and some curious things came to light. For instance, a considerable quantity of atropine."

"Well, do you think that maybe I'm an atropine addict—if there is such a thing?"

If Levy seemed changed, so did Norma. She took another cigarette, and leaned back, crossing one leg high across the other, showing a long stretch of bare, slender leg; the dressing-gown had gaped open, in a very low neckline. Her tone was flippant; she looked disheveled, almost wanton.

"Last night," said Levy, "two women were standing on the corner below here; one was waiting for a bus, and the other was keeping her company. One of them states that at this time, Miss Hamilton and Mrs. Vanderbilt were talking to you in this room."

"How could they know that?" asked Norma.

"One of them was your former maid, Regina—"

"Last night?"

"She came back here, and entered the house through a window in the kitchen—"

"She had no *right* to come in here!"

"No right at all," Levy agreed. "I told her so. I told her she had committed a trespass and could be so charged."

"She will be, too," said Norma. "I'll see to that. Sneaking around my house, dropping a shoe—I'll take it to court."

Biddy's shoe, Brophy thought. I suppose she gave them to Regina. But Norma... Doesn't she realize Levy's got a warrant to arrest her, on a murder charge, and she's talking about taking Regina into court.... Is she so completely innocent she doesn't realize...?

"These two witnesses," Levy continued, "both state they saw a woman leave this house by a side door, and run along the path to the rock garden.

They both state that this woman was carrying a bottle, and that she threw it behind the rock. Perhaps she did not know that the pile of glass formerly there had been removed, and she was disturbed by hearing no crash. In any case, both the witnesses state that they saw the woman lean over the fence and take several beer bottles from a refuse container in the street, the property of the people in the next house. These bottles she threw down on the one already there, and there was a crash of broken glass. She returned to the house, and shortly after, Regina followed her. She hid for a time in the attic, and later concealed herself behind what she called a 'garment bag' in the late Mrs. Brophy's closet."

"And of course, she recognized me in the garden, in the dark," said Norma.

"The bottle the aforementioned woman threw out had contained chloral hydrate. It was a prescription given by Doctor Griffin, and made out for Miss Norma Crockett."

"I *told* you about that. I said I'd thrown away the bottle. Very well. Maybe Regina found it and kept it. Why should you believe every word that clumsy, stupid servant says, and never believe me? Why are you so sure that she didn't put that bottle there herself, and just invent the rest of it?"

"There were two witnesses, you know, Miss Crockett."

"And they both recognized me, in that garden, with all those trees? Why, your whole case against me is nothing but nonsense—servant's gossip, a lot of farfetched talk about bottles."

Brophy was glad to see her grown angry. It was a sign, he thought, that she was beginning at last to understand, to see the danger that faced her. He thought himself that everything so far brought against her was flimsy enough, but there might be more.

"The second witness stated that she would not be able to identify you."

"Then it's just Regina!"

"The two witnesses are both in agreement on one point, Miss Crockett. The light from the open side door gave them both a clear view of her costume."

There was a silence, and it worried Brophy. He glanced at Norma, and she no longer seemed angry. She was smoking, her eyes were lowered. How does she look? he thought. It's not so easy as writers make out, to read people's faces. Is she exhausted, sick of the whole thing? Or thinking, about something that's just occurred to her? Anyhow, she doesn't look nervous, or at all frightened.

"Well!" she asked, in her usual quiet voice. "What was this mysterious woman's costume, Lieutenant?"

"Both witnesses agree that she was wearing a purple robe," said Levy.

The two uniformed policemen stood near the doorway, carefully not looking at anybody; Levy sat, leaning forward, in an armchair, facing the sofa; Brophy sat on the edge of a table. And among those silent and almost motionless men sat Norma, in her purple robe.

"Officer Bascom rode to the hospital in the ambulance with the late Miss de Paul," said Levy. "He is prepared to make a sworn statement of what Miss de Paul said to him, or in his presence. Officer Bascom!"

A young policeman with a freckled face and neatly sleeked-down red hair stepped forward a few paces and saluted.

"Officer, kindly repeat what you heard Miss de Paul say, in the ambulance."

"It was sort of mumbly-like," said young Bascom, "and a lot of it you couldn't make out at all. But she said, a lot of times, 'A purple robe,' she said a lot of times. Running in the garden, she said, a lot of times, and carrying a bottle, and she had on a purple robe."

Norma had risen; she stood there, with her hand on the back of the couch, facing them all in her purple robe.

"There was an intern in the ambulance who will corroborate Bascom's statement," said Levy. "Go on, Bascom."

"Well, there wasn't much more," said Bascom. "Only a kind of a moaning noise. Then she'd put her hand on her throat, and she'd say—it burns me; and she put her hand—" He could not, apparently, find a word sufficiently delicate. "Here," he said, stretching his big hand over his midriff. "'It burns me,' she'd say, and then she'd say, 'She said take some more whiskey, and you'll feel fine in a few moments.' But she didn't talk long; she was out cold, before we ever got to the hospital."

"All right, Bascom," said the Lieutenant. "Send in the matron."

He turned to Norma. "The matron will go up with you while you dress, and pack a bag—a small bag."

"You—you're arresting her?" cried Brophy. "No! Wait! Look here! Wait, and I'll get a lawyer. I'll have bail for her. Don't— Look here! Don't take her to jail!"

The matron came into the house, stout and pale, with a crow-like smile.

"Norma, look here!" said Brophy. "I'll—find out what to do."

"They can't do anything to me, Jimmy," she said. "I haven't done anything wrong, ever."

She spoke in a tone that was almost preposterously lofty. But that's the way she feels, poor devil, thought Brophy. Anything she does is right. Has to be, because she can always bring out such a noble motive.

"So don't worry, Jimmy," she said, with a pleasant social smile, and turned away to mount the stairs, followed by the matron.

"How does it look for her, Lieutenant?" Brophy asked, when the door upstairs had closed. "I mean, d'you think she'll come out of this all right?"

"I think we have a pretty strong case, Mr. Brophy."

I think so, too, Brophy said to himself. I think she killed Billie, and I think she'll be convicted of it. And certainly she'll make the worst impression anyone could make on a jury.

"And," Levy went on, "if this charge doesn't stick, we'll bring up the other one. In fact, I'd have had the warrant made for that one, if I'd had Regina's story before tonight."

"What—other one?"

"Your wife's murder, Mr. Brophy."

"Good God! You mean you think *Norma...?*"

"We don't often get an eyewitness in a murder case, Mr. Brophy. But if we're going to believe this girl's story—and she seems like a decent, honest girl—"

"Let's have it."

"She says that just before the cocktail party she saw you prepare a dose of medicine for your wife."

"Regina wasn't there. She was downstairs, helping."

"You can only say that you didn't see or notice her upstairs, Mr. Brophy. She is willing to attest under oath that she saw you prepare the medicine, and then go downstairs. She further states that directly you were gone, deceased's sister Norma Crockett entered the room, and knocked the cup off the table. Miss Crockett apologized and offered to prepare another and deceased gave her permission. The girl Regina states that Miss Crockett carried the cup and saucer into the bedroom, and a few moments later returned with it, filled with the liquid, which deceased drank."

The aforementioned Regina was not upstairs, thought Brophy. And there wasn't any cup and saucer, just a medicine glass. Why, for God's sake, did Regina tell him that lie?

Now I'll have to tell him the truth. I can't let Norma be accused of *that*. But she will be, unless she's convicted of Billie's murder. No. If I tell Levy now, it'll only make it worse for Norma. How she switched the bottles, tried to help her sister's murderer....

"I didn't suspect Miss Crockett, at first," said Levy

"Well, then.... Who?"

"You," Levy answered, amiably.

"But—why?"

"I had quite a lot of reasons," said Levy. "But after I found out that your sister-in-law seemed rather addicted to poisoning, and breaking bottles, and after I'd heard Regina's story, I felt I'd been mistaken." He smiled. "I'm very glad I was, Mr. Brophy," he said. "Good-night, sir."

It was growing light outside, the sky a dark violet. The night is over, Brophy thought, but he did not know how it had passed, whether he had slept, or whether he had simply sat all the while, in this chair. It seemed to him that he never stopped thinking, and always the same thought.

Norma's in jail. And Levy thinks she killed Lulu, but I *know* she didn't. It was me. I've got to tell him. Get it off my chest. You can't do a thing like that, and just go on living, without a word. You have to speak the truth. And Norma's in jail.

All right. The truth won't help her now, won't get her out of jail. And I don't think they'd believe me, if I told the truth. I mean, about its being an accident. They'd find plenty of people to say Lulu and I hadn't been happy together. Plenty of people who'd heard some bit of gossip about Biddy and me.... Biddy'd be dragged through the mud, and one—I might even go to the chair. Nothing in my favor, except Regina's story.

And why did she tell that story? Why was she here in the house?

A bird, which seemed to him enormous, went flailing past the window. Making a lot of effort, he thought. Well, that's because it's extinct. It seemed to be dark-blue, with gold linings to its gigantic wings. It's the Roc, he thought. The Roc that Sinbad rode on, to get out of the Valley. Full of jewels, wasn't it? I don't remember whether Sinbad got any of them....

He opened his eyes, and the sun was high now. Regina was coming toward him with a tray; he smelled coffee.

"You shouldn't be here," he said.

"Miss Biddy sent me, sir, and she said that she and her mother are coming over later, to see can they do anything."

The giant Roc and the Valley of jewels drifted out of his mind, and then he thought of Lulu; he had some of the hot, strong coffee, and then he thought of Norma in jail.

"Why did you come here last night?" he asked.

"'Twas to get my little fur jacket, sir."

"Why did you have to creep around, like a ghost? You could have come, perfectly openly, in the daytime to get anything that belonged to you."

"No, sir, I could not. If Miss Norma seen that little fur coat, she'd have took it off me."

"She wouldn't, Regina, if it belonged to you."

"Indeed and it did belong to me, for didn't Miss Lulu herself give it to me? But she done told me before, sir, Miss Norma did. It was a fine little necklace that Miss Lulu gave me and Miss Norma, she took it off me. If Mr. Melton gives my sister a nice present, she says, you've no right to take it from her. She took it, and she never give it back to Miss Lulu. It's up in her dressing-table drawer, this moment, and I've seen it there, with my own two eyes. Last night, oh, it was a terrible temptation.... I'd be saying to myself, it's mine, and I've a right to it. But then I'd remember it would be no better than stealing, and that I'd not do, even from *her*."

So that's it, thought Brophy. She heard what we said last night, and she twisted it into that tale of hers.

"Regina," he said, and stopped.

"Sir?"

"Nothing," he said. "I'd like another cup of coffee, thanks."

THE END

## *The Best in Mystery & Noir Fiction Past & Present*

1-933586-26-5 **Benjamin Appel** Sweet Money Girl / Life and Death of a Tough Guy $21.95

1-933586-03-6 **Malcolm Braly** Shake Him Till He Rattles / It's Cold Out There $19.95

1-933586-10-9 **Gil Brewer** Wild to Possess / A Taste for Sin $19.95

1-933586-20-6 **Gil Brewer** A Devil for O'Shaugnessy / The Three-Way Split $14.95

1-933586-24-9 **W. R. Burnett** It's Always Four O'Clock / Iron Man $19.95

1-933586-31-1 **Catherine Butzen** Thief of Midnight $15.95

1-933586-38-9 **James Hadley Chase** Come Easy--Go Easy / In a Vain Shadow $19.95

0-9667848-0-4 **Storm Constantine** Oracle Lips (limited hb) $45.00

1-933586-30-3 **Jada M. Davis** One for Hell $19.95

1-933586-43-5 **Bruce Elliot** One is a Lonely Number /

                     **Elliott Chaze** Black Wings Has My Angel $19.95

1-933586-34-6 **Don Elliott** Gang Girl / Sex Bum $19.95

1-933586-12-5 **A. S. Fleischman** Look Behind You Lady / The Venetian Blonde $19.95

1-933568-28-1 **A. S. Fleischman** Danger in Paradise / Malay Woman $19.95

1-933586-35-4 **Orrie Hitt** The Cheaters / Dial "M" for Man $19.95

0-9667848-7-1 **Elisabeth Sanxay Holding** Lady Killer / Miasma $19.95

0-9667848-9-8 **Elisabeth Sanxay Holding** The Death Wish / Net of Cobwebs $19.95

1-933586-16-8 **Elisabeth Sanxay Holding** The Old Battle Ax / Dark Power $19.95

1-933586-17-6 **Russell James** Underground / Collected Stories $14.95

0-9749438-8-6 **Day Keene** Framed in Guilt / My Flesh is Sweet $19.95

1-933586-33-8 **Day Keene** Dead Dolls Don't Talk / Hunt the Killer / Too Hot to Hold $23.95

1-933586-21-4 **Mercedes Lambert** Dogtown / Soultown $14.95

1-933586-14-1 **Dan Marlowe/Fletcher Flora/Charles Runyon** Trio of Gold Medals $15.95

1-933586-07-9 **Ed by McCarthy & Gorman** Invasion of the Body Snatchers: A Tribute $19.95

1-933586-09-5 **Margaret Millar** An Air That Kills / Do Evil in Return $19.95

1-933586-23-0 **Wade Miller** The Killer / Devil on Two Sticks $17.95

1-933586-27-3 **E. Phillips Oppenheim** The Amazing Judgment / Mr. Laxworthy's Adventures $19.95

0-9749438-3-5 **Vin Packer** Something in the Shadows / Intimate Victims $19.95

1-933586-05-2 **Vin Packer** Whisper His Sin / The Evil Friendship $19.95

1-933586-18-4 **Richard Powell** A Shot in the Dark / Shell Game $14.95

1-933586-19-2 **Bill Pronzini** Snowbound / Games $14.95

0-9667848-8-x **Peter Rabe** The Box / Journey Into Terror $21.95

0-9749438-4-3 **Peter Rabe** Murder Me for Nickels / Benny Muscles In $19.95

1-933586-00-1 **Peter Rabe** Blood on the Desert / A House in Naples $21.95

1-933586-11-7 **Peter Rabe** My Lovely Executioner / Agreement to Kill $19.95

1-933586-22-2 **Peter Rabe** Anatomy of a Killer / A Shroud for Jesso $14.95

1-933586-32-x **Peter Rabe** The Silent Wall / The Return of Marvin Palaver $19.95

0-9749438-2-7 **Douglas Sanderson** Pure Sweet Hell / Catch a Fallen Starlet $19.95

1-933586-06-0 **Douglas Sanderson** The Deadly Dames / A Dum-Dum for the President $19.95

1-933586-29-X **Charlie Stella** Johnny Porno $15.95

1-933586-39-7 **Charlie Stella** Rough Riders $15.95

1-933586-08-7 **Harry Whittington** A Night for Screaming / Any Woman He Wanted $19.95

1-933586-25-7 **Harry Whittington** To Find Cora / Like Mink Like Murder / Body and Passion $23.95

1-933586-36-2 **Harry Whittington** Rapture Alley / Winter Girl / Strictly for the Boys $23.95